THE DYING HOUR

JANE JESMOND

Storm
PUBLISHING

Ebook ISBN: 978-1-80508-165-4
Paperback ISBN: 978-1-80508-167-8

Cover design: Ghost
Cover images: Adobe, Shutterstock

Published by Storm Publishing.
For further information, visit:
www.stormpublishing.co

ALSO BY JANE JESMOND

On the Edge

Cut Adrift

Her

A Quiet Contagion

Gone to Earth

To Mr G, from his number one oppo

ONE

JOSH MASON

MONDAY NIGHT

The call from the switchboard came through to Sergeant Beresford at Thorpe police station at around 6.30 p.m. on Monday. Multiple complaints about dogs howling and barking all day at Cooper's Stables. Someone claimed they'd been bitten. And now two of the owner's dogs had been caught worrying the young pheasants in their woodland pen at the Stainthorpe Shoot. One of them had bitten Edward Lambert, the manager. Please send officer to check.

Beresford chewed the corner of his mouth. It wasn't unexpected. Not at all. But it would be much easier for him and everybody else if one of the complainers had thought to go and check themselves. Not that he was surprised. Charlie Cooper who ran the livery yard and riding school near Thorpe had a nasty temper. He'd managed to make enemies of all his neighbours, particularly the pheasant shoot and Boyes, a nearby farmer. It was slightly odd Johnny Boyes hadn't called too. He was usually the first to complain about Cooper, especially when he'd had a few.

Who should he send? He checked the roster. PC Josh Mason? Not a bad idea. He was a capable youngster. He'd shown some initiative as well as a degree of common sense when he'd been sent to investigate reports of illegal waste chemical dumping by the river, and managed to get the Environment Agency to intervene before it had got into the water. Beresford, who'd guessed who the perpetrators were, had spoken to them and told them to be more careful. It would be interesting to see how he dealt with the problem of the Coopers.

A couple of hours later, Josh leaned out of the car window and pressed the buzzer at the gate to the stables. He'd persuaded an angry Ed Lambert at the pheasant pens not to shoot Cooper's dogs and to keep them locked up until Josh could get Cooper to collect them. Josh had decided to go with him to avoid any violence. It was a pity because he'd planned to treat himself to a takeaway tonight. He'd squeezed in a run this morning and he'd walked a fair bit while carrying out welfare checks on some of the elderly living out of town, who were still without electricity after Storm Beatrice on Friday night, the first one of the winter. If he ended up getting back to Thorpe late, he'd be too hungry to wait for a Deliveroo from his favourite Indian in Harrogate. It would have to be a burger from Sean's van in the square at Thorpe. Or he could forgo the takeaway and eat one of the healthy meals he'd stocked up on when the waistband of his trousers had become uncomfortably tight. He probably should, given he'd already bought himself a bag of home-made shortbread as a reward for the run.

A long, narrow tarmacked driveway led down to the stables. No lights peered through the evening dusk. Horses grazed in the fields on either side. It was still warm enough for them to be kept out, although they wore coats. The large one with huge feet – some Shire ancestry there – stared at him. It had ripped part of its water-proof coat off. And, as Josh watched, it tossed his head back and seized a ribbon of torn material and pulled again. Josh eyed the fence. He wasn't keen on horses. He'd had the obligatory couple of riding lessons as a boy but had hated the way the pony dipped its head to snatch at the grass when he was on its back, making him feel he might slide down its neck. He didn't have much of a head for heights anyway.

The horse cantered over to him. The fence looked neither high enough nor strong enough to stop it from getting out if it wanted to. A small elder tree had fallen and smashed the top rung. Damage from Storm Beatrice probably. It had whistled through the exposed eastern side of Thorpe at a great rate. Josh had been off duty but his colleagues had been full of stories of trees blocking roads and smashing roofs.

No answer from the intercom. He tried the gate again in case it had been silently and electronically unlocked, but no. A notice told him the stables were open from Tuesday to Sunday and there were strictly no visitors nor owners allowed on the yard on Mondays.

Today was Monday.

He pressed the buzzer again and held it down for a few seconds.

The noise of dogs howling and barking greeted him. How many dogs did Cooper have? He hoped they weren't loose as well. He wasn't that keen on dogs either if he was honest, although he tried to keep it well hidden.

Still no answer.

He tried the buzzer again, this time holding it down until it left the tip of his finger curiously flattened. Then he sounded the car horn several times.

Nothing. Except the dogs. He wasn't surprised the neighbours had complained. Some freak of acoustics made the noise echo round the surrounding hills. Clearly the Coopers weren't there. Probably taken advantage of the warmer autumn weather for a day out or gone into Harrogate for a bit of shopping.

What should he do?

It was a question he asked himself a lot. Somehow his studies at police college hadn't quite prepared him for the reality of everyday policing. There were a lot more grey areas than he'd been led to believe. It wasn't easy to know the right thing to do, and Josh was determined to do the right thing. Joining the police had been his childhood ambition. He wanted to do well though, and there hadn't been much opportunity to impress his superiors stuck, as he was, in Local Policing, hoping for a chance to move to a more interesting department. He wasn't going to end up like Sergeant Beresford, who'd spent his whole working life at Thorpe police station, and who everybody told him loved running the Local Policing team. Josh wasn't so sure. He'd caught a look in Beresford's eyes when yet another junior PC announced a promotion and headed off to Northallerton or York to join Traffic or Crime. It had taken him aback. Not the least because a couple of things Beresford had let slip implied that he saw Josh as a suitable replacement when he retired.

So he wasn't going to ask Beresford what to do. No, he'd check the place over first. He glanced at his phone. Just time for a look round and still make it back for the promised chat with his aunt. With Kezia, he reminded himself. She'd told him to stop calling her Aunty when she moved into his flat. She was quite young for an aunt anyway, much younger than his mother – theirs had been a large family.

At first, he'd regretted letting his parents persuade him to offer her the spare room of his newly acquired flat. They'd known he'd have to rent the second bedroom out to cover the mortgage, so when Kezia and David had divorced – and not amicably – they'd pushed him. He'd probably never see her, they'd said. Their hours were so different. She was broke and she was family. It wouldn't be for ever. Long enough to let her get back on her feet and find a proper job. And they'd contribute. Although Kezia mustn't know.

He knew they were taking advantage of him but he couldn't say no. They'd helped him financially with the flat purchase and Aunty's— Kezia's only other option was to stay with them. Except his father couldn't stand her. Chalk and cheese they were, according to Mum, and she'd begged him privately to take pity on her and do this one thing, promising she'd sort it if it went on too long.

It was a year now, though. Mainly it had been OK. His

colleagues had stopped mocking him for living with his aunt and his friends had got used to her presence. She was hardly there anyway; she spent a lot of time at the small warehouse she used as a photographic studio and when she was in she kept out of his way.

Perhaps she was planning to leave and that was why she wanted to talk. Strangely enough, the thought of finding someone else wasn't as welcome as he'd thought it would be.

He'd find out soon enough – provided he checked the stables quickly.

He clambered over the gate and walked down the track, keeping to the far side as he passed the black horse. It stopped chewing and stared at him, then turned and walked alongside him. Sweat broke out under the heavy material of his uniform. He sped up but the horse matched him pace for pace.

So he was relieved when he reached the gate into the yard and found it unlocked. He shut it firmly behind him. Buildings surrounded the concreted yard. A large barn with rolls of black-plastic-covered haylage on his left, then lower buildings on the other two sides. Some were stables, but on the right the near doors were marked Tack Room and Office. To the side of the building, stairs led up to a first floor squeezed beneath a low roof. All doors were firmly closed, including the one keeping the dogs in. The noise was deafening as, encouraged by his presence, they barked even more. The door rattled against the lock as they hurled themselves against it. He wondered how the two he'd seen at the pheasant shoot had escaped.

Josh waited for a pause and shouted. No answer apart from even more frantic barking. There was no one in.

He thought quickly about the Cooper family. He knew them vaguely in the way he knew most of the old families in and around Thorpe. He was Thorpe born and bred himself. Everybody knew everybody here.

Charlie Cooper ran the yard and stables. He had a wife but Josh couldn't remember her name. A thin woman, he thought, prone to whinging about things. Or at least she had that sort of face. And a son and a daughter. Giles was the son. Four years older than Josh. He'd left secondary school the year after Josh started and gone to catering college. The daughter was much younger, but he couldn't remember anything else about her.

He opened the wooden door on his left, thankfully not locked, that led to the Coopers' cottage, and walked through a small York stone-paved courtyard containing a benched table, a barbecue and an array of plants in pots. The back door was locked, so he banged on it, the force of his knocks inspired more by annoyance than a belief anyone was in. No one could have ignored the noise the dogs were making. Not even the thick walls of the cottage would keep it out. Besides, no one locked their back door here if they were in.

'Police,' he called a couple of times for good measure. No answer. What now? Leaving a note didn't quite feel right. He'd noticed French windows in the courtyard, so he picked his way through the flowerpots and shaded his eyes as he looked inside.

It was dark but his eyes made out two large green sofas in a V shape and a child's playpen all facing a chimney with a pile of logs dumped on the hearth. Narrow stairs curved up on the left. There was a lump on the carpet in between the fireplace and the stairs. Dark and long, with what looked like a huge red flower growing out of one end. Had one of the plant pots that lined the inside of the French windows fallen and spilled a mound of earth on the carpet? Then what he'd taken to be broken pieces of earthenware at the other end of the mound resolved themselves into brown leather slippers. He hesitated, unsure of what his eyes were telling him, then tapped on the glass and shouted. A small cloud of flies rose and buzzed around for a few seconds before settling down again on what he realised was a body. Shock coursed through his blood as sharp as the pain of a wasp sting.

What had happened?

He peered again at the body. Charlie Cooper? Probably. The old-man slippers gave it away. Had he fallen and knocked a plant pot over?

He broke down the door in the end – it was surprisingly hard and took several runs before it gave way. He stepped into a porch, which was crammed full of coats and boots, and called although it felt stupid after the racket he'd made breaking in, but he'd been well brought up. Then opened the inner back door that led to the kitchen.

The smell hit him. Pungent but sweet and unmistakeable. Then the noise. A buzzing noise. More flies.

On the floor by the stove, Mrs Cooper lay face up in a pool of blood. It had matted her hair into thick spikes, giving her a punk-like appearance. A pan of Bolognese sauce on the hob echoed the colour of the blood. Some part of Josh's consciousness registered that the gas was turned off and that a wooden spoon also lay on the floor tiles. It had clearly been dropped by Mrs Cooper as she fell and had left a spatter of sauce drops where it had hit the ground.

Another body slumped face down at the kitchen table. The newspaper beneath the head had soaked up the worst of the blood and dried a deep and ruddy brown, the colour of freshly fallen autumn leaves.

Josh became aware he'd been standing and staring for quite some time. He pulled himself together and called the station.

'Recent?' Sergeant Beresford's voice was at its most clipped.

Josh forced himself to think logically.

'Don't think so. The blood has dried. And there are flies.'

'Is it the Coopers?'

'The woman is probably Mrs Cooper and I guess the other body is Giles, her son. It's a youngish man but—'

'OK. Don't touch them. Check the rest of the house. Then secure the premises and wait outside. I'll set the ball rolling.'

He'd been right about the body by the French windows in the sitting room. Shot in the face and clearly at close range. Some freak circumstance had caused the bullet to open a wound like a flower. A huge red lily with thick bulbous petals and a dark centre.

Josh thought the image would never leave him.

He saw the younger woman over by the stairs as soon as he looked away, horror briefly overwhelming him. For a brief and stupid second he hoped she was alive. That coming down the stairs unaware, the shock of what she'd seen had made her faint and tumble – but, when he turned her over, he saw the great hole in her chest. The carpet had soaked up the blood.

She held something in her hand. Cards, he thought. Quite large ones and colourful. Tarot? He took a closer look. The top card showed a naked child riding a grey horse while up above a huge yellow sun gazed serenely down. The Sun. A joyful card. Except someone had defaced it. Two red slashes, the pen so forcibly applied it had dug into the surface, were scratched over the child's face. It made Josh think of the corpse by the window with its head blown half away. He couldn't see the second card and he knew better than to touch them.

His radio crackled.

'Sarge?'

'Found anything?'

'Another two bodies in the sitting room. Both dead. Mr Cooper, I think, and a younger woman.' He forced himself to remember his firearms training. 'Shotgun, I suppose. Close quarters. It's... it's...'

He couldn't find the words to describe the face.

'Aah. You OK?'

'Yes, Sarge.'

'Sounds like Charlie Cooper, and probably his daughter, Chloe. The mother's name is Elaine.'

'I've found the whole family then.'

'Not quite, I'm afraid. There's a child. Under two, we think. Chloe Cooper's son. You'll have to check the rest of the house for him.'

Josh remembered then. Chloe had barely left school when she'd had a baby. The father was one of Giles's friends. Charlie Cooper had been furious.

Less than two years old! He didn't think he could bear to discover the small body mutilated like the others. Like the child on the tarot card. He forced himself to check behind the sofa, then went to the stairs. He noticed now they were spattered with mud and his misgivings ratcheted up a notch. It was unlikely the family would walk through the cottage in muddy boots. It looked as though someone else had gone upstairs. He checked his own boots. He didn't want to add to the mud. But they were clean. Then, stepping round the mud, he went up to the bedrooms. They were the only place the child might be. The cottage was little more than a two-up two-down with the downstairs rooms knocked into one and a kitchen extension added.

He hesitated on the landing. Three doors. The first opened into a small shower room. Empty. Fresh air poured in through the window, banishing the stench of blood. He took a few deep breaths. Back on the landing the smell hit him again. Not only blood but something rotten. Two doors remained. Both ajar. Only two bedrooms. He wondered about the family's sleeping arrangements. There must be another bedroom somewhere. Maybe in the yard. Above the stables.

A rustling noise came from one of the rooms. Rats? They were everywhere, especially in a stables. Nesting in the straw. Stealing the horses' feed. Rats ate corpses. Especially small ones.

It took him every ounce of willpower to push the door open. The smell was even stronger here. It must be Chloe's, the daughter's, bedroom. A small room with a single bed and a wardrobe and, over by the window, a cot. A quilt-covered lump inside it. Moving.

He stamped his foot, clapped his hands and shouted, to scare away what was inside. Anything rather than pull the quilt back and see— But small hands thrust the quilt down and a head popped up. Its mouth opened into a round at the sight of Josh, then the face crumpled and the child yelled.

Josh picked up the screaming youngster and fled the house, burying the child's head in his shoulder as he walked through the sitting room and kitchen and outside. The shock of the cold shut him up briefly and Josh heard sirens in the distance.

'Shhh,' he murmured into the child's sweaty hair.

The smell was the full nappy the child was wearing, now

leaking all over his uniform. How long had the kid been alone? He was probably starving. Maybe he should go back into the kitchen. Try to find him something to eat. But he couldn't face it. Besides, what would he do with the child? He wasn't going to take him back into the cottage.

Blue flashing lights turned in to the drive. Help was on its way.

'It's going to be all right,' he muttered to the little boy. 'Just you see, everything's going to be all right.'

It occurred to him that, with his mother, uncle and grandparents all dead, it probably wasn't.

TWO

JOSH MASON

SAME NIGHT

Seven hours later, dressed in borrowed sweatpants, T-shirt and trainers that pinched his toes, Josh climbed out of his car and opened his front door. His front door. The phrase still gave him a momentary surge of pleasure. OK, it was only a small and boxy flat over a chemist's in the centre of Thorpe. A bit soulless and dull. But his own. His very own. Not many people could say that at the age of twenty-five.

It was only a start though. The first step on the ladder whose top rung was a warehouse conversion flat. All bare bricks, high ceilings and strange pillars remaining from its previous life. In the centre of Leeds, he thought, or maybe York. A big city, anyway. Somewhere away from people who'd known him since he was a baby.

He put his car keys in the Faraday pouch on the windowsill and wondered what to do. He was very tired. The waiting around while the team from headquarters had organised the scene and the CSI officers had started their laborious job had been long and tedious. Someone from Social Services had taken the child. Not that Josh had been completely confident in the woman. When he'd told her, slightly anxiously, that he'd fed him a whole bag of short-bread, she seemed to have little idea as to what a child of that age could and couldn't eat. It had been one of the CSI staff who'd told him the kid was old enough to eat anything.

'What will happen to him?' Josh had asked.

'He'll go to an emergency foster carer now, but his father is local. We're trying to get hold of him.'

Once the child was in safe hands he'd hoped to get away, but he was told to wait until DCI Carter arrived. Josh had a sense that everybody was waiting for him even though the routine work of processing the scene continued. When he finally showed up, entering unhurriedly and unobtrusively, it was only the sudden stiffening of the officer at the gate that made Josh look twice, inter-ested to see the famous DCI Carter who'd spectacularly failed to solve the murder of eleven-year-old Peter Walker a year ago – a case that had left its mark on Thorpe. Josh could see little of him in the grey greatcoat with its wide collar turned up against the chill as he passed through the gate into the cottage.

Ten minutes later, he was told Carter wanted Josh to walk him through the scene. Normally Josh would have been nervous but thrilled to talk to the head of Crime, but going into the cottage again didn't appeal. Not that he had a choice. He put the hooded white suit on and stretched the slip-on covers over his boots. It seemed a bit pointless as he'd tramped through the whole cottage already. However he was glad of the clothing when he went into the kitchen, full of CSI and forensics officers examining the bodies and photographing everything. Along with the camera flashes and the low murmur of officers going about their job, it distanced him from his surroundings, and he was able to give Carter a coherent account of his discoveries.

The DCI listened but made no comment. It was hard to tell what he was thinking. He barely looked at Josh anyway but nodded occasionally, his floppy fringe of brown and grey hair rising and falling on his forehead until he brushed it out of his eyes and tucked it under the suit hood. His gaze rested on each element of the scene without blinking for a few seconds as though committing it to memory, then swivelled to the next as Josh gave his account of discovering the bodies.

The work of discovering, recording and cataloguing was focussed on the kitchen and when they went through into the sitting room they were alone. Josh had found his rhythm though. He explained how he'd seen Charlie Cooper's corpse through the window and how he'd mistaken the mangled face for a huge red flower. For the first time Carter looked at him properly. Josh regretted his words. They sounded overwrought and fanciful.

But Carter nodded and squatted down over the body. 'I've not seen anything quite like it before,' he said. 'The effects of a shotgun at close range hitting the centre of the face and forcing the outside to explode open, I imagine. But Forensics will explain better. Looks as though he's been shot twice.' He pointed to the shoulder and waved away a few flies that had circled upwards from Cooper's corpse as he leaned over. 'Not an easy thing to find, though.'

Josh shook his head.

They crossed over to Chloe Cooper's body. Josh explained he'd turned it over, hoping for a brief and stupid moment that the young woman was only injured. Carter's gaze was fixed on Chloe Cooper's hand and the cards it still clutched.

'Tarot,' Josh said helpfully.

'I know.'

He thought of telling Carter the top card's name but decided not to. He didn't want to explain how he knew. His mother's penchant for doing impromptu tarot readings after a few drinks at a party was a source of embarrassment to his father and, therefore, to Josh.

Carter bent down and removed the two cards from Chloe's hand. The second was one of the kings. He sealed the cards inside an evidence bag, wrote on it and put it in the pocket of his paper suit. Something remained in Chloe's hand. Carter prised it out of the stiff fingers.

It was a note. A very short note. Typed on a scrap of mauve

paper that had been torn from a bigger sheet. Josh had time to read it before Carter dropped it, in turn, into a plastic pouch.

For Freddy, it said. *Tell Giles.*

Carter looked directly at Josh.

'Local Policing, aren't you?'

'Yes, sir.'

'Based in Thorpe?'

'Yes, sir.'

'Mason, you said?'

Josh only said yes this time. He thought he'd probably said sir enough.

'You found the boy upstairs?'

'Yes. Is his name Freddy?'

'I would imagine it is. Do you know the family?'

'Not really.' Josh racked his brains for something useful to say. 'Charlie Cooper was known to have a fiery temper.'

'No gun here though. So unlikely he shot his family and then killed himself.'

Josh followed Carter upstairs, both men using the clear plastic stepping plates laid out to prevent the mud on the stair carpet being disturbed. Josh wondered if the murderer had gone upstairs but been unable to shoot Freddy.

Despite the slipperiness of the shoe coverings they wore and the narrowness of the plates, the DCI padded upstairs easily. He was a big man, towering over Josh, and with the breadth and depth of a Viking. Probably not from round here. The Yorkshire Dales and Moors bred tough, thickset men but on the whole they were shortish.

Carter examined all the surfaces, then opened drawers and boxes and rifled through the shelves in the wardrobe. He was quick and deft. He bagged nothing though. When he'd finished, he stood by the cot and stared through the window, set into thick, thick walls. He pulled at the fingers of his gloves, letting them snap back into place with a crack.

Josh waited.

'That'll do for now, Mason,' he said without turning. 'Report to the crime scene manager so your uniform can be bagged, and I'd like you to write a brief statement while it's all fresh in your mind. Give it direct to me tomorrow.'

Josh wasn't quite sure how he was supposed to do that. Crime headquarters were at Northallerton with a significant presence in York, but he didn't know where Carter was based. It was probably one of those things he should know. He thought about asking Carter, then decided he'd speak to Sergeant Beresford in the morning.

But when he got back to the station, dressed only in a fresh paper suit after he'd handed over his clothes to Forensics and promising himself he'd always carry a spare set in the car from now on, Beresford was still there. The investigation would be based in Thorpe – at least initially – and he was overseeing the clearing of the big room on the first floor they hadn't used since the Walker case, ready for the arrival of the crime team tomorrow. He found Josh some old clothes and waited while he completed his statement, then took it, saying he'd give it to Carter first thing and Josh wasn't to come in until late morning.

So yes, here he was, home finally and very tired, although he didn't think he'd sleep. Not yet. He should eat something, and he fancied a cup of tea. He stood on the landing, unable to decide what to do first and almost wishing he was back at his parents' where there was every chance his mother, Zina, a light sleeper, would have been woken by his arrival and fussed over him with tea and food. Above all, he realised he'd like to tell someone about it all. Someone who wouldn't make him feel he needed to be cogent and professional.

So he was quite pleased when Aunty— when Kezia opened her bedroom door, her eyes blinking in the unexpected light, and asked him if everything was all right.

'Sort of,' he said. 'Sorry I'm late. Something came up at work.'

'I guessed that,' she said. A slight smile lifted her colourless face, still pinched with sleep.

'I didn't mean to wake you,' he added.

'You didn't.'

There was a pause and he realised she wasn't going to explain why she was awake at two in the morning.

'I found some dead bodies.'

'I see.'

'It was bound to happen eventually but it was a shock.'

She came right out of the bedroom now and closed the door behind her. Beneath her thick green-checked dressing gown, she was wearing white silky pyjamas. His mother had the same pair but she wore them with a brightly coloured kimono.

'I'll make you tea. Have you eaten?'

'I don't think I could eat but tea would be lovely.'

He sat at the tiny table he'd squeezed into the kitchen and found himself telling her about the call to go to the stables while she filled the kettle. She interrupted him straight away.

'Cooper's Stables? Is that where the dead bodies were?'

'Yes.'

He remembered she used to keep her horse there.

'Who? Who's died?' she asked.

'The Coopers. All four of them. Not the child.'

'No one else?'

'No.'

She breathed in and out a few times, then poured boiling water into the mugs and put them on the table. She'd made it exactly how he liked. Strong with a dash of milk and a teaspoon of sugar. He wrapped his hands round the comforting heat of the mug, then launched back into his account. He told her all the details. He couldn't help himself. Mr Cooper's face through the window, the pool of blood beneath Mrs Cooper's head, his terrible fear for the child when he saw the mud on the stairs and the awful, awful stench.

'The smell,' he said. 'It's like it's impregnated my skin and hair. I had a shower at the station but I can still smell it.'

'Blood?'

'Mainly.'

'And aging blood. Starting to rot. The stench of anything rotting is powerful and sweet too. It's designed to attract the things that might find the corpse useful.' She looked at him as though trying to decide whether to go on. 'I imagine there were flies.'

'Quite a few. And the smell, you know, it reminded me... We went to Kew Gardens once when I was a child. One of the plants there, a huge strange-looking thing, they said it smelled exactly like a rotting corpse.'

'Titan arum,' she said. 'The corpse flower.'

He nodded. His mind back in the bloody cottage. 'Well, they were right. It does smell exactly like a dead body.'

She smiled. She never gave much away, and her lack of horror was somehow comforting. It made her easy to talk to now, and he found himself telling her how he'd wondered – very briefly – if he could simply leave the scene and pretend he'd found nothing.

It crossed his mind this was the first proper conversation they'd had. If you could call it a conversation. It was mostly him talking but she said enough to show she was listening acutely. The only time she showed any emotion was when he mentioned the tarot cards in Chloe Cooper's hand. Something flickered across her face at that point. Disgust maybe. She'd never shared his mother's love of tarot. Which was surprising really given that their mother had taught all the daughters to read the cards.

He gulped the tea down now it was cooler. He was thirsty. She took the cue and busied herself making another as he told her about the endless hours at the police station shivering in a paper suit.

She put two mugs on the table in front of him.

'That one's Yorkshire Tea again. I know that's what you like. And this is a mixture of mine.'

The liquid in the other mug was the colour of yellow autumn leaves turning brown. He didn't fancy it. He wasn't much in the way of herbal teas.

'What's in it?'

'Mint and sage and chamomile and a few other herbs. Plus a little ground cayenne pepper. Chilli. They're all good for shock. Try it, please.'

She fixed her greeny-grey eyes on him. Dad said they were the colour of dirty pond water, but he said a lot of unkind things about her. Josh found he couldn't refuse. The tea had a strong but warm and cleansing fragrance that banished the lingering odour of the cottage. He breathed in deeply a few times. It was probably his tired brain conjuring up stuff but he did feel a bit better. Less wired. He might be able to sleep. He took a sip. Not bad actually, tasting mostly of mint with a sharp underlying flavour and a kick of heat he guessed came from the chilli.

Kezia put the jars of dried herbs back into her cupboard and the Yorkshire Tea back in its place by the kettle, then wiped a few specks of herbs from the worktop. She was very tidy. He liked that about her because he was too. It was the upside of sharing your flat with an older woman.

And at least, at her age, she wasn't likely to bring strange men back to the flat. He didn't fancy making polite conversation over breakfast with someone he didn't know. Plus the walls of the flat weren't that thick. He'd been a bit ill at ease the first time he'd brought a girlfriend back but Kezia had let it slip later that she liked to listen to music in bed, so she always wore headphones. He'd have to make sure he woke her if the fire alarms he'd installed went off. It crossed his mind she couldn't have been been wearing headphones tonight, because she'd heard him come in.

It was quite sad for her really, he thought. Divorced and broke, and with little chance of finding another man. Lesley, one of the PCSOs he worked with, blonde and vivacious, and divorced too, said it was a crowded marketplace. You had to put the work in and get yourself out there. Kiss a lot of frogs. The stories she told about the no-hopers she dated were hilarious. He couldn't imagine Kezia on a date. She was too serious, rarely smiling. Not that she looked too bad. For her age, anyway. Still slim and lithe, and with little grey in the black hair that framed her face in waves. Somehow though you didn't notice her. Her only remarkable feature was the crooked tooth at the front of her mouth. The left one overlapped the right. Maybe that was why she always smiled with her lips shut.

And then he realised he'd forgotten to think about the cottage for at least ten minutes and he'd drunk the rest of her tea without noticing. He yawned.

'I think I'll go to bed now.'

'Good idea. One thing though. Could you find out what's happening to the horses?'

'Of course.'

'Good night then.'

But he lingered, not sure why.

'I'm not due in until late morning,' he said.

'Well, I'll be quiet when I get up.'

'You always are. How's the photography going?'

'It's slow but I'm scraping a living. I'm with Zina tomorrow morning. She wants to refresh the salon pictures.'

His mother owned and ran a successful hairdressing business in the centre of Thorpe. He wondered whether she really wanted new pictures or whether this session was another attempt to help Kezia without her realising.

Something about the look she gave him made him guess she was aware of his thoughts.

'Then in the afternoon, I'm meeting Hamish about a new client.'

'Hamish?'

'Hamish Aitken.'

Hamish had carved himself out a role as Thorpe's local reporter, filing articles for the Yorkshire papers and the occasional story on regional TV news. He published a weekly bulletin grandly called the *Thorpe Gazette*. Sergeant Beresford hated him because he was always criticising the police and the local council. His journalism wasn't quite enough to sustain a living, so he also turned his hand to publicity and, over Covid, had created websites and social media presences for local businesses.

'You won't tell Hamish what I've told you. About Cooper's Stables. In fact, please don't tell anyone.'

He probably shouldn't have poured it all out to her in the first place.

'Of course not. Not that it will make much difference. It'll be all over Thorpe by lunchtime.'

THREE
LAUREN

TUESDAY

Lauren looked at herself in the mirror. Zina, the salon owner, had been right. Short hair suited her. And Zina had kept her promise that it would be easy to look after. A quick flick of hair gel and a few minutes with a dryer were all it had taken. Zina had done her make-up for the photos as well. She must take a note of the products and the colours because it looked tons better than when Lauren did it. She guessed they were probably expensive, but maybe Sean might buy her a voucher for her birthday. If she gave him a strong enough hint. The thought of Sean and her upcoming birthday sent her brain down frequently travelled pathways. The relationship wasn't that old, but she was already having doubts. Partly because of her age. At twenty-nine about to be thirty, her time for having children was running out. No children was the one thing Sean was adamant about. Even though the miracles of modern medicine meant they could test to see if the baby carried Sean's illness. She'd been sure she didn't want children until recently, and now she was in two minds. It was all right for Sean to be against. He already had Freddy.

'All done,' the photographer said.

'Perfect timing,' Zina said. 'Lunch? You too, Lauren?'

Really she should get back. She'd received a shipment of kid leather from China yesterday. It had been expensive and the sooner she made it into something to sell the sooner she'd get a return on her money. Gloves probably. It was too soft for the sort of handbags her Thorpe clientele liked.

'It'll have to be quick,' the photographer said. 'I'm meeting Hamish this afternoon.'

'Oh yes?' Zina said. 'Has he got some work for you?'

'Yes.'

'What would that be?'

'Photos for someone's website. A Mrs Monroe. Tomorrow.'

'Not the thing I saw in the *Gazette* on Sunday. The clairvoyant woman offering a free session in exchange for photos? Really?'

'Yes.' The photographer's reply was short and off-putting. 'Exactly like the shoot I've just done for you.'

Lauren had realised from their conversation during the photo-shoot that the two of them were sisters. You'd never have guessed though. Zina was lovely. With her beautifully cut hair, a casual blend of honey and gold tones which was wound in a tight yet ornate chignon today, and perfect complexion (Lauren's skin still had a tendency to break out in spots round her nose whenever she was tired), plus her ability to put unusual colour combinations of clothes together, she always looked amazing. Whereas the photographer – Lauren didn't think Zina had mentioned her name – was dim beside Zina's glow. Her hair – long and dark with a few grey threads running through it and tufting out at odd angles round her sharp face – was the thing you noticed mostly about her. That and the deft way she handled the camera equipment.

And then Lauren remembered she had seen her before. At the Christmas panto rehearsals. She'd come for a couple of the Sunday sessions and taken lots of photos, not only of the actors fumbling their lines onstage and arguing with each other over where to stand, but of everybody, including the scenery crew Lauren was part of.

'I'd love lunch,' she said. 'But I'll have to be quick too.'

'I'll get something from the burger van in the square then, and we can eat in the back room here while the salon is closed.'

'I don't fancy a burger much,' the photographer said.

'They do lots of other stuff – salads and nice sandwiches,' Zina said before Lauren had a chance. 'Sean Price has really taken it upmarket. He's Lauren's partner,' she added with a smile at Lauren. 'His mother came in the other day for a colour top-up and I promised I'd give it a try.'

'You colour Annie's hair?' Lauren said.

Annie, Sean's mum, had curly hair, deep chestnut apart from a thick streak of blond at the front. She'd had it since she was born.

'Yes. It's complicated because of keeping the blond streak au naturel.'

'You probably shouldn't have told me because she swears blind she doesn't colour it.'

'Does she? Oh well. So shall I see what Sean can offer us?'

'All right,' the photographer said. 'I mean great. Sounds lovely.'

'My treat,' Zina said quickly as she reached for her handbag.

The photographer's handbag was one of Lauren's. A model she hadn't made for a few years and, despite the scuffs on the leather, it looked fine, which was pretty good going. The strap was coming away from the bag at one end though.

'I could mend that for you,' she said. 'Your handbag. It's one of mine. I have the leather shop off the square.'

'It's fine as it is.'

'I'll pay for it, Kezia,' Zina said. 'I think I bought it for you in the first place.'

Kezia, that was the photographer's name. Unusual. Lauren had heard it before. She tried to remember where.

'I wouldn't charge Zina, nor you,' Lauren said. 'Not after my free haircut.'

'I said no.' Kezia turned away and busied herself taking down the lights she'd clipped to the mirror. Zina shook her head slightly, caught Lauren looking at her and gave her a papering-over-a-diffi-cult-moment sort of smile and shrug.

There was an awkward silence until Lauren thought of something to say.

'Would you do my tarot cards again, Zina?'

Zina had given her a reading at a party a few months ago when Lauren had been having her first doubts about Sean. She'd drawn the Seven of Swords. A card Zina had said could mean deceit and betrayal. Someone was maybe being dishonest with her. She'd laughed it off at the time, but the memory of the card had returned when she'd discovered the true extent of Sean's gambling. He'd stopped now. Or at least he said he had. Not that she cared. It was his money and if he wanted to waste it that was fine with her. She'd made certain they had separate finances ever since.

'I don't have any cards at the salon.'

'I brought some along,' Lauren said.

She pulled out the colourful packet of cards and passed it to Zina, who opened it and spread them out on the table with a swift and practised gesture.

'Must we?' Kezia's voice was surprisingly sharp.

'It's just a piece of fun. Don't get so worked up. You used to love them, don't you remember?' Zina turned to Lauren. 'Touch them and shuffle them and think about what you want to ask while I go and order food.'

They decided what they wanted to eat and Zina left.

Kezia stared at the cards as Lauren picked them up. She remembered where she'd heard the name Kezia before.

It was the name of David Kingsley's first wife. Becky, his second wife, had mentioned it, although she normally referred to her as the ex. If Kezia was the first wife, David had married two very different women. Becky, one of Lauren's best customers, was self-centred, gorgeous and magnificently lazy unless she wanted something. Then her pursuit was as tenacious as a saltwater croc-odile's jaw gripping its prey.

David had come into the shop last Christmas to buy Becky a

handbag. Becky had primed Lauren to show him the two she liked best and to suggest he bought both. Lauren had disliked him as soon as he walked into the shop, slightly sweaty and in a slightly too tight three-piece suit – really they needed to fit impeccably to look good. He'd paid cash and tried to knock the price of the handbag down because of it. People often asked for a discount but the way he'd gone about it had ruffled her, especially as he was known to be well off. It wasn't difficult to guess what Becky had seen in him. The man had little in the way of personal charm.

She couldn't imagine him and Kezia together.

She shuffled the cards slowly, concentrating on Sean. The trouble was, there were things about him she really liked. Like his ambition and talent. Like the fact he didn't work nine to five and he understood she didn't either. Like the way he was happy to follow her lead in bed. That part of their relationship was good. In fact, it was better than good.

She sighed, then remembered she wasn't alone. Kezia was still gazing at the tarot cards, though.

'They help me think about my life,' Lauren found herself saying.

'Do they?'

'Yes. That's all really.'

'Can't you do that without them?'

'I suppose so. But they're helpful.'

'So long as you know they're only bits of card with pretty pictures on. Pictures that can be interpreted in many different ways.'

Lauren laid them out face down on the desk, but before she could pick them up again Kezia turned one over. It showed a scene in a medieval village. A man in a red hood, surrounded by vases of flowers, held out a bunch to an older-looking woman.

'Six of Cups,' Kezia said.

Lauren realised the vases were large chalice-type cups.

'What does it mean?'

'Whatever you want. What do you think?'

Lauren stared at the card. 'Well, the man is giving flowers to the older woman. Maybe she's his mother or another older relation. So something to do with family? With visiting them.' She thought again. Normally the cards had a meaning beyond the obvious. 'Or revisiting your past. Dealing with something in your distant past? When you were a child. Unless it's some weird thing to do with toy boys and cougars.'

Kezia smiled thinly. 'No toy boys. The rest is pretty accurate. Something unresolved from your past but there are lots of variations. Do you have anything that would fit that?'

Lauren thought a bit more. 'We all have unresolved things from our past and childhood.'

'Exactly! So it will mean something to everybody.'

It occurred to Lauren that Kezia had drawn the card. Not her.

Kezia picked the deck up now and shuffled it, then spread the cards out on the desk. Her movement was as practised as Zina's.

'Try another,' she said.

But as Lauren leaned forward to choose a card, Kezia's hands twitched as if an electric shock had passed through them.

'Wait,' she said. 'Count them.'

She watched as Lauren did as she was told.

'Seventy.'

'Check. There should be seventy-eight.'

But Lauren counted seventy again. Kezia took the cards, turned them face up and sorted them into five rows.

'What are they?'

'The five suits,' she replied tersely. 'Four suits of fourteen cards – Cups, Swords, Wands and Pentacles – they're the minor arcana. And twenty-two cards in the major arcana. They're probably the ones you know best.'

'The Hanged Man and the Wheel of Fortune.'

'Yes, that's two of them.'

She counted the major arcana.

'Death, the Sun and the Tower are missing.'

She sorted each suit into chronological order, then sighed.

'The Ten of Swords is missing too.'

'Which one's that?'

'In this deck – the classic Rider–Waite one – the Ten of Swords shows a corpse lying on the ground stabbed by ten swords.'

'Nasty.'

Kezia sighed again. 'It's not a happy card, always associated with pain and endings, although not necessarily violent death. The stabbing and the corpse are symbolic.'

'Can we do the reading anyway?'

'No point with all these cards missing.'

'What else is missing?'

'The four Kings. A strange mix. I wonder—'

But whatever else Kezia was going to say was drowned out by Zina bursting back into the room. She plonked a tray of salads and sandwiches on the desk.

'Lauren,' she said straight away. 'I'm so sorry. I've just heard. You should have said. We could have done this some other time.'

'Heard what?'

A small strand of Zina's chignon had escaped the confines of its plait and curled over her forehead. She poked it back into place as she stared at Lauren.

'You really don't know, do you? About the Coopers? And Sean?'

'What?' Lauren said guardedly.

'The Coopers are dead.'

'What do you mean?'

But Zina stared at her helplessly.

'Not Freddy.' This was Kezia. 'Freddy's fine. The rest of the family have been shot. But Freddy is fine.'

'You know about—' Zina said, but Lauren interrupted her.

'Freddy's OK? You're sure?'

'He's fine.'

'Sorry, Lauren. I should have said first of all that Freddy was all right. But I thought you'd know. With Sean being his father.' Zina had found her voice.

'But the others— I mean, all of them? Chloe, as well?'

'I'm afraid so. Someone broke in and massacred the whole family. And the thing is, Lauren, the police have taken Sean in for questioning.'

Thoughts raced through Lauren's mind. Mainly that the police were bound to interview Sean. Everybody knew how much he hated Giles. And Charlie Cooper. Especially since the big falling-out when Charlie had threatened to shoot Sean and his mum if they came round again. The police would let him go. Charlie Cooper had alienated half the local population anyway.

'When?' she asked. 'When did it happen?'

'No one knows.'

She hadn't actually spoken to Sean since Sunday morning. He'd stayed over at his parents' on Sunday night and gone straight to work from there. He always finished late on Mondays and started late on Tuesdays, so she'd been asleep when he came in and he was asleep when she left.

Not that it mattered.

'I expect it's nothing,' she said. 'I mean the police taking Sean in. There's history between him and the Coopers. He and Giles used to run a catering business from a burger van until they fell out. An old van. Not like the one Sean has now. And of course Charlie Cooper hated him because of Chloe. But he'd never...'

Sean was still bitter about the souring of his relationship with Giles, although it had been as much his fault as anybody's. He should have been more careful with Chloe. Especially as she was so much younger than him. In any case, setting up with his own van had been the making of him. He'd borrowed the money from his parents and the business, thanks to his hard work, was slowly becoming very successful.

'I'm sure it's nothing,' Zina said. 'The police will be interviewing everyone with connections to the Coopers. Remember how they pulled in everybody who'd driven down the Bishop Sawley Road after...'

Zina ground to a halt. No one liked to talk about young Peter

Walker's death. The eleven-year-old had disappeared while cycling home from school one afternoon and his dead body had been found a couple of weeks later on the moors. Word was he'd been shot and very recently, but the police had never released details. Nor had they charged anyone. No schoolchildren cycled or walked alone to school anymore.

'It's OK,' Lauren said. 'I'll give Sean a call.'

But he didn't answer. Of course, he couldn't if he was with the police. She tapped the phone against her teeth and wondered what to do. His parents. Maybe they'd heard something. And if they hadn't, she should warn them.

There was no answer from the house but Sean's mum answered her mobile – in itself a miracle as Annie usually treated it as something to be used only when she wanted to call someone.

'Lauren,' she said.

'Annie, have you heard?'

'Of course. Sean rang me this morning. It's terrible.'

She didn't sound as though she thought it was all that terrible, but then Charlie Cooper had treated Sean and Annie appallingly, fetching his gun and shooting over their heads when they'd gone round to try and make some sort of peace. Only Annie's insistence had stopped Sean reporting him to the police. She'd said there was still a chance Chloe would let them see Freddy without her father knowing and, in any case, Chloe would leave home at some point. She'd been right too.

'Someone told me the police have taken Sean in. Have you—'

'Is that why he isn't here? I've been waiting for ages. They've arrested him.'

Lauren tried to insert herself into Annie's diatribe to explain she didn't think they'd arrested Sean, but gave up, pressing her phone tight to her ear so Kezia and Zina wouldn't hear Annie ranting on about Charlie Cooper's despicableness. She came close to saying he deserved to die, but managed to swerve and say that she wasn't at all surprised that someone had killed him.

'Where are you?' Lauren managed to ask.

'Social Services.' She spat the words out. 'They called Sean this morning and told him about the Coopers. They've taken Freddy into care. Sean was supposed to meet me here.'

'I suppose the police picked him up before he could.'

'The social worker won't talk to me without Sean being present. It's absolutely ridiculous. I'm Freddy's grandmother. Poor little love. He was in that house of death all night and all day. On his own. Twenty-four hours with nothing to eat or drink. I can't bear the thought of it. And now they won't even tell me how he is other than he's being looked after by one of their most experienced carers. But it's not the same as his family, is it Lauren?'

Lauren felt sorry for Annie. She didn't particularly like her but her love for Freddy was very real. As it was for Sean.

'I'll go to the police and see what's happening,' Lauren said.

'No, don't worry. I'll go. I'll tell them about Charlie Cooper shooting at us. That should make them see sense.'

'No, Annie. Don't do that. Please don't.'

Zina and Kezia were both staring at her but looked away quickly when she caught their eyes.

'Don't mention Charlie threatening you. It will make things worse,' she muttered. 'Look, I'll meet you at the station.'

FOUR

KEZIA HERON

SAME DAY

Zina accused me of forgetting how much I loved the tarot cards as a child. I hadn't though. We didn't have much as children. When you move from place to place at a moment's notice, things get left behind. But we always had the tarot. It was my mother's way of making a living when all else failed.

That along with a few other grifts and scams.

I loved the cards. Each with its snippet of a different story. Enough to spark a daydream full of adventure and peril and heroes and villains. Most children had books. I had the tarot and my imagination. I drew a card every morning. Not to see what the day would bring. That's for the fools who believe in it. No, I drew one to escape into a daydream.

Until I grew up and stopped. Until I realised our life was all wrong. And left.

I hadn't picked up a deck since.

But I took the ones Lauren brought with her to the salon. She left in such a rush, she didn't notice.

The missing cards worried me.

And now back at the flat, I counted them again and again and checked the little marks I'd seen. The marks were still there and there were still eight cards missing. And, once again, I thought of Josh's strange story of finding two tarot cards in Chloe Cooper's hands. He hadn't told me what they were. It was probably a coincidence. Nothing to do with this deck. Except I thought I knew where one of the other missing cards was.

Leave it. It's the past. It's over.

Hamish had cancelled our meeting. Too busy, he'd said. Doubtless using every contact to find out about the Coopers' deaths. He shouldn't have cancelled our meeting as I probably knew more than anyone.

Not that I'd reveal what Josh had told me.

I didn't even want to think about it myself.

The edges of the tarot deck bit into my hands. I spread them in a wide arc on the kitchen table. I hadn't lost the knack. I shut my eyes and took one. I couldn't stop myself. It wouldn't count though. Not if it came from a pack with so many cards missing.

The Knight of Cups.

The picture shows a knight in armour riding a grey horse and offering a cup to someone unseen. Noble and upright, he was often the hero of my stories as a youngster.

Like David was the hero of my story as an adult. Until he wasn't.

I wouldn't think about him now.

Of all the horses and riders in the tarot – from memory, there are eight – the Knight of Cups is the only one who looks as though he knows how to ride. He is in the correct classical seat with perfect shoulder/hip/heel alignment and a loose rein. Exactly how I was taught. Back in the days when I'd had a horse. My lovely Bathsheba. I wondered if she was still in Cooper's field down from the stables. She'd be OK though. Because Marty would look after her. Like he was when I last saw her...

FIVE
KEZIA HERON

SIX MONTHS AGO

I thought Bathsheba might not know me when I crossed the lane and approached the field she shared with Harding. It had been nearly a year since I'd seen her. I was wrong though. Horses don't have large brains, but the part devoted to memory is big and well developed. It's why they're good at learning complex actions. Bathy's head shot up as soon as I neared the fence and, when I called, she came straight away and pushed her head into my shoulder.

I sat on the fence now and waited for Marty. The day was warm – for a Yorkshire spring day anyway – and it was good to feel Bathsheba headbutt my knee every few minutes as though she too needed to be sure I was really here. The new grass must be coming through, because the sound of Harding tearing and munching the spring growth was clear through the fluting trill of the curlews out on the nearby moors and rustle of trees in the woods opposite. The coconut smell of the gorse softened the air. The world was waking from its winter stillness.

How very poetical I sounded! Like someone who had no idea that rural life was as full of shit as life everywhere. I shouldn't have come here. It brought back too many memories. Especially Bathsheba's presence. I ran my fingers over her mane from the soft hair at the base and then through the coarser strands. It felt heavy but smooth. Someone had been grooming her. Probably Marty.

Giving her up had been a hard thing. But Charlie Cooper who owned the livery stables had taken me aside a year ago – a chillier spring day than this one when I'd come back from a hack on the moors and Bathsheba's coat was damp with exertion and the fine mist held in the air – and told me David hadn't paid the livery bill since before Covid. A lot of clients had struggled financially during the pandemic but all except David had sorted their debts out and most were now up to date. He still had bills for feed and farriers and vets to pay. I'd cut him off then and asked how much.

It was a lot.

I'd no idea keeping a horse was so expensive. But then I hadn't had much idea about anything. Somehow, over the twenty-five years of our marriage, I'd got used to leaving all that to David. He told me to leave it to him again. He said he'd have a word with Giles, Charlie Cooper's son, because Giles owed him money.

But when Charlie Cooper asked me again, I knew David had done nothing. I realised I had to stop leaving things to him. I couldn't afford to keep Bathsheba. I owed Charlie Cooper a lot of money. It was as simple as one and one make two. I told Charlie Cooper to sell her and use the money to pay what we owed. Then I walked away and never went back.

I did the same with David two months later because... because he wasn't the man I'd thought he was.

The sound of footsteps. Harding, who'd left Bathsheba and me alone to say hello, perked his ears up. A low whistle followed and he snuffled and shook his head as though reluctant to leave the succulent grass. Marty came into view, crossing the lane from the woods, and Harding shook himself again and ambled over to join us.

'You've got mints,' I said as Harding nosed Marty's pockets.

'For this guy, always.' Marty put the tack he'd brought from the stables on the grass and patted Harding's dark neck, then flicked his own blond fringe off his forehead. It was damp with sweat and he smelled of straw and exertion. He pulled the green bandana from round his neck and wiped his face. I smothered a smile. At least he'd grown out of wearing a Stetson.

'Listen,' he said now. 'Bathy's new owner has broken her leg. She's asked Mr Cooper to exercise Bathy for her. He's only too happy to let me do it in my free time.'

Of course Cooper was. And make money out of it. Charlie Cooper charged for every extra service he could.

'So I thought you could ride her rather than just say hello. It means I get more time to ride Harding.' He patted the horse's nose and fed him a mint, along with a few scraps of fluff from his pocket. Harding didn't seem to mind. 'Don't I, boy? I brought Bathsheba's tack down with me. And there's a spare helmet here.'

Marty and I had always got on, despite the age gap, and when I'd bumped into him in Thorpe a couple of days ago, he'd told me Bathsheba had been moved to be with Harding in one of the fields away from the stables. Charlie Cooper used it over spring and summer for the horses whose owners came infrequently to the yard. There was an old barn here, used for storage as the horses were overwintered up at the stables.

Marty held out Bathy's bridle to me.

Ride? I was wearing jeans and ankle boots, but I could. God, I wanted to. So, so much. So very, very much. *Say yes. Say it. What harm are you doing?*

I hesitated.

If Charlie Cooper found out, he'd probably sack Marty. And if there was one thing I'd gathered from all the times Marty and I had chatted, back in the days before I sold Bathsheba, when I could go riding whenever I wanted, when Charlie Cooper's temper meant nothing to me because I was an owner who paid the stables to look after my horse, it was that Marty loved this job. He was only a stable lad and the only stable lad, cheap because he was officially an apprentice, extremely cheap because he worked far longer hours than his contract stipulated, with Cooper begrudging him the time he spent at college and studying, but he was happy. It radiated off his stocky body and the dry, coarse hands stroking Harding's mane.

The buzz of a moped broke the peace. We turned to look, but the rider swerved off the road and down the track that led into the woods opposite, avoiding opening the heavy gate by slipping through the gap at the side that Marty had appeared through. He barely missed my car, parked in the space between the lane and the gate.

Mr Cooper won't be happy about that,' Marty said.

'He had a Deliveroo bag. Is the catering business back at the yard?'

During Covid, Giles Cooper and Sean Price had run a take-away service from their burger van parked at the stables, but Charlie had made them move elsewhere when the stables had reopened completely after the pandemic. David had lent Giles money to buy the van and I thought this was the money Giles owed him.

'I thought Giles sold it. I haven't seen it up at the stables but maybe he's keeping it in the woods. Even so, the bridleway is for walkers and horses. If Mr Cooper catches him, there'll be trouble.'

'Don't the woods belong to the pheasant shoot?'

'Only on the left of the bridleway. The land on the right belongs to the stables, but it's no use for anything so Mr Cooper doesn't bother maintaining it. Well, are you going to ride with us?'

I said yes before I could stop myself and, as we tacked up the horses, I avoided thinking about the decision. I focussed on Marty, whispering sweet nothings to Harding. Marty loved Harding. He loved most of the horses, but he and Harding understood each other. It was his dream, he'd confided in me, to buy Harding once his owner, an elderly man who'd moved to York to live near his family, accepted that his riding days were over and finally decided to sell him. He saved every penny of the pittance Cooper paid him. Once upon a time, when I thought we were well off, knowing that not even the most parsimonious existence would enable Marty to buy Harding, I'd thought of buying him myself so Marty could use him. But that was before. And now was after.

'Let's go then,' Marty said.

We rode out, down the lane a short way and onto the trail that led to the moors. The field Harding and Bathy lived in looked out onto the moors, but Charlie wouldn't spend the money to put a gate in for direct access and Marty wouldn't risk jumping the fence. It was low enough for both horses to get over, but if Harding knew he could jump it he'd go off on his own. He loved the moors, you see, and he gave a soft whicker as we left the road behind us.

'All OK?' Marty asked.

'I think so.'

I hadn't ridden since I'd told Charlie Cooper to sell Bathy. Long enough for me to be sore tomorrow – but not for muscle memory to fade. The connection between me and Bathsheba clicked back into place as soon as I settled into the saddle. I told her to canter without thinking and I felt the familiar movement pull my hips forward and back, smooth as silk.

Out here, on the moor, we were on top of the world. A world of big skies. Around us vast expanses of heather rippled into the distance, only broken by the occasional copse of blackthorn nestled into a hollow and already blooming with white flowers. Bathsheba relaxed into her stride. I relaxed too and lost myself for a while in the currents of sweet air brushing my face.

I'd had Bathsheba since she was two – an ungainly youngster, all legs and not very beautiful, with the typical black limbs, mane and tail of a bay. But she'd grown into her body and turned out to have the sweetest nature. Now, at twelve years old, she was the equivalent of my age – forty-seven – although she still felt younger than me.

We came to the highest point of the local moors. A few black-faced sheep grazed. It was a place of rough grass and stony outcrops where the only signs of civilisation were the dry-stone walls curving through the land. Nothing had changed here for centuries.

Harding quivered with excitement. Bathsheba snorted and threshed her head up and down as though agreeing with him. To one side of us was a gentle slope free of stones where we let the horses gallop, and Harding loved to gallop. Some horses are like that.

Marty laughed. 'OK, boy. Let's go.'

The two of them moved off, building up speed smoothly until Marty lifted himself off the saddle and bent forward as Harding stretched into a gallop. They tore away, mane and hair flying, Harding's legs barely touching the ground.

Bathsheba watched them for a few seconds, then lowered her head, waiting for me to decide what we were doing. Not galloping, I thought. If I asked her, Bathsheba would oblige, and enjoy it, but I found I didn't want to. Today I wanted to be calm and just enjoy being here.

'Thank you,' I said to Marty when we'd brushed the horses and washed them. 'That was very special.'

'Listen, Kezia. No one but me comes down here. You could ride Bathy any time. I'll leave her tack here. The only person you'd have to be careful of is Giles. He comes down to the barn in the woods opposite from time to time. He's not interested in the horses, but he'd recognise your car if you parked there.'

My car was a bog-standard Fiesta I'd bought cheap after the divorce. Cheap because its previous owner had had it sprayed a vile shade of orange. Not that I cared.

'No,' I said. 'No.'

'Why not?'

'Because Bathsheba doesn't belong to me. It would be theft or fraud.'

He shrugged. 'Can't see it'd do any harm. In fact, it would save me a chore. Not that I mind exercising her.' He reached over and ran his stubby fingers through her mane.

'Maybe,' I said.

But afterwards, when Lou Reed's 'Perfect Day' came on the car radio, I knew I wouldn't. It had been a perfect day. Except I'd broken the rules. Broken the law, probably. Nudged at its boundaries, anyway. And if there was one thing all the awfulness of the last few months had been about, it was holding on to rectitude and obeying the law. One and one make two. One step down the wrong path and you're lost.

SIX

JOSH MASON

TUESDAY

'You're to go straight up to Crime,' Sergeant Beresford told Josh when he came in the day after discovering the bodies. 'Report to DCI Carter. He's asked for an officer from Local Policing to be seconded to the investigation. I managed the liaison last time but he wants a dedicated officer this time.'

Neither of them mentioned that last time had been the Walker case.

'And try to look as though you've learned something about policing in the months you've been in this department.'

The gossip was that Carter wasn't easy to work for, prone to changing his mind and not sharing much with his officers.

'Carter doesn't like stupid policemen,' Beresford said. 'Or policewomen, for that matter. Or whatever we're supposed to call them now.'

'Police officers, Sarge,' Josh said.

'That's exactly the sort of comment to avoid making in front of Carter. And you know what I mean.'

Josh wondered if he should have reread his report as he

climbed the stairs to the room Crime had taken over. He didn't want to make a fool of himself. He'd like to work in Crime one day but so did most entry-level police constables, so he was under no illusion about how competitive it was.

Sergeant Beresford had worked miracles. The big room was empty of all the clutter stored there and looked as though it had always been an office. Tables and chairs were scattered around and the walls lined with whiteboards. It was empty of people though, apart from him and a busy detective constable who seemed to be fielding all the phone calls.

He wandered over to one of the whiteboards while the DC was on the phone. It was the 'persons of interest' board. Most of whom he knew, or knew of. But then they all came from Thorpe.

The Coopers' next-door neighbour was there. If you could call him that. Johnny Boyes's farm was a few hundred yards away. It was no secret Boyes and Cooper hadn't been on cordial terms. Boyes was an old acquaintance of Sergeant Beresford and often rang him direct to complain about the stables. One of Boyes's dogs, a fully trained sheepdog, a beautiful animal and worth a fair bit, had been injured and lost half a leg. Boyes blamed Cooper, although Josh didn't think he'd made an official complaint. Nevertheless he couldn't believe that Boyes, grumpy and touchy as he was, had been responsible for the bloodshed at the stables. Although there had been gossip about his drinking since his wife died.

Lambert, the manager of the Stainthorpe Shoot on the other side of the Coopers', was on the list too. Wanda Stainthorpe, the owner of the pheasant shoot, and the Coopers were – or had been – in dispute over the bridleway running through the woodland where they kept the young birds' pens. She claimed riders left the path and trespassed in the woods. Someone had wrecked the pens, letting a fox come in and kill a large number of the birds.

When Josh had been young, the land had belonged to old man Stainthorpe, who'd scratched a living from a mixture of dairy and poultry farming, and had a few sheep grazing on the common land up on the nearby moors. But when he died Wanda, who'd gone off to do something other than farming – Josh thought she might have joined the army – had sold the animals and mortgaged the land, raising enough money to start the shoot and a holiday cottage business. Word was it was successful. Word begrudgingly given though. People didn't like seeing farming land taken out of food production. Wanda had spent a few years setting it up and then put it in the hands of a manager and was rarely there.

'PC Mason, isn't it?' The DC had finished his call, and came over to join Josh.

'Yes.'

'Lovell. DC Lovell. I'm managing the office. You live in Thorpe, don't you?'

'Born and bred and still here.'

'Can you tell us anything about these people?' He gestured to the board.

Josh thought for a moment. It was difficult to explain to an outsider how permanent the grudges and bad feeling were between certain families who'd always lived in Thorpe and the surrounding villages. The Boyes and the Coopers had been at loggerheads for centuries. It was constant but low-level. Part of the fabric of life but unlikely to flare up into a murderous attack. Except...

'Johnny Boyes,' Josh said. 'He's a sour man. Especially after a few drinks. And he often has a few drinks. He's been banned from owning a gun.'

Which was Cooper's fault. He'd made an official complaint about Boyes threatening him and his family. More fuel to the ever-seething fire of their feud.

'Whoever did it used Cooper's gun, we think. It's missing. How about this lad?'

Josh hadn't clocked Marty's name on the board. Martin Appleton, they'd written. He was Cooper's current stable lad.

'Why have you included him? He's a good lad.'

'What makes you say that?'

'Well, I've never heard anything bad about him. He's not one of the youngsters who hang around the centre at night.'

Josh knew most of them. They were the ones who'd left school as soon as they could and then found that working life suited them no better. If they could get a job. Many of them were on benefits or spasmodically employed as Deliveroo or Uber riders. A few of them ended up as delivery boys for the families in Leeds and York who ran the drugs trade. Beresford said it was worse since Covid. The organised crime groups had used the pandemic to expand the delivery side of their business, more than doubling online ordering. The effects were becoming obvious in Thorpe. Nowadays if you saw kids – even those of middle school age – on bikes, they were likely employed by one of the organised crime groups. It was a serious problem.

'Martin Appleton's family are known to us,' Lovell said. 'His dad's done time. And Cooper had just sacked him. Some of the horse owners were there when it happened. Plus Martin had plenty of opportunity and would have known where the gun was.'

'Where was it?'

'In a gun safe in the tack room. Locked, of course, but it was no secret that Cooper kept the keys and ammunition in the next-door office. Neither room was ever locked.'

'No secret? So lots of people would have known?' Josh asked.

'Possibly. But Marty lives on the premises. Not in the cottage but in a room over one of the old stable blocks. There's a couple of bedrooms and bathrooms up there. We've brought him in as routine, of course, to make a statement. Carter's interviewing him now.'

'You'd be better following up Boyes,' Josh said.

'We are. But his story checks out. He was at the pub. And noticed there. What about Sean Price?' He pointed to the next name on the board. 'What do you know about him?'

Josh knew he and Giles had fallen out, but that was an old story.

'He's the child's father,' Lovell added.

'Freddy? Sean is Freddy's father?'

He did some quick maths. Freddy must have been conceived and born while he was at uni.

'Sean Price lives in Thorpe.'

There was a faintly accusatory note in Lovell's voice.

'I don't know everything about everybody in Thorpe, you know.'

'He stands to get a lot of money. The kid inherits the lot and Sean will have control over it. There's not a great deal of cash but the stables with the land will fetch a fair bit. Cooper owned the place outright.'

'You think he'd kill the whole family, including the child's mother, to get his hands on his son's inheritance?'

'There'd been a big falling-out. Sean wasn't allowed to see his son.'

Josh tried to look as though this wasn't news to him.

'There was bad blood between Sean and Giles too,' Josh said quickly. This he did know about. Sean had bent his ear often enough when he'd been buying supper from the van.

Before he could tell Lovell the whole story, two officers came into the room and the phone rang again. One of them answered it. The other came over.

'You can take Ed Lambert off the board,' he said, and pointed to the manager of the shoot's name. 'He says he spent Sunday with a friend.' He checked his phone. 'Jon Rutherford from over Masham way. Picked him up around six thirty and went to the Red Bull. The barman at the Red Bull has confirmed Lambert came in shortly after seven, neat as a whistle, with Rutherford. The two of them left just before nine thirty. And here's the interesting bit. According to Lambert, Rutherford called in at the Coopers' on the way back. He wanted to have a word with Charlie about payment for some fencing he'd done. Lambert stayed in the car, as Cooper wouldn't have been pleased to see him. He says Rutherford told him the cottage was dark and there was no one about. They went back to Rutherford's after that and Lambert left around eleven.

Rutherford's coming in to be interviewed but I think it'll check out.'

'Add it to the timeline board, will you?'

Once the officer had finished, Josh went over to take a look.

<u>Sunday</u>

15h00: Giles returns (Napier) and rows with Charlie Cooper

16h00: Charlie sacks Martin Appleton

19h00: Beginning of Time of Death window (Pathologist at Scene)

TBC: When did last owner leave?
When did Chloe Cooper return (Pantomime)?

21h45: Ed Lambert & Rutherrford at stables – no-one about

23h00: End of Time of Death Window (PaS)

Josh assumed the blank space between 19h00 and 21h45 was when the murder had taken place. Sunday. That meant the bodies had been lying there undiscovered for twenty-four hours when he'd arrived. No wonder there'd been flies. He reached up and rubbed out the extra R in Rutherford.

'Don't go fiddling with that,' the officer who'd added the information about Lambert barked at him. 'Who are you anyway?'

'PC Mason. I was first at the scene.'

'Carter wants him on board.' This came from Lovell. 'He works in Local here.'

'God, just what we need.'

Between the news that Carter wanted him 'on board', whatever that meant, and the hostility of the other officer, Josh didn't know what to reply.

'Who's Napier?' he asked.

'Thought you were local,' the officer said

'I am.'

'Well, Napier's one of your local electricians. Giles called him out because Storm Beatrice had knocked out the power to one of the barns. Napier was one of a queue of helpful locals who turned up here as soon as word of the killings got out.'

He didn't sound as though he'd found them helpful at all.

'How long have you been in the force?' he asked now.

'Eighteen months.'

'And before that?'

'Leeds University.'

'Degree in Professional Policing, I suppose?' He made quote marks with his fingers round the words Professional Policing.

'Yes.'

'Lay off him, Burden. We all have qualifications these days,' Lovell said.

Burden muttered a couple of things to the officer with him. They both laughed.

'Put him onto the hunt for the burger van,' he said. 'I'm off to see Rutherford.' They left.

'Who was he?' Josh asked.

'DI Burden. Old school. He's a bit of an acquired taste, but a good officer.'

'Burger van? What was that about?'

'Nothing. The man who lives opposite the entrance to Cooper's Stables thought they'd seen a burger van parked at the entrance to the stables. He suggested someone might have been stealing the dogs and got caught in the act by the Coopers – hence the slaughter.'

'Why stealing the dogs?'

'The caller doesn't have a very high opinion of the quality of the meat in the burgers the vans sell.'

Josh laughed.

'Anyway,' Lovell went on. 'The neighbour wasn't a hundred per cent sure what day it was.'

Josh took a deep breath. He liked Sean, but he was a professional policeman now and Price was a person of interest.

'Giles used to own an old burger van. He ran it with Sean Price. Until the two of them quarrelled. I was going to tell you when Burden came in.'

'What did they quarrel about?'

'Money, I think. Giles had borrowed some – a lot – to buy the van and he was under pressure to repay the loan. And Sean didn't think Giles was pulling his weight. Plus I suspect things were already awkward, because Chloe must have been pregnant by then.'

Sean hadn't mentioned this side of the story to Josh.

'There was no van at the stables.'

'I suspect Giles sold it.'

'Maybe. Anyway, we don't think the burger van is relevant.'

Josh remembered some stray gossip.

'What about Giles? There was a lot of talk about him locally. Mixing with the wrong people. Letting seedy friends use the stables to store drugs.'

'Ah. Local knowledge, you see. Always useful. We'll look into it. Murder seems to strike out of the blue but if you look hard enough it's never really that sudden. Death has been creeping up on the victims, stealthy step by stealthy step, for a while. An unfortunate concatenation of factors that makes their murder more and more essential to someone until - wham - the scales tip, the killer strikes and the victims' dying hour arrives. And it's our job to look into victims' lives and unpick them until we discover exactly what the factors were that led to that dying hour arriving. Once you know why, you know who the killer was.'

Lovell wasn't much older than Josh but he had an air of confidence Josh hoped he'd acquire eventually.

'Did he see anyone else? The man who lived opposite, I mean.'

'He saw you arrive on Monday night. We think the killer came up the bridleway through the woods. There was mud all over the living room carpet and up the stairs.'

'That would make sense. I walked down the drive and my boots were clean. You think the killer went upstairs?'

'Looks like it.'

'Talk me through everything,' Josh said. The phone rang once more. 'If you have the time, that is.'

Lovell ignored the phone. 'Well, I've walked you through the persons of interest. Unless there's anyone you think we've missed?'

Josh shook his head.

'Timeline wise, it's early days yet but progress is very good. The pathologist at the scene put time of death as between nineteen hundred hours and twenty-three hundred hours, although that's to be kept quiet. We're asking people to account for their movements from Sunday afternoon until you discovered the bodies on Monday. We're finding out when the last owner left the yard. The family must have been killed within a short period of time. There are no signs of struggle. The quicker we can narrow the time of death, the better. Someone somewhere has a missing hour. An hour when they vanished, went to Cooper's Stables and slaughtered the family, then left and picked up the strands of their life again. Chloe Cooper went to a rehearsal for the pantomime. Know anything about that?'

'Not really. Except it's *Puss in Boots* this year.' Josh tried to dredge up something helpful. 'You should speak to Raymond Mason – he's the director. He'd probably know when Chloe left.'

'Mason. Relation of yours?'

'A cousin of sorts.'

He remembered Kezia had asked about the horses.

'What's happening to the horses? And the dogs?'

'The owners have been asked to organise the horses' care. Luckily they're still out in the fields. But it's tricky because they've got no access to the tack and feed rooms on the yard. So the quicker they get the horses moved the better. The RSPCA took the dogs.'

'And Freddy?' Josh felt guilty that he'd asked about the animals first.

'Social Services.'

'And it definitely wasn't murder–suicide?'

'There was no gun found at the scene.'

A phone rang. Lovell cast a quick glance at it.

'I'll have to get that.' He picked a sheaf of papers off his desk and passed them to Josh. 'Initial crime scene report. Read it and see if we've missed anything.'

Josh read and reread the report. It took him quite a while. Partly because the words, although written in the most uncolourful language possible, brought back memories of the scene. They hadn't mentioned the smell, he thought. Nor the endless flies. Stray ideas distracted him. Like no wonder Freddy had wolfed down the packet of biscuits in his car. The poor kid must have been starving. Up there in his cot all night and all day. Josh supposed he'd have cried and cried. But no one had come.

'Any thoughts?' Lovell asked in between calls setting up times for owners to come in and give statements.

'Not really. You could ask the local farmers for access to their CCTV though. A lot of them have cameras watching the entrance to their farms. Boyes, for example. His farm is near the bottom of the bridleway you think the killer might have used. You're searching it, presumably? Anything could be in those woods.'

'Happening right now. And good point about the CCTV.' Lovell made a note.

'And there are things missing from the list of evidence. There were a couple of tarot cards in Chloe Cooper's hand. And a note. It's in my report.'

'I didn't know you'd seen those.' Lovell sighed. 'Keep quiet about them for the moment. Carter doesn't want it generally known. Even amongst the officers working on the case.'

Josh knew they often held back details. It was a quick way to check that the nutters who rang up or came in to confess to the crime were just that. He'd never understood why a crime like this attracted them but there was no denying it did.

'I see,' he said. Although he wasn't quite sure why it had to be kept secret from the other officers.

'A link to the Walker case, I think,' Lovell said. 'You remember it? This time last year it would have been.'

'Yes. I'd not long started here.'

It had been discussed endlessly at home as well. Mrs Walker had been one of his mother's clients.

An eleven-year-old boy, Peter Walker, from a farm a little north of Thorpe, had disappeared while cycling home from school. The press and the police had taken it seriously from the start and mounted searches, but they hadn't been thorough enough. It had been Peter's father who had found his bike and a torn school bag on the side of the road a few days later.

And the following week, the boy's body had been discovered on the moors. He'd been shot very recently but a knife had been inserted into his chest after death. No one had ever been arrested and progress on the case had come to a complete halt.

'A tarot card was found near the boy's body,' Lovell said. 'The King of Swords. We always thought the family weren't being entirely open with us,' Lovell went on quietly. 'And after the body was found with the card, they closed up completely. They sold the farm shortly afterwards and moved away. Carter re-interviewed them recently but they had nothing to add. We thought they'd been got at. They had two more young sons and a daughter.'

He opened a drawer and pulled out the two evidence bags Carter had used the night before.

'Take a look at the note, will you. At its back, I mean. It's been typed onto a bit of paper torn off something else and there's some print on the back.'

Josh looked again. He hadn't noticed the back last night, but he recognised it immediately.

'It's been torn from the *Thorpe Gazette*.'

Lovell looked no wiser.

'It's a weekly news-sheet, comes out every Sunday, produced by Hamish Aitken. He's a reporter. Of sorts. He prints it on whatever paper is going cheap, so it's always a different colour. Funds it with local advertising. The back of the note is an advert for one of the Thorpe restaurants.'

He wondered why anyone would send a note on a piece of paper torn from the *Gazette*.

'Damn,' Lovell said. 'So there's no point Forensics checking it for prints. Any number of people could have touched it.'

'Is it necessarily anything to do with the shootings, anyway?'

Lovell shrugged. 'We check everything.'

'And the tarot cards? Did they come with the note?'

'There was no sign of a pack on the premises. Carter searched himself. But it could be a coincidence.'

DCI Carter swept into the room, which had been slowly filling up as Lovell talked, silenced the chatter with a raised hand and started speaking before the door had slammed shut behind him.

'Lovell,' he said. 'Get Martin Appleton's statement distributed asap. Burden, I want you to go down to the crime scene. Martin Appleton's bedroom. It's one of the rooms above the stables on the left. Search it. There are still plenty of CS officers there.'

A buzz of questions threatened to drown him out. He raised a hand.

'You'll understand when you read Martin Appleton's statement. For now, I want us to get on it fast.'

He distributed tasks at speed. Other officers were to go to Martin's father's house in Acer Lane, Thorpe, search it and talk to the neighbours about the family's comings and goings. Lovell was to chase up Forensics then check how long it would take to cycle from Cooper's yard to Acer Lane.

The room emptied until only Josh, Lovell and Carter remained.

'Sean Price, sir,' Lovell said.

'What about him?'

'Your interview with him. Anything new?'

'He has an alibi. It's still to be checked but we've let him go.'

'And what about Mason?'

'Who?'

'PC Mason.' He nodded his head towards Josh. 'You asked for him to be seconded to Crime.'

'So I did. Well, find him something useful to do.'

And Josh found himself clutching a newly printed copy of Martin Appleton's statement and a list of owners to call.

WITNESS STATEMENT
– MARTIN APPLETON

1. I, Martin Appleton, of 11 Acer Lane, Thorpe TS1 6LK, worked at Cooper's Stables, Thorpe from September 2023 to Sunday 13 October 2024. I was employed as part of a course I am studying in stable management. I live on the premises in a room above the stable block – one of three that used to be part of a bed and breakfast business run by the Coopers. I am seventeen years old.

2. Sunday 13 October was a normal day. My hours are fluid but Saturdays and Sundays are our busiest days as most of the owners want to ride their horses and the visiting instructor, Mrs Botham, gives lessons on both those days.

3. Mr Cooper seemed particularly stressed on Sunday. A couple of trees had come down on the fences during the storm and he was trying to do emergency repairs and deal with the normal Sunday work. Plus we'd had a delivery from Carrs Billington that was wrong and he needed to check it against the order before Monday.

4. I was aware that Giles Cooper returned mid-afternoon. I don't know the exact time but I was wiping down the school ponies so it must have been after the last children's lesson, which finishes around two. The children had all left so probably close to three as they are expected to remove the ponies' tack, clean it and put it away. Giles and Mr Cooper had an argument in the haylage barn. You could hear them in the yard although I didn't hear what it was about. I don't suppose it was anything important as they often argued. Mr Cooper thought Giles should help more. Normally they don't argue when there are owners around.

5. Mr Cooper and Giles seemed OK when they came out of the barn though. Mr Cooper told me I should have finished the ponies. I wasn't happy. I'd been run off my feet all day. I said something. I can't remember what but along the lines of how it wasn't fair to treat me like that. He told me it wasn't working out and I could go. Then he said he was sacking me. He told me to pack my things straight away and leave. I was too stunned to do anything and I thought it would be best if I went home and asked my dad what to do. (Police note: Martin's father is Henry (Harry) Appleton). My course requires me to have a job, so it meant I wouldn't be able to continue because it isn't easy to find a job. There's lots of casual work but nothing permanent.

6. Giles helped me pack, although I couldn't take everything because I was on my bike. He was quite nice to me. Normally he ignores me. So I think he was as shocked by Mr Cooper sacking me as I was.

7. I arrived home at around seven. But my dad wasn't there. I'd forgotten he was away in Edinburgh for the weekend. I spent the rest of the evening playing video games and fell asleep on the sofa. I don't know what time that was.

8. I didn't go back to the stables to get the rest of my stuff. My dad wasn't due back until today (Police note: Tuesday 15/10) and I needed him to take me in his car. Anyway I wanted to talk to him first of all.

I believe that the facts stated in this witness statement are true.

SEVEN
ANNIE PRICE

WEDNESDAY

Annie Price cast an eye over the other people waiting with her in the small room. She hoped this wasn't going to be tedious. They'd discussed coming along at the panto sewing club on Sunday when Cora had read the announcement in the *Thorpe Gazette*.

An Afternoon Beyond the Veil with Mrs Monroe

Step into the shadows and discover what lies beyond…

Join renowned spiritual medium **Mrs Monroe** for an intimate **Seance** absolutely free of charge. With decades of experience and a gift passed down through generations, Mrs Monroe invites you to connect with loved ones who have crossed to the other side.

Limited spaces available

FREE to attend – in exchange for your kind **permission to be photographed** during the session.

Wednesday at 2 p.m.

Whether you come seeking comfort, curiosity or connection, all are welcome to this peaceful gathering where the veil is thinnest. Spaces are limited – **reserve your place** and step into something extraordinary.

Ages 18+ only.

Cora was keen. Her husband, Bill, had had a stroke in one of the clothes shops in Thorpe – the one opposite the chemist – and died in hospital two weeks later. Which was awful enough. But there'd been talk of him spending a lot of time in the lingerie part of the shop. Someone claimed to have seen him fingering the bras.

It was all very awkward and Annie guessed Cora had heard the gossip. Which was probably why she wanted to go so badly, hoping Bill would speak to her and explain. Annie had said she'd go too. Not that she was at all interested in discovering if there was any truth in the rumours.

No one else had seemed keen once Annie announced she'd accompany Cora.

Dennis, her husband, had persuaded her not to cancel at the last minute although, really, she had every reason to. She was in such a state about Freddy. They were so close to getting him released. There was no other way to put it. It was shameful the way Social Services had kept him from them. Insisting on interviewing Sean before they'd let her even see Freddy. He was her grandson for heaven's sake.

Luckily the police had released Sean quickly. And now they'd checked out his alibi, there shouldn't be any more problems. Good thing the waiters in the Italian restaurant she'd gone to with Sean had remembered Annie complaining her pasta wasn't cooked properly.

It looked as though everything was going to work out. Provided Lauren's flat passed the Social Services inspection this afternoon.

The last hurdle to jump. She was sure it would, although she'd had to be firm with Lauren. The second bedroom had to be cleared of all the shop stuff stored there to make a proper bedroom for Freddy. Lauren had claimed she had nowhere to put it so Annie had told Dennis to store it in the cottage, make some space amongst all the fishing rods and the like and, no, she didn't care if it wasn't very convenient. This was their grandson they were talking about. Dennis had said he would but only if she left him and Sean to move everything with Lauren.

She'd been glad to. So long as Lauren's was clear, she didn't care where they put it. She didn't even like the cottage. Too many memories of being forced to spend every holiday there because Dennis didn't enjoy going places with lots of people. She'd told him he should make an effort. For Sean's sake as much as hers. But Sean had turned out to enjoy fishing too. Well, she wasn't going to make the same mistake with Freddy!

She couldn't wait to give him a big hug. The thought of him alone with the corpses for all that time threatened to make her weep again. She couldn't bear it.

She made herself look round the room. There were six of them waiting. Cora, of course, all sparkly with hope. Two other women, her age, probably widows hoping for a message from their departed husbands like Cora. One of them wore a wedding band and old-fashioned engagement ring, but the other didn't and never had judging from the smooth shape of her ring finger. Years of wearing a wedding ring thinned the flesh where it'd been. What brought this woman? A dead parent?

A younger woman and man who held hands made up the numbers. Had they lost a child? She'd have liked to ask them but Mrs Monroe had suggested they wait quietly and focus on what they wanted from the seance.

Well, Annie didn't want anything.

She looked around at the room. It was quite nice, really. It must be Mrs Monroe's sitting room. A couple of sofas and armchairs. No television, unless it was in the wooden cabinet by the corner. There was an open folder with letters from grateful clients on the coffee table. Annie flicked through them. Quite impressive. Mrs Monroe certainly seemed to have a knack for helping people. And the certificates on the wall too. Annie had no idea that there were colleges teaching psychic studies. But then what did she know? There were all sorts of extraordinary courses now. One of Cora's granddaughters was studying computer game design.

Mrs Monroe had seemed fine too. She'd expected someone a bit stranger – more mystical. Instead she reminded Annie of the woman who'd run HR at Dennis's old company. Very kind as well as confident and organised. In her sixties, but not trying to look any younger. Grey hair and specs. A slight smell of cigarette smoke, but Annie didn't mind that.

She glanced at her watch. They'd been waiting a long time. Mrs Monroe had asked them to bring something along that belonged to the departed. Something special. Annie had brought an old ring of her mother's, although she wasn't particularly keen on having a conversation with her. She'd never forgiven her mother for the things she'd said about Dennis when Annie had decided to marry him. Still, Mum had paid for those comments in full when Annie had refused to visit with Sean, saying it was too far to drive on her own and, as the sight of Dennis made her mother sick – which was what her mother had meant although she hadn't used those exact words – she couldn't ask him to bring her.

Cora had brought Bill's cufflinks. She'd let Annie have a look at them in the car on the way over. Frankly they could have done with a bit of a clean. They'd been a present from Bill's parents for his twenty-first. Gold. Cora had had them engraved with his initials and a little rose on their twenty-fifth wedding anniversary. Because they both loved roses. They'd placed the objects on a tray, covered with a crisp white embroidered cloth, and Mrs Monroe had taken it away with her. Only for a short while, she'd explained. A time when it was just her and the spirits. She'd call them in as soon as she felt ready.

EIGHT
MRS MONROE

SAME DAY

Once she'd welcomed the consultation participants and left them in the front room, Mrs Monroe checked her lipstick in the mirror. The twenty minutes or so they spent waiting gave them a chance to read all her certificates and letters and reframe their perceptions of her. She wanted them to see her as a professional – a kindly one, of course, like the sort of family doctor that didn't seem to exist any more.

In the mirror, she caught sight of the photographer – Kezia Heron – staring at her. She had a very intense gaze that Mrs Monroe didn't like. She was probably checking light levels. They'd already had a slightly difficult discussion about how many lights she could put up. Mrs Monroe didn't want them to be too bright. It would destroy the atmosphere. Luckily Kezia herself was fairly self-effacing. One of these people you forgot you'd met when you bumped into them for a second time. Mind you, that was happening to her more and more often. She turned sharply and winced.

Her hip was having a bad day, and that would mean heaving herself in and out of the old captain's chair she used when working, which was almost too much for her arm muscles. Really she ought to lose weight like her doctor said. Except he'd also told her to give up smoking and, when she'd asked him which she should concentrate on, after much humming and hawing he'd told her to stop smoking but not to put any weight on. As this was clearly impossible, she'd put off doing either.

She checked her watch again. Plenty of time for a ciggie before the session began. Something about the look on Kezia's face when she'd lit up prior to the participants arriving had told her the photographer disapproved. But she thought the woman disapproved of her, full stop. She opened the windows and leaned out so the smoke wouldn't impregnate her hair and clothes too much, and took a deep and blessed inhale. How on earth was she going to stop? In her more rational moments she knew she had to. It was so expensive. And according to the doctor it was a poison in the blood that would raise her chances of infection and blood loss when she had the hip operation.

If it weren't for the ciggies and the hope that she might save up enough to go private and get her hip sorted straight away, she'd retire. She could live off her pension, although there'd be no extravagances. That was what all this malarkey with the photographer was for. She was investing a bit of money in her business in the hope of saving up a little nest egg. It meant making a website and a Facebook page. She drew the line at all the other things Hamish had suggested.

She wondered again if it was a mistake. Hamish was very reasonably priced though, and he seemed to know what he was doing. He'd recommended Kezia for the photographs. Said she was good value and really smart at getting arresting shots. Mind you, they'd disagreed about what sort of photographs to use. He, of course, had wanted something mystic and gipsyish. At her age she wasn't going to start dressing up in a shawl and wearing big earrings. Besides, she might not be up to date with the latest marketing techniques, but she knew her clientele and they'd be totally put off by anything like that. Part of her appeal was her ordinariness. She looked like the sort of person you'd be comfortable chatting to while you were waiting at the bus stop. She'd dressed up a little when she was younger, but subtly. Enough to give a hint of a Romany background. Not that she had one. Her father and mother had been staunch members of the local Scottish Presbyterian church and would have been horrified if they knew how their daughter made a living.

'I'm ready now, so whenever you want to inspect the tray of objects is fine with me.' Kezia interrupted her thoughts.

It was amazing how much you could glean from the objects people brought in.

'Like this?'

She stared down at the tray and its sad collection of relics, feeling the familiar sense of pity that this was all that remained after death. It reminded her of Kim's Game. They played it when she was a child. You had to memorise a set of random objects on a tray and write them down after the tray had been taken away. Today's youngsters would probably stare at you in disbelief if you explained this had been thought of as entertainment.

Kezia moved silently round the room as she looked. Only the sound of clicks told Mrs Monroe where she was. There was a teddy bear on the tray that must have belonged to a young child, a man's watch, old and used, which would belong to someone's dead husband. A ring, which was quite pretty. A real diamond, even if it was only small. Probably someone's mother or sister, but a woman anyway. And, of course, a set of cufflinks. She couldn't remember the last time she'd done a consultation without cufflinks being on the tray. They too normally meant a dead husband. These ones were worn and stained.

'Could you pick something up and look at it?'

Mrs Monroe jumped. Kezia was leaning over and looking into the tray, much closer than she'd realised.

'Not the teddy bear,' she added. She pointed towards the cufflinks. 'What about those? They're a bit stained but if you turn them away from the camera...'

CUFFLINKS

Bill doesn't like women's clothes shops much, particularly not small and rather snooty ones like this, where the assistants look you up and down when you enter and decide whether to welcome you with a smile or watch you with tight eyes and mouths in case you leave grubby finger marks on the pristine silks and satins. But Cora loved the blouse when she saw in it the shop window. So he's braved the disapproving stares to buy it for her birthday. It's something she wants, unlike the cordless vacuum cleaner their daughter persuaded him to buy last year. It'll be just the thing for Mum, she'd said. So practical. Save her having to bend down to plug and unplug the old one. Well, she'd been wrong. Although Cora pasted a smile onto her mouth, her face fell as soon as she realised what it was. And he understood. She wanted something pretty rather than practical. And why shouldn't she?

The price of the blouse shocked him. Although that wasn't what gave him a funny turn on the way to the cash desk. He felt quite dizzy for a few minutes, had to shut his eyes and hold on to one of the displays. The assistant was glaring at him when he opened his eyes afterwards.

He doesn't feel all that good now as he waits in the queue to pay. He loosens his tie. It's hot. He supposes it has to be, so that the women trying on dresses behind the tightly drawn green curtains at the far end of the shop – the ones guarded by another sour-faced assistant – don't feel cold. He undoes the top button of his shirt, wishing he hadn't eaten a second piece of toast at breakfast. He's feeling a little sick now. If only the woman in front of him would stop yakking on about how the new supermarket will destroy the high street and pay. He's going to have to say something. Because he needs to get outside. Into the fresh air. Now.

The words won't come though. In fact he can't open his mouth. And the dizziness is overwhelming. He reaches out to grab the counter as his legs give way. But misses. Something sharp tears the back of his hand as he falls.

He's aware of a sudden silence broken almost immediately by sharp cries. He can't speak though. He doesn't know why. His mouth won't make the shapes that produce words. He reaches his arms up towards the counter so he can grab it to lever himself off the floor but only one works. And it's shaking. It waves in the air. Like a drowning man's. He's ripped the skin on the back of his hand as he fell and a trickle of blood crawls down the skin and into his shirt cuff. Cora won't be happy about that. Heavens above, he mustn't bleed on the blouse. Where is it? But it's OK he has it in the other hand. The one that's lying inert and useless on the chocolate-brown carpet. The pattern is pretty. She'll love it. An assistant bends down and he thinks she's going to help him up but, instead, she takes the blouse from him.

The shocked voices are fading. The bright lights of the shop dim. Is he going to sleep? He does feel tired. So very, very tired. And as his vision darkens all he's aware of is the smell of roses. The little tight buds of pink roses that opened into small but perfect flowers on the climber he and Cora had in the garden of the first house they lived in. You can't buy roses that smell like that any more.

NINE

ANNIE PRICE

SAME DAY

It was a long wait before Mrs Monroe called them into a room overlooking what was quite an attractive garden at the back. Nicely kept lawn and well-tended borders. Annie knew how much work that was. They sat themselves round a large rectangular table, with Mrs Monroe in the middle of one of the longer sides rather than the end. She winced as she sat down. She didn't look quite as well put together as she had before. One of her cardigan cuffs was slightly askew and her hair looked as though she'd run her fingers through it repeatedly.

The photographer wandered round the room taking pictures. Annie was glad she'd had her hair done. It was her best feature and the streak at the front gave her a distinguished look. People didn't forget her in a hurry, but for good reasons. Whereas the photographer was a real nonentity. She was pale too. Very pale, with almost bloodless lips. She caught a glimpse of Annie staring at her and smiled slightly.

'This is Kezia.' Mrs Monroe introduced the photographer. 'Please try to ignore her. She'll only be around for the very beginning.' She smiled reassuringly. 'Now let's begin.'

She launched herself into what Annie recognised as a well-rehearsed speech thanking them and saying how privileged she felt they'd come to her seeking contact with their loved ones. She'd do her best but sometimes things weren't perfect. The spirits were often as lost or confused as those they'd left behind.

They all nodded.

She would need their help, she told them with a rueful smile. She couldn't raise the dead. That wasn't what she did at all. She could only hear their loved ones if they wanted to communicate. Communication – that was what this was all about. And they'd need to talk back. To have a conversation. Sometimes even start the conversation. After all, they knew their loved ones better than she did. She took a moment to explain how her gift worked.

'I'm clairaudient,' she said. 'I don't see the spirits but I hear them, so I can't describe them. And it's not the same as hearing in the physical world. Sometimes the words are garbled or I misunderstand them. It can be like listening to a foreign language you only partly understand.'

They all nodded again.

Annie thought it was a load of rubbish but she nodded too.

And then Mrs Monroe started. And, really, it was quite extraordinary. No messing about. It was as though she had one of those earpieces people on TV wore and she was listening to someone through that. Her eyes narrowed and she looked out of the window as she listened, nodding from time to time.

'I'm talking to someone who has a connection with the south,' she said finally. 'Maybe this country, maybe further afield. They're talking about beautiful countryside. Could be somewhere they've lived. Maybe where they come from? But it was important to them.'

One of the women suddenly smiled. 'That'll be my Arthur,' she said. 'His family came from Cornwall and we spent every holiday there. He never stopped going on about the place. The last holiday was just before he died. We knew he didn't have long then. Please tell him how special it was for me.'

After that it was as if Mrs Monroe had Arthur on the phone and was relaying his words – sometimes not completely correctly, but his wife managed to understand.

Annie began to feel uneasy. Just a little. She didn't believe in all this. But you never knew and she didn't want her mother speaking her mind to anyone about what she called Annie's selfishness. Just because Annie thought it was important to stand up for yourself. They were always banging on about human rights these days. And Annie didn't see why she shouldn't have any.

The young couple were next. Sister and brother, it turned out, and their older brother had died. Abroad but after a long illness. The teddy bear was all they had of him. It was confusing because initially he spoke to Mrs Monroe in the voice of a young child. Once they'd established who he was, she explained that those who had passed sometimes used the guise of a child when they spoke to siblings. It was a way of reconnecting with their shared childhood.

The sister and brother exchanged memories with their brother via Mrs Monroe. They'd had a difficult time as children. The sister and brother wanted reassurance that their brother had recovered from the experience. He had, he told them, and his only regret was that he'd not been in touch in recent years.

Annie noticed the statements the dead brother made via Mrs Monroe were often very general. Most people had times when they grew apart or lost something important. And even the more specific things could be true for everybody. Like having a stash of photos they'd never got round to putting in an album, or having long hair or a beard for a while. Mrs Monroe let the people in the room fill in the details. Annie relaxed. It was all a scam. No need to worry about her mother coming back from the dead, so to speak.

At some point the photographer slipped out. The atmosphere changed because, quiet as she was, the clicks had been intrusive. Even Mrs Monroe had kept on glancing at her. Now she too appeared to settle.

'I've got someone whose name begins with W, I think.' There

was a new note in Mrs Monroe's voice. A sharpness. An eagerness. 'His voice is very quiet.'

Cora gave Annie a nudge. Bill had always spoken quietly. It was all too easy though. Mrs Monroe had the cufflinks with his initial on.

'No, he's telling me everybody called him Bill. He's talking about a shop, I think. A shop for women. Yes, one that sells women's clothing. I think I know the one he means. Claire's Fashions on the high street here. Something happened there. He felt very ill and fainted? Does that mean anything to anyone?'

Annie couldn't believe it. There was no way Mrs Monroe could have guessed all this.

'And, he hurt his hand when he tumbled. It bled quite a bit.'

'It's Bill,' Cora said. 'He had a stroke in that shop, a few months ago. And he hurt his hand when he fell. There was blood everywhere even though it was only a little scratch. It bothered him. He kept on rubbing it and making it bleed all the time he was in hospital.'

'He was buying you something. For your birthday, I think. He wants to know if you got it.'

'No.'

'No, that's right. He hadn't got as far as paying for it. He says it was a blouse. One you'd said you liked.'

Annie remembered the blouse. Normally Cora made her own clothes. Like Annie. You knew what you were getting then. Cora had taken a photo of it in the shop window and asked Annie if she'd seen any similar material. Pretty and silky, with little pink flowers.

'I'm getting a scent of roses,' Mrs Monroe went on. 'Those lovely old-fashioned ones. Not like modern ones with no smell whatsoever.'

'Yes. The blouse had roses on. We always loved them. Bill gave me a bunch every anniversary and we were married under an arch of them.'

Now Cora had started talking to Bill she couldn't stop. All sorts of things poured out. And he understood them all and sent comforting messages via Mrs Monroe. The conversation took a long time. Thank heavens. Because Annie was having misgivings again.

'Tell him,' Cora said. 'He didn't need to buy me something so expensive, although I'd have loved it.'

She waited while Mrs Monroe gazed into the distance.

'He knows all that. But he wants you to buy the blouse. A last present from him.'

'Oh, Bill.'

The others blinked or dabbed their eyes. Annie contented herself with sniffing a little and, under the guise of lifting her hand to brush away a tear, cast a discreet glance at her watch. Not much longer.

TEN

JOSH MASON

SAME DAY

Raymond Mason was as fat as Josh remembered from Christmases as a child. When his father's mother had been alive, his extended family had always gathered together for gargantuan Christmas lunches. Josh had loved them and so had his mother. Only his father had been pleased when they'd stopped a couple of years after his grandmother's death.

Uncle Raymond, although he was really a second cousin of sorts, had always organised games and charades after the meal, somehow getting everybody to their feet despite the vast amounts of turkey, roast potatoes and Yorkshire puddings they'd consumed. Josh still remembered his grandmother's Yorkshire puddings. Great pillows of hot, crisp batter with a soft interior. All with her ruddy and gleaming gravy... His mouth watered at the memory.

Lovell had asked him to do the interview and told him to go to the old church the pantomime used as a rehearsal space, workshop and venue. It had been unused for decades until the council stepped in a few years ago, did a few vital repairs and, at a loss to know what to do with the building, announced it could be used by Thorpe associations. It had been a free-for-all the first couple of years, but Uncle Raymond, employing the same techniques he'd used to get the Mason family on their feet after Gran's famous lunches, had charmed and bulldozed the other associations into letting the pantomime have sole use of the church rather than cluttering up the other rooms and halls. A skill acquired from years of persuading amateur actors that learning lines was as important as the fit and colour of their costume and whether they occupied the most visible position on stage. Besides, Thorpe was proud of its Christmas panto. It was far and away the best of the local offerings. People had been known to come from Harrogate to watch.

Raymond heaved himself out the pew, where he'd been working at a table cut to fit over the ones in front, and shook Josh's hand.

'It's been a long time,' he said. 'Tea? I always bring a flask.'

His voice echoed off the bare granite walls. It would have been a dour space were it not for the huge and colourful flats painted to resemble magical castles, tangled forests and seascapes dotted around its walls.

'No thanks, er...'

Josh didn't know whether to call him Raymond or maybe Mr Mason, as he was here on official business.

'I presume you know why I'm here?'

'Chloe Cooper?'

'Yes.'

Raymond sighed and pulled at the silk scarf round his neck.

'Poor child,' he said. 'She wasn't much more than a child, really. Very talented too. She was going to study musical theatre in London. But then Freddy came along.'

Josh nodded. He wondered why Chloe had kept Freddy. In this day and age it wouldn't have been difficult to terminate the pregnancy and, even if she'd left it too late, there were families crying out to adopt.

'I believe she was here last Sunday.'

'Yes. She was playing Puss. *Puss in Boots*, you know. That's this year's panto. I wasn't sure. It can be a mistake to do the traditional versions after Disney has had a go. But Chloe was brilliant. In the film Puss was played by Antonio Banderas and she came up with the idea of him being a renegade Spanish cousin who continually phoned her for tips on what to do. It would have been very funny.'

He sighed again.

'We'll have to carry on, of course. We're too far down the road to do another panto. I was just making some alterations to the script because it'll have to change now Chloe's... I know it sounds hard-hearted but—'

Josh thought he'd been going to say, *Life must go on* but stopped himself.

'It won't be the same.' Raymond smoothed his crumpled shirt. 'Life won't go on quite the same, I mean. These things mark a community. Especially coming so soon after young Peter Walker's killing. If the panto were next week, we'd cancel. As it is, I'm making sure there's nothing in it to remind the audience. We'll cut all the stage blood and make the fights less violent. You need to find out who did this one, Josh.'

Josh nodded.

'So,' he said. 'Sunday.'

'Sundays are when we all get together. There are rehearsals during the week, and the backstage crew get on with stuff as well. But it's good if we're all together once a week. Costume fittings and trying out props, you know. Plus they can all see what the others are up to. It's worth it even if we don't get as much rehearsal done as I'd like. The carpenters and painters have to use this room and they will chat. Not as bad as the costume ladies though. Their machines are noisy and some of them like to sing, so they use the vestry. Can't complain though. They do a fabulous job. Annie Price organises them and she's very clever.'

'Chloe was here, then.'

'Of course. She never missed a Sunday. I don't think she got out much because of Freddy, but she brought him along on Sundays. I told her to. Plenty of people happy to look after him for her.'

'When did she arrive and when did she leave?'

'Is that— Did it happen on Sunday night? After she left?'

'I can't tell you that.'

'Damn.' He sucked his cheeks in until his lips bulged. 'Damn, damn, damn... I know we all have to die sometime. The bible tells us the hour of a man's death is fixed from the moment he is born. But not like this. Please God, not like this.'

'No.'

'Right. Chloe. She arrived at around two. She gets— got a lift with Jim, our set designer.'

'Full name, please. And a contact number.'

Raymond scribbled them down on the back of an old copy of the *Thorpe Gazette*.

'And did he give her a lift home?'

'Normally, yes. We finish at seven. They always left promptly because it was late for young Freddy.'

Josh thought quickly. Probably half an hour from here to Cooper's yard. That meant Chloe hadn't got home until seven thirty at the earliest.

Raymond's phone rang. 'Do you mind if I answer this?'

'Go on.'

The call gave Josh time to run through the mental checklist he'd prepared. Had he missed anything? He didn't think so.

'That was Annie Price,' Raymond said when he'd finished the call. 'She was supposed to meet me to discuss altering Chloe's costume but she's just heard that Sean can pick Freddy up from Social Services, so she wants to go with him. It's good news of a sort. How long was the poor child alone with the...'

Josh shook his head. 'Thank you, Mr Mason,' he said firmly. 'That's helpful.'

'For heaven's sake, Josh, call me Raymond.'

He stood up to leave. Raymond didn't though. He gazed into the front of the church, where the altar had been but which was now just an empty stage with a clutter of chairs in the middle.

'Unless there's anything else you want to tell me.'

'There is something. Not sure if it's relevant though.'

'What's that?'

'Chloe had a private word with me on Sunday. I promised I wouldn't tell anyone but...' He shrugged. 'She was going to London next weekend. Supposedly to see a friend. Well, she was seeing a friend but she had another reason. She'd contacted the college who'd offered her a place to study before Freddy was born. They still had room on this year's course and told her the place was hers if she wanted it. She does— did want it. So she was going to check out the college crèche and accommodation and so on. She told me because it would mean she couldn't be in the panto. It was a bore. A real bore. She didn't want anyone to know until she'd decided. Frightened of her parents finding out, I think.'

'Her parents?'

'Her father really. He has quite a temper on him. There's no possibility he did it, is there?'

'No.'

'And killed himself?'

Josh shook his head. Really he shouldn't have said anything, but the memory of Charlie's Cooper's face had forced the word out. No one could have done that to themselves. Could they? No. In any case, the gun was missing.

'Oh well. If you're sure. But I'd have thought he was the obvious person.'

ELEVEN

JOSH MASON

THURSDAY

'Carter wants to see you,' Lovell said to Josh as soon as he arrived the following morning.

Josh wondered why. Everything had gone well enough yesterday. Or so Josh thought. He'd called the set designer immediately. Jim worked at the Water Rat on the river, over the footbridge from the old church. The manager had been happy to let him take a break to talk to Josh.

'Anything to help the police,' he'd said. 'The Walker case affected trade badly. People felt uncomfortable about going out and having fun. Plus they wanted to keep their families close. My daughter babysits for pocket money and she didn't have a booking for eight months. You need to catch the killer this time.'

The conversation with the set designer had been quick. He'd picked Chloe and Freddy up at the entrance to the stables at around one thirty and dropped them both back there at seven forty-two. He knew the exact time because he'd checked his phone. He'd promised the Water Rat he'd work from eight that evening and he was worried about being late. He'd left her at the end of the drive. She'd said it was OK, although he'd have been happy to take her to the cottage, but she knew he was in a hurry to get to work.

'It was kind of you to take her home anyway, given that you were working near the old church.'

'I'd do anything for Chloe. I was sorry to hear she was leaving Thorpe. She's a lovely girl.'

Which was quite an epitaph.

Josh had passed all the information on to Lovell and then been sent to the stables to help with the search of the barns and the land. Burden had allocated him to the team in the woods, which had been OK, if a little dull. He'd remembered the words his father endlessly spouted. *Keep your eyes and ears open and your mouth shut*. Burden was exactly the sort of old-school copper who wouldn't appreciate the benefit of Josh's more up-to-date take on policing. He'd come away impressed by Burden's thoroughness though. And by Charlie Cooper's management. All the buildings were impeccably maintained and their contents organised. Even the empty barns were clean, including the one in the middle of the woods.

They hadn't found the gun.

'Why does Carter want to see me?'

'He didn't say,' Lovell replied. 'But then he rarely feels the need to explain his reasoning to the DCs.'

Josh felt himself flushing. 'Where is he?'

'Watching Martin Appleton's interview.'

'He's been brought in already?'

'After what was found at his home yesterday? Of course he has. We don't hang about in crime. It's not like Local Policing.'

Josh nodded and walked away, hoping he didn't look as stupid as he felt. The interview rooms were in the basement. Carter sat inside the smallest one watching a monitor. He gestured for Josh to sit. Apart from the two seats and a table with a speaker and monitor, the room was empty. It was more of a large cupboard really, windowless and painted with the kind of thick cream paint that looked dirty as soon as you put it on. They didn't have much need for two interview rooms in Thorpe. He looked at the monitor.

Burden was interviewing Marty. Although the officer with him, a DC Josh didn't know, was asking all the questions. He was currently taking Marty through his statement and getting the youngster to confirm all the details were correct.

'That's his father.' Carter pointed to the man sitting next to Marty. 'Harry Appleton. Chip off the old block.'

It was true that Harry was as chunky as his son, but there the resemblance ended. Marty was strawberry blond and ruddy with an openness about him. His feelings were clear in every look and gesture. Whereas his father was dark and contained.

'He's been inside, hasn't he?'

Carter nodded curtly and Josh realised he hadn't said sir. It was too late now to add it. Not without drawing attention to the fact that he'd forgotten. Carter didn't look unduly bothered though. He leaned on one elbow, his fringe just falling short of his eyebrows.

'Mr Cooper wouldn't listen to me,' Marty was saying. 'Said he wanted me gone there and then. I could take whatever I could carry and come back for the rest on Tuesday.'

'That must have been tough.'

Marty went as though to say something but his father interrupted him.

'Marty rang me. And I told him to go home. That I'd be back on Tuesday and we'd go over to the stables together and talk to Charlie. I was away on a job up in Edinburgh and staying over.'

'We're not really interested in your movements, Mr Appleton.'

'You've checked though, haven't you? You've checked I was where I said I was. You can't be too careful with someone like me, can you? I mean with my history.'

Burden stared at Harry, who'd stood up, until the man sat down again.

'Get on with it,' Carter muttered.

'Like I said,' the DC continued. 'Getting the sack must have been quite a blow, Marty. We've heard you had big ambitions. Wanted to run your own stables. Have your own horses. Even enter those competitions where they make horses dance.'

'Dressage,' Marty said.

'That's it. Did you dream of becoming an Olympic star, then?'

'All youngsters have dreams.' This was Harry.

'Shouldn't he have a solicitor?' Josh asked Carter.

'Refused one. Or his father did. Said they're either useless or corrupt unless you've got lots of money.'

'And after Mr Cooper sacked you, you left straight away?' Burden asked.

Marty nodded.

'Please speak for the recording.'

'Yes.'

'And you didn't go back?'

'No.'

There was a long silence.

'Not at all?' the DC asked.

And before Marty could answer, Burden broke in. 'You see, Marty, we've had some initial forensics back from the scene. Fingerprint reports. From the kitchen.'

'Marty's fingerprints are bound to be everywhere. He ate with the family.'

'Please stay in your seat, Mr Appleton. The fingerprints were found in Giles Cooper's blood. On the kitchen table.'

Burden gave Marty a couple of beats to answer then, when he didn't, went on.

'And there were traces of blood in your father's washing machine. As though someone had tried to wash bloodstained clothing. We've taken your damp clothing, Marty. And your wet trainers. Washing machines don't get rid of blood completely, you know. We'll find evidence.'

Another pause.

'We will find blood, won't we, Marty.'

Some tension left the youngster's body. He sighed and nodded his head.

'For the recording, Martin Appleton nodded.' This was the DC.

'Yes,' Marty said. His face flushed. He was a beacon of colour in a grey room. It crossed Josh's mind how out of place the boy looked. There was something intrinsically open-air and healthy about him.

'Marty?' Harry turned to his son.

'I didn't leave straight away, Dad.'

'He's not answering any more questions.'

'I want to.'

'No. We'll get a solicitor.'

'Do you want a solicitor, Marty? We can call the duty solicitor. It'll take a while.'

'Yes, he does—'

'No. I want to get this over and done with. I didn't leave straight away. Well, I did. But I only went down the bridleway. Mr Cooper has a couple of fields at the bottom. Where he keeps horses whose owners don't visit often. I look after them mainly. I went down to see them.'

It was Burden's turn to wait.

'I stayed there for a bit and calmed down. Thought about it all. Sometimes I said things to Mr Cooper that annoyed him. Suggested we tried some of the newer methods I learned at college. His ways were very old-fashioned. I tried not to but occasionally it just came out. But he really needed me. I do lots more hours than I'm supposed to. I don't mind. It's all good experience. He'd never manage on his own, though. So I thought now he'd had time to cool down, if I went back to apologise, he might change his mind.'

The silence was broken by Harry leaning abruptly forward and burying his face in his hands.

'So you went back to the stables?'

'Yes.'

'And when was this?'

'I don't know. I wasn't paying attention. But it was dark by then. I had to use my phone to see the bridleway.'

The DC made a note. 'So you didn't cycle back to the stables?'

'No. Too muddy. I'd had to push my bike down. I left it in the field with Hard← with the horses.'

'And?'

'The stables was very quiet. The owners had gone. Which was fine. Mr Cooper was always more relaxed when they weren't around. He was brilliant with the horses, you see, but not so good with the owners.'

Everyone waited. Carter had stopped breathing.

'Marty.' This was the DC. 'You need to tell us what happened next.'

'I went into the cottage. And found them.'

'Them?'

'Giles and Mrs Cooper. In the kitchen.'

He stopped, his eyes blinking rapidly. Harry put an arm round him.

'It's not very clear after that.'

'Did you go into the rest of the house?'

Marty shook his head. Then remembered the recording and said, 'No.'

'How long did you stay in the kitchen?'

'I don't know. I was... frozen like.' And then after a while: 'I don't remember much. Except the bodies. But I must have left and cycled home. Because I remember getting home and realising my sleeve and my jeans had blood on them. And my trainers too. So I washed them.'

'You locked the door to Cooper's cottage.'

'Yes. I have a key.'

'And why did you do that?'

'I don't know. Maybe so no one else would stumble on them. Like I had.'

'And it didn't occur to you to alert the authorities? To call an ambulance? Or us?'

'I did.'

'You did what?'

'I called the police. I didn't think of an ambulance. I was sure they were dead.'

'You called the police?' Burden's voice was sharp. 'When?'

'After I'd locked up. But...'

'But what?' the DC said after a while.

'I couldn't say it. That they were dead. It didn't seem real. I didn't think they'd believe me. So I just said that the dogs were out and had bitten me. I thought they'd send someone round to check. And I let two of them out... the two that like to go for the pheasants. I knew that'd bring Ed Lambert round.'

The DC made a note, but Carter picked up his phone. 'Lovell,' he said. 'I want the record of all calls made to us about Cooper's dogs on the Sunday and Monday.' He listened for a while, turning the sound down on the speaker. 'Ask him to come down here,' he said and rang off.

He looked at Josh. 'Mason, isn't it? Why are you here?'

'You asked to see me, sir. Lovell sent me down.'

'Oh yes. What do you think of him?' He jerked his head towards the screen. 'Martin Appleton. He's local to Thorpe, isn't he?'

'Yes.'

'Know anything about him?'

'Not really. Nothing bad anyway.'

'Pity. Local knowledge is always helpful.'

'My aunt knows him.' Josh felt himself flush. Just like Marty. As though admitting he had an aunt wasn't the done thing. 'In fact, she used to have a horse at Cooper's Stables.'

'Used to?'

'She sold the horse. Couldn't afford to keep it. She's divorced now.' Josh shook his head. None of this was relevant. 'But she knew Marty.'

'What did she think of him?'

'She said he was kind. She was talking to my mother about her horse being sold. She said the horse was staying with Cooper and Marty had promised to look after her.'

'Maybe kind to horses. But not so kind to the Cooper family.'

'You think he did it?'

'All the indications are that he did. Everybody else can account for their whereabouts.'

'Sean Price, the child's father, too?'

'Yes. He took his mother for a meal and then they went to Fountains Abbey for some light show or other. They were seen. We need to find where Marty left the gun.'

He stared back at the screen. The overhead light settled his face back into harsh lines.

'One other thing.' Carter didn't turn round as he spoke.

'Yes, sir.'

'The tarot cards. Lovell told you not to mention them.'

'Yes, sir. He explained about the Walker case.'

'He did, did he?'

Josh wanted to say that if there was a link to the Walker case then surely Marty couldn't be involved, but he suspected this was one of those moments when he should keep his mouth shut and his ears open.

'Heard anything about tarot locally?'

'No, sir.'

'I don't mean as an officer. Just people talking about tarot. People having tarot cards.'

'No, sir. Well, except for my family, that is.'

'Your family?' Carter still brooded over the screen, where Burden was asking Marty where he'd left the gun.

'My mother reads them. Just for a bit of fun, though. That's how I knew one of the ones at the stables was the Sun.'

For once Carter looked interested.

'And its significance?'

Josh thought for a second. 'I think it's normally a very happy card. It often means something good is going to happen to you.'

He couldn't remember what each element of the picture

meant. The child on the horse was something to do with joy though.

'I could ask my mother, if you like. Or Kezia. That's my aunt. She knows about tarot too.'

Carter turned to look at him.

'The card didn't look quite right though,' he added.

'Yes, someone had disfigured the child's face. Could have been Freddy scribbling. Probably doesn't mean anything.'

Josh shut his mouth.

'What did you say your aunt's name was?'

'Kezia, sir.' He thought of explaining that the whole family had odd names, but didn't.

'Kezia? You said Kezia?'

'Kezia Heron, sir.'

Carter stared at him for a while. Or seemed to. But Josh realised he was looking straight through him, lost in some thought process. The sound of footsteps coming down the corridor broke him out of his reverie.

'The tarot cards at the Coopers' are a dead end,' Carter said. 'Just one of those things, but keep it quiet. That'll be all, Mason.'

Josh left. Although he was burning to argue.

A man in a dark suit passed him in the corridor. Josh didn't know who he was but that meant nothing. He didn't know half the officers who were currently based here. He watched him walk past. Carter stood as he entered the room, then closed the door behind them.

Someone senior to Carter then.

TWELVE
ALAN CALVERT

SAME DAY

Alan looked up from bagging the wood ash after his weekend's bonfire in the incinerator when Kezia passed by his allotment. He'd guessed it was her as soon as he'd heard the rapid footsteps. He wondered if she'd heard the news. Mrs Vine, who had an allotment right by the entrance, had told him. She was always the first to know everything, although he'd been expecting it ever since he'd been told the police had turned the Appletons' flat upside down.

The feeling of triumph had shaken him. He knew it was un-Christian to take such pleasure in someone else's misery, but surely in this one instance it was fair enough. Harry Appleton had never paid in full for the years of loneliness and unhappiness he'd bestowed on Alan. And for the blow to be dealt him via his son was the icing on the cake. Alan allowed himself a few minutes of deep satisfaction.

It was a good thing all round.

He'd heard the murmurs about Sean Price. It was ridiculous, of course. But gossip like that was poisonous. Alan had been at the cottage with Dennis when Annie had rung with news of the killings and to tell him the police had picked up Sean. The two of them had been fishing and Dennis's fingers had trembled as he packed away his fishing gear. Poor Dennis. He had more than enough to deal with as it was. Mind you he'd felt surprisingly shaky himself. He must remember to give Dennis the spare key to the cottage back.

He wished he had someone to share the feeling with. Maybe he could tell Kezia. She didn't stop though. Just gave him a quick wave and passed by.

Hers was the end allotment, a corner one, next to his. It was surrounded on three sides by a tall hedge, and a large part of its area was taken up by a damp ditch full of nettles and weeds that often smelled rank. She had jumped the queue when she applied four months ago because no one else was prepared to take it on.

He'd been faintly put out at first. He'd quite liked the solitude. Not that Kezia had shown any inclination to disturb it. She'd introduced herself the first time she'd come down and he'd thought the shortish woman, slim with dark, slightly untidy hair and high cheekbones, unremarkable. She'd never encroached, contenting herself with a friendly wave as she passed.

In fact, he'd been the one who'd become curious about her and what she was doing in her allotment.

He'd satisfied his curiosity about the allotment easily enough. She hadn't done much, as far as he could see from peering through the gaps round the wooden gate set into the boundary hedge and when he'd been fixing the roof of his shed and been able to look in from the ladder. She'd hacked down the hedge on the south side, which adjoined his allotment, to a manageable level, keeping it just high enough to prevent anyone looking over but also letting the sun shine in. She couldn't do anything with the other hedges because they belonged to a couple who'd bought the neighbouring farm and were rewilding it – much to the bewilderment of the local farmers. Apart from that the allotment looked as unkempt as ever.

Finding out about her hadn't been so easy.

Initial gossip at the monthly allotment-holders' meetings was that she'd divorced last year. Her ex-husband was a successful solicitor in York. He'd had an affair and wanted out of the marriage. Same old story. No children to make him feel he should stay. Alan had wondered about that. Whether there was some reason for her childlessness. Some tragedy in her past?

She was friendly enough, stopping to exchange a few words when he waylaid her, an expression of interest as he explained what he was doing on his allotment. And that slight smile. The one with the lips closed over her mouth that made her seem so mysterious.

And over the months since, his interest had grown from mild curiosity to wanting to get to know her. He hadn't felt like this for years. If he was honest he'd thought he'd spend the rest of his life alone. Well, not alone exactly. He had friends. And social activities. And they'd been enough.

Until now.

He wasn't that old, after all. Mid-fifties, fit and slim. He still had all his hair. She was late forties. It wasn't too big a gap. So he'd started chatting to her a bit more. And giving her fruit and vegetables. She'd let slip she loved old Bette Davis films and he'd noticed one of the independents in York was doing a retrospective. He'd wondered about asking if she'd like to go with him to see a couple.

And then he'd felt guilty. He'd always thought he'd stay faithful to Janice's memory. And Samuel's. But he'd told Janice about Kezia and what he planned when he'd taken the flowers to the grave she shared with Samuel a few weeks ago. Twice a week he went. Even if the weather was dreadful. Afterwards he'd felt at peace about it. As though she'd given him her blessing. Then, it was only a question of waiting for the right opportunity.

Just it never seemed to arrive.

Well, he'd go over now. Ask her if she'd like some of the wood ash from his incinerator. For her allotment. And then lead it into it. What was the worst that could happen? She'd say no. And it wouldn't be the end of the world. He was aware though of an uneasy feeling in the pit of his stomach.

'Kezia.' It felt stupid to knock on the gate set into the hedge arch, so he called her name.

'Coming,' she called.

She dragged the battered gate open over an overgrown patch of grass.

'Sorry,' he said. 'I didn't mean to disturb you.' He looked around. It was worse close to. If she didn't sort it out, she'd lose the allotment. There were strict rules about keeping weeds under control. The committee would give a lot of leeway because of its state when she took it over, but there were limits.

'I've been picking herbs,' she said with a defensive note in her voice. 'To dry.'

She pointed towards the table outside her ramshackle shed, piled with leafy stalks and bits of twig and what looked like nettles.

'It's a good time of year to start digging out the beds for next spring.' He couldn't help giving her the benefit of his experience. 'Let the frost break up the soil over winter. And give you the chance to get lots of compost in. I could give you a hand if you like.'

'I read somewhere it's best to leave a garden for a year before tackling it, so you can see what might be hiding under the surface.'

They both gazed round. In his heart of hearts Alan knew nothing was going to suddenly break the earth here except more weeds.

'Well, let me know if you change your mind. I popped over because I've been doing some clearing and burning. So I've got a lot of wood ash if you'd like some. Quite good as a nutrient. Plus your soil is probably acidic.'

He pointed to the coniferous hedge. She didn't understand, so he explained about the pH value of soil and how coniferous plants raise its acidity and that most vegetables didn't like this.

'Thank you,' she said when he paused. 'I'd like that. Would you like some herbs? When they're ready, I mean. They need to dry first. I do it at my studio. It's too damp here.'

'Sage?' he asked. 'I like a bit of sage in a stuffing for a chicken. And thyme is always useful.'

'Yes. And I grow rosemary and bay at the studio. In pots.'

'That would be nice.' He stared into the distance for a few seconds, trying to think what to say next. 'I'll get you the ash,' he said eventually. 'A bag for here and maybe a small bag for the herbs at the studio. They won't want a lot.'

'That would be nice.' She repeated his words.

'I'll get them now.'

She left the gate open as he walked down the brick path that bisected his garden and round the back of the pristine shed to the small incinerator he used for burning the bits of plant that were too woody for his compost heap. He wished he hadn't tried to explain about soil acidity. He'd bored her, he was sure. He shook his head as he shovelled grey ash into a black rubbish sack and a smaller amount into a plastic bag. He'd just ask her straight out about the retrospective when he went back, before he got sidetracked onto anything else.

She was tying string round the end of what was definitely a bunch of nettles. What on earth for? He remembered his resolution and opened his mouth to tell her about the Bette Davis retrospective, but at the last minute he couldn't find the right words. Instead he heard himself tell her Mrs Vine's news.

'I hear they've made an arrest in the Cooper's Stables killings.'

He had her attention now.

'Who?'

'The stable lad. Martin Appleton.'

'Marty? No!' The words exploded out of her.

'Do you know him?'

'Yes. He's a lovely lad. Why though? Why him?'

He repeated what Mrs Vine had told him. Charlie Cooper had sacked the lad and the killings had been some sort of revenge attack.

'That's ridiculous. It's a mistake. I'm sure of it.'

She pulled the knot tight on the last bunch of nettles and added it to the pile, then rested her full weight on the table. It wobbled slightly before settling.

'The Appletons are bad news,' he said. 'Always have been always will be. Behind every break-in in Thorpe. And Harry Appleton's the worst of the bunch.'

Should he tell Kezia what Harry had done to him? Surely she knew. Everybody in Thorpe knew. But she spoke first.

'Who told you they'd arrested Marty?' And when he hesitated, 'Mrs Vine, wasn't it?' She picked up the small bag of ashes and put it into a basket, then swept the bundle of herbs and nettles in on top. 'Right, I'm heading off.'

'To see Mrs Vine?'

'Amongst others.'

He followed her out of her allotment and watched as she strode away.

He realised he hadn't asked her out.

THIRTEEN
JOSH MASON

FRIDAY

Josh didn't feel too bad when he woke on Friday morning. Surprisingly. Although he had gone easy towards the end of the evening. Burden had sneered when he'd opted for water during the last couple of rounds, but Lovell had also asked for water, and a couple of the other DCs too. A decent breakfast would clear away his faint hangover. It wouldn't do his diet any good. But neither would the pints he'd drunk last night. Nor the burger he'd had from Sean's van on the way home.

He'd hoped Sean wouldn't be there, that his assistant Megan would be on duty with one of the array of casual staff who never seemed to last more than a couple of weeks. Beresford had warned him it could be tricky navigating friendships when the friends had been involved with the police. Not that Sean was a friend exactly. But after his evening in the pub, he didn't feel up to fielding remarks if Sean was annoyed about being brought in to the station for an interview.

Sean was there though. But fine. In fact more than fine. He left Megan to make Josh's burger and came out to lean against the counter and roll a cigarette. A big man, but triangular-shaped with narrow hips and broad shoulders, although the white apron he was wearing disguised most of it.

'I hear you've made an arrest?'

Josh nodded and felt a faint belch of beery gas escape the confines of his stomach. Probably wiser to say nothing and change the subject.

'So you'll be back to traffic duty and delivering anti-crime leaflets,' Sean said.

Josh forbore to tell him that those duties were more often carried out by PCSOs and nodded.

'Maybe you could tell Sergeant Beresford that the car park behind the Co-op is being used by people without permits. I was going to have a word with him about it.'

Sean paid a not inconsiderable sum for the use of the charging facility and water in the square while he was open and to park his van overnight in the car park behind the supermarket, and he wasn't happy that other vans and trucks seemed to park there without paying.

'Nobody's policing it, Josh,' he said.

'It's not really the police's job to, er, police the car park. It's the council's.'

'Well, they don't. The old van Giles and I used to run was there all of Monday and Tuesday.'

Josh remembered the mysterious van the Coopers' neighbour had seen outside the stables at some point in the last few days.

'Does— did Giles still have it?'

'Don't think so. I think he sold it. He'd no chance of running it by himself after I walked out. He couldn't organise a piss-up in a brewery, let alone a catering business on his own.'

It wouldn't do any harm to find out a bit more about Giles.

'You walked out?' Josh asked.

'Yes. The van belonged to Giles. I supplied all the skills. That was the deal. But David Kingsley was pushing for his money back – he gave Giles a loan to buy the van, although the interest rate was extortionate. So Giles wanted to go over to the dark side. That's why I walked out.'

'Dark side?' he asked.

'Dark kitchens. They're going to put me out of business.'

And before Josh could ask what he meant, Sean started going on about how difficult everything was with the regulations and the inspections.

'I told Beresford, but he said dark kitchens were nothing to do with the police.'

That phrase again. 'What are dark kitchens?'

Megan came over with his burger as Sean's phone buzzed. 'I've told you, Sean. And Beresford has. They're not illegal.'

'Order for two pizzas,' Sean said.

'You do them. I'll finish this order. Hi Josh. How are you?'

He'd been in the same class as Megan at school, although you wouldn't recognise the scrawny kid she'd been in the young woman who'd smiled when he arrived and was now chopping salad for his burger.

'Fine. And you?'

'Good.'

She piled salad into the bun. 'Here's your burger.' She turned to put the rest of the salad back into the fridge.

'So what are these dark kitchens?' Josh said quickly. 'Sounds very mysterious.'

'Not really. Everyone orders takeaway now, from Uber or Deliveroo. We take orders from them. People think the food comes from the restaurant, but more often than not it's made at separate premises set up only for takeaways. They're called dark kitchens. It's all perfectly legal. But Sean thinks some of them don't register and escape scrutiny.'

'They don't pay rent. They don't pay council tax.' Sean swung a pizza base round on one finger and slapped it back onto the stainless steel work surface. Josh had taken his burger and left before he could start up again.

It had been fun catching up with Megan, he thought as he

turned the stove on. Maybe he'd get another burger tonight. He'd just have to buy some new trousers.

He cracked the eggs that were the *pièce de résistance* of his breakfast into a mixture of butter and oil. Oil meant they'd have crispy edges and butter for the taste. His mind wandered back to work. At least he'd been asked to come to the pub. He'd heard stories about newbies being excluded from celebratory drinks. Not that there was much opportunity for celebration in Local Policing. And Martin Appleton's arrest was a stunning success. A terrible massacre solved in three days.

'*Nobody's promised tomorrow,*' he sang along to the radio and shovelled the contents of the pan onto a warmed plate on the table. Kezia appeared at the door, dressed in her work attire – loose cotton trousers and a T-shirt under a V neck sweater. All in neutral shades.

'Want some breakfast?' he asked.

'No. Everybody's saying you've arrested Marty. Is it true?'

Her voice was tighter than normal.

'You know I can't say. Help yourself to coffee. I've made plenty.'

'Is it true?'

'We have made an arrest but the person's name will not be released. You always have tea in the morning, don't you? I'll put the kettle back on. Actually it's probably hot enough still.' He sat down at the table to give her room to make tea.

'So it is Marty. But why?'

He felt slightly winded by her unexpected forcefulness.

'Like I say, the person's name will not be released.'

She spooned tea into the pot she'd asked him not to use for his normal tea.

'So, tell me why you've arrested this person.'

'I can't. You know that.'

'Josh.'

He remembered how much he'd already told her.

'There was evidence they'd been present at the scene. Modern forensics, you know.'

'What evidence?'

He put a forkful of beans in his mouth and chewed. He wasn't going to tell her anything else.

'Evidence he'd been at the scene?' she said. 'What could that be? Blood? Yes, blood on his clothes?'

He ignored her and cut his sausage into bite-sized bits.

'No! He must have discovered the bodies. He did, didn't he? Oh, poor Marty. Poor, poor Marty. How awful.'

This was too much. He swallowed the food.

'So this person says now. But only after he was confronted with a fi— proof that he'd been present after the shooting from the crime scene staff – top blokes by the way. Strangely enough though, he doesn't remember what time this was. He doesn't remember how long he spent in the cottage, nor what he did there. He says he was frozen and it's all jumbled up in his mind. Very convenient for him. Means he can change his story if we find any more evidence.'

Josh was aware that he was repeating Burden's scornful words. He didn't care.

'And get this – instead of reporting it he locked the cottage door and cycled home. Then washed his bloodstained clothes and trainers. Shocked people don't carefully lock a crime scene up and flee.'

He hadn't meant to tell her all this.

'They might,' she said. 'People do strange things after a great trauma.'

He carefully balanced another mouthful of fried egg and bacon onto a square of fried bread, smeared tomato ketchup on it and ate it. She sloshed water into the pot. He sliced a round of black pudding but somehow didn't fancy it. Left it on the side of his plate and ate some more fried bread and bacon. She watched the teapot.

'You're very quiet now,' he said. 'You clearly aren't happy about it.'

'You seriously think Marty'd blast an innocent family to death because he'd lost his job—'

'You heard he'd been sacked then?'

'Everybody's talking about it. Doesn't seem much of a motive.'

She poured herself a cup.

He was aware of a feeling of unease. The plate of sausages, bacon and eggs suddenly seemed less appetising.

She was staring at him with a look of distaste on her face.

'And don't tell me how he comes from a bad family,' she added. 'The Appletons. How locally there's a saying: "*The Appleton never falls far from the tree.*"'

He was about to say background played a part, then remembered her ex-husband. David came from the worst of worst backgrounds. The Kingsley family was well known to York police. David's uncle, Miles Kingsley, was behind most of the serious and violent crime in the area. David had made good though. Stuck it out through school and got into college. Qualified as a solicitor and worked for the stuffiest and most proper of firms in York before setting up for himself.

'Motive isn't everything,' he said. 'I'm speaking generally, you realise. I couldn't comment on the Cooper killings.' He avoided looking at her. 'Sometimes we – the police – never understand what drove someone. However, I will tell you, the person we've arrested behaved very weirdly. Something was off the first time we interviewed this person. They were hugely jumpy.'

'Don't you think any youngster might be a bit jumpy and weird after being linked to a slaughter like the one you described to me?'

'Look, they lied through their teeth the first time they spoke to us. Why would they do that if they didn't have something to hide?'

A little voice in Josh's head reminded him people lied to the police all the time and for the strangest reasons.

He gave up on his breakfast.

'The CPS won't prosecute unless there's a case to answer,' he said finally. 'Lots of water still to flow under the bridge.'

He scraped the plate into the bin and ran water in the sink.

'Besides,' he added. 'Everybody else is accounted for.'

That shut her up. And made him feel better. Everyone had

alibis for the appropriate time. Not that the police had released the exact time when the murders had taken place. People had been asked to account for their movements until Monday evening when Josh had discovered the bodies. The neighbours, Boyes and Lambert, had been in the pub and vouched for by any number of people. Sean Price at some event at Fountains Abbey with his mother. It crossed his mind that they hadn't actively searched for any other suspects or followed up on Giles's dubious connections, but really everything pointed to Martin Appleton.

'What about the tarot cards?'

Shit. He'd forgotten he'd told her about them.

'Kezia. I shouldn't have mentioned them to you. I shouldn't have mentioned any of this. You haven't spoken about it, have you?'

'No.'

'Then please don't. It's confidential.'

'Why?'

'Er... Connection to another case.'

He could see the question forming in her brain. What did another case have to do with Marty shooting the Coopers?

'I can't talk about it,' he said quickly. 'It's irrelevant anyway. Just something Chloe Cooper happened to have.'

Had he told her about the note? The one with the card. *For Freddy*, it had said. *Tell Giles*. And the fact that one of the cards had been disfigured. He didn't think he had. He wondered what all that was about. Just another loose end. Like the gun. They hadn't found it. They probably never would. But Martin had had lots of time to get rid of it. According to Lovell and Burden, there were always things you couldn't explain. The general public, bless them, didn't get it. Too used to watching detective shows where everything was neatly tied up at the end. They didn't understand the realities of policing.

Kezia was quiet. And still. Not even drinking her tea. He was aware of its aromatic smell now he'd got rid of his breakfast. It was quite pleasant really. Sort of fresh but calming. He glanced at her again.

She gave so little away. Very different to his mother. In every way. Small and dark whereas Mum was tall and blond. And vivacious. You always knew what Mum was thinking. She said it came from being one of a large family. You had to be quick and loud to be heard. Not that Mum talked a lot about her childhood. Just occasionally when Dad wasn't around, she let a few things slip. Enough to make him realise her family was a bit... ramshackle, was the best way to put it. They'd never stayed in one place for long. Moving from one strange group of people to another. New age communes and gipsies, he supposed. She never spoke of her father. It occurred to Josh for the first time that she and Kezia probably had different fathers.

Kezia wasn't happy. He was aware of that. Just as he was aware some of her words had stirred up his own doubts. It made no difference though. He laughed at the idea that he, PC Josh Mason, newest of the new, had any sway in the crime department of a busy police force. Maybe one day.

'What are you up to today?' he asked.

She looked startled at being addressed, but answered readily enough.

'Someone's coming to the studio for some head and shoulder shots this afternoon. A Mrs Monroe. For her website. I took some shots of her working a couple of days ago.'

'Mrs Monroe? Scottish?'

'Not sure. But I expect she could be if you wanted her to.'

'What do you mean?'

'She's a con artist. She makes a living out of telling people what they want to hear and charging them for it.'

Josh had never heard Kezia sound so scornful.

'Go on. What does she do that's annoyed you so much?'

'She claims to be a medium. You know, someone who gets messages from dead people for their loved ones. Although she doesn't see them, she only hears them. Much less likely to get something wrong if you're only describing someone's voice.'

'You mean a seance? You went to a seance?'

'Yup. Only to get some photos of her in action.'

'What was it like?'

'Horrible. Half a dozen sad people desperate to make sense of the death of someone they loved.'

'And did the dead speak?'

'Of course.'

'You sound very sceptical.'

'I am. The majority of the people who attend are women of a certain age, so it's likely at least one of them is a grieving widow. She'll say she has a message from a husband and you can tell pretty quickly from their faces who is hoping for that. And then there are all sorts of techniques for drawing information out of them and giving them what they want to hear.'

Kezia sounded really angry, although not with him now. He'd have liked to ask her how she knew all this, but decided not to chance his luck. Probably something she'd come across during her ramshackle childhood. Like his mother, she didn't like talking about it.

'Mind you, she was kind,' Kezia added. 'The messages she gave were all pretty comforting, so it could have been worse. But it's still all wrong.'

And with that she whisked out of the kitchen and disappeared into her room, muttering something about getting ready.

FOURTEEN

KEZIA HERON

SAME DAY

Marty hadn't killed the Coopers. I knew he hadn't. But I couldn't do anything about it. Anyway, I needed to go to the studio and get ready for Mrs Monroe. I hoped she'd recovered from Wednesday afternoon. She'd been shaken up by what had happened – whatever it was – her voice thin and quivery although she'd managed to get it back under control before the seance started. Not that the experience had left me untouched. I'd got through the shoot as quickly as I could and left.

I took my coat from the wardrobe and saw the tarot deck on a shelf. I should have asked Josh which tarot cards had been in Chloe Cooper's hands. He might even have told me. He wasn't great at keeping things to himself. Never had been. Especially not when pushed. I wasn't sure I wanted to know though. What if they were two of the cards missing from this deck?

I shut my eyes, laid them out on the bed, face down, and picked one. A spur-of-the-moment thing, done before the rational part of my brain kicked in. The Knight of Swords. What was it with the knights – the action heroes of the tarot? Why did I keep picking them?

They reminded me of David.

And the Knight of Swords even more than the others. Always charging after something and never reaching it.

He's a knight in armour, holding a sword high and urging his horse onward. Things I hadn't noticed as a child leapt out at me now. The way the horse rolls his eye back to look at the knight. No wonder, really. The rider's seat made him very unstable. If the horse stumbled, he'd go flying.

Oh, David. David and his restless search to become someone.

First he saw himself as a successful businessman, all three-piece suits, handmade shirts and cufflinks. He started collecting watches and we went to endless charity functions and Rotary dinners. He asked me to give up my array of low-paid jobs then. He wanted a wife with hobbies and time for charity fundraising rather than a barmaid and shop assistant. To be fair, I was only too happy.

And then he reimagined himself as a country gentleman. Tweeds and shoots. Boring, boring days of killing birds and drinking too much. He was never very good at it. So he bought us horses. We went hunting and he wasn't bad. That hobby lasted longer than many but he tired of it eventually and became an athlete. Lycra and gym memberships and personal trainers, hours spent comparing running times and drinking juices. I didn't join him though. He might have given up on riding but I had found something I loved. And to be fair, he didn't mind. Maybe it was easier for him without his wife casting a sardonic eye when he gushed about his latest craze.

But the thing is, it all costs money. And we didn't have any. As I discovered when I started looking into our finances after selling Bathy to pay the stable debts. We'd never had much. David's practice as a solicitor was nothing like as successful as I'd imagined. And there was worse.

I'd thought we'd discuss it. That David would see things had to change. We'd come up with a plan together. But instead he reinvented himself as an unhappy husband with a demanding and lazy wife and took up with Becky, marrying her the day after our divorce came through.

I wasn't sure what persona he'd adopted since.

I put the card back in the deck and noticed the marks again. Checked the others.

Maybe I needed to find out what David had become. And now.

FIFTEEN

BECKY KINGSLEY

SAME DAY

Becky Kingsley looked at her watch again. Davey had promised the old kitchen would be picked up before nine a.m., but it was nearly eleven and it still sat on the pavement where Davey had left it last night after he'd finished ripping it out. Any minute now the neighbours would sound off. They didn't like her. They were very off when she popped over to say hello after she moved in. How was she to know they'd been big friends with Davey's ex?

Since then, they'd complained about everything.

She'd called Davey twice already and he'd said he'd ring his cousin who was sending the men and a van to take the kitchen away. Why Davey couldn't have let the company installing the new kitchen take it out, she didn't know. It would only have cost a couple of thousand more. Davey hadn't wanted a new kitchen but she'd insisted. His ex had had the old one put in and while the oak and Gothic vibe might have suited her Becky didn't like it and you know what they say – Happy Wife, Happy Life.

She'd have liked to move to a new house, modern with clean white walls and lots of glass and preferably not in Thorpe. Their road ran past the church with a cemetery opposite, filled with ancient plane trees and wonky gravestones. The house itself looked vaguely church-like with its arched porch and pointy windows. But Davey had said no and nothing she could say would persuade him to change his mind. No idea why. It would have made perfect sense to move to York, where he worked as a solicitor.

Still, she'd managed to change a lot of things and cleared out huge amounts of junk the ex had left behind. The local charity shops knew her well.

Maybe she should broach the subject once more. The recent murders at the stables hardly made Thorpe a desirable place to live. A regular bloodbath it had been. Only the toddler had been spared. Even Davey had been shocked. He'd snapped at her to make sure the door was locked at all times and not to open it to anyone she didn't know. But then he was permanently in a bad mood now. Maybe she wouldn't mention moving again.

The phone rang. She let it go to voicemail and listened in. Sure enough it was next door, wondering how much longer they'd be leaving their rubbish on the pavement. Right. Enough was enough. Davey had asked her to wait until the men came but she wasn't going to. She'd go out.

She'd get a couple of coffees from Sean's van and go and see Lauren. Her shop was open on Friday mornings. Lauren knew lots about the murders at the stables. Her boyfriend, Sean, was the toddler's father, although he and Chloe Cooper had split up before the child was born. Sean hadn't wanted children, been furious when Chloe insisted on keeping the baby, Lauren had said. He had some medical condition, which he might have passed on, although Becky hadn't seen any evidence of it on the odd occasion when she'd met him. He looked quite normal really. And apparently the child was fine.

She couldn't wait to hear what Lauren knew about the boy they'd arrested. The stable lad.

That reminded her, Lauren had met Davey's first wife. She'd blurted it out when Becky had been describing the awfulness of the old kitchen. She'd been very tight-lipped when Becky had expressed a perfectly natural interest in the woman. Becky had seen her a couple of times at the office herself. Before she and Davey got together of course. But not since. As soon as she and Davey split up, she'd abandoned all their joint friends. Which was a relief really.

Becky checked her face and got her coat, but, when she looked out of the window to be sure the neighbours weren't lying in wait for her, a woman was standing on the opposite side of the road and staring at the house. Well, at the stuff on the pavement really. She looked shocked and a bit angry. Shit. Becky hoped she wasn't from the council.

The woman crossed the road and walked around the pile. She didn't look like council. She was dressed in loose cotton trousers and an old raincoat, with a battered handbag over one shoulder and a hessian bag over the other. Probably not council. They normally wore those yellow jackets. Maybe she was looking the old kitchen over with a view to helping herself. It had been good quality according to Davey. He'd wanted her to try to sell it on Facebook but it was too much faff. Well the woman was more than welcome. She could take the whole lot as far as Becky was concerned.

The woman glanced up at the house and saw Becky at the window.

It was Davey's ex. The Kezia woman.

How weird was that! Her appearing at the same moment as Becky had been thinking about her. Was she stalking Becky? First meeting Lauren and now this?

A black car suddenly pulled up. Davey's cousin got out and sauntered in through the gate. She checked her make-up again and wished she had washed her hair after all.

'Hi,' she said as she opened the door. Behind him a white van arrived. Two men got out and started throwing the kitchen into its back.

'Sorry we're late,' he said 'Traffic.'

It was so nice to look up to a man. Even though he was two steps below her, he was still taller. Davey was so short.

'What was *she* doing here?' he asked.

'Who?'

'Kezia. She scarpered when she saw me.'

'No idea. Maybe she heard we were replacing her kitchen and wanted a souvenir.'

'I thought she'd moved away.'

'No, she lives in Thorpe. Renting a room from her nephew, I think Davey said.'

'The local copper?'

'Is he? I didn't know. Davey never said.'

'Does Miles know?'

Becky shrugged.

SIXTEEN

MRS MONROE

SAME DAY

The session had gone well, Mrs Monroe thought, as she scrolled through the images on Kezia's computer. She looked kindly and welcoming but at the same time confident and serious. And just a little younger. Which was nice. Growing old was tiresome. Bits of her body didn't work as well as they used to and she was sick to death of the way young people's eyes slid over her and away as they instantly classified her as elderly. She didn't feel any different to how she'd felt when she was their age. And one day they'd feel the same. The certificates and thank-you cards Kezia had told her to bring made a perfect backdrop to some of the pictures. Kezia was a clever woman in her own quiet way.

Kezia drew back the black curtains covering the huge arched window at one end of the studio. The building had originally been warehousing for the canal but had fallen into disuse. The developers had kept the basic structure intact and filled the large arches, which once would have contained wooden doors, with glass. Mrs Monroe looked around as daylight broke into the space again.

It was one large room with two smaller ones off it. One used for storage and the other a washroom. The walls were lined with photographs of objects. A couple were recognisable: a piece of glass with its edges smoothed by the sea and its surface cloudy; an ancient slate arrowhead. But most were bits of stone and wood.

'No people?' Mrs Monroe said.

'I like things. Objects. I like feeling their shape and texture and seeing what they tell me. And then I see if I can capture that on film.'

Mrs Monroe looked again, but honestly they were just photos of objects. Maybe the lump of granite had a heaviness that made you realise how long it had been around.

'Let's do some shots of you looking more relaxed and less businesslike,' Kezia said. 'Something more personal. Clients like to know a little about the person behind.'

Hamish had said that too, so she'd included a little biography for the website. Nothing too revealing but enough to make her sound human.

'Fine,'

'Do you have any hobbies?'

'Well. I like reading. Crime fiction mainly.'

'Maybe not. Anything else?'

'I used to enjoy walking the dog, but since my hip started bothering me I can't do long walks any more. Luckily he's an old boy so he's quite happy pottering around with me in the garden.'

'Have you brought him? Left him in the car?'

'No. My neighbour has a key. She goes in and lets him out if I'm not there.'

'Gardening then. That's a nice hobby.'

'Wholesome, you mean? Unlike my day job.'

Mrs Monroe suspected Kezia thought she was a fraud. Maybe she was. But maybe she wasn't. To be honest, the seances and tarot readings were second nature now and much of what she said was rote, learned from years of practice. Little was inspired by the spirit world. But there was one. She believed that. Where else did the things she knew without being told come from? Maybe the impression she gave of the dead speaking directly to her wasn't a hundred per cent accurate, but her clients needed an explanation of her gifts they could understand. Like the tarot readings. She'd learned what the cards meant. But, really, they were a vehicle for the insights she had about the people who came for guidance. Most of them just needed to talk anyway. The answers they were looking for were staring them in the face.

She waited for Kezia to respond but if she disliked Mrs Monroe's profession she didn't want to reveal it.

'I've got a little garden in my courtyard,' she said. 'Let's see if we can get a couple of photos there.'

It was delightful. A little suntrap and sheltered. Kezia had large pots of plants along one wall, most of which Mrs Monroe recognised although some were unknown to her. She wondered whether she dared light up. After all, they were outside now. Then she remembered with a pang that the cigarette she'd had before coming in had been the last in her packet and she'd sworn she wouldn't buy any more.

'What's this?' she asked, touching the dark leaves of a bush with curious fruits sprouting along its stems and trying to banish the thought of a cigarette. It had a strange smell that reminded Mrs Monroe a little of wet dog.

'Ashwagandha. Or Indian winter cherry.'

'I've heard of it. Good for stress, isn't it?'

'Amongst other things, yes. This one nearly died a few months ago, but I've nursed it back to health.'

Mrs Monroe looked closer. Most of the plants Kezia grew had a use, often medicinal rather than culinary.

'Here you go,' Kezia said, and she passed Mrs Monroe a small trowel and a pair of gardening gloves along with a bag of something grey. 'It's wood ash. You can dig a little into the soil of some of the big pots and I'll photograph you. It'll look more natural than if I try to pose you.'

Mrs Monroe did as she was told while Kezia took what seemed like hundreds of pictures.

'That'll do,' she said eventually.

Mrs Monroe straightened her back and winced. Bending over Kezia's pots had been painful, and with a wave of depression she wondered how long she'd have to wait to get her hip done if she couldn't scrape together enough money to go private. She really needed the new website and publicity to pay dividends soon.

'I don't think your ash has been burned very well,' she said, stripping the gloves off. 'There's what looks like partially burnt material in it.'

She pointed to a large piece she'd half buried in the soil around the ashwagandha. They both bent over to get a better look.

BURNT MATERIAL

Charlie Cooper has never liked this carpet. His wife chose it and, as they'd already argued about the floor tiles in the kitchen and she'd given in to him as she generally did, some rare streak of affection had made him hold his tongue. She'd shown him the sample with evident trepidation that he'd crush her again. Her fingers had stroked it and he'd known how much she liked it.

It's no better close up. In fact, with it right by his nose, he can see it's worn badly. The backing is visible in parts, stained dark red. Has he dropped a glass of wine? And the pile is scratchy against his skin. Why is he lying on the floor?

And his memory returns like a great bird swooping down out of the sky and digging its talons into his shoulder. He'd scream with the pain if he wasn't so terrified. Because the person with the gun is still in the room. He can see their feet at the top end of his vision.

He'd been by the fireplace, thinking he should clean it out. Get Giles to give him a hand sweeping the chimney. If Giles could spare him the time. Giles always has something better to do than help his father. He wrenches his thoughts away. He won't think about the mess Giles has got them into.

Yes, he was getting the fire ready when he heard a loud crash from the kitchen. Followed by a strangled cry. Elaine had dropped something, he thought. Typical. He hoped it wasn't supper. He was hungry. And then another crash.

The door into the kitchen opened. He expected Elaine to come in. Maybe weeping. She wept a lot these days. Not for any reason that he could see. She wept when she ran out of sugar. She wept if he was the slightest bit morose. She wept because Chloe had become a mother so young. In fact it was rare to see her without tears running down her face or her cheeks and mouth puckered in an effort to hold them back. He hadn't looked up when she came in. Just waited for her grating voice to moan about whatever the latest mishap was. If supper was ruined he'd go to the pub in Thorpe and have a pie and a pint. Or maybe fish and chips.

Then someone gave him a great shove. Knocked him over and, he thought, kicked him in the shoulder. But now, he realises he's been shot. Not Elaine. Surely not. Surely her strange moodiness wouldn't make her go that far. The feet he can see are clad in dirty wellingtons. Brown and stained, with mud clinging to the edges. Not Elaine, then. She wears slippers in the house. She's always on at them to take their boots off before they come in. And saying they should use the kettle in the tack room if they want a quick coffee. But he needs to get away from the bloody clients sometimes. With their endless worrying about the welfare of their horses, they're wearing. Most of them don't have a clue. Not a clue about their horses. He loves the beasts, you see. Not in the irritating way the owners do, treating them like pets or children. Horses are complex and individual. They need respect and they need to feel secure. Endlessly stressing about them is all wrong. It irritates the hell out of him. Especially when his knee is bothering him – which it is most of the time now. The doctor's told him he should get it done but it would mean being laid up for months. And who'll run the stables if he's out of commission? Elaine doesn't understand how tiring the pain is though. None of them do. He snapped at Chloe this morning when she tried to talk to him and he saw her shrivel and turn away.

He needs to focus on the here and now instead of letting his thoughts wander. He's been shot. He needs help. Police. Ambulance. That sort of help. Except he can't do anything while the shooter is here. They're just standing there. Why are they waiting? They must think he's dead. Hardly surprising given the amount of blood that's leaked out of his shoulder and all over Elaine's carpet. It's slowing now. Which is good. He doesn't want them to remember dead men don't bleed.

Why are they still here?

His gaze travels up from the wellies and he realises the dirt isn't just mud. Not unless the socks folded over the top of the boots are white with red splashes on them. Blood. From the kitchen, he supposes. And he realises for the first time that his wife has been shot too. And Giles. He was in the kitchen with her, wasn't he? The two crashes he'd heard. Now he thinks about it, they came from a shotgun. He should have recognised the noise. Except you don't expect to hear it in the house.

Giles. He's sure this is all Giles's fault. Giles hasn't told him everything.

He tries to shift his head a fraction of an inch. Not enough to be noticeable but enough to see what the owner of the feet is doing. The great bird of prey digs its claws further into his shoulder and he just about manages not to scream.

No, best he lies here quietly and waits for them to go.

There's a sound from upstairs. Chloe is up there. Giving young Freddy his bath and putting him to bed. Is that what they're waiting for? Not Chloe and not Freddy. Please no.

He can't help himself; he lets out a cry of protest. And then another. Maybe he can warn Chloe. She can lock them both in the bathroom. She'll have her mobile with her. She always does. Yes. That's what he'll do. He gathers up his strength and lets out a bellow. Except it arrives as a soft groan. He takes another breath. He must do better.

They've moved. The feet have moved. While he was trying to shout. They're right by his head now. When he shifts his eyes upwards all he can see is the barrel of the gun a few inches from his head, its two round holes sharp and black. He tries to focus beyond the barrel. To see who's holding it, but his eyes won't shift. He knows what's coming next. He knows he has no chance of surviving it.

With his last remaining strength, he reaches his good arm up. Maybe to beg for mercy. Maybe to push the barrel away. Or seize it. But his arm is feeble. The strength that means he can still push up the lorry ramp and carry a couple of saddles has drained away. He *tries again. This time his hand finds something. Something soft. Not the gun but something the shooter is wearing. He seizes it and pulls. Something flutters at the edge of his vision*

 A sharp intake of breath.

 Then nothing.

CALL TRANSCRIPT

Operation: Bracken
Message No.: 0347
Date/Time Received: 18/10/24 – 17:14 hrs
From: Mrs Monroe
Taken by: PC 1643 Jones

Call Handler: *North Yorkshire Police, Operation Bracken Incident Room – how can I help you?*

Caller: Is this the right number for the… the inquiry into the Cooper murders?

Call Handler: *Yes. Do you have some information for us?*

Caller: Well, I think so. But it's a little hard to explain.

Call Handler: *All right. I'm listening.*

Caller: It's just I've had… I suppose you'd call it a message. A message from Charlie Cooper.

Call Handler: *I see. Could you tell me a little more about this message?*

Caller: Well, it was a vision really. As though I was there at the cottage when the murders took place and was seeing it through his eyes. And… it's hard to explain.

Call Handler: *OK. Can I take your name?*

Caller: Er, Mrs Monroe.

Call Handler: *And your address and phone number?*

Caller: 54 Sycamore Avenue, Thorpe. My phone number is Thorpe 546689.

Call Handler: *Thank you. I've made a note of them. And a note of your call.*

Caller: But don't you want me to tell you what I saw?

Call Handler: *I've made a note of the information you've given. Someone will get in touch if we need to follow it up. Thank you for your call.*

Caller: But I haven't told you anything. I'm a medium, you see. A professional medium. And what I saw was important.

Call Handler: *All information is logged and reviewed by the investigation team. Thank you for your call.*

SEVENTEEN
JOSH MASON

SAME DAY

Josh unlocked the front door to his flat and took a deep breath. He wanted nothing more than to change out of his uniform and have a beer. He shouldn't really. He'd caved in at lunchtime and had fish and chips in the canteen. He'd spent the day wading through CCTV footage on his own, mainly to see if any of Martin Appleton's movements had been recorded. They hadn't. Josh wasn't surprised. There were paths through the woods and alleys in town that a bike could use as short cuts. A white car had headed past Boyes's Farm and returned around the right time but, apart from that, nothing had broken the monotony. The camera hadn't picked up its number plate.

Kezia's reaction to Marty's arrest that morning had left him feeling on edge. Some of the other officers felt the same. He'd overheard Burden muttering to Beresford about Carter being desperate for a result. All in all it hadn't been a great day and he was looking forward to switching off.

Kezia burst out of her room and startled him. Something had upset her. Her face was even whiter than usual with deep shadows under her eyes, but before he could ask her what was up she launched into the most ridiculous story about the medium she'd been photographing and visions and messages from the dead.

If he didn't know her better he'd have wondered if she'd taken something. Her pupils were large and dark and her gestures strangely jerky. God knows, drugs were readily available in Thorpe. Local youngsters thought nothing of taking MDMA and amphetamines at the weekend. It was impossible to stop the supply. No sooner had they shut off one route than another opened up.

He put his keys in the Faraday pouch and made himself reply gently.

'So,' he said. 'Let me see if I've got this right. But let's sit down first.'

But as soon as he went into the sitting room, with her following, he regretted it. She didn't come into this room much and, even to his eyes, it was a bit of a man cave, with half the space taken up with his gaming computer and accessories. He made a space at the small dining table they never used. She sat down and faced him.

'So first,' he said. 'Have you told me this story as Josh, your nephew, or as a police officer?'

'As a police officer, of course. Don't you see, it changes everything? Marty didn't do it. We called the station but they wouldn't listen.'

He sighed to himself.

'Let me recap and see if I've got this right. You were at your studio taking photographs of a psychic, Mrs Monroe, because she's doing some publicity.'

He waited for her to acknowledge this. She nodded.

'And during the course of this photography, Mrs Monroe suddenly collapsed and started speaking as though she was witnessing the murder from Charlie Cooper's perspective.'

She nodded again but shivered at the same time, then wrapped her right hand round her left shoulder and massaged it.

'Are you OK? It must have been a bit of a shock.'

'It wasn't gentle. The strain of Charlie Cooper's intrusion made her body jerk and thrash about. As if she was having a fit.'

He was curious about the so-called visitation. It had clearly upset Kezia. But that wasn't really the point of this conversation.

'In a nutshell, you're telling me Mrs Monroe had a – let's call it a vision – a vision concerning the murders at Cooper's Stables. The vision's contents don't correspond with the arrest you think we've made, nor with the crime scene investigation that led to that arrest.'

He was aware of how pompous he sounded but she needed to see how ridiculous this all was. He desperately didn't want her to insist on him reporting it.

'I know you think we've arrested Martin Appleton and I can't confirm or deny you're right. But, assuming you are, the key elements of the scene that make you think the police have made a mistake are, firstly, that the perpetrator didn't seem to be acting out of rage. They waited for the daughter to come downstairs rather than charge up and shoot her as violently as the rest of the family. Secondly the perpetrator definitely wasn't wearing trainers. Unfortunately Mrs Monroe – or Charlie Cooper as she thinks she was at that moment – only saw the murderer's lower legs and feet. Correct?'

'Yes.'

'Wearing muddy wellingtons with white socks over the tops?'

'Yes.'

He wanted to ask her why on earth she believed this Mrs Monroe after everything she'd said about her being a fake, but he couldn't quite bring himself to. Instead he tried to find a way to let her down gently.

'Look, you've probably heard stories about the police using psychics to assist them. But that's all it is. Just stories. Modern policing requires evidence.'

'You spoke to one in the Walker case.'

'The Walker case.'

'Last year. The missing boy. His body was found on the moors.'

'I know the Walker case. Everybody in North Yorkshire Police remembers it. Besides, Mrs Walker was one of Mum's clients, so it was endlessly picked over at home. I didn't know about the psychic though. Are you sure?'

'Yes. Hamish told Mrs Monroe and she told me.'

'Well, it can't have been helpful, because we've never found out who was behind Peter's abduction and murder.'

He knew he sounded petty.

'That psychic was a charlatan. In it for the publicity.'

'Of course they were. But why do you think Mrs Monroe is any different? You said she was having publicity photographs taken.'

She thought for a second.

'Because I was there, Josh. I saw the terror and pain reflected on her face. She spoke Charlie Cooper's thoughts out loud. No could have invented what she said. And afterwards she was sick with the horror of it all. Honestly, Josh. She wasn't making it up.'

She read the scepticism he felt in his face.

'I know,' she said. 'I know some people are very suggestible. They can will themselves into having fits and visions. But this wasn't like that.' She paused again. 'It's called psychometry. It's the ability to read an inanimate object. To get information about an event or a person who was associated with the object. We all leave traces behind us. You know that as a police officer. Fingerprints or bits of hair or blood. Science has ways of reading them now that would have seemed magical a couple of hundred years ago. Try to think of this as another branch of the same thing. Just one that's hard to explain.'

He ignored the psychobabble and homed in on the key point. 'An object inspiring the vision. What was it?'

'Ashes. Some ashes I got from the allotment. There was a bit of cloth in amongst them. Charred but not totally burnt. When Mrs Monroe picked it up the— er, vision began.'

'You're not saying this bit of cloth belonged to Charlie Cooper, are you? His clothing was intact.'

'I think it belonged to the murderer. But it had Charlie Cooper's blood on it. That's why it spoke so strongly to Mrs Monroe.

Some psychics are very sensitive to blood. Charlie grabbed at the killer's clothes. Maybe he wiped some of the blood off his hand at that point?'

Josh leaned back in his chair and looked at the ceiling. Mrs Monroe had been right about Cooper being shot twice, but he'd put that down to coincidence. He had a feeling the crime scene reports mentioned one of Charlie Cooper's hands being wiped clean of blood.

'Where did you say the cloth came from?'

'In ashes. From the allotment. They're a sort of fertiliser. My next-door neighbour gave them to me.'

'Who is that?'

'Alan Calvert. But you can't think he had anything to do with it. Anyone could have dumped something in his incinerator.'

Alan Calvert. Now that was interesting. Alan Calvert's wife and baby son had been killed by a speeding youngster, high on drugs, who'd lost control of his car. He was fairly sure the youngster had been Harry Appleton, Marty's father. He toyed with the idea of Calvert killing the Coopers and implicating Marty. Family feuds lasted a long time in Thorpe. Through generations, until no one remembered what had sparked the enmity in the first place.

No. It was too unlikely.

'You could ask him,' she said.

She thought he was taking her seriously. That he was going to do something about her story.

'Kezia. There's no point my reporting this. My superiors will see it as a nonsense and me as a fool for listening to you. I'm sorry but that's how it is. If you'd said one useful thing. One thing we could follow up. I might consider it. Mrs Monroe can't even tell us what the killer looked like.'

'She can only recount what Charlie Cooper saw and he didn't look up.'

He shook his head.

'So you won't do anything?'

'I'm sorry.'

She stood up to leave then, still clutching her left arm, but stopped at the door.

'One other thing,' she said. 'The tarot cards. In Chloe Cooper's hands. Was one of them Death?'

'No.'

'Or the Sun?'

He stopped himself in time. 'I'm not going to let you go through all seventy-eight cards of the tarot deck until you come to the right one.'

'It *was* the Sun then.'

He shook his head. He didn't think he'd given it away.

'And the other one – a King?'

But this time he was in control of his face.

A few seconds later, the front door slammed. This startled him. Firstly because Kezia had shown no signs of going out tonight, but mainly because she never slammed doors.

He wondered how she'd managed to guess the tarot cards so accurately.

EIGHTEEN
SAM THE TAXI DRIVER

EARLY SATURDAY MORNING

It was a vile night. Sam peered through the torrent of water running down the windscreen. The road she was parked on was busy, even at this time in the early morning, and the glare of headlights and the rain made it impossible to see anything. She needed her wipers on. Her battery was on its last legs though, so she turned the engine on and the wipers sprang into action. She'd have to put the car in for a service this week and get a new battery too. It would probably use up the weekend's profit but she had no choice.

Kezia appeared on the pavement in front and waved. She unlocked the doors.

'I'm a bit wet,' she said as she settled herself in the passenger seat beside Sam. 'Good thing you've got the covers on the seats.'

Sam smiled. 'At least you're not going to be sick. I turned one fare down earlier. She was already vomiting in the gutter. I hate doing it, but her friends promised me they'd walk her home and see she got there safely.'

She heard the click of the seatbelt and pulled out. Kezia settled down and was quiet for a while. Sam wondered if she'd gone to sleep. It wouldn't be the first time. Once she'd had to wake her up when they reached Thorpe. But as soon as they'd left the worst of the Leeds traffic behind, she spoke.

'How's Ellie?'

Sam gave her a rundown of her daughter's activities over the last week.

'I'm going to have to change babysitter though,' she said. 'Ellie asked to come with me tonight. When I pushed her she said the current sitter's friends make a lot of noise when they come over. Which is not supposed to happen.'

And they chatted about the difficulty of finding good childcare. During the week, Sam only worked while Ellie was at school. But doing the late shifts for the taxi company in Leeds at the weekends made her twice as much. They were always looking for women drivers. It was only worth doing if she used teenagers after some pocket money to babysit, especially since the price of diesel had rocketed. Many of the other taxi drivers were investing in electric cars, but that was way out of Sam's reach.

They'd met around six months ago when Kezia had booked a woman driver and got Sam a couple of times. They'd started talking and realised Thorpe was nearly home for Sam. If Kezia could time her return for when Sam finished her shift, it would be advantageous for both of them.

Over the months since, they'd chatted about everything. Kezia might not have any children, but she understood the difficulties of being a single mum and it was easier to talk frankly to her because she had no connection with the rest of Sam's life. Kezia seemed to feel the same freedom. She certainly enjoyed bitching about the men she met via the dating apps. Sam had grasped quickly that Kezia wanted something uncomplicated and short-term, which was why she dated away from her home.

'I've been married,' she said, one night. 'And got it very wrong.'

'Another woman?' Sam had asked.

'Yes, but it's more complicated than that.'

Sam had waited.

'No sudden, earth-shattering revelation, just the slow understanding that I'd been blind to lots of things and the life I'd built with him was a fantasy. We both come from difficult families and I thought we'd put them behind us. I thought our respectable but fulfilling lives were proof you could do that. Me with my horses and photography and him with his successful career. But I was wrong.'

She'd paused, then said, 'But I miss bits of being married. Only bits though.'

And they'd both laughed. Which was the thing Sam associated with Kezia. Laughter. Strange, really, because she didn't have much to laugh about and Kezia didn't either. She'd let slip a couple of times that money was tight and she didn't like living in Thorpe. She hated the way everybody knew everybody. Sam wondered why she hadn't left. And why she didn't get a proper job, or at least one that paid better than her photography clearly did.

Kezia was unusually quiet tonight though, just reacting to what Sam told her and asking questions from time to time.

'Everything all right?' Sam asked. 'Not a good night?'

'No, it was fine. Although I think it will be the last with him.'

'Ah. Not going anywhere?'

'That doesn't bother me. I don't want anything permanent. Although I might have met someone who'd like to be.'

'Who? Tell me who.'

'No. I'm probably wrong. And, anyway, it would be very unfair of me. I'm sure he means well.'

'Kezia.'

'Ok then. Someone at the allotment. The man with the next-door plot. He was very stand-offish at first. Which was fine. I thought he was as solitary as I was. But recently he's started chatting. Which is fine too. Although he keeps trying to suggest things I should do with the allotment.'

It didn't sound very interesting to Sam.

'Some lonely old codger who likes an audience.'

'He's not that old. Only a few years older than me. He lost his wife and his son quite a long time ago. Dead, I mean. Not divorced. I don't know how.'

'He still sounds like he could just be lonely.'

'You're probably right. Anyway, I've been careful not to give him the chance to ask me out.'

For the first time that evening, they started laughing.

'I think this will be my last outing for a while, Sam,' Kezia said as they neared the outskirts of Thorpe. 'Like I said, it wasn't much fun tonight. Probably my fault. Things on my mind.'

'I'll miss our chats.' This was true but Sam knew better than to suggest they met up outside work. 'Anything I can help with? Give you a different perspective?'

She heard the creaking of the seat cover as Kezia turned to look at her.

'Maybe,' she said. 'Maybe you could. There's a youngster I know. From the riding stables where I kept my horse. He loves horses like I do. And he's a lovely lad. Gentle and hard-working. When I had to sell Bathsheba – that was my horse – he understood how hard it was.' She paused. 'He's in trouble.'

Sam waited. She had an inkling she knew what Kezia was talking about.

'Real trouble,' Kezia added.

'Is this the seventeen-year-old who's been charged with the killings at the stables?'

Kezia was silent. The lights of the oncoming cars shone through the rain-stained windscreen, robbing her face of all colour and leaving marks like tears running down it.

'Yes,' she said.

'I don't see what you can do about it.'

'That's what I thought, except...'

'Except what?'

'I know he didn't do it.'

Sam wasn't sure what Kezia meant by *know*.

'If you know something relevant, you should tell the police, Kezia.'

'I've tried to. But they're not interested. It's not exactly factual.'

Sam was about to ask her what she meant by factual when Kezia put her head in her hands and muttered something.

'I didn't catch that, sorry.'

'Never mind. Between the bits I can't talk about and the bits I don't understand, it's difficult. I'll just have to wait and hope it sorts itself out. Nothing I do is going to help.'

They drove without speaking for a while. Sam would have liked silence to absorb what Kezia had said, but the background noise of rain drumming on the car and the wipers' swish and squeak intruded on her thoughts. Kezia's last words had rattled her.

'Look,' Sam said in the end. 'Maybe you're right about nothing you do helping, but—'

'I should try? Yes?'

'Yes. Make the police listen to you. Put pressure on them somehow.'

'I know. As soon as I said I'd have to wait and see, it was suddenly clear. I can't do that. No, I can't.'

They drove the short distance to the market square in silence. Sam stopped the car.

'What will you do?'

'I don't know. No, wait. What day is it?'

'Friday. Well Saturday really now.'

'Maybe not too late.'

She thought for a few seconds, then muttered, 'Yes.'

'What, Kezia?'

'I'm going to get us a bit of publicity. See if that makes the police take notice.'

Sam waited.

'It'll probably annoy a few people and may be useless, but I don't care. I don't care at all. I'll do it.' She opened the car door. 'Thank you, Sam. You were right. I needed to talk.'

'Kezia,' Sam said on impulse, as Kezia swung her legs round to get out. 'Things sound difficult at the moment. You know, if there was anything I could do, I would. Just call me.'

Kezia poked her head back into the car.

'Thanks. I mean it. Thanks. And I will.'

NINETEEN
KEZIA HERON

SATURDAY

Saturday afternoon. A day of warmth, the autumn sun golden and lush, after last night's downpour.

It felt all wrong.

Josh and I were avoiding each other. Or rather I was avoiding Josh. He thought I was sulking like a mortally offended teenager because he'd refused to report the vision, but in truth I couldn't face him. It felt underhand to act normally when I knew he'd be furious with me tomorrow.

I hoped I'd done the right thing.

I should go for a walk. Anything would be better than hanging around listening to him humming as he cooked a selection of healthy meals for the week. Meals he'd more than likely leave in the fridge untouched and throw away next weekend.

Yes, I'd go for a walk. Or maybe not. Maybe I should stop avoiding the other questions I wanted answers to.

I pulled the tarot deck out from the drawer in my bedside table and laid them face down on the floor in a great arc. I examined them.

You'd never notice the marks. Not unless you were looking.

The backs of this deck had a design of circles and squares against a background of shooting stars and the signs of the zodiac. A little scrape in one of the astrological signs, easily done with a sharp knife, showed the card's suit. And a nick in one of the squares showed its number. One of my mother's lovers had taught us how to do it.

And Zina marked her decks so she knew which card was which. You see there are ways of presenting the deck that encourage people to choose specific cards and Zina was also adept at exchanging cards when she swept the deck away after they'd chosen. She told me it was more fun that way.

No point my picking a card. Not unless I shuffled them and laid them out with eyes closed. No point anyway, because I knew which card I wanted.

Number 15 of the major arcana.

The Devil.

He dominates the card. A malevolent figure, half man half goat with the wings of a vampire bat to show how he sucks the lifeblood out of everyone he touches. Chained to him are a man and a woman, both with devil-like tails and horns themselves. The man's tail ends in fire to signify lust and the woman's in grapes to signify pleasure and its darker side, addiction.

The card doesn't need much interpreting.

It reminds me of David's uncle.

Miles Kingsley. Fat and hairy under his smart suits and expensive cologne, with a gaze that raked the skin from your body. A man, who, if David was correct, ran the drugs trade in North Yorkshire and had a finger in every illegal and violent money-making crime that took place. The kingpin of David's family. The family he was as desperate to leave behind as I was mine. The backgrounds we both swore we'd help each other escape from.

And I thought we had. Until Charlie Cooper told me about the money we owed and I started looking into our life.

The Kingsleys had put work David's way for years and he'd taken it. Nothing illegal, he told me. So he represented some criminals, but everybody had the right to representation. His family paid well and we needed the money. Did I think it was easy running a law firm? The overheads were massive: secretaries, offices etc. etc. And they had to be paid every month. Even during Covid. I had no idea how hard it was. And how stressful. His name didn't help either. The police were always popping in for a chat. Clients didn't like it. Not the supposedly respectable ones anyway. And supposedly was the right word. Most of them were as ready as his family to bend a few rules to make money. Why did I think they needed a solicitor in the first place?

I said nothing. There was no point. He'd broken his promise. And that was that. I hung around for a bit, not sure what to do, but I think he knew it was over because a while later he told me he'd met someone else and he wanted a divorce. Besides, I'd worked out it was much worse than he said because Miles had lent him money. A lot. I couldn't see how he was ever going to pay it back.

And now I was going to have to ask him if he had and how.

TWENTY

BECKY KINGSLEY

SAME DAY

Becky had chosen the sofa with its back to the window and made Davey's ex sit facing the full glare of the late afternoon sun. It didn't seem to bother her though. She'd put her head back and shut her eyes while they waited for Davey. He'd offered her a drink, as though this was a pleasant social get-together. And when she'd said tea would be nice in that scratchy voice of hers, he'd looked over at Becky, expecting her to get up and make it. So she'd said she'd love one too and there'd been an awkward few seconds before it dawned on Davey that he was going to have to make it himself.

The ex pressed her fingertips into the pale skin round her closed eyes. Becky noted the red marks left behind with a dash of pleasure. A sign of aging skin.

Davey came in, carrying three mugs.

'Not those hideous things,' Becky couldn't stop herself exclaiming.

Brightly coloured and rustic in shape, she'd consigned them to the back of a cupboard when she'd moved in and bought some smart bone china ones in York.

'I rather like them,' Davey said.

'What about sugar?' she added.

'Neither of you take it. Unless…'

'No,' the ex said. 'I still don't.'

And then there was another silence. Becky sipped at her tea. She wasn't going to break it. The ex had asked to come and see Davey. It was up to her to speak.

'So Kezia, how have you been?' This was Davey. She heard the irritation in his voice. It was probably because of Becky's presence, but the woman wasn't going to know that. When Kezia texted him a couple of hours ago and asked to meet up, he hadn't liked Becky insisting on being present.

'I've been fine,' the ex replied.

Another silence.

'And what brings you here?' Davey asked.

The ex sat up at that and darted a quick look at Becky. Yes, Becky thought, you weren't expecting me to stay, were you? Then she looked at Davey, who didn't react.

'I see,' the ex said. She ran her tongue over her teeth as she thought. They waited. Finally she spoke.

'The tarot card,' she said. 'You remember it, David?'

'Tarot card?' Becky said.

'No,' he said, but quickly. Too quickly.

'Aren't they the big ones with the spooky pictures on?' Becky asked.

They both ignored her.

'A woman came round with a tarot card,' Kezia said. 'I'm sure you remember. Said she was returning it. To you.'

'I told you at the time she was a nutter. I'd probably won a case against her. You know that people often blame the solicitor.'

'She said to tell you she wasn't scared. And then she left.'

Davey shrugged in that infuriating way he had when he didn't want to discuss something.

'The card was the Tower.'

'So?'

'Who was the woman who brought the card round?'

'As I told you at the time, I have no idea.'

'A tall woman with faded blond hair? And a scar running through her eyebrow. Early forties, I think.'

'I don't know.'

'It looks like a terrible card. The picture shows a bolt of lightning hitting a tall, stone tower bursting into flames with people jumping from it and clearly about to be dashed to death on the rocks below. But like all tarot, there are lots of different interpretations. Some people see it as representing a sudden moment of clarity or revelation that your life has been built on a false foundation. Zina does.'

'Zina?' Becky said. Not many people were called Zina.

'My sister.'

'Zina who owns the salon? She's your sister?'

The ex nodded.

A ripple of anger ran through Becky's body. Zina cut her hair. Davey should have told her she was the ex's sister. She banked the rage though. She'd take Davey's failure out later and see what it could be used to obtain.

'What is all this about, Kezia?' Davey asked.

'Someone gave me a tarot deck but there are some cards missing, including the Tower.'

'So.'

'You had a deck of tarot cards here. One of Zina's. You asked her for it after a party when she did a few readings. Have you still got it?'

'I have no idea.'

'Because the deck I was given was definitely one of Zina's.'

'How could you possibly tell?'

'Zina marks them. Not all of them. The ones she likes to talk about.'

'Maybe you should ask your sister about it then.' Davey's voice was squeezed of all life.

A stray memory flickered into Becky's mind. A strange card on Davey's desk. At the office. Before they got together. A picture of a black skeleton on a horse. That had been a tarot card. The Death card. She stored the information away to examine later.

'Ask your sister.' Becky echoed Davey's words.

Time to get rid of the ex. She stood up.

'If the tea's not to your liking, let me take it away.'

The ex handed her the full cup but remained seated. Then Davey handed her his tea. He'd not touched it either. For a few seconds she stood like a fool with a cup in each hand, before realising she'd have to take them to the room they were using as a kitchen while they waited for the new one to be finished. She left the door wide open though.

It was still open when she came back. And the two of them were still sitting in the same postures. Had she missed something? She hadn't heard them speak. She'd never seen Davey look like this before. The sun pouring through the window had cast a dark veil over his face, accentuating his eyes and teeth. And his teeth were clenched in a smile. But it wasn't nice. Not nice at all. She shivered and felt glad it was directed at his ex and not her. He flicked his eyes at her and, all of a sudden, she decided to leave the matter of his ex's sister being her hairdresser alone for a while.

The ex moved her head and the light caught a trace of wetness on her cheek. Like the trails the snails left on the garden path. Then she slung her bag over one shoulder and stood. It was one of Lauren's bags. Becky recognised the little silver L on the clasp. It was old, though. It crossed her mind as she saw the ex out that Davey might have bought it for her.

'Well, that was weird,' she said to Davey. 'Mind you she is a bit weird. I hope you don't mind my saying that.'

'I need to phone someone,' he said. He pressed his lips together until they went white.

'Who?'

'It's a family thing.'

She decided not to ask him any more. Besides, she wanted a bit of time on her own to process everything that had just happened.

CALL INTERCEPT REPORT

Case / Reference: 2025-00987 / Operation Lieder
Investigation: Suspected class A drug supply
Audio file ref: Exhibits/Audio/2024-10-19_Call_0001.mp3
Date(s) of call: 2024-10-19
Local time (start): 2024-10-19 118:03:21 (BST)
Duration: 00:04:48
Call type: mobile (voice)
Call direction: incoming (from +44 7xx xxxx xxx to +44 7yy yyyy yyy)
Authorising warrant / authority: WRT-2025-441 (Home Office) 2024-09-11

Call Transcript

[00:00:00.000] SPEAKER A (+44 7xx xxx xxxx): **Hello?**

[00:00:00.300] SPEAKER B (+44 7yy yyy yyyy): **It's me. Can we meet?**

[00:00:04.120] SPEAKER A: **Is it important?**

[00:00:07.000] SPEAKER B: **I think it could be.**

[00:00:10.250] [PAUSE — 1.2s]

[00:00:11.450] SPEAKER A: **Not another schedule disruption?**

[00:00:15.080] SPEAKER B: **No, no. Nothing like that. Someone came to visit.**

[00:00:17.000] [BACKGROUND: vehicle passing; horn]

[00:00:18.300] SPEAKER A: **Our friends in blue?**

[00:00:19.100] SPEAKER B: **No. But she lives with one.**

[00:00:23.200] SPEAKER A: **Ah yes. Your cousin mentioned that. It would have been useful to know.**

[00:00:26.300] SPEAKER B: **I didn't think it was important.**

[00:00:28.400] SPEAKER A: **Let me be the judge of that next time. So?**

[00:00:31.300] SPEAKER B: **The friend she lives with. He was the one who discovered the... the...**

[00:00:35.900] SPEAKER A: **I understand.**

[00:00:37.300] SPEAKER B: **I'm concerned he might have spoken to her and she's put things together. She asked me a couple of difficult questions.**

[00:00:41.100] SPEAKER A: **We'll sort it.**

[00:00:42.250] [PAUSE — 2.3s]

[00:00:46.300] SPEAKER B: **What will you do?**

[00:00:48.400] [CALL ENDED]

Summary and Key Timestamps

- **Summary:** Brief exchange about visitor. Potential threat to visitor. No explicit reference to alleged supply of drugs in this call. Speaker A identified as Miles Kingsley. Speaker B unknown.
- **Key timestamps:** 00:00:11.450 — reference to 'another schedule disruption'. 00:00:18.300 — reference to 'boys in blue'. 00:00:41.100 — reference to 'we'll sort it'.
- **Investigative suggestion:** Review known female associates of Miles Kingsley.

TWENTY-ONE
JOSH MASON

SUNDAY

When Josh entered, DCI Carter was creating a chain of paper clips from the pile on the desk, although his gaze was fixed on the far wall. Josh had knocked, of course. But Carter didn't seem bothered at being discovered doing such a childish activity.

'Yes?'

'PC Mason, sir. You asked to see me.'

'Ah yes. Sit down. Let me just finish this paperwork, or HR will be on at me again.'

He patted round the mounds of paper on his desk until he found a pair of glasses, and put them on. Josh realised he must wear contacts normally. Rumour was that women found Carter attractive. Josh examined his superior officer carefully. Hunched over his desk, with his left arm curled over the papers as he breathed heavily, Josh couldn't see why.

He was oldish, for a start. You didn't make DCI without reaching a certain age. In his fifties, Josh thought, and he looked every day of it today. Not that age ruled out being attractive. Look at Brad Pitt. Or George Clooney. In their sixties but still women liked them. Even when they wore bright pink or yellow as Pitt had started to do. Josh was sure he'd be laughed at if he tried. But then he had a shrewd suspicion Brad Pitt in pink might be laughed at in Yorkshire.

Yes, he'd like to see him walking down Thorpe High Street in pink.

The thought cheered him, because it was tough waiting for DCI Carter to finish. He hadn't done anything wrong that he knew of, but he couldn't help feeling Carter might not think that. Nothing was ever as straightforward as you thought it was going to be at college.

'So, PC Mason.'

Josh realised DCI Carter had finished his papers and was addressing him.

'Yes, sir.'

'Not Perry, is it?'

'Perry? Sir?'

Josh could only think of the pear cider they sold in the Swan in York. How did Carter know he liked it?

'Perry Mason. I wondered if it was your name.'

No, sir. It's Josh. Short for Joshua. An old family name. No Perrys in my family.'

'Never mind.'

Carter pushed his chair back and stood, stretched his arms above his head until his shoulders clicked in protest, then ambled over to the window and looked down at the river that ran past Thorpe police station and through the town centre. He appeared lost in thought.

Josh waited.

'You're from Thorpe?'

'Yes, sir.'

Carter knew this.

'Maybe you've seen today's edition of the *Thorpe Gazette*?'

'No, sir.'

Carter passed it over. Hamish had printed it on yellow paper this time. The front page was mainly concerned with the Thorpe pantomime. They wanted donations of fur coats or collars to help with the costumes for *Puss in Boots*.

'What am I looking for, sir?'

'Other side.'

And there it was, surrounded by little squares of advertising from the local trades and shops.

POLICE IGNORE OFFER OF HELP IN COOPER MURDERS

Mrs Monroe, a well-respected local psychic (www.Monroe-Psychic.com), has told us how Yorkshire Police have ignored her requests to talk to them about the terrible massacre at Cooper's Stables last week. She has information casting doubt on the guilt of the 17-year-old arrested and charged with the murders.

The events of last Sunday have caused widespread alarm within the community and the *Gazette* feels the police should leave no stone unturned in their efforts to uncover the truth. We would urge the police to remember the case of Peter Walker, the missing boy whose body was found on Melkin Moors. Early mistakes in the investigation and false assumptions meant valuable time was lost. More than a year later and the police are no closer to finding the culprit. Let's not make the same mistake again.

Mrs Monroe told us, 'I informed the police I had knowledge I needed to share with them and I would be happy to try and glean more. Obviously there would be no charge. I was offering my help as a concerned citizen.'

When approached for comment about this new development the father of the youngster arrested and charged with the crime told us, 'This is typical of the police's attitude throughout the investigation. They decided early on that my child was guilty and have done everything they can to make the evidence fit. They've refused to investigate any other leads.'

While many people may be sceptical of the assistance a psychic could offer, there is a long history of cooperation between psychics and the police and surely the police should be welcoming any offer of help with open arms.

Josh felt the colour flood his face as he finished reading. Kezia was behind this. How could she? And to speak to Hamish Aitken, who everybody knew was a left-wing lunatic with an innate hatred of every institution.

'I see you do know something about this.'

'Yes, sir.'

'Tell me about Mrs Monroe, then.'

'I don't know much about her, sir. It was my aunt who er... brought the subject to my attention.'

'Your aunt? Kezia Heron?'

'Yes.'

'And does Ms Heron claim to be a psychic too?'

'No, no, not at all. She's a very quiet and normal sort of person,' Josh said quickly. 'She takes photographs for a living and that's how she met Mrs Monroe,' he added. 'She told me because I was the only police officer she knew.'

'And you decided it wasn't worth drawing my attention to it.'

'She said Mrs Monroe had rung the incident room. The call would have been logged and reviewed. So...'

'You decided to let someone else decide if it was worthy of my attention.'

Josh couldn't tell from Carter's tone whether this had been a good decision or not. Surely Carter agreed the whole thing was rubbish. So he contented himself with merely saying Yes and then, a couple of seconds later, Sir.

'Why don't you tell me exactly what your aunt told you. Don't dress it up in the kind of jargon they taught you to use at college. Just plain and simple words will do.'

Josh retold Kezia's strange story.

'Psychometry?' Carter said when Josh had finished. 'That's what she called it?'

'Yes.'

Carter crossed over to his desk and appeared to write the word down, his awkward writing style made even more awkward because he was standing. It reminded Josh of the brainbox at school writing during exams. All hunched over to stop anyone copying his answers.

'Thank you, Mason. Get that written up into a statement and on my desk before the end of the day.'

It wasn't a question but Josh still said Yes.

Carter sat back down behind his desk and Josh realised he was dismissed. He wanted to ask if Carter was going to do anything, but something stopped him. He stood quietly and headed for the door.

'Mason,' Carter said suddenly.

'Sir.'

'I don't think we need to see Mrs Monroe. It all sounds a bit feeble to me.' He stopped and appeared lost in thought.

Josh really, really wanted to leave it at that, but some part of him knew he wouldn't feel the same when he had Kezia in front of him.

'My aunt thought you might have spoken to a psychic during the Walker case.'

'Did she now? Well, that's true. The family begged us to. He was no help though. None at all.'

He picked up the chain of paper clips and started undoing them. Josh waited until he roused himself to speak again.

'Maybe suggest to your aunt that any more contact with the press would be unfortunate. There is an offence of wasting police time. Not that it really applies, but she won't know that.'

'Yes, sir.'

Josh left. He'd call Kezia straight away. How could she have done this? Not that it had done her any good. He almost looked forward to telling her.

BURNT MATERIAL

She tries to keep some sense of herself as the vision unrolls this time. But it's hard. As soon as she found her eyes staring at the living room carpet at Cooper's cottage she knew it would be the same. She'd like to speed through the moment when the pain and terror hit Charlie Cooper. They're worse because she knows they're coming. She can smell the blood, this time. And feel its sticky warmth.

She focusses on what's happening outside Charlie Cooper's body. The murderer is in the room and she concentrates on the sounds Charlie must have heard although they'd made no impression on his consciousness, overwhelmed as it was with shock and fear. There's nothing, except the noise of Charlie's breaths. His lungs grab oxygen as though it can mend the terrible wounds the gun has inflicted. It can't, and instead it feels as though the gulps are tearing his body apart.

He shifts his eyes just like last time and she sees the shooter's feet. In wellies. Dirty wellies. Just like last time. What type are they? She can't tell. Then their socks. What are they wearing above the socks? But Charlie never looks up.

Why are they just standing there? What are they waiting for?

Charlie lets out a cry of protest and then tries to shout to warn his daughter. The feet move closer. Every part of Charlie's awareness is taken up by the dark holes of the barrel a short way from his face. He tries, and so does she, to see beyond the gun to the shooter's face, but it is impossible.

He reaches up his hand to grab the gun and she focusses on his fingers. They grab cloth. Soft material. Cotton? It's thin. Nothing like jeans. Charlie must have grabbed something the killer was wearing. If only she could see it.

She is aware suddenly of a scent that banishes the sickly smell of blood. It is sharp and fragrant. Herbs?

But that makes no sense.

Again something flutters at the edge of Charlie's vision.

A sharp intake of breath.

Then nothing.

TWENTY-TWO

MRS MONROE

SAME DAY

Mrs Monroe watched as Kezia's gloved hands placed the piece of burnt cloth carefully back into a plastic bag, which she sealed. The pain and terror had seemed as intense as the first time, even though she'd known what was coming. The recovery had been quicker, although her left arm still shook with a memory of the pain. And it had been a waste of time. Nothing new. She wished she hadn't let Kezia persuade her to try again. Something was driving her that Mrs Monroe didn't understand. First of all getting Hamish to print an article about the police's refusal to talk to them in the *Gazette*, then wanting to revisit Charlie Cooper's vision.

'I'd like to find one useful thing the police could follow up,' she'd said. 'If they decide to talk to us.'

That reminded Mrs Monroe.

'There was nothing about tarot cards,' she said. 'You asked me to look out for that.'

Kezia nodded. She looked as exhausted as Mrs Monroe felt.

'What was the killer waiting for?' she said.

She disappeared into her thoughts and sipped at the herbal tea she'd brought with her. Had the fragrant smell at the end of the vision come from the tea? Kezia had made it in advance and let it steep to give the herbs time to infuse.

Mrs Monroe's mind wandered back to cigarettes. A whole forty-eight hours since her last one. She didn't know how she'd got through them. Especially last night. She'd woken every two hours regular as clockwork to go to the loo and been consumed by the urge to drive to the all-night garage for a pack.

Think of something else, she told herself.

The new website was up and the Facebook page, plus Hamish had run a Facebook advertisement. She'd been agreeably surprised by the number of enquiries from that. And apparently a lot of shares – whatever that meant. Some of the comments on her page had concerned her, but Hamish had assured her that all publicity was good publicity and this morning's article in the *Thorpe Gazette* would only help. A rosier future seemed to be opening up.

'They still haven't phoned.' Kezia's words broke through the agreeable fug inside Mrs Monroe's head.

'The police, you mean?'

'Yes. I thought the article would stir them into action.'

'It is Sunday.'

'The police work on Sunday. Josh was on duty today.'

'Can't you call him?'

Kezia didn't seem to be too keen to speak to Josh.

'I'm going to find out where the cloth in the ashes came from.'

'What?'

'I told you. The ashes came from my neighbour's incinerator at the allotment.' She held the plastic bag of material up to the light. 'Look. There's a pattern in the cloth. Can you see it? Flowers? Leaves?'

Mrs Monroe looked. 'Maybe specks of dried blood.'

'It's too regular.'

Kezia rattled her nails on the table. Something had changed in her. She was less, well, retiring. It might be an old-fashioned sort of quality, but Mrs Monroe had liked it.

'I'll have a poke round his allotment tomorrow. There might be other fragments. Maybe telling other stories. He's never there on a Monday. Goes fishing. Do you want to come with me?'

Mrs Monroe began to wish she'd never met Kezia. It was hard to say no to her.

But the sound of her doorbell saved her from answering.

Kezia lifted her head, her face avid, like an animal catching an alluring scent.

'Maybe it's the police. Come to talk to you?'

Mrs Monroe hoped not. It was all very well going to the police station for a chat with the detectives, but she didn't want police cars and uniformed officers parked outside her house.

'It's probably my neighbour. She often comes in for a cup of tea on a Sunday.'

But when she opened the door, it was neither the police nor her neighbour. A middle-aged man stood there. Thickset and ill at ease, dressed in jeans and a jacket – a combination Mrs Monroe particularly disliked. It was neither one thing nor another. Probably trying to sell her something. And on a Sunday too.

'Mrs Monroe?' he said.

'Yes,' she said. Then something about the dark shadows round his eyes and the way he held the jacket tight round himself softened her. 'Yes,' she said again. But more gently.

'Harry Appleton. Hamish told me to come and talk to you. I read the article in the *Gazette*.'

'Harry Appleton?' Kezia had come up behind her. 'Marty's father?'

'Yes.' Harry looked curiously at her.

'Kezia,' she said, and thrust her hand out at him. 'I'm a friend of Marty's.'

'Kezia,' he said. 'I think he's spoken about you.'

He took her hand and shook it.

'Come in. Come in.'

Mrs Monroe had no option but to watch as Kezia ushered Harry into her house and sat him down.

'Have you seen Marty?'

'Yes.'

'Where is he? How is he?'

'He's in what they call a young offenders' institution. And it's not good. He's not tough, Marty. Not like I was.'

Mrs Monroe dredged around in her head. 'What about bail?'

'Every solicitor says the same. No chance. Not with what happened at the Stables. He'll be there until the court case. And that could be months away.'

He stopped talking. Abruptly. And stared at his hands splayed out on the tablecloth. The sides of his forefinger were stained yellow with nicotine. The outline of a pack of cigarettes was visible in the pocket of his shirt.

'If you knew him,' he said to Mrs Monroe, 'you'd understand he couldn't have done it. He's— well, he's a teenage boy and they're not always the easiest. But Marty's a gentle kid. He was bullied at school. Not badly. Low-level stuff. Pushing and name-calling. But he never retaliated. Just put up with it. It's not possible he did this. Besides Cooper wasn't popular. There are a lot of people who had reason to bear him a grudge. People who knew one end of a gun from another. Which Marty didn't. But the police have refused to look at anyone else.'

Mrs Monroe couldn't help thinking Harry Appleton was hardly unbiased.

'Why did Cooper fire him? Isn't that what had happened?' She sounded sharp, but she'd caught a whiff of cigarette smoke oozing out of Harry's jacket and the temptation to ask him for one was driving her mad.

'I think he'd have changed his mind. Maybe Marty got a bit lippy. He's a lad. He was a bit outspoken about some of Cooper's methods. They taught him differently at college. I told him to keep his mouth shut, but he didn't find it easy and Cooper was always very quick to take offence.'

Kezia's phone rang.

'It's Josh,' she said. 'I need to take this.'

She disappeared into the front room.

Harry patted the cigarette bulge in his pocket.

'Do you mind if I smoke?'

Part of her nearly snapped out a *Yes. She did mind*. But she stopped herself.

'Fine,' she said. But go outside, please, and keep the smoke out of the house.' She took a deep breath. 'I've just given up. Two days ago, in fact. And... it's absolute torture.'

'Have you tried gum? Or patches?'

'Patches?'

'Nicotine patches.'

She remembered now. The doctor had mentioned them. And the gum. She'd been dead against it. She couldn't start chewing gum at her age.

'They're supposed to help. You can get them from the chemist.'

She'd go to the chemist's first thing. She might get the gum too.

'I started smoking in prison,' Harry said. 'And I've never managed to kick the habit. You'd heard I'd been in prison, I expect.'

'Well, yes.'

'I deserved it. Not like Marty. Dangerous driving but I killed someone. Two people, in fact. A mother and a child. It was almost a relief to be sent down for it. It was completely my fault, you see. I was high and angry with it. Driving like an idiot. Squealed round a corner and lost control. She was pushing a buggy. I'll never forget her face. She turned for a brief flash of time before I hit her.'

He told her how he'd done his time in a relatively easy prison but had seen and heard enough to decide he was never going back. He'd grabbed every opportunity to learn. His schoolteachers would have laughed to see him sweating over books and writing essays, but he knew by then that they'd been right and he'd been wrong.

He seemed to have forgotten about his cigarette. She suspected he needed to talk.

'I wanted something different for Marty,' he went on. 'And he's only wanted one thing since he was a child and that's to be with horses. He's worked hard to do that. He helped out at Cooper's as a lad in exchange for the odd lesson, getting up early every morning and spending all his weekends there. Cooper got a bargain when he gave him a job. Marty's a hard worker and brilliant with the horses. He puts the hours in too. Far more than he's supposed to and all for an apprentice wage.'

Kezia came back and sat down heavily.

'What did Josh say?'

'No. No and no. And he's furious with me. That's the police,' she said to Harry. 'They won't talk to Mrs Monroe.'

Mrs Monroe would have been quite relieved to hear this an hour ago. Part of her had dreaded talking to the police. But the look of despair on Harry's face stopped her.

'Tell me what you know anyway,' he said. 'Tell me what this information that will help the police is. The information you mentioned in the *Gazette*.'

He was disappointed when Mrs Monroe recounted the vision.

'A pair of wellingtons instead of trainers. Is that all?'

Really when you put it like that, it did sound weak.

'With socks,' Kezia added. 'White socks turned over the tops.'

'Marty doesn't have white socks.'

'There you go.'

'But I'll never prove that.'

'I'm sorry. I'd do anything to help Marty.' She sank into thought for a few seconds. 'There is something I could do. Something I should check. It might help.'

'What?'

'I can't tell you. Not until I'm sure. Some of it was told to me in confidence. But I could go and ask today. Yes, I'll do that.'

She stood up and put an arm into one sleeve of her coat.

Harry fingered the cigarettes again.

'Before you go,' he said. 'There is something else. Something Mrs Monroe could do.'

Mrs Monroe waited.

'Hamish said that all the media are interested in the story.'

Because of the goriness of the killings, she thought. How awful people were.

'He thought you could get more publicity. The more we undermine the police case the better, and maybe more coverage might bring someone forward. Someone who knows something that would help Marty.'

'Of course,' Kezia said. 'We'll talk to Hamish. We'll go and see him after I've— If Mrs Monroe doesn't mind.'

They both turned to look at her. She realised she'd have to say yes.

TWENTY-THREE

LAUREN

SAME DAY

Lauren watched Annie walk down the aisle and wait until the fight onstage paused as Rachel, Chloe's understudy, once again dropped her sword. Then she whisked over the stage to the old vestry. The sound of singing briefly flooded the church as she opened and closed the door to the sewing group's den.

'Let's take it from the top.' Raymond's tone was encouraging. 'Looking good, Rachel.'

Lauren seethed.

She stuffed the brochure Annie had given her for Sean into her bag and went back to spattering paint onto the castle walls, alternating between the pots of cream, grey and a darker brown she was using to break up the grey she'd already daubed thickly over the tree-painted scenery from last year's panto, *Babes in the Wood*.

Of course a child-friendly holiday at Center Parcs for all the family would be perfect. But Sean should have discussed it with her before talking to his mother.

Really it was all getting too much.

She'd had to totally clear out her second bedroom for Freddy. Not that she minded at all. But surely a small child could cope with a few boxes in his bedroom. He did nothing but sleep there. In any case, it didn't look as though he was going to be sleeping there very often. Annie looked after him most of the time and it was far easier if he stayed the night with her.

She forced herself to be rational. Annie had been terrified Social Services would refuse to hand Freddy over to Sean. They'd all been worried. No wonder she'd wanted Lauren's flat to be impeccable when they inspected it. But now all the stock and supplies she didn't have room for in her shop were stored in Dennis's fishing cottage. It was over an hour away, making it utterly impractical for her, and her stuff took up most of the room downstairs, so Dennis wouldn't be able to use it until she found another solution. She'd have to talk to Sean about moving some of it back now.

At the thought of Sean her mood dived even further down. All sorts of little things about him were getting on her nerves. Things that wouldn't matter if there was something at the heart of their relationship, and she wasn't sure there was any more. They did nothing together really. Except have sex. And even that wasn't as good as it had been.

'That's probably enough, Lauren.' Jim, the set designer, came up behind her. 'Let's leave it to dry and I'll pop in during the week and sketch out the blocks. We can paint the mortar in next Sunday.'

'What do you want me to do now?'

'Can you try and make the rock look a bit more...'

'Like a rock?'

He laughed. The rock was a huge construction of papier mâché whose shape was somehow wrong. It just didn't look like a rock. Successive pantomime crews had tried adding bits that either made it worse or fell off. Every year Jim said they'd make a new one, but they never did.

'I wondered if some green moss might make it a little more craggy. Can you see if you can work your magic?'

Lauren thought it was unlikely anything would help, but she nodded all the same.

'Bit thin on the ground this afternoon.'

'Hardly surprising, with it being the first rehearsal without Chloe. I thought Raymond might cancel.'

'She needs all the rehearsal she can get.' Jim jerked his head at Rachel and the actor playing the ogre on stage. 'There has to be a first rehearsal without Chloe at some point, so it might as well be sooner rather than later.'

Lauren agreed. The sooner things got back to normal the better. For Freddy and for Sean.

'Have you seen today's *Gazette*?' Jim asked.

'Not yet.'

'Some psychic woman stirring things up, claiming the Appleton boy couldn't have done it. He gave a forced laugh. She needs to be careful. Not sure I'd be so keen on advertising the fact I thought someone else had done it. Not if that someone was still out there.'

The doors opened, letting a swoosh of wind and fragmented leaves into the nave. Lauren shivered.

Two women entered. One sat down in a pew by the door while the other headed towards Raymond, now patiently walking Rachel through the part where Puss kills the ogre. Lauren realised it was Kezia.

What did she want?

It was easy enough to hear her talking to Raymond. The church acoustics were wonderful, making even the quietest actors loud and clear. Kezia was asking if they wanted updated photos.

'I can't do it right now,' she said. 'We're off to see someone. But I'd be happy to do them.'

She was right. The publicity photos showed Chloe as Puss in Boots. They'd have to be redone. Along with the costume Annie and her team had slaved over and were now taking apart.

Kezia and Raymond arranged a session in November. Kezia looked around.

'I'll grab a few shots for the archive while I'm here. Nothing posed.'

Lauren daubed green paint on the rock's ridges. Maybe a few silver veins might perk it up. She went to find the metallic paint from their store. When she came back Kezia was staring at the rock.

'Hi Lauren. What's this you're painting?'

'Guess?'

'A dragon curled round its treasure? You're painting it green.'

'No, it's a rock. That's moss.'

'Oh.'

She took a few photos nevertheless. Then hung about watching Lauren.

The sound of singing burst out of the vestry again. Rachel dropped her sword for the umpteenth time. Freddy ran out onto the stage, closely followed by Annie. She reached him and swept him up into her arms.

'Sorry Raymond. We didn't shut the door properly. I'll make sure this monster doesn't escape again.' She tweaked Freddy's nose and the little boy giggled as she took him back into the vestry.

'That was Freddy, wasn't it?'

'Yes.'

'And who was that with him?'

'Scan's mum.'

'I've seen her before. She was at the seance I was photographing. She's very easy to remember.'

'Because of her hair?'

'The Mallen Streak.'

Lauren didn't know what Kezia was talking about.

'Are you too young to have heard of Catherine Cookson?' Kezia asked.

'No.'

'She wrote some books about a family who had all had a white streak in their hair. Like Annie's. A family called Mallen.'

'Annie's family name is Evans. She's Welsh through and through.'

'It's only fiction.' She fiddled with one of the buttons on the camera. 'Freddy seems fine though.'

'He is during the day. The nights are not so good. He wakes up and calls for his mum. Annie says it comes from being left alone for more than twenty-four hours. She's wonderful with him though. She spends half the night talking and playing with him until he goes back to sleep. I don't know how she keeps going during the day because he's full on.'

'Doesn't he go to a crèche or something? I mean, with the money Freddy's going to inherit. Presumably Sean can pay for that.'

'Maybe. But he's a bit funny about using the money. He's got debts, you see. And he thinks the bank will call them in if he suddenly seems to have lots of money.'

Besides, Lauren knew Annie felt it was better Freddy was looked after by family for the moment, and she was probably right.

'Debts?'

Lauren loaded a brush with silver paint and started to trace a threadlike vein over the papier mâché.

'He gambles. Well, gambled. He claims he's stopped but he still owes money.'

Why had she said he *claimed* he'd stopped? Didn't she believe him? She realised she had her doubts. Well, she knew exactly which of his friends wouldn't be able to lie convincingly if asked.

Jim came over and looked at the rock. 'That looks better already.'

Lauren and Kezia looked too. Neither of them said anything.

'Break time,' he said. 'I heard Mrs Vine made parkin.'

The sewing group came out of their vestry, clutching Tupperware boxes, and crossed the stage as a member of stage management wheeled a trolley of mugs and urns out from somewhere behind them. It squeaked and jolted over the nave floor's uneven tiles.

'You going to have a cup of tea with us?'

'No thanks. We're meeting someone. I was passing so I thought I'd drop in to see Raymond.'

It crossed Lauren's mind that, for someone who had just dropped in, Kezia had hung around quite a bit.

'Don't forget to bring your handbag in to be mended.'

'Maybe I will. And, Lauren, where did you get the tarot deck you brought to Zina's – the day of the photoshoot?'

'One of the charity shops in The Warrens.'

'Can you remember which one?'

'Not sure. I go into so many. On the lookout for old leather I can cannibalise.'

'Could you try and remember?'

'Does it matter?'

'They might have the missing cards. Maybe they fell out.' Kezia stared up to where the old chancery window had been, now boarded over and painted black. 'It seems a pity to throw them away.'

'Probably Sue Ryder. Yes, it was. I remember now the assistant commented on them.'

'OK. When was that?'

'The morning of the photoshoot at Zina's salon.'

Kezia nodded, then walked away, pausing only to wait for the older woman who'd come with her to heave herself out of the pew.

Lauren joined the others round the trolley. The parkin was as good as usual, dark, rich, moist and spicy. And Annie had brought some of her curd tarts. Lauren snaffled one before stage management could scoff the lot.

Annie stood slightly apart from the others and seemed to be staring into space. For once she looked tired. Lauren felt a pang of guilt. Annie could be deeply annoying, but the main burden of caring for Freddy had fallen on her and she never complained.

'Love these tarts,' she said. 'How did you find the time to make them?'

'I had some leftover pastry. And Freddy likes them too.'

They both looked over to where Freddy sat on a pew, his legs jutting out in front of him, cramming a tart into his mouth with both hands.

'I'll clear the mess up after,' she said. 'He needs a bit of comfort food at the moment. But then so do we all.'

It was true. The home-made cakes always disappeared during tea break, but today little was left but crumbs already. Already, the atmosphere felt less strained. People were starting to talk about everyday things rather than the horrors of Cooper's Stables.

'Some people thought I should have left Freddy behind today,' Annie said. 'But the sooner people stop looking at him and remembering, the better. We need to put it behind us.'

Lauren realised how true this was. Everyone was relieved the police had arrested the stable lad.

'What was that photographer doing here?' Annie asked.

'Arranging a time to take some fresh photos. With Rachel.'

'And why did she bring the medium?'

'The woman with her?'

'That was Mrs Monroe. She's a psychic. I went to one of her séances with Cora.'

'So that's her? She's in the *Gazette* this morning?'

'Is she?'

'Claiming to know the lad they've arrested for the murders didn't do it.'

'Really. I haven't seen the *Gazette* yet.'

'Jim's got a copy. Ask him.'

But Annie just pushed and pulled at the pins sticking out of a pad round her wrist. She looked tired again. Lauren thought about offering to have Freddy tomorrow. She could take the day off.

TWENTY-FOUR

ALAN CALVERT

MONDAY

Alan Calvert put the *Gazette* down with a sigh. Just Hamish sounding off. He had a bee in his bonnet about the police. Never shaken off his radical days at Glasgow Uni. Well, he needed to be careful. The local community would only take so much of his bellyaching, and he relied on advertising from Thorpe shops and trades to keep his so-called newspaper afloat.

Or at least Alan hoped. He didn't want people starting to question Marty's arrest.

He tore the paper in half and put it in the compost. Best place for it.

He'd seen Harry Appleton coming out of the butchers yesterday. He'd looked awful. A warm feeling of satisfaction had washed over Alan. It was only natural. Harry's son charged with murder and taken to the youth remand centre in Leeds – that must bring back bad memories for Harry. And Marty wouldn't be getting out after a few months like his father.

He dragged his thoughts back to the present and looked around, wondering what he should do today. He'd dig out the bed at the front of the allotment. Get it ready to plant broad beans. A bit of healthy activity would take his mind off everything.

Kezia came along the path as he was leaning on his spade and considering leaving the rest of the digging for tomorrow. The earth was damp and heavy to dig. She stopped dead when she saw him. Alan wished he wasn't so sweaty. He wiped his forehead with his shirtsleeve and smiled.

'Morning, Kezia.'

'Alan. I didn't expect to see you. Don't you go fishing on a Monday? With a friend.'

He remembered he'd shown her the latest fly he'd made and explained how soft materials gave it a more natural feel.

'Dennis cancelled,' he said shortly. 'He's got a lot on at the moment. What with looking after Freddy.'

She stared at him and blinked her eyes rapidly a few times. Her mouth was slightly open. Like one of the fish he'd landed last Monday. A particularly large brown trout that had seemed thunderstruck at being caught.

'You mean Freddy Cooper?' she said.

'Yes. Dennis Price is Freddy's grandfather and Sean's father. Didn't you know?'

'No.'

Her eyes slipped out of focus and she gazed beyond him.

'Are you OK?'

'Yes. Yes. A bit spaced out, I suppose. I had a migraine yesterday. So I didn't sleep well.'

'Painful things. Never had one myself.'

'It can be but I have what they call a hemiplegic migraine. It's a weakness in my limbs mainly. I can't feel anything with it. But it passes after about an hour and then I'm just shattered.'

'Sounds horrible,' Alan said.

Kezia seemed very happy to chat. Normally he had the impression she was itching to disappear behind her high hedge.

'Those Bette Davis films you were talking about,' she said. 'The retrospective. Are they showing *Now, Voyager?* Do you remember?'

'That was one of them,' he replied and took a deep breath, but she got there before him.

'I'd love to see it.'

'So would I,' he said quickly. Although he couldn't remember which one it was. He'd looked them all up but the details had slipped out of his memory. 'Maybe we could go together. Take one car. Mine of course.'

'What a good idea. If you don't mind, that is. When is it on?'

'The brochure's in my shed. Come and have a cup of tea and I'll find it. Maybe there's another film we fancy as well. They're on all week.'

She smiled and followed him to the shed, where he whisked a pile of bags off the chair, dusted it briefly with his sleeve and offered it to her.

He could have kicked himself. Obviously she'd been hoping he might ask her to go. Poor woman. He made tea with the hot water he brought in a Thermos and they had a lovely chat about the films on next week. He didn't think she noticed when he muddled up *Jezebel* and *Dark Victory*.

'You wouldn't have any more of the wood ash, would you?' she asked.

'Of course. But you shouldn't use too much of it, you know.' And he heard himself give a long and boring monologue about soil nutrients and acidity. Once he'd begun he couldn't find a way out. Why did he do this? She cut him off gently.

'I'll be careful,' she said. 'But I could do with a little more.'

He took her round to the back where he kept the incinerator and removed the lid. They both stared in at the grey powdery mass at the bottom.

'Should I have sieved it before I put it on my pots at the studio?'

'It shouldn't be necessary. It's only wood, so if there were any bits that hadn't quite burned through they would eventually rot down.' He managed to resist the urge to explain his incinerating process to her. It was something he'd devoted a great deal of time and effort to perfecting, but not everybody was as interested in it as him.

'But maybe it looks a bit unattractive in pots,' he added.

'There was something else in the ash. Not wood. Maybe some cloth.'

'Definitely not. This lot was old raspberry canes, the prunings from the blackberry bushes and some potato stalks. I don't like to put the potato detritus in the compost. It can spread disease. But I always wait until the incinerator is at its hottest. It's amazing how quickly it can burn even very wet stuff then.' He made a Herculean effort to stop there. 'Look.'

He picked up a stick and stirred the remaining ash. The wood thwacked the metal sides and gave off an eerie clanging as a cloud of ash rose up and made him cough.

'Just ash,' he said.

'I'm sure. Maybe someone else put something in without you knowing.'

'Why would they do that?'

'Just a thought.'

'In any case, I never leave the incinerator unattended when it's burning. That would be irresponsible. And dangerous. You never know with a fire.'

'Of course. And no one gave you anything to burn?'

'No.'

'You're sure?'

'Absolutely.'

She looked as though she'd have liked to ask him more and he felt a little irritated by her persistence.

'Did you see the piece in the local rag?' he said. 'About the Cooper killings? Hamish Aitken has surpassed himself this time.'

'Yes.'

'It's modern journalism at its worst. Giving a – what do they call it – a platform to charlatans like that wretched psychic woman.'

'Ah. I see.'

'It's very hard on the innocent people who've been caught up in the tragedy.'

He dug his spade deep into the earth and turned over a particularly heavy sod.

'Like your friend Dennis, you mean.'

'Yes.'

'Alan. Can I ask you something a bit complicated.'

'Of course.'

'I'd rather be honest than try to... I don't know.' She laughed suddenly, then smoothed her hair back from her face and rewound the band holding it in place. 'Maybe it would be easiest if I just tell you what I want.'

He stuttered a bit because... well, because he had no idea what was coming.

'It's about the Cooper murders.'

Whatever he'd expected it wasn't this.

'Yes.'

And she plunged into an incredible story about the psychic woman and a vision. He struggled to get his head round it. She seemed to believe in it too. He'd thought beneath the scatty exterior she had a core of sense. But that was women for you. Always unexpected. Suddenly revealing bits of themselves you never knew about. Really, he'd been stupid to expect her to be as clear-sighted as Janice.

A delightful fantasy took over his thoughts as he imagined the two of them together, with him gently guiding Kezia. Patiently but kindly showing her how misguided some of her beliefs were. He emerged from these pleasant thoughts to realise she was talking about investigating the murders herself. He nearly laughed but realised, in time, this would not be the best response. Really people like that psychic woman were dangerous. Putting stupid ideas into people's heads. They should be stopped. He opened his mouth to say this, then understood she was asking him for help. Could he help her meet the Prices? She knew Sean's partner. A little. But it was difficult to ask her without telling her why.

'But why do you want to meet them?'

'Well. Sean's a suspect, isn't he? I've got to start somewhere.'

He started to look for words to let her down gently. Dennis Price was a friend, after all. And then another agreeable vision came to him. The two of them, him and Kezia, working together to solve the case. Going to see Dennis and Annie. Then discussing everything they'd learned afterwards. Besides, it would give him a chance to keep an eye on her. Which might be a very good idea.

'Of course, I can organise that. I'll give Dennis a call tomorrow. Make some excuse to pop over and you can come with me,' he said.

She looked startled at his enthusiasm.

'We can't let a miscarriage of justice happen,' he added.

'Thank you, Alan. I've got to do something. Marty's not good. His father, Harry, he's—'

'I know Harry.'

'Of course you do. I forget how everybody knows everybody in Thorpe. Harry's desperate to get Marty out of the remand centre. He's a lovely man and devoted to his son. I'd do anything to help them.'

Alan didn't like that. Not at all. She sounded far too keen on Harry. Was that why she was determined to investigate the killings? Well, all the more reason for him to get involved.

'Alan.'

Her voice pulled him back from the dangerous thoughts invading his mind.

'Sorry. Just thinking of a reason to see Dennis.'

'Does he have an allotment?'

'No. He has small veg patch in his garden.'

It occurred to him she probably didn't know about Dennis's illness.

'He doesn't go out much. Never has. Worked from home a lot before he retired. His firm was very good to him. Mind you, I think they'd have done anything to keep him. He was an electronic design engineer. A brilliant one. He helped develop the latest rigid-flex PCB boards.' He managed to stop before he started explaining what a PCB board was and forced himself back to the point. 'He has a condition. Neurofibromatosis. It means he has growths on his face. They're little tumours really. Little benign ones. But people stare. Nevertheless he's done very well for himself. Not short of a bob or two but not silly with it.'

She nodded.

'I sometimes borrow his rotavator. That'd be a good reason to pop in to see him.'

'Does he give you stuff to burn?'

'No. They collect garden waste where he is. Why?'

'No reason really.'

For once she didn't look straight at him with the piercing gaze that made him think she could see right into his head, but glanced down at her hands. They were slim and elegant despite the red and rough skin on her palms. He wished she'd stop harping on about the incinerator. It bothered him.

Her phone rang. She glanced at the screen and smiled.

'I'll have to answer this,' she said. 'Hello, Hamish.'

And, phone pressed to her ear, she whisked out of his allotment and down the path into hers.

He'd take a break from the digging and sort some ashes for her.

The ones at the bottom of the incinerator were hard to scrape up, so he scooped some out of the bag he'd prepared for another allotment holder. Kezia was right. There was something mixed in with it. Shreds of cloth. Not completely burnt. He thought rapidly. He hadn't been careful enough. The more he thought about it, the more he realised going with Kezia to see Dennis would be a good idea. He needed to keep an eye on things.

He went back to his digging. He'd catch Kezia on the way out and give her the ashes. But as he leaned his weight on the spade, two men sauntered past.

There was only one place they could be heading. Kezia's allotment. Unless they'd made a mistake. Something about them made him think twice about asking them though.

Both wearing dark T-shirts and jeans, they were youngish – thirties or forties – with the sort of build that came from hours in the gym. There the resemblance ended. The first and younger of the two, whose stride never paused as he passed by, wore an expensive jacket and an air of confidence. The second, older and rougher round the edges, gave Alan a nod and a half-smile that made him feel observed, then dismissed as pointless. A waft of cologne stung his nose.

They reached the gate in Kezia's hedge. The first one stepped back and gestured to the second, who gave it a sharp push with his shoulder. It flew open over the overgrown grass. They entered, shoving it shut behind them.

Alan waited.

But whatever was happening behind Kezia's high hedge was silent. Even close to, he heard nothing.

Thirty minutes later, they sauntered out past his allotment again.

Kezia came out an hour later, but she sped down the path before he could give her the ashes and maybe ask who her visitors had been.

DI VINCENT DOUGLAS

To: DCI Carter
re: PC Josh Mason – request for background check

Following your call last week, I can confirm PC Josh Mason has a
connection to the Kingsley family. As you surmised, Kezia Heron
is David Kingsley's ex-wife and Mason's aunt.

We have no record of PC Mason nor his aunt having any involvement in organised crime. Nor for that matter has David Kingsley
ever been implicated in any crime although his firm has represented several people linked to the Kingsley family. Nevertheless
further investigation will be carried out.

Your hypothesis that an officer was/is passing information onto the
Kingsleys during the Peter Walker investigation warrants further
examination and I will liaise with the Independent Office for
Police Conduct who, as you know, are conducting a review into the
management of the Peter Walker case.

I have noted that PC Mason was working in Local Policing at
Thorpe station where the Peter Walker investigation was based.
Your comments that boundaries between the two departments,
Local Policing and Crime, were operationally blurred and
PC Mason would have had access to the details of the investigation
are useful.

I understand you intend to test out Mason. Please keep me informed as to any developments.

Yours,

DI Vince Douglas
Anti-Corruption Unit North Yorkshire Police

TWENTY-FIVE
MRS MONROE

TUESDAY

'And then,' Mrs Monroe said, wishing the lights weren't so bright in her eyes and trying to look at the camera like they'd told her to. She took a pause for effect before she launched into the final part of the vision, but the presenter cut across her.

'I'm afraid we'll have to wait for the rest of Mrs Monroe's vision. We've received news of a serious accident on the A642 through Swillington involving an oil tanker. Police have declared a major incident. Over to James Dunn at the scene.'

She listened to her earpiece for a few seconds, then leaned over to Mrs Monroe. She could smell the thick make-up covering the woman's face.

'Sorry about the break and just as you were getting into your stride, but that's breakfast TV for you. Have to go with the flow. Just hold on to your last thought.'

Mrs Monroe fixed a smile on her mouth. You never knew when the camera on you would suddenly be live. She'd never in a million years thought she'd be on the television. Even when Hamish said he could probably fix it, she still hadn't thought it would come off.

The presenter signalled to her that they were back on air and

Mrs Monroe tried to remember what she'd been saying when she'd been interrupted.

'Devastating news for the residents of Swillington, James. We'll keep you updated on a rapidly evolving situation. But for now, let's go back to my studio guest, Mrs Monroe, and her fascinating take on the recent tragedy at the stables near Thorpe. For viewers who've just tuned in, a reminder that the entire Cooper family were the victims of a shocking and bloody rampage. Police were swift to arrest and charge a local youngster. But the question is, *Were they too swift?* Mrs Monroe, a noted psychic, thinks so. She is convinced that she has a message from Charlie Cooper with information the police should at least listen to. Mrs Monroe, you were telling us the final part of Charlie Cooper's ghostly appearance.'

Mrs Monroe swallowed her irritation at the woman's characterisation of her vision as a ghostly appearance. She supposed it was easier for the general public to understand than psychometry, which she and Kezia had decided to steer clear of mentioning. She recounted the rest of the scene that Charlie had witnessed.

'Something fluttered at the edge of Charlie's vision as he clutched imploringly at the killer's clothes, desperate to save his daughter and grandson's lives. And then...'

'And then?'

Mrs Monroe realised that the woman was actually interested. She'd been about to say, *and then he knew no more.* But that didn't seem sufficiently exciting. She thought quickly.

'Fluttered at the edge of Charlie's vision,' she repeated. Something Kezia had asked her to look out for came into her mind. 'And as he stared at it, he realised it was a tarot card. It spun round and landed beside him. Giving him a glimpse of its terrible picture. He looked back up to see the killer's gun trained on his face. And then, he knew no more.'

That had gone well. Her voice had had just the right level of drama without going over the top. It wasn't strictly true but no one was going to know. Even the presenter, continually distracted by people talking in her ear, had appeared to focus on her words.

'And the tarot card,' she asked now. 'Did you recognise it?'

'Of course. I'm an experienced tarot reader and very sensitive to the cards.'

The presenter was waiting for her to say something.

'But that,' she announced in the most mysterious voice she could summon, 'is a detail I will only share with the police. If they deign to talk to me. And let's hope they do because I predict there will be more deaths if not.'

She was pleased with her quick thinking.

'Well, let's hope the police will listen now.' The presenter echoed her words, before moving onto a segment about the dumping of illegal chemicals along a little-used road between Harrogate and Thorpe.

Mrs Monroe hoped enough people had caught her name. Hamish had promised that, if anyone googled it along with the title of the show or any words to do with her practice, they'd find her Facebook page and website.

The assistant came over to escort her out of the studio as soon as the next segment started.

'There's a car waiting to take you home,' she said.

Mrs Monroe wondered if Kezia would still be there. She'd turned up yesterday evening and asked if she could stay the night. Something about not wanting to go back to the flat. Maybe Kezia's nephew was still angry. Well, he wasn't going to be happy about her television appearance. Was that why Kezia had suddenly seemed less keen about it herself?

'Do you do tarot readings?' the assistant asked.

'Of course.'

'Maybe I could book one?'

Mrs Monroe felt pleased. This was all working out better than she'd hoped.

TWENTY-SIX

JOSH

WEDNESDAY

Josh was furious with Kezia. He'd waited for her to come home for hours last night so he could tell her exactly what he thought. He'd given up around two and gone to bed.

Her coat had been by the door when he surfaced this morning.

It was probably a good thing he'd gone to sleep rather than accosting her in the small hours when his brain had kept on coming up with words about how she'd betrayed him, which sounded altogether too emotional. He was calmer now.

She appeared in the kitchen around eight o'clock. She looked as though she hadn't slept. Probably nervous about what he was going to say.

'Morning,' she said, and busied herself spooning the revolting dried herbs she called tea into a pot.

'You told that bloody medium,' he blurted out.

'What?'

But he could see she knew what he was talking about, because her hand froze for a second en route between the caddy and the mug and when it started up again she scattered herbs over the counter.

'The tarot card. You told your friend Mrs Monroe. And she spouted about it in the interview, even though I'd told you to keep it quiet.'

Before she could reply, her phone rang. She answered it, and slipped out and into her bedroom where he couldn't hear her.

'You told Mrs Monroe about the tarot card,' he repeated when she came back a few minutes later.

'Is that why your colleagues want to see her?' she said. 'Because of the tarot card.'

'What?'

She wrapped her arms round her waist in a gesture that made him think she might be cold.

'That was Mrs Monroe on the phone,' she said flatly. 'The police have asked her to come in and talk to them.'

'You haven't answered my question. You told her about the tarot card, didn't you?'

'She wants me to go with her.'

'No, you mustn't.'

'Why not? You're allowed a friend aren't you? Is there a way in through the back?'

'What?'

'Mrs Monroe doesn't want any fuss,' she said quickly.

He realised she'd sidetracked him from the question.

'Did you tell Mrs Monroe about the tarot card?'

It was his phone's turn to ring. Work. He answered it. And by the time he'd finished the call, Kezia had left the flat. She hadn't drunk her tea.

She'd have to find out for herself that Carter had asked him to be present at the interview.

He hoped she wouldn't let slip he'd told her about the tarot card. Really he should have kept his mouth shut. She'd been behaving very oddly in the last couple of days. He was sure she hadn't come home at all on Monday night. And she didn't seem as happy as he'd have expected about Mrs Monroe being interviewed by Carter.

TWENTY-SEVEN
JOSH

SAME DAY

Carter paused before he opened the door, drew himself up to his full height, not easy as he was clutching a jug of water, four glasses and a sheaf of notes, and plastered a smile across his face. He was cleaner-shaven than usual and his floppy hair had been smoothed back from his face.

'Ladies,' he said as he entered. 'Thank you for coming in. So sorry to keep you waiting.'

Josh kept his face from reacting to this geniality from the normally morose DCI and observed the two women sitting at the table as he'd been told to do. Carter hadn't explained why he wanted Josh present but had merely told him to keep his mouth shut and watch.

Mrs Monroe and Kezia looked uncomfortable in the windowless room. It was usually reserved for interviews under caution as it was fully equipped with recording equipment. Carter had specifically asked for them to be brought here despite Beresford offering him one of the far more pleasant offices where discussions with people helping the police generally took place.

Mrs Monroe patted her hair. She looked exactly like the photos on her website, the ones he supposed Kezia had taken, elderly but shrewd. Very similar to the host of older women with unmoving helmets of grey hair and smart outfits who attended the local church. As a child, Josh had never been able to distinguish between them. Mrs Monroe looked at him. For a second Josh thought a sardonic gleam flashed in her eyes. Had she read his thoughts? Surely she couldn't. Of course not.

Carter introduced himself and then Josh before sitting at the other side of the table. Kezia didn't react to Josh's presence.

'So, Mrs Monroe.' Carter started immediately. 'You know why you're here. Why don't you take us through the insight the spirit world has given you into the Cooper murders.'

Mrs Monroe needed no further invitation. She plunged in with the eagerness of someone psyched up to brave the crowds for a bargain in the January sales.

'The visitation came on me all of a sudden. They can take me unawares like that, although I'm always reaching into the unknown in case someone who's passed has an urgent message. A connection clicked over the great divide. A sudden linking of minds. And I was lying on the floor in the living room of Mr Cooper's cottage, soaked in blood and in great pain, while the killer stood—'

'How, may I ask, did you know you were in Cooper's cottage?'

Mrs Monroe, cut off in full flow, gaped at him.

'My apologies. I interrupted you. I imagine Mr Cooper imparted that information when the two of you established your, er, link. I'm right in saying it was Mr Cooper who contacted you?'

'Yes.'

'And presumably, Ms Heron, who used to be a regular visitor to the stables, could confirm the room you were in was at the Coopers'?'

'Well, yes. But I mean, I knew anyway. Just as I knew it was Charlie Cooper.'

'Thank you. I wanted to have it clear in my head. We have very down-to-earth minds in the police, I'm afraid. Please do continue.'

But Mrs Monroe had lost the thread of her dramatic spiel and simply told Carter how Charlie Cooper had seen the killer's feet. And they'd been wearing muddy wellingtons and thick socks. How he'd tried to warn his daughter and then been shot.

'And that's all?'

'Well, yes.'

'According to PC Mason, something called psychometry inspired your vision.' He shuffled through the notes he'd brought. 'Ah, yes. "The ability to read an inanimate object. To get information about an event or a person who was associated with the object." I understand the object in this case was a piece of burnt cloth, found in some ashes. You didn't mention psychometry in your television interview.'

Clearly the DCI had done some research.

'It's not an easy thing to understand,' Mrs Monroe said.

'Didn't want to confuse the general public.'

'And we'd have had to say what the object was and where it came from. We didn't think it was a good idea.' This was Kezia. 'But I have it here. Maybe you could...'

She pulled a plastic bag containing a dark piece of cloth from her pocket.

'Do some tests?'

'Yes.'

Carter took the plastic bag and examined the blackened shred for a few seconds.

'I doubt we'll get anything from it, but thank you.'

He placed it on the table.

'I know where it came from.'

'Yes, you told PC Mason. Mr Calvert's incinerator in the next-door allotment.'

'Yes.'

'Are you accusing Mr Calvert of being the gun-toting wearer of bloodstained wellingtons?'

'No. But someone could have put something in his incinerator.'

'Presumably you've asked Mr Calvert?'

For the first time, Kezia looked directly at Josh. 'I have,' she said. 'But he said no one could have accessed the fire. But maybe he's wrong.'

Carter sighed. 'Another dead end nevertheless. But that's police work for you.'

He put his glasses on and looked again at his notes.

'Ah yes. A tarot card. In your television slot, Mrs Monroe, you said something about a tarot card. Let me see.' He quoted, '"*Something fluttered at the edge of Charlie's vision. And as he stared at it, he realised it was a tarot card. It spun round and landed beside him. Giving him a glimpse of its terrible picture. He looked back up to see the killer's gun trained on his face. And then, he knew no more.* I think I've got that right, haven't I?'

'Yes.'

'Thank you for keeping the actual card to yourself, but we're longing to hear which one it was. Aren't we, PC Mason?'

Josh had to nod agreement.

'I only caught a glimpse, so I couldn't be sure.'

'But you're an expert tarot reader. You must have recognised something.'

Mrs Monroe looked at Kezia. 'Can you remember what I said?' She turned back to Carter. 'Kezia was present while I was in the trance. I describe everything while I'm under and it helps to have someone make notes as to what I say. I don't always remember.'

Josh waited. If Kezia said it was the Sun he would have to admit he'd told her. The fallout wouldn't be good. Thank God Mrs Monroe hadn't mentioned two cards.

Kezia reached for the water jug and poured herself a glass. When she eventually spoke she didn't look at Josh but kept her eyes trained on Carter.

'Let me see. You talked about a corpse on the card. With a red cloak. Stabbed, you said. I noticed it because up to then you'd only mentioned gunshots. Stabbed with lots of swords. All upright. Does that help, Mrs Monroe?'

Ten of Swords, Josh thought. He realised he'd been holding his breath.

'Ten of Swords,' Mrs Monroe said.

It occurred to Josh that Kezia knew very well which card she'd described.

'Probably from the Rider–Waite deck,' Mrs Monroe continued. 'Although it's one of the cards that is very similar across all decks.'

Carter poured himself a glass of water, drank and grimaced.

'Yorkshire water,' he said. 'You'd expect it to be wonderful but it's always disappointing. Faintly disinfected and difficult to swallow. Anything else you can tell us?'

Mrs Monroe shook her head.

'No other information from beyond?'

'No.'

'No hint as to whether Mr Cooper recognised the killer?'

'No.'

'Could you try and re-establish contact with him and ask? It would be very helpful.'

'It doesn't work like that. I-I can't control what they tell me.'

'Ah. My apologies. I thought you generally asked the spirits questions on behalf of their loved ones left behind.'

Mrs Monroe merely pursed her lips at this and shot a glance at Kezia.

'Will you look at the case again?' Kezia addressed Carter directly.

'Nothing you've told me opens up any useful lines of enquiry, I'm afraid. But thank you for coming in, Mrs Monroe.' Carter turned to Kezia. 'And you too, Ms Heron. What exactly is your role in all this?'

'I'm here as a friend of Mrs Monroe's.'

'We're not as brutal as television crime series would have you believe. Mrs Monroe would have been perfectly safe with me and PC Mason. But, of course, you know PC Mason, don't you?'

'Yes. He's my nephew.'

'You're not at all alike.'

'Josh— PC Mason takes after his father. I'm his mother's sister.'

'And the two of you share a flat.'

Carter knew a surprising amount about Kezia.

'I rent a room. Surely what Mrs Monroe saw makes it unlikely Marty Appleton was the killer. They were wearing wellingtons. It was Marty's trainers that were bloodstained.'

'And how do you know we've arrested Marty Appleton, Ms Heron? And why do you think his trainers might have been stained with blood?'

The sharp back and forth of Kezia and Carter's conversation came to an abrupt end. Silence. Not quite silence. The hum of traffic from the busy interchange outside penetrated even this windowless room buried in the depths of the station. And some freak of acoustics channelled an echo of a tap running from the gents' above them. Only part of Josh's mind registered them. The rest of it was focussed on not looking at Kezia. He was afraid she'd glanced at him when Carter had asked the question.

'Harry Appleton, Marty's father, told me about the trainers. And everyone knows you've arrested Marty.'

Josh looked up sharply.

Kezia's voice was as matter-of-fact as if she was recalling a conversation about the bus timetable.

'People change their footwear, Ms Heron.'

He sipped at his water.

'And the tarot card. An odd thing for the Coopers to have,' Kezia went on. 'Was there a tarot deck found at the stables?'

'I can't divulge details of a crime scene. As PC Mason will confirm, that would be a shocking piece of misconduct.'

Josh stammered an agreement.

'You used to ride at the stables, didn't you? Any other insights into Cooper's character you'd like to share?'

Kezia shook her head.

'Why did you leave?'

'I sold my horse.'

'Ah yes. That would be a few months before you divorced, I suppose. Divorced David Kingsley.'

Kezia's silence this time was deliberate. She looked down at her hands resting on the table and examined a nail.

Josh looked down at his own hands. How did Carter know? Had he done more research? It wouldn't have been difficult to find out.

'Have you discussed the Coopers with your husband?'

'My ex-husband.'

'Your ex-husband. No love lost between you then?'

'We're civilised.'

'That bad? Maybe you wouldn't mind coming in and talking to us in connection with another inquiry.'

Whatever Josh had expected it wasn't this. Kezia didn't seem surprised though.

'You've always had it in for him, haven't you?'

The exchange had gone far beyond a polite chat. Carter was still genial and Kezia composed, but an edge of some other emotion sliced through their words.

'I've never met your husband.'

'My ex-husband. And you know full well I don't mean you personally. I mean the police. He can't help his background. He did his best to put it behind him. Make something of himself. But you never let up, did you. Picking him up for a "friendly chat" every now and then. Visiting his offices at all times of the day and night. Making life as difficult for him as you could. Because you could. Because you can. Because you can't believe someone like him can make good. So you make it doubly hard for him to get away.'

Kezia was not so composed now. Josh didn't think he'd ever seen her so fired up. She shook with what he supposed was anger.

'It is true that your husband—' Carter waited a second. 'Your ex-husband, I should say. He does come from a very unfortunate family. A family that – to speak frankly – is behind the majority of the drug trade, prostitution and violent crime in this area. So you'll have to forgive us if we wonder about your husband. If we think having an ostensibly upright solicitor at the Kingsley family's service is exactly what they'd like. There is a certain feeling... How can I put it? Yes. A feeling that blood will out.'

Mrs Monroe coughed into the ensuing silence, then reached down into her handbag and brought out a folded square of handkerchief that she patted her lips with. They all looked at her.

'Let's go,' Kezia said. 'This is pointless.'

The effect of her late night showed in the shake of her arm as she pressed down on the table to lift herself out of her chair and the white, almost haunted look on her face.

'Let me see you ladies out. But think about what I said, Ms Heron. I have an open mind. A very open mind. And I'm ready to overlook a certain amount of criminal involvement, in exchange for useful information.'

'I have never been involved in anything criminal.'

'Of course. But the offer applies to any member of your family.'

'My ex-family.' She spat the words out.

'Anyone.'

Kezia stomped to the door. Carter was quicker though. He opened it for her but, once in the corridor, he asked a passing DC to see Mrs Monroe and Kezia to reception, then stood and watched them both leave.

'So, Mason, what did you think? I suppose it's difficult for you as she's your aunt. You need to see beyond that.'

Josh couldn't tell anything from Carter's voice. Part of him wanted to point out how much of Mrs Monroe's vision was accurate. Cooper had been shot twice and in the living room. Giles and Elaine in the kitchen. Chloe at the bottom of the stairs. But they were all details he'd given to Kezia and he thought Carter suspected this.

Had Kezia told Mrs Monroe? He didn't think she'd would. But it was possible that whatever Mrs Monroe had seen was shaped in the retelling – even unconsciously – by Kezia's knowledge.

'What did you think? Sir.'

'What did I think? Not a word of truth from either of them. They fed us a lot of rubbish, concealed in smoke and mirrors. I spoke more truth than the two of them combined. And Mrs Monroe's in it for the publicity.'

'Will you test the cloth?'

'What would be the point? It's hopelessly contaminated as it is. No chain of evidence either.' Carter stared at him moodily for a few seconds. 'I expect you wondered why I asked your aunt if she might help us with our enquiries into the Kingsleys.'

'I don't think she knows anything.'

'You think that, do you? But, of course, she was very angry about the suggestion. Maybe a little too angry, didn't you think? I did wonder if she was afraid. Is that possible?'

He waited but Josh couldn't think of a suitable response.

'Still,' Carter went on. 'She might change her mind. My door is always open to people with information. Even if they're not completely clean themselves. I can be very discreet. And we can offer round-the-clock protection. Tell her that. The same applies to anybody with information about the Kingsleys.'

Once again he looked at Josh as though expecting a response. None came to Josh's mind.

'Well, bear it in mind, Mason. We can dispense with you in Crime now. Job's winding up. The investigation is moving back to York. Local Policing can have the benefit of your expertise. Sign off with Lovell and hand back anything unfinished.'

And with that he strode off.

Josh went back upstairs and gave Lovell his log of the CCTV footage. He'd pretty much finished anyway. He wasn't sorry to see the back of it.

'Anything?'

'A couple of cyclists near Appleton's flat around half ten on Sunday night, but I don't think either is Martin. And the camera from Boyes's Farm shows a white car heading towards the stables around eight, then returning after nine.'

'Registration?'

'Not visible. Boyes's camera is set up to catch people coming onto the farm. It only caught the top of the car. It's all in my log.'

'No burger vans then?'

'No.'

The burger van was a running joke after the elderly chap living opposite the stables entrance had rung on another three occasions to report a sighting. The last two had turned out to be the mobile lab the crime scene investigation team had insisted on using. They'd been plagued ever since by officers knocking on the window and asking for a burger and chips.

'OK. Drop the drives into the evidence store on your way down.'

Lovell's mobile rang. He answered.

'Sir?'

He listened, then started scribbling on a pad of paper.

'Yes, sir. I'll get on it right away.'

He listened to the response, then finished the call.

'Carter?' Josh asked.

'Yes. Don't worry about the drives, I'll take them. I've got to get something from the evidence store myself.'

Josh headed downstairs in a thoughtful mood, but stopped on the ground floor and went to the coffee machine outside the evidence store.

Sure enough Lovell came down a few minutes later, carrying the box of drives Josh had worked through. He went into the evidence store. When he came out, he had two evidence bags. Even with the coffee machine blocking most of his vision, Josh saw enough to be sure Lovell had collected the two tarot cards found in Chloe Cooper's hands. Lovell went straight back upstairs.

Taking the cards to Carter. Josh was sure that was what he was doing. The question was why. Why had Carter suddenly asked Lovell to fetch them and what had he said to Lovell that had made the DC write Rider–Waite and Walker on his notepad?

TWENTY-EIGHT
JOSH

SAME DAY

DI Burden was chatting to Sergeant Beresford when Josh went into his office a little while later. They turned to look as Josh came in.

'I'm to report back to you from now on.'

'Carter finished with you, then?' Beresford asked.

'Yes, Sarge.'

'Did you enjoy your time in Crime?' This was Burden.

Josh thought for a few seconds. Burden was clever and liable to use his speed of mind to turn an innocent phrase of Josh's into a weapon to cudgel him with.

'It was good experience.'

'And working alongside DCI Carter?'

'It was interesting, sir.'

'Very diplomatic. Bit of advice though. From one who's been kicking round the police force for quite a while.'

'Yes, sir. Thank you.'

'The Carters of this world. They come and go. He's got his sights set on bigger things than being a DCI in North Yorkshire. You understand me?'

Some trickle of common sense told Josh it would be wise to keep his mouth shut. Despite Burden's almost friendly smile. And despite feeling Carter's conduct during the interview with Kezia and Mrs Monroe had been very strange.

'Yes, sir.'

'You live in Thorpe, don't you?'

'Yes, sir.'

'Not happy here, are they?'

'I don't listen to gossip.'

'And the psychic woman? You were in the interview, weren't you? Anything useful?'

'Waste of time, sir.'

Burden's current sidekick, a permanently worried DC, appeared at the door and the two of them left.

'It'll be good to have you back, Mason,' Beresford said.

Josh felt a bit warmer.

'Being one officer short has been difficult.'

'I see, sir.'

'Burden said you were useful, by the way. He can be a bit abrupt but he knows what he's talking about.'

Burden and Beresford must be about the same age. Only a couple of years away from retirement. A lot in common, then.

'Carter was in the running for the ACC job. In West Midlands. Until the Walker case fiasco. He's desperate to get away from here.'

Josh nodded. At the moment, he felt much the same.

'Professional Standards are looking into the Walker case. Particularly the way Carter managed it.'

Josh remembered the officer who'd come to see Carter after the interview with Marty. Was he from Professional Standards?

One of Josh's friends from college had gone to work for IOPC headquarters in Canary Wharf. Josh toyed with the idea of asking him what was going on.

'Was it mishandled, Sarge? I'd not long started and wasn't...'

Beresford sighed. 'The case was handled initially by Missing

Persons but assessed as high-risk, so Crime were involved. With Carter as officer in charge. As you know, the search team missed the abduction site when checking Peter's route home from school.'

Josh remembered the discarded bike and ripped school bag that had been discovered eventually by Peter's father who'd gone out to look for himself.

'And keep this to yourself, but Carter was convinced Peter's disappearance was linked to drugs. His early hypothesis was that Peter was a county lines delivery boy who'd fallen foul of his bosses or got caught up a gang fight over areas. He wasted a lot of resources investigating that even though Peter's family, his school, his friends – everybody said it wasn't possible. No wonder the family refused to talk to him afterwards.'

'And the tarot card? The one found with Peter's body?'

'You know about that then?'

'Lovell told me.' He made a decision. 'Because I found two at the Cooper murder scene.'

'Yes. I saw it in your report. What of it?'

'Surely it means the two cases are linked.'

Beresford was silent.

'It can't be a coincidence. Why aren't we looking into it?'

'It could be. You'd be surprised how many people have tarot cards. Let it go, Josh. For once, Carter has got the right person. And next time some dodgy psychic uses you to get publicity, come and see me first.'

'What do you mean?'

'Local press and television were outside the station waiting for her to come out so they could interview her. We didn't tell them she was coming in, so she must have.'

It was entirely possible. Especially as Hamish Aitken was involved with her.

'It was your aunt who came with her, wasn't it?'

'Yes.'

'She was very put out by the all the media interest. Looked terrified.'

Josh nodded. Should he tell Beresford about Carter's strange behaviour towards Kezia? Carter hadn't asked him to keep anything quiet.

He poured it all out to the sergeant, who, for once, didn't interrupt him with kindly but patronising advice.

'Carter's got a bee in his bonnet about the Kingsleys,' he said when Josh had finished. 'Of course, they are a major problem. But it's starting to affect his judgement. Your aunt was absolutely right to keep out of it. You're due some time off, Josh. Why not take it? Things are calming down here now the investigation's moving back to York.'

'I'll think about it, Sarge.'

The phone rang. Beresford answered it. His voice took on a veneer of patience. 'Yes, Mr Boyes. I'm sorry to hear this. Just one minute.'

He put his hand over the mouthpiece. 'Drunk,' he said. 'Dog's dead. Take all the time you need, Josh. Is there anything else?'

Josh shook his head. He decided to go home and forget about it all but as he left his phone rang.

TWENTY-NINE
JOSH

SAME DAY

'He really isn't going to do anything is he?' Kezia said to Josh when she opened the door of Harry Appleton's flat to him.

'If you mean DCI Carter,' Josh said. 'No. But it was never very likely.'

He followed her into Harry's sitting room. She'd rung him and begged him to come over.

'Not even test the cloth?'

'No.' There was no point avoiding the truth. 'He didn't believe a word Mrs Monroe said. He thought she was only interested in publicising herself.'

Too late he realised Mrs Monroe was there, settled in a low armchair. She flushed, then puffed herself up like a frog deterring an attack and launched into a speech about how she'd never misuse her gifts. Kezia cut her off.

'I know. I know. But that doesn't help us now. We have to find another way of persuading the police to reopen the case.'

'No point,' Josh said. 'Carter won't. And he's the only person who can. He's— He needed a quick success and he's got it with

Marty. You'd do better concentrating on building a good defence for the case.'

'But that won't be for months and Marty can't wait that long.' This was Harry. 'I saw him this morning. He— he was very quiet. I hoped it meant he was coping better. But Marty's never quiet. And his eyes were dull. Like an ill animal. I think he's giving up.'

'We need to find the killer.' This was Mrs Monroe, her soft cheeks still red. 'Because they're out there. Probably thinking they've got away with it. Someone shot that family in— Kezia, do you think we should try the cloth again? See if something new—'

'No. We got nothing last time. Anyway, I left it at the police station.'

Mrs Monroe glared, her jaw moving furiously. Josh realised she was chewing gum.

Kezia spun round. 'Why are you here, Josh?' She was wired too.

'Because you asked me to come.'

'I didn't think you would though.'

'Maybe I owe you something.'

'Ha! Yes. We would have been far more believable if we'd got the tarot card at the Coopers' right, wouldn't we?'

'Yes. So like I said, I owe you. Why did you say Ten of Swords though?'

She stopped pacing for a couple of seconds and stared at a print of Constable's *The Hay Wain* as though she'd just noticed its beauty.

'No reason. Why do you ask?'

Should he tell her about the King of Swords found by Peter Walker's body? Of course not. He'd already told her far too much. And in a sudden flash of insight, he saw he'd always been prone to sharing his thoughts and worries. With Zina, with his friends, with Kezia. Well, he couldn't any more. At least not police affairs.

'Just wondered,' he said. 'No reason.'

'But do *you* believe us?' Kezia asked.

This was tricky. He didn't know what he believed.

'I don't think you're lying.'

'But you're not sure if we're right.'

'No.'

'Sean Price needs money,' Kezia said.

'What?'

'Sean Price gambles. His girlfriend said he'd lost a lot of money. Everyone says Freddy will inherit the Coopers' money.'

Harry looked hopeful.

'Kezia? What are you suggesting?'

'If we can't persuade the police Marty is innocent, we'll have to find out who did kill the Coopers.'

'But you can't be—'

'And Sean Price strikes me as a suspect.'

'Sean Price has an alibi.'

'What was it?'

'He took his mother out for a meal on Sunday night and then to Fountains Abbey, to see the light show. And I shouldn't have told you that.'

But he had. He'd done it again.

'So they *were* killed on Sunday night?'

He remembered that the details of when the murders had happened hadn't been released.

'I didn't say that.'

But he had really.

'Have you checked his alibi out? Mothers lie for their sons.'

'Of course we have. They were seen together at the restaurant.'

Kezia started pacing again. Less restlessly though. More as though she was working something out and needed the movement of her body to settle her mind. She stopped suddenly, picked up her handbag from the sofa and pulled sharply at the handle. It came away in her hand.

They all stared at her but she shook her head.

'So who else might it have been?' Mrs Monroe asked.

'You can't ask Josh that,' Kezia said. 'It's not fair.'

'All the other suspects have rock-solid alibis. I'll tell you that.'

'Who were they?'

Josh shifted his weight from one foot to another as he thought. He didn't want them racing around asking questions. They might get into trouble.

'You could work it for yourselves by asking around but I'll tell you. That's all though. Johnny Boyes. He has the land next door to—'

'I know Johnny,' Harry said. 'I've done work for him. Rewiring. I don't think he—'

'It doesn't matter what we think, Harry.' Kezia cut him off. 'What's his alibi?'

'Pub. The Red Lion. All evening.'

'Who else?'

'Ed Lambert. He manages the Stainthorpe Shoot. Their land borders the Coopers.' There'd been ongoing disputes over the bridleway through the woods where the Stainthorpe Shoot put the release pens for the young birds. Someone vandalised them. Foxes got in and massacred the lot. Lambert accused Cooper of being behind it.'

'And what happened?'

'Cooper denied it. And we couldn't prove anything. Anyway, Ms Stainthorpe told us to let it go. Said the insurance had paid up, so it wasn't worth pursuing.'

'Ms Stainthorpe?' Kezia asked.

'Wanda Stainthorpe.'

'I don't think I've met her.'

'You'd remember if you had. Ex-army and tough as— Quite impressive. She's not been around for a while. Leaves Ed Lambert to run the shoot now.'

'Tough?'

'Well. No-nonsense. Not the sort to suffer fools.'

'A tall woman with faded blond hair? And a scar or something running through her eyebrow?'

'That's her. You've met her?'

'Maybe. Any other suspects?'

'No, but Giles, Cooper's son, had a bit of a reputation.'

'I know. But anything specific?'

'Not really. Mixed with the wrong people. Not averse to easy money. Rumours he let the stables be used to store illegal substances. Once you get involved with the drug trade, it can go very wrong. Especially if you want out. I was surprised they – we – weren't looking harder at Giles.'

They were silent for a few minutes. Josh thought about drugs and, of course, the Kingsleys. It was a natural progression. Then he remembered something Sean had said. About David and Giles. David had lent Giles money for the burger van Giles had run with Sean. There'd been sightings of a mysterious van. And Sean thought Giles had been using it as a dark kitchen. Mind you, there was nothing illegal about that.

'Josh,' Kezia said. 'You should go.'

She was planning something. Something she thought he shouldn't know about. Part of him didn't want to know what and part of him worried about... Well, he was just worried.

'Just one last thing,' Kezia asked. 'Did they find a tarot deck at the stables?'

Josh hesitated.

'No,' he said eventually.

'It was the Sun in Chloe Cooper's hands, wasn't it?' she said. 'And the Rider–Waite deck?'

But Josh shook his head. He would say no more about the tarot cards. He'd been told to keep it to himself and that was that. Although of all the things they'd discussed it was the one that needed looking into. Tarot cards at the scene of both the Cooper killings and the murder of Peter Walker. There had to be a connection. Why wouldn't Carter investigate?

He made a decision. He was going to look into it himself. But on his own. No more confiding in other people. Time to trust his own judgement.

'I'm going to see Boyes,' Harry said. 'I have good reason as he hasn't paid me yet for the last job I did. He might not be the killer but he knows things about the Coopers. Maybe other people who they'd fallen out with.'

'No,' Josh said. 'Leave it to the police.' He knew it was hopeless, though. Nothing he said was going to stop them. And actually he didn't blame them for trying.

'I'll help too.' Mrs Monroe's voice was low but vehement. 'That man insulted me. He should be ashamed of himself.'

'Are you talking about DCI Carter?' Kezia asked.

'Yes. He said I was a liar.'

'So he did. And me, too.'

'What was all that about your ex-husband?'

'I don't know.'

'That Carter man was very persistent.'

'Like I said, I don't know.'

Josh found himself repeating Sergeant Beresford's words. 'Carter has a bee in his bonnet about the Kingsleys. Everyone knows that. He even told me to let you know the police could offer you round-the-clock protection if necessary.'

Kezia stopped pacing.

'The Kingsleys?' This was Harry.

'You know them?'

'My own family aren't exactly pure as the driven snow. Strictly petty stuff though. And they'd never tread on the Kingsleys' turf.'

'We might have to,' Kezia said.

Josh tried again. 'The Kingsleys are dangerous. Leave them alone. Don't get involved. Leave the investigating to the police.'

They stared at him, all three of them with no intention of doing what he asked. He knew there were no words that would persuade them otherwise.

'Not the Kingsleys, Kezia. Please promise me you won't go near them.'

'He's right,' Harry said. 'You don't see it like I do. You've no children and even if you did they'd be aiming for university and good careers. There's not much in Thorpe for kids like Marty and his friends. The Kingsleys – or their low-life employees – prey on the youngsters, fill their heads with ideas of money and status, then set them to work delivering drugs. Every time you see a kid speeding somewhere on a bike or a scooter, they're not heading off to Scouts or football or tennis, they're working for the Kingsleys. And once they're in they'll never get out. They end up in prison or as addicts on the street. They get beaten up and killed, either by the people they're working for or caught up in rival gang warfare. Life is very cheap to people like the Kingsleys.'

He took a deep shuddering breath.

'Why don't your lot do more to stop them?' Harry addressed Josh.

It was unanswerable. They tried but it was hopeless. The OGCs carried on operating from prison. Or rival gangs took over. It crossed his mind for the first time that he might be better staying in Local Policing. At least you had a chance of helping.

Harry turned to Mrs Monroe, who'd been chewing along to every one of his vehement words.

'Could you get back in touch with Charlie Cooper?' he asked. 'See what else your vision might tell you. Is that possible?'

'Not without the cloth,' Mrs Monroe said. 'We need it.'

The anger provoked by the thought of Carter had faded from Mrs Monroe's face, leaving only lips compressed in a rigid line and a certain mulish quality to her eyes.

Kezia stared at her for a few seconds. 'There is something else we might be able to do,' she said. 'But only, I think, if we're desperate.'

'I am desperate,' Harry said.

'We should try everything else first. Talk to Boyes and investigate Sean. And if nothing comes of that... We'd need your help though, Josh.'

Once again all three of them turned to look at him.

THIRTY
LAUREN

SAME DAY

Lauren looked up from the roll of fabric she was cutting into trapeziums, laid out to get the maximum number possible. Normally she enjoyed the mathematics of economical cutting even if it only saved a fraction of a penny per handbag. But today she was feeling a bit grim after the last couple of days' drama. She'd made the right decision though. No point going over and over it. She forced her mind back to the cutting. This material had been a bargain – an end of line she'd picked up cheap, knowing its dull colour but faint sheen was perfect for her more classic handbag models.

Someone peered in through the array of handbags, gloves and belts displayed in her shop window. Lauren bent back down over the fabric as the door opened. She would have liked to get this cutting finished before dealing with a client. If it was a client. She was still being pestered by people wanting to gossip about the Coopers. The sooner word got round that she'd split up with Sean the better.

'Hi, Lauren.'

It was Kezia.

'Sorry to bother you, but you said you could mend my handbag and I'm here to take you up on it because the handle has come away completely. And I brought a couple of the photos I took of you at the salon and at the panto.'

She passed her bag over to Lauren. The handle had separated from the body of the bag, tearing a square of leather away with it. It wasn't going to be so easy to mend now.

'Did someone try to snatch it?' Lauren asked.

Kezia shook her head.

'It's been given a good wrench. I can mend it but I don't have any leather the same colour.'

Given that the bag was a patchwork of different leathers, it probably wouldn't matter. She went into her back room and returned with the scrap box.

'Let's see what would work.'

She gathered a handful of leather pieces and held them to the bag.

'What about this?' She held out a rectangle of burgundy leather.

Kezia rubbed it between her fingers, then sniffed it. It seemed a strange thing to do; the place smelled of leather anyway. Rich and warm. Lauren took the piece from her fingers, folded it into a square and held it in place on the handbag.

'I think this looks good.'

The lining of the handbag had torn away too.

'Maybe I could give you this too?' Kezia hauled a grubby plastic bag onto the counter and pulled out a corner of furry material.

'I don't use fur.'

'It's not real.'

'Even so. I—'

'It's not for you. It's for the pantomime. They were asking for fur for the cat costume in the *Gazette*. I guess they need it even more now they're having to replace...'

'Chloe?'

'Yes.'

'How's that going?'

'Fine. Luckily Rachel had already started learning the lines as Chloe was probably leaving anyway. Going to London. Some drama course. She was very talented.'

'I didn't know she was going.'

'Not many people did. She didn't want her father to find out until it was sure. He wasn't keen on her acting, thought it was a waste of time.'

Kezia rubbed the burgundy leather back and forth through her fingers.

'Well, could you give the fur to Sean to give to his mother? Didn't you say she sewed for the panto?'

'Sean and I have split up. As of last Friday evening.'

Kezia looked at her steadily and blinked a few times.

'Ah. I see. Why?'

'I found out he'd been lying to me.' She didn't see why she should lie about it. 'I told you he gambled?'

'Yes.'

'He swore to me he'd stopped but something didn't add up. So I asked a friend of his. And he's been playing poker again. For money. And lost a lot. But that's not why. I've kept our finances completely separate since the first time. I don't even care if he gambles. But I hate being lied to. So I'd rather you gave it to his mum yourself. She— Things aren't easy between us at the moment.'

To put it mildly. She'd hoped Annie would maintain a dignified silence, but she'd made a few very nasty digs when she and Dennis had brought all her stuff back to the flat from their cottage. It would pass. Or at least Lauren hoped it would. Annie had a reputation for never letting anything go when it came to protecting her family.

She went back to the handbag.

'I'll have to replace the lining,' she said.

She rummaged through the box of scraps. A length of cotton

caught her eye. It was printed with a pattern of leaves and twigs and flowers. Herbs, she thought, as she looked closer. Thyme and rosemary, and the rest of the common ones used in cooking. It was pretty, and perfect for Kezia's bag.

'It's a remnant but there's enough,' she said. 'People give me bits and pieces. The leather's most useful but I use the fabrics for linings.'

Kezia didn't say anything.

'Do you like it?'

'Yes, it's fine.'

She hadn't really looked at it.

'Look Lauren, I know it's an awful thing to ask. And you don't have to answer me. Everyone knows Sean and Charlie Cooper had fallen out. But Sean has an alibi, right?'

'Oh, yes. He was somewhere else all right.'

'And you're sure.'

'I'm sure. Every moment of Sunday night is accounted for.'

Kezia's breath hissed through her teeth.

'Why are you asking me all this?'

'Because I don't think Mar— the boy they've arrested is guilty.'

'Kezia. You need to be very careful about going round saying things like that.'

'I know. Believe me, I know. But... Sean knew the Coopers. Maybe he knows who else might have...'

She tailed off again.

'Sean had very little to do with the Coopers after Chloe and the pregnancy and then falling out with Giles.' Lauren thought for a moment. 'He did say the police should have investigated Giles. He was always a bit dodgy. Charlie Cooper's land extends into the woods south of the yard. They're useless for the horses but Giles used the old barn there for storing things he maybe shouldn't.'

She piled the fabrics and leather back into the box.

'And Sean's falling-out with Charlie?'

'Charlie Cooper decided Sean's reluctance to become a father justified him making it difficult for Sean to see Freddy. It all came to a head last year. Sean and his mum went over there to try to sort something out. They had a blazing row and Charlie Cooper got his gun and threatened to shoot them both if they didn't leave straight away. It shook Annie to the core.'

Kezia's eyes were fixed on the doorframe behind Lauren, as she took in what Lauren had said.

'I need to get on, Kezia. Will you leave your bag with me?'

'Of course. How much—'

'I told you, no charge. A thank-you for the photos, if you like.'

'If you're sure. One other thing. Did Sean ever mention the Coopers having tarot cards? Or anything to do with tarot?'

'Tarot? No. But I don't really know. Why?'

But Kezia shrugged.

'I'll go out the back way. It's much quicker.'

'Sure. I'll bolt it after you.'

And with a quick thank you, Kezia left.

Lauren watched her go. She'd changed. Hard to put your finger on, but she couldn't imagine the quiet woman of the photoshoot at Zina's salon asking all those questions. She'd said she didn't think the lad they'd arrested was guilty. She was the most unlikely person to be investigating a murder.

She went back to her trapeziums, but something niggled at the back of her mind. Something Kezia's questions had awoken. And it came to her.

Just she wasn't sure what to do about it. Except the police should be told.

THIRTY-ONE

KEZIA

SAME DAY

Harry's words echoed in my thoughts. *I am desperate,* he'd said. So was I. Otherwise I wouldn't be sitting here on the bed in Marty's room in Harry's flat clutching the tarot deck with the missing cards and fighting the urge to ask them for guidance. I'd learned little from Lauren and I suspected my trip to see Sean's father, Dennis, with Alan tomorrow would be equally fruitless.

I'd grabbed the tarot deck and a few clothes when I'd risked going back to Josh's flat last night. I didn't dare go back again.

They'd turned up at the allotment. After I'd been talking to Alan. Two of them. Told me Miles Kingsley wasn't happy about me living at Josh's. That I was to keep away from him and the police. Told me to stop harassing David. Told me they'd be watching me. So politely that at first I hadn't understood I was being threatened. It was only when the bigger one had pulled a knife and carved a broken heart on my table that I'd got the message. *To remind me,* the other one had said, letting his smooth veneer crack for a few seconds so I saw the threat underneath.

Going to the police with Mrs Monroe had been dangerous. But she wouldn't go without me.

I'd followed their instructions to the letter until then. Kept away from Josh. Kept away from David. Stayed at Mrs Monroe's the first night and only gone back to the flat in the early hours this morning. And when Mrs Monroe had asked me to go to the police with her, I'd walked round Thorpe for a couple of hours first until I was sure no one was following me.

I'd forgotten about Hamish though. The press outside the station when we'd left had been a nasty surprise. I was in the background of some of the photos. All I could do now was lie low and hope they were right when they told me they'd know every word I said if I went to the police.

Because I'd been very careful when I'd spoken about David. Some of it had even been true.

I shut my eyes, laid the cards out and picked one.

I didn't look.

I am desperate, Harry had said.

I looked.

The Empress.

Not what I was expecting. And not helpful at all.

The Empress is a full-figured woman with a peaceful aura, surrounded by lush forest and golden wheat. She wears a robe patterned with pomegranates – the ancient symbol of fertility – and she is, indeed, the personification of fertility, femininity and abundance.

She always reminded me of my mother, who adored babies. Everything about them, from conception, through pregnancy and birth. She loved them.

She wasn't so keen when they started to have minds and wills of their own, so every three years or so she found another lover and fell pregnant again. I was her last. Or almost her last.

She became pregnant once more after me. I must have been four or five because I remember her big, swollen belly getting in the way of climbing into my place on her lap. I remember her breath in my hair as she whispered that my little brother or sister was inside and waiting to come out and play with me.

Zina said the baby was born dead.

And afterwards, whether it was an early menopause or infertility caused by the stillbirth, she never had another pregnancy. Eventually she gave up and searched for something else to fill the emptiness. For a while it was a commune living off the land in the north of Scotland. Then a big house with bare floorboards and no doors in a city by the sea – maybe Brighton – probably a squat. A time spent walking and camping in old Scout tents with a group of hippies. None of them ever lasted.

I put the card back into the deck. Thinking about my mother wasn't going to help me find out who killed the Coopers.

THIRTY-TWO

MRS MONROE

THURSDAY

To be honest, Mrs Monroe was having second thoughts about visiting Boyes with Harry. She'd said she'd go when she was still fired up with annoyance at the horrid police officer who'd told Kezia's nephew they'd both been lying. She should be used to people doubting her gifts. On bad days she doubted them herself, aware that the flashing insights of her youth came rarely now. It was mostly her instinctive understanding and ability to read people that got her by.

She only did good though. The sad people who came to her, desperate for some message from their dear dead, went away comforted. And the ones seeking enlightenment about their future spent time considering themselves and what they really wanted. It was all for the best.

So Carter's casual dismissal of them both had stung. But mainly because he was wrong about them lying. Wrong, wrong, wrong. And she should know.

She looked out through the rain-coated windscreen. The wiper on the passenger side of Harry's van barely worked, simply smearing the water over the glass to give a soft edge to the grey day outside and blur the stark lines of tree branches and fence posts that punctuated the passing countryside.

'How will you get Boyes to talk about the Coopers?' she asked Harry.

'I'll start with the money he owes. Tell him I need it because of paying for lawyers for Marty. It'll be easy to lead on to the murders and the Coopers.'

True enough.

'That's Boyes's Farm,' he said.

He drove straight past.

'Aren't we going in?'

She looked back and saw a car pulling out of the farm entrance.

'No, I want to check something first.'

He pulled up a little further along the lane and parked next to a track leading into the woods on their left. On the other side two horses, their manes flattened by the rain, gazed at them over the hedge.

'Where are we?'

'To get to Cooper's Stables by car, you drive up this lane, turn left onto the main road, then left again into the stable entrance. But if you were on foot, or a bike, you'd cut up the old bridleway here. It goes through these woods to the back of the stables. That's what Marty used to do. I'd pick him up here on the nights when he had college the next day. He'd see to the horses over there first. He's very fond of the big one.'

Mrs Monroe glanced over at the horses. They both looked pretty big to her.

'I went to the Red Lion yesterday evening to check Boyes's alibi. He was very drunk that night, so they took his keys away and told him to walk home. The shortest way would have been the bridleway – I think anyway, and I want to check I'm right. The Coopers were already dead when he left the pub but he might have seen something.'

Mrs Monroe looked at the track the other side of the gate. The ground looked very muddy and she didn't fancy a walk in the rain.

'I'll wait in the van.'

He opened the glove compartment, pushed aside a carton of cigarettes and pulled out a key. 'I might have a look in Cooper's cottage while I'm there. I brought Marty's key.'

Harry was a long time.

A very long time.

Mrs Monroe sat in the passenger seat with her knees less than a foot away from the glove compartment.

If only it wasn't raining, she could get out and walk. Go and say hello to the poor horses in the field. Surely they should have coats on or something. There was a barn of sorts on the far side of the field. Why they didn't go and shelter in there?

There wasn't much else to look at apart from the horses. Nothing to distract her. That was the problem with the countryside. Once you'd seen a few trees and hills, you'd seen them all really. She didn't mind a drive out on a nice, sunny day, especially if it involved a coffee somewhere in a pleasant café or even a shandy in a pub – and a cigarette.

No.

No, no, no.

Tomorrow would be a week since she'd stopped. She couldn't cave in now. Damn Harry. Her hand reached towards the glove compartment.

A car drew up alongside the van. A big pickup. With two black retrievers in the back. Its window slid down. A woman with scraped-back blond hair stared down. A scar bisected one of her eyebrows and gave her a lopsided look. She gestured to Mrs Monroe to open her window. The van was sufficiently old to have a handle, so Mrs Monroe obliged.

'You can't park here,' the woman said. She looked beyond her into the van. 'Where's your driver?'

The lifelong habit of politeness, drummed into Mrs Monroe by her parents, suddenly left her.

'Why not? It's a public highway.'

The woman got out of the car, slamming the door behind her. The sudden noise startled the dogs and they barked. She silenced them with a swift hand gesture.

'You're blocking my access.'

'It's a bridleway. No vehicles allowed.'

'Not the first part. That's my land.'

Mrs Monroe looked beyond the gate. The woman was quite right. A second gate led off the beginning of the path, with a short track beyond.

'Well, you'll have to wait. The driver'll be back in a minute. I don't have the keys.'

Which was a relief. She didn't fancy trying to manoeuvre Harry's van.

'Where is he?'

'Round about.'

She waved her hand around. And to her relief Harry appeared. The dogs barked again. The woman darted her hand into her car and grabbed something.

'We need to move, Harry. This woman wants to get through the gate.'

Harry turned to the woman.

'No vehicles allowed up there,' he said.

'I'm not going up the bridleway, just onto my land.' The woman withdrew her arm from her car. A shotgun was now visible, leaning against the driver' seat.

'I'm Wanda Stainthorpe. I own the land on the left side of the bridleway.'

'The pheasant shoot.'

'Yes. I manage it.'

So this was the Wanda Stainthorpe that Josh had mentioned. He'd said she'd gone away but clearly she'd come back.

'What happened to Lambert?' Harry asked.

'He left. I'm running it now.'

And probably very well, Mrs Monroe thought. But then

women generally did. Especially ones as tough and capable as Wanda seemed in her battered Barbour and practical boots.

'And I won't stand for anyone driving up the bridleway,' Wanda added.

'We weren't going to.'

'Good.'

She silenced the dogs again, got back into the car and drove a short way down the road, then stopped.

Harry got into the van.

'Let's go see Boyes,' he said. 'I'm sure he'd have taken the short cut and it leads straight past the stables.'

'Did you go inside?'

'Yes. The place was deserted. Just lots of police tape everywhere.'

'And?'

'Nothing to see. Here, you take the key. You'll need it.'

Mrs Monroe took it reluctantly. She'd told Kezia she wasn't prepared to go along with her idea, but she couldn't bring herself to tell Harry.

He turned the van sharply, throwing Mrs Monroe around. Really, it couldn't be good for the steering to squeal so much.

'Wanda Stainthorpe's right to keep an eye on the bridleway though. Something's driven down it and it's been churned up badly.'

Boyes's Farm was a grim place. Harry said Boyes farmed sheep, but there weren't any present. Probably out on the moors or wherever sheep lived. No dogs either. A stack of cans marked *Sheep Dip* was all that revealed the farm's function.

Harry knocked on the door. No answer.

'Let's have a look round.'

There was no sign of Boyes in any of the ramshackle outbuildings filled with the detritus of what Mrs Monroe supposed was modern farming. Mainly an astonishing array of chemicals and methods of applying them to the poor sheep.

A quad bike with a trailer attachment was parked over by a

long-neglected garden, although a small patch of newly dug ground showed someone had recently made an effort. Not that they'd got far. The patch was small and humped. Like a child's grave. Mrs Monroe shuddered.

'He's not here,' she said. 'Let's go.'

'Let's try the house again.'

Harry hammered on the door this time. 'Boyes,' he yelled. Still no answer.

'Must be out with the sheep.' He winked at Mrs Monroe and tried the latch. The door opened. He went inside.

Mrs Monroe hesitated, then followed Harry in. The door led straight into the kitchen, a cold and dank room.

'What are we doing?' she asked.

'Just having a quick look.'

Harry crossed to the dresser and rummaged through the piles of papers and letters dumped on it. The stove hadn't been lit for a while judging by the rust running round its rim. Boyes obviously cooked on the old gas hob whose surface was spattered with dark grease blobs and bits of cooking detritus. A smell that was both stale and damp permeated the air.

'Nothing here,' Harry said, dropping the pamphlets in his hand back onto the dresser. He knocked a vase with some dead flowers onto the floor. It survived the fall. As he picked it up and put it back, something caught Mrs Monroe's eye.

'I'm going to have a look in the rest of the house.'

'Do you think we...'

But Harry had disappeared through a door on the far side of the kitchen. After a few seconds Mrs Monroe followed him. It led into a corridor. First on the right was a bathroom as unsavoury as the kitchen. A quick peep behind the mildewed shower curtain revealed Boyes used the bath to wash the worst of the mud off his boots. Harry appeared in the doorway.

'We have to go,' he said. 'Now.'

His face was white, emphasising the dark bristle coating his chin.

'Has he come back?'

'No. We're going now.'

'What's happened?'

'Boyes. I found his body. He's dead. No, don't go and look. I'm sure.'

She pushed past him, down the corridor to the sitting room.

For a moment she thought Harry was wrong. Boyes was merely asleep. Nodded off with his face in his meal. Drunks did that all the time, and the table bore the same medley of glasses and bottles as the one in the kitchen. But the red spots she'd taken to be splatters of tomato ketchup were too many and too large. Nevertheless she nudged his shoulder. He didn't move.

'We have to go now.' Harry's voice from behind made her jump.

'What are we going to do?' she said when they stepped out into the yard.

'I'm trying to think.'

'We should report it.'

Harry's eyes fluttered with the speed of his thoughts.

'He was shot, wasn't he? I think he was shot. And with a shotgun. Like the Coopers were. It must have been the same person. Don't you see? Marty couldn't have done it. The police will have to reopen the case.'

'Can we report it anonymously?'

'Why?'

Mrs Monroe wasn't sure.

'They'll know I was here anyway,' Harry said. 'I touched the doorframe and some of the bottles. They have my fingerprints. Did you touch anything?'

She thought quickly. The bathroom door had been open already, and the shower curtain so disgusting she'd pushed it aside with her arm.

'His shoulder.'

'I doubt they'll get prints off his jumper. You go. No one need know you've been here.'

But she hesitated.

'Go on. I need to report it now. There'll be CCTV of my van on its way here. They'll work out when I arrived.'

He was right but there was something she had to check first. She turned without a word and went back inside, into the kitchen and over to the dresser. There they were. They'd been covered by the vase Harry had knocked over. In the middle of some leaflets from West Cumberland Farmers and Carrs Billington.

Two tarot cards. In a plastic bag.

Kezia had mentioned tarot cards. Several times. Mrs Monroe looked carefully. The Death card was one of them, with its skeleton in black armour on a white horse. The card people feared the most, although they didn't need to. It had its positive side, meaning the end of a part of your life that was no longer right for you and the beginning of something new and exciting.

The other card was the King of Pentacles. A strange one to find here. It represented wealth and success. Grapes and vines adorned a richly dressed king on a carved throne with a sceptre and golden coin.

Neither card made any sense.

She thought about taking them but changed her mind. Much better to let the police find them. She left them in a prominent place on the dresser and told Harry about them.

She was a fair distance out of the farm and up the lane when the first police car drove by. A very quick response.

She hoped Harry would be all right.

THIRTY-THREE
DENNIS PRICE

SAME DAY

Dennis drove the fork into the ground and turned the earth, giving the worms time to wriggle away. The soil was good here where he'd made his vegetable patch. He took care of it though. There was a plentiful supply of well-rotted manure available locally. If he was quick enough he'd get a wheelbarrow-load in before the dark clouds heading towards him from Thorpe dumped their cargo of rain. He needed the exercise anyway. It would help him sleep. The arrival of his sixties had heralded the impossibility of sleeping all through the night. Mostly it was his bladder that woke him, and he'd yet to acquire his wife, Annie's, ability to get up, pee, then go straight back to sleep.

Now the child kept him awake.

Not quite two, Freddy didn't think the nights were for sleeping. It was fine to snuggle down in bed all pink from his bath and sleep for a few hours, but a few hours were all he needed to recharge his batteries. He woke Dennis every night around three trying to climb out of his cot. When he failed, he'd wail for Annie. Even with both doors shut, Dennis heard Freddy giggling as she chanted 'Five Little Pigs' to him or played endless games of Peep Bo.

And since Sean had moved back in, after his sudden break-up with Lauren, Annie seemed to look after Freddy full time. Sean really wasn't cut out for fatherhood. In fact, he suspected Sean's reluctance to become a father was as much due to his lack of interest in children as his fear of passing on neurofibromatosis.

Annie told him Freddy's sleeplessness wouldn't last. He was traumatised after being so long without food, water or company in that house of horrors. Dennis's mind veered away from thinking of the slaughter at the stables.

He'd suggested Sean spend some of the supposed hundreds of thousands young Freddy was going to inherit on childcare, but Sean had mumbled something about it looking bad if he asked the estate for money straight away. Dennis understood his reluctance. He'd had a nasty few hours while Sean had been with the police. Such a relief when he'd said he was with Annie and, of course, they'd both been seen in the Italian restaurant. He leaned on his fork until the breathlessness passed. He didn't like to think what the police might have thought otherwise.

The threatened rain started and Dennis put the fork in the shed and went into the house. He'd hoped that the rain would hold off until Alan and the woman with the strange name came round to pick up the rotavator. He was happier with strangers outside. There was more space. Easier for them all. He hoped Alan had warned her. Nothing was worse than seeing people's shock if they saw his face without having been told about it.

He unloaded the dishwasher, then wondered if he had time for a short nap. Probably not. Which was a pity because the house was quiet. Annie had taken Freddy round to show him off to some friends. He hoped she wouldn't come back before Alan had gone. Freddy was the same age as Alan's son when he and Alan's wife, Janice, had been killed by an out-of-control car.

Harry Appleton had been the driver. And now Harry's son had been arrested for the Cooper murders. Alan had said nothing, but Dennis had sensed his satisfaction when the news had broken. Dennis had felt relieved too.

If only that medium woman would stop spouting her nonsense about the killer still being out there on live television. Alan was right, people like her shouldn't be given a platform. They could do immeasurable damage.

Dennis heard the noise of a car turning into the cul-de-sac. It was Alan. And driving his old Jaguar Mark X. Fancy that. He never normally took it out if there was a risk of rain. He stood outside the front door, making sure his face was easily seen. Better to give the woman a chance to get used to it.

She walked up the drive steadily though, and held out her hand to him. Her gaze never left his face.

'Hello,' she said. 'I'm Kezia.'

'Dennis,' he said. And because she was still holding out her hand, he shook it. 'Mine's a bit lumpy and bumpy, I'm afraid. But I expect Alan warned you.'

He was surprised and pleased to see that she didn't hesitate before saying yes, Alan had told her about his neurofibromatosis.

The second surprise was that Alan had fallen for her. His expression gave him away. Dennis had thought Alan would never get over his wife's death. God knows, enough of his friends had tried to match him up with single women – or their wives had. Maybe he'd finally – how did the therapists put it? – achieved closure.

He invited them in, thinking he should make an effort to get to know her, and sat them down in the front room, still mercifully clear of the child paraphernalia that had taken over the rest of the house, although Annie's sewing machine filled the bay window and bits of the fur coats she was taking apart to remake the cat costume for the pantomime were strewn over the back of the sofa. He piled them onto a chair already covered with remnants of the cottons she used in her dressmaking, knowing she'd be annoyed as there was probably a reason they'd been laid out like that.

'My wife does the costumes for the panto, you know. She's a wonderful sewer, makes all her own clothes.'

Kezia smiled. She looked familiar. But that was Thorpe for you. Not in the least bit like Janice. No, she was small and dark and awkward. Maybe unwell? Or was it the impression given by her pale skin and her eyes, the colour of fading bruises, that shifted around, never resting on one place more than a few seconds.

'Is your grandson here? Alan told me about him.'

'No, Annie's taken him out.'

'And how is he? I mean after the ordeal.'

'He's fine.'

'Children are so resilient, aren't they?'

'It seems so.'

He'd thought she'd taken his appearance in her stride, but now she seemed to be ill at ease and covering it up by asking a myriad of questions.

'He's nearly two, isn't he? It's an exhausting age.'

'You have children?'

'No. You've just got the one son? Sean, isn't it? And the one grandchild?'

'Yes, Freddy's the only one, and he's a bit of a lucky chance. Sean never wanted children.'

He wished he hadn't said that but it had seemed only polite to explain. Now, though, he'd opened himself to a horde of questions about why Sean hadn't wanted children. He turned quickly to Alan. 'I see you came in the Jaguar. How is the old girl?'

Alan droned on about ride quality and handling and how he'd taken the suspension apart. As Dennis had known he would.

'Did Sean not want children because of the neurofibromatosis?' Kezia asked when Alan paused for breath. 'I'm right in thinking he has it, doesn't he?'

'Yes.'

Sean had seemed perfect when he was born, but they'd tested him all the same and the results were positive for the condition. He'd developed the coffee-coloured patches on his skin very early on but nothing else. His teenage years had been a nightmare. Every outbreak of acne meant a trip to the specialist in case it was the tumours that had disfigured Dennis's face so badly.

'And what do you think of Alan's Jaguar?' he asked. 'They don't make cars like her any more.'

'Er, it's very nice. Not that I know much about cars. I wondered—'

'What do you drive?'

It was a stupid question but the first one that came to his lips.

'I have an old Fiesta – bright orange.'

'Kezia lives in a flat in the centre of Thorpe, so she walks everywhere,' Alan said.

'And how do you find that?'

'I— It's fine. Very convenient.'

'It's one of the new flats,' Alan said. 'Round the back of the Co-op. Got their own parking spaces in the Co-op car park too, which is very useful considering how difficult parking in town is. They need to get the buses sorted.' And Alan was off again on the shortfalls of local public transport.

For once, Dennis was glad Alan had an opinion on everything. Nothing deflected Kezia though. She interrupted him.

'Living there is very convenient,' she said. 'So Freddy doesn't have neurofibromatosis?'

'No, only fifty per cent of children who have a parent with it are born with the condition. Freddy was one of the lucky ones.'

'There are tests, aren't there? Before they're born? Didn't—'

He cut her off.

'Yes, there are tests.'

And then he closed his mouth and fixed his eyes on her face, daring her to probe further. For once her pale skin showed a hint of colour. She looked away first.

Of course there were tests. But by the time they'd learned Chloe was pregnant, Sean had fallen out with the Coopers. Not that Annie had wanted them to discuss the options with the family. Testing had been available when Annie was pregnant. They'd tried it the first two times and Annie had miscarried. Probably because of the tests, so she'd refused to have one for Sean.

'Word is the stables are worth a lot of money.' Kezia's embarrassment hadn't lasted long.

Even Alan looked put out by this comment.

'Sean won't touch Freddy's money,' he said rapidly.

There was a brief silence, but Dennis had the feeling Kezia was building up to another question.

'Did you remember the key, Alan?' he said. 'You've still got the key to the cottage.'

'I forgot. Sorry. I'll bring it with me next week. You still on for fishing on Monday?'

'Sean must have been relieved when the police arrested the killer so quickly.'

Kezia's face was devoid of anything but a friendly smile. Surely she realised what she was implying.

Alan did.

'I think we all were, Kezia,' he said. 'No one liked the thought of a killer rampaging round the countryside.'

'But everyone knew the killings were personal. Homicidal lunatics are few and far between. Don't you think so, Mr Price?'

'Yes,' he said shortly. And then, because explaining might shut her up, 'Sean had an alibi for the whole evening. In case you were wondering. Luckily for him he took his mother out.'

'How lovely. Where did they go?'

Again nothing on her face to suggest this was anything other than a friendly question.

'They had a meal at Mario's in Thorpe and then on to the light show at Fountains Abbey.'

'The light show's wonderful, isn't it?'

'I didn't go.'

'It's definitely worth a visit.'

'I don't like places with lots of people. It's why I like fishing. I have a cottage out near Leyburn on the River Burn. Lovely place. Alan and I fish there every Monday. Salmon, grayling and, of course, trout. We both make flies, you know. It's a bit of a speciality of ours.'

He sounded like Alan in full flood but nothing else would shut her up. She was eyeing him already, waiting for him to take a breath so she could get a word in. Well, he wasn't going to let her. He could talk about flies and the different types and how you made them for an eternity.

Her phone bleeped, enough to distract him briefly, and she took advantage of his hesitation.

'I went to the light show a few weeks ago,' she said. 'It was absolutely packed though. I was meeting up with friends but I couldn't find them. I hope Sean and your wife weren't trying to meet anyone.'

Dennis was saved from answering by the sound of a key in the front door. Sean came in.

'Where's Mum?' he asked, ignoring Alan and Kezia.

'She's taken Freddy to some friends. You remember Alan, don't you? And this is a friend of his. Kezia.'

Sean nodded abruptly.

'Your father was telling us about your trip to Fountains Abbey. The show's wonderful, isn't it?' Kezia said.

'Er, yes.'

'My favourite part was the rotating globe.'

'I— Yes, it was good.'

'Is something wrong, Sean?' Dennis asked.

Sean's normally settled face was twitching with different expressions.

'Mum isn't answering her phone.'

This was hardly unusual. Annie only answered when it suited her.

'And there's been another killing. The old guy from the farm near the Coopers. Shot, just like them.'

'Boyes? Johnny Boyes?' This was Kezia.

'Yes.'

'When?'

'I don't know.'

She got up and left the room. Dennis saw her appear outside the back window, with a phone pressed to her ear.

These killings unsettled everyone and made them want to check in with their loved ones.

Like Sean.

He rang Annie. Just to be sure. To be absolutely sure. And she answered. Then told him in great detail how all her friends had thought Freddy was wonderful. He managed to extract the information that she was on her way home, then finished the call.

'Your mum's OK.'

'I worked that out.'

'How did you hear about Johnny Boyes?' Kezia had come back in.

'Carrs Billington driver delivering. He said the police were all over the farm. He thought they'd arrested someone already. Caught in the act.'

'They think it happened this morning?' Dennis asked.

'I don't know, Dad. Not for sure. Although someone said Boyes was at the abattoir first thing today, so possibly. I'm in the clear if it was. I've been at the van with Megan since the crack of dawn. Surrounded by people. No way I could have nipped off to Boyes's place.'

'You think they're linked? Boyes's killing and the Coopers'?' This was Alan.

'Stands to reason, doesn't it?'

'Then Marty Appleton couldn't have done it. He's locked up,' Alan said.

Dennis tried to think what that meant for his family.

'I suppose the police will let him go,' Alan added. He looked at Dennis.

Had Alan guessed he might be as unhappy about the thought of Marty Appleton being released as Alan was?

'I'm not so sure.' Kezia stared into space. 'The police are going to suspect the worst.'

'Could you ask your nephew?' Alan turned to Dennis. 'Kezia's nephew is a police officer.'

Dennis realised why she was familiar. The police. There'd been pictures of her in the papers outside the station. She'd been with that dreadful psychic woman. The one who'd been insisting the police had got everything wrong.

He began to suspect the troublesome medium had sent her here to ask all those questions about Sean, about his illness and his alibi. He didn't like it. He didn't like it one bit.

THIRTY-FOUR

JOSH

SAME DAY

Josh peered in through the window of his mother's salon, holding a copy of the *Yorkshire Post* over his head to protect it from the drizzle. If the salon was too busy, he'd wait until later. He didn't want to deal with her clients – many of whom had known him since he was born – interrogating him about the Cooper murders, the police force in general and his love life.

It was quiet though. One of the juniors swept while the other polished the huge mirrors lining three sides of the salon. No clients apart from two women reading with their heads under the dryers. And no sign of his mother. She was probably in the office.

He went in, gave Mrs Vine in one of the dryers a quick wave and shot into the office before she could open her mouth. His mother was staring at the computer screen on her desk. She looked up and a start of pleasure lightened her slightly sad-looking expression.

'Everything all right, Mum?'

'Yes, yes. Just trying to get the accounts ready for the accountants. VAT time. So what brings my favourite son in to see me?'

'Just fancied a chat, you know. Haven't seen you for a bit.'

'Yes, I noticed.'

'Mum.'

'I know, you're busy. Was there anything in particular you wanted to chat about? Or is this really a social call?'

She knew him too well.

'How's Dad?'

'Bored. It's too wet for golf and half his cronies have skipped off to catch some late sun. And don't you start. He doesn't stop complaining that we can't do that because I'm still working.'

His dad, a decade older than his mum, had taken early and well-funded retirement from the accountancy firm he'd owned and had been stunned when Zina hadn't immediately followed suit.

'But you've not come to ask about your father, have you? What is it, Josh?'

'Mrs Walker. She was a client, wasn't she?'

'Do you mean... Peter's mother? The boy—'

'Yes, I do. They sold up and moved a few months after his death. Do you know where they went? I thought, if it was nearby, she might still come to you.'

He'd noticed women were perfectly happy to change doctors when they moved but reluctant to leave their hairdresser.

'She came a couple of times. But it was too far really. Plus this place – Thorpe – reminded her of everything.'

'So where did they go?'

'Is this police business, Josh?'

'No. I could probably find out by asking at work but I'd have to explain why.'

'And you think I won't ask you?'

He shrugged and waited until she laughed.

'Mrs Walker asked me for details of how I coloured her hair before she went. So she could tell her new hairdresser. In Skipton. Although they went to a village nearby. Embsay. A cottage by the reservoir, she told me. On the Devonshire estate.'

'Thanks Mum.'

'Anything else I can help you with?'

She was laughing at him. He was sure.

'Yup. You can tell me what the King of Swords means.'

'Really?'

'Yes, really.'

'Er. Well, quickly, it's about clarity of mind and intellect. Generally it means you should use your brain, use logic, to navigate the way ahead. Maybe call on expert help to guide you.'

Josh could see no way in which this related to an eleven-year old's body found shot in a ditch on the moors. With a knife thrust into his chest afterwards.

'Does that help?' she asked.

'No. But never mind. I didn't think it would.'

He stood up to go.

'Mrs Walker asked me about tarot,' she said.

Josh stopped. 'Really?'

'A couple of weeks before Peter disappeared. She wanted to know what a certain card meant.'

'The King of Swords?'

'No. She didn't know which one it was. But from her description, I knew it was the Ten of Swords. It's unmistakeable with its picture of a corpse full of swords.'

Ten of Swords. The card Kezia had described to Carter. Did she know something?

'Did Mrs Walker say why?'

'No, but I thought she looked desperately worried.'

He was glad he'd waited out the worst of the rain in Embsay village shop. It hit as he left Thorpe, turning what should have been a gentle hour's drive into nearly two hours of crawl as he peered through the water pouring down his windscreen. The wipers were useless.

The road from Embsay to the reservoir was narrow, but passable at first. However, as it left the intimacy of the close-knit village cottages behind and wound up and onto the moors, it became rougher and rougher, until Josh feared for his tyres. In between stretches of muddy tarmac, where his car slid from one side of the lane to the other, large potholes waited. The underside of his car scraped the edges and added worry about the sump to his other concerns.

He took advantage of a patch of road that had been resurfaced in the last fifty years to squeeze one of the Cadbury's Chocolate Eclairs he'd bought while waiting in the shop out of its wrapper and into his mouth. They were probably his favourite sweets. You could either crunch them straight away and savour the chocolate and caramel together, or let the toffee soften in your mouth until the chocolate oozed out.

He was so concentrated on the road that he missed the house. It was high off the road and set back, only visible when he realised he'd gone too far and turned round.

He stopped at the bottom of a driveway leading up to the house. It struck him as strange that the Walkers had chosen to move to somewhere so deserted and surrounded by the moors where Peter had died. He left the car at the bottom of the driveway and walked up.

She was waiting at the top, wrapped in an ancient mac, her feet shoved into wellingtons and carrying a stick. The hair gave her away. It was one of his mother's favourite shades, a streaky mixture of warm and sombre tones of brown that looked almost natural until you noticed a large number of the women in Thorpe had the same colour.

'Mrs Walker,' he called.

'Stay right there,' she yelled back. 'What do you want?'

'Just to talk to you.'

'Who are you?'

'Josh Mason. Zina's son. Zina your hairdresser in Thorpe.'

She walked towards him. The stick he'd thought she carried was a shotgun.

'So you are. Well, Josh Mason, what brings— You're a police officer, aren't you?'

'I'm not here in an official capacity.'

The words sounded pompous to him as soon as they'd left his mouth.

'I am here because I think you might be able to help.'

Before he'd got to Embsay, he'd debated with himself how best to approach the Walkers. And decided he wasn't prepared to lie.

'You heard about the Cooper murders? At the stables.'

She nodded.

'And how a youngster had been arrested?'

'Martin Appleton. Yes, I'd heard.'

He wondered if there was anyone who didn't know Marty Appleton was the youngster they'd arrested.

'Some of us believe he's innocent. And that there might be a connection to... to Peter. You asked my mother something. Before Peter was taken. Something about tarot. You asked her what the Ten of Swords meant and I wondered why.'

'Zina knows a lot about tarot. That's common knowledge.'

'But why did you want to know about that card? Why that particular card?'

'No reason.'

He didn't believe her.

'What's it got to do with the Coopers anyway?' she asked.

'There seems,' he said carefully, 'to be a lot going on with tarot cards that we don't understand. And I think it might have a bearing on the Cooper case. It might mean that Martin Appleton is innocent. None of us want to see him go down for something he didn't do. So will you tell me why, out of the blue, you asked my mother what the Ten of Swords meant?'

She walked over to the stone wall that marked the start of the steep descent to the road and laid the gun on top of it. He followed her. On a clear sunny day, the view would be stunning. Even today, with low cloud and a landscape in grey it reminded him of a Turner painting, all moody and melodramatic. The road was visible all the way down to the reservoir. Was that why they'd moved here? Had something happened to make them wary of unexpected visitors?

'We're leaving, you know,' she said. 'This place was only ever a stopgap. We're going to Australia. They want farmers there, unlike here, but the paperwork has taken a long time. It's finally come through. Only immediate family know. We're flying out on Sunday.'

'I see.'

'The children will be safe then. We thought, once we'd gone, we might try and tell the police everything we know.'

Josh waited. Something told him pressurising her wouldn't work. Besides he had no levers to force the truth out of her. Only the hope that she'd want to do the right thing.

'Except we didn't know who to trust.' She spoke in such a low voice, he almost missed the words.

'Who to trust?'

'You see, every time we reported something to the police it got back to some people who were threatening us. They knew. They knew every little thing we said. And that's why Peter was killed.'

Josh's phone vibrated insistently against his hip bone. Someone was trying to call him. They'd have to wait.

'Will you trust me?' he asked.

'Will I trust you? I don't know. Who sent you?'

'No one. No one knows I'm here. You could shoot me and bury my body out on the moors, or dump me in the reservoir, and no one would know.'

He thought the idea almost amused her. She stretched out her hand and stroked the gun with a half-smile on her face.

'I'd quite like to kill someone,' she said. 'But not you, Zina's son. Not you. Or at least, not yet.'

She kept her hand on the gun while Josh waited.

'You'll have to swear not to tell anyone what I say until Sunday afternoon. Until we're out of here.'

'I promise.'

Her grip tightened on the gun. She picked it up and pointed it at him. It was all he could do not to flinch.

'And I swear,' she said. 'That if you break that promise, I will use this gun. Not on you. Or, at least, not straight away. I'll kill your family first and let you try to live with knowing it's all your fault.'

'I won't break my promise. I wouldn't have even if you hadn't threatened me.'

She took a few breaths, forcing them out of her body noisily, and then spoke. She didn't put the gun down.

'It started a few weeks after we bought the farm, summer of last year. We should have guessed there was a reason it was so cheap but at the time we just thought we'd been lucky. They came round on a Sunday evening after the kids had gone to bed. Two of them. They spoke to Ken. Told him they'd had an arrangement with the previous farmer to use one of the barns up the top of the farm, quite a way away. It had been renovated with hard standing and a proper access road. Power and water as well. They told us they'd run a takeaway fast food business from it but had to move elsewhere when the farmer sold up. It wasn't as convenient so they'd like to move back. Ken would appreciate the rent they were prepared to pay.'

She looked out at the view as she talked, although she kept the gun trained on him. He hoped the safety was on. Her clenched and whitened fingers looked all too likely to slip and press the trigger. Better not to interrupt her, although he was desperate to ask who 'they' were.

'Ken refused. We had plans for the barn. And we didn't like the men. But they kept on coming back to see if we'd changed our minds. A series of things went wrong. Dogs killed a lot of our sheep and machinery was vandalised. Then someone broke in one night while we were asleep and took one of the kids' photos from the fridge and left it on the kitchen table along with the tarot card – the Ten of Swords. That was when I asked Zina what it meant. We guessed it was a warning. Ken rang the police and made an appointment to go in and talk to someone the next day. We didn't want them to come to us.'

Josh waited.

'That was when they took Peter.'

He still waited.

'Straight away. Ken rang in the morning and they snatched Peter on the way back from school. Somehow they knew.'

Finally she put the gun down. With a dismissive gesture as though it disgusted her. It clattered onto the top of the stone wall. She was quiet for a long time. Until Josh felt he had to speak.

'I see,' he said.

'Do you really?' She turned to him. Her cheeks and nose flushed red. 'Do you really see? Because we didn't. We didn't see it coming. And we couldn't see what to do next.'

Josh's phone vibrated again. Just once. Just a message. He was glad she couldn't hear it.

'So we reported Peter missing but nothing else,' she went. 'And prayed. Until we couldn't bear it any more. Until people started hinting Peter had been involved in delivering drugs. Until we thought we could trust the officer in charge. He seemed like a good man. He came round a lot. At the end of the day, when he could have been going home. We had a liaison officer, of course, but he still tried to talk to us himself. So we decided to tell him.'

She rammed her knuckles into her mouth and bit them hard. Josh had questions. Some he thought he knew the answer to. Others he wasn't sure. He didn't want to ask this woman, teetering on the edge of madness, any of them but he had to.

'Was that when...'

'When Peter was killed? Yes. It must have almost immediately. He'd not been dead very long when they found his body.'

'You said, "they". Who were they?'

'They never told us their names. They said they were from the Kingsleys.'

'Did you recognise them?'

She shook her head.

'You know Giles Cooper? Knew Giles Cooper?'

'Not well but yes.'

'And he wasn't one of them?'

'No. The main one was older than him. And smarter. The other, a nasty bit of work, but not Giles.'

'And the senior officer?'

'Carter was his name. Detective Chief Inspector Carter. We rang him and asked him to come over and the next day Peter's body was found. They said he'd been shot and a knife put in his chest afterwards. And the King of Swords was pinned to his sweater. They didn't know why but we did. In case we were stupid enough to think someone else did it.'

THIRTY-FIVE

JOSH

SAME DAY

Josh drove until he was beyond the reservoir and back in Embsay village. He stopped in a car park overlooking a tired-looking children's play area and checked his phone. Kezia had called, several times. And honestly he wasn't sure if he could face calling her back. It would either be another demand for help that he couldn't fulfil or to share some information she thought was vital to the investigation but which would confuse everything even more. He needed time to think. To consider what Mrs Walker had told him. And then come up with a plan.

He put the phone back on the passenger seat and stared out at the rusty swings. It rang immediately. It was Kezia again. He sighed. He'd have to answer it.

Her voice was quiet and firm though when she spoke. Wiped clean of all emotion. She told him Harry and Mrs Monroe had gone to talk to Boyes but found him dead at his farm. Harry had reported it but Mrs Monroe had slipped away, and Kezia was on her way to pick her up.

He realised she didn't expect him to do anything.

Which was a relief.

'There were two tarot cards there, Josh.'

'What? Where?'

'At Boyes's. Two tarot cards in a plastic bag. As if he'd saved them.'

More tarot cards. What did they mean?

He remembered that Boyes had called Beresford yesterday. Had he been calling with information about the Coopers' murders? Because if he had, the sergeant would have put him straight through to Crime.

And Carter.

Was that why he'd been killed?

'Which cards?' he said.

'The Death card and the King of Pentacles.'

Black-armoured death riding a white horse, with corpses on the ground and people begging for mercy.

And the King of Pentacles. Lush and rich, with its meaning of worldly success.

Was the Death card a warning? Like the Ten of Swords sent to the Walkers? Probably. Both sent with Kings.

And then he saw it.

The Kings were simply calling cards.

A King to mean the Kingsley family.

'There's something else,' Kezia said. 'I've got the deck those cards were taken from.'

'What deck? Where did you get it from?'

'From a charity shop.'

'But why didn't you tell me before?'

'Because I wasn't sure and because it's one of Zina's.'

'Mum's?'

'Yes. A Rider–Waite deck.'

'It's a common enough deck. You can't be sure it's hers.'

'But Josh, I *am*. Look, Zina doesn't believe in the power of the cards any more than I do. It's only a bit of fun for her. So she marks the cards. We were both taught how.'

Josh tried to think what it meant.

'There are eight cards missing from this deck including Death and the King of Pentacles. You wouldn't tell me which card was found at the Coopers', but it was the Sun, wasn't it?'

'Yes.' The time for keeping quiet was long gone. Especially if his mother was somehow involved.

'It's one of the missing cards.'

'What are the rest?'

'The other three Kings.'

Shit. No.

'And?'

'The Ten of Swords and the Tower.'

The Ten of Swords. He felt sick. It was too much of a coincidence. Kezia must have the deck the cards had come from.

'You can't think my mother is involved. She'd never...'

'Of course not. Listen, I think David had the deck. I think he took it from Zina, ages ago.'

He waited.

'He always liked it when she did readings. And...'

'And what, Kezia?'

'And then I think he might have given the cards to his family. And they must have used them.'

'You said he had nothing to do with them.'

'I was wrong about that. Very, very wrong. A woman came to the house, you see. My old house. Before I moved out. She gave me a tarot card and told me to tell my husband it didn't scare her. David said she was a nutter and to ignore it.'

'Which card?'

'The Tower.'

Josh tried to think of something to say.

'So I went to ask David about the tarot cards. A couple of days ago. And afterwards... Afterwards Miles Kingsley sent two of his bullies to threaten me. They told me to back off.'

Blood hammered in his ears. How could she have been so stupid?

'You went to see David! What possessed you?'

'He wouldn't hurt me. Besides, he had nothing to do with the Cooper deaths. I asked him, Josh. I asked him straight out. He promised me he didn't. I'd know if he was lying. But he must have warned his family.'

She took a deep breath.

'So would you tell your DCI Carter that I will come in and talk to him. About David and his family. But I'll need protection. You said Carter could arrange it.'

For a moment his mind went blank. He stared at the swings, remembered the thrill of being at the top of the curve as gravity dragged the seat back down but his body felt as though it might fly away.

'Josh?'

His thoughts settled with a thump. She couldn't talk to Carter. Not while there was a chance Carter was passing on information to the Kingsleys as Mrs Walker thought.

'I'd keep Zina out of it,' she said. 'Not mention it was her deck. Just tell them about David.'

He picked his words carefully.

'I will tell my— my colleagues. But I need to think how. There are... You probably know there is corruption within the force. People who feed information back to the families like the Kingsleys.' And worse, he thought. 'So we need to be careful. Promise me you won't talk to anyone. And give me some time to think about the best way to handle this.'

'Can we discuss it later?'

'No. And don't go back to the flat. Go away. Stay in a hotel somewhere far away.'

'I can't do that. Not while Marty's in prison. I've got things to do. Especially if you don't want me to talk to the police.'

'But Kezia—'

'No, Josh. I'll call you later. I'm going to need your help.'

She cut the call.

He scrabbled through the glove compartment until he found an old envelope, and made a list of the cards Kezia told him were missing from his mother's deck. And what he knew about them.

Ten of Swords – Sent to Walkers. Warning?

King of Swords – On Peter Walker's body

The Sun – Sent to Chloe Cooper with note. Warning?

A King – Also sent to Chloe Cooper

Death – Sent to Boyes

King of Pentacles – Sent to Boyes

Tower – Sent to woman who accused DK of trying to scare her?

Seven cards. Seven cards out of the eight missing. Only one of the kings unaccounted for. It was probably sent to the woman along with the Tower.

Kezia was right. David's family was behind all this, although he wasn't sure exactly what *this* was.

Who could he tell? No one here in Thorpe. It was too dangerous.

THIRTY-SIX
MRS MONROE

SATURDAY

The wind was cold tonight. As soon as Mrs Monroe got out of the car, it nipped at her ankles in the gap between the trainers and sweatpants Kezia had made her buy. She wanted them to wear brand new clothes. Less chance of leaving some trace of themselves behind that could be tracked back to them. It's called Locard's Exchange Principle, Kezia had said. It's a forensics thing. *The perpetrator of a crime will bring something into the crime scene and leave with something from it.* We can't be too careful.

Mrs Monroe had wanted to say that they weren't perpetrating a crime, but she knew Kezia would point out that breaking and entering was still a crime whatever their motives.

She peered around for Kezia, who had the torch and had shot out of the car before her. No sign. Well, she wasn't moving until Kezia came back. She remembered this place from when Harry had parked here to check the bridleway to the stables – the same path they were going to take to avoid leaving the car at the stables gate. It had been muddy then and it certainly wouldn't have dried out in the wet weather they'd been having ever since.

The thought of Harry sent her brain down another pathway.

He'd been arrested straight away on Thursday and kept in custody ever since; the police had applied for an extension this morning. Apparently Boyes had not long been dead when the two of them arrived, so Harry was the prime suspect. Everyone in Thorpe believed he'd killed Boyes either because Boyes knew something damning about Marty or for the simple reason that Marty couldn't have. People were even saying that Harry had got the idea from Mrs Monroe irresponsibly predicting more deaths on television.

So suddenly it was all her fault.

She'd said she'd tell the police she'd been with Harry, but Kezia had been adamant that they must keep away from them. They were unlikely to believe her anyway and would probably arrest her as an accomplice.

The tarot cards she'd seen at Boyes's hadn't been found, according to Josh. No sign of them. Her mind ran back over the conversation.

Was she sure she'd seen them?

Of course she was.

It had been dim inside the cottage and she'd had a great shock.

She'd seen them.

It was a pity she hadn't thought to take a photograph.

Well, she hadn't. She wasn't one of these youngsters who took photos of everything. What did Josh expect? A selfie with the tarot cards in situ and her grinning face beside them?

A sudden movement by her side and Kezia reappeared.

'Where did you go?'

'Over the road. To see the horses. I promised Marty I'd check them. I went to see him yesterday.'

'How was he?'

'Awful. He didn't know about Harry. I had to tell him.'

Suddenly Mrs Monroe felt readier to deal with what lay ahead.

The path was muddy and overgrown and also littered with tiresome stones. Mrs Monroe tripped over a few of them in the dark. Kezia wouldn't use the torch unless it was absolutely necessary. She was terrified someone might see them. But, really, who was going to be out on the bridleway on a night like this? It was all right for Kezia. She wound her way between the rocks like a lithe black cat, her wellies never tripping her up. Mrs Monroe followed her closely, but she still bashed her ankles and once a swathe of stinging nettles scourged their bruised skin.

They reached the gate into the Coopers' yard. Kezia climbed over it. Mrs Monroe sighed and managed to heave herself up and over too. They were right by a heap of muck and straw, which someone, Cooper, Mrs Monroe supposed, had shaped and smoothed into a ramp so a wheelbarrow could access the top of the pile.

'Nearly there,' Kezia said in a low voice. 'Need to be careful of the security lights.'

They edged round the side of an open barn filled with black plastic-covered rolls. Mrs Monroe's eyes were getting used to the night, although her nerves still jumped and twanged at the slightest noise. Josh had said the place was empty. The remaining liveries had been dispersed to the outermost fields and were being cared for by a lad employed by the solicitors and charged to the owners. The few Cooper had owned were in a large stables near Harrogate.

The place had been busy after the killings, with forensics and crime scene techs photographing, logging and taking samples. But once the investigation had finished, the police didn't have the resources to keep watch, according to Josh, so they'd secured the premises and left. Securing the premises meant locking up and extensive use of warning tape and signs, as far as Mrs Monroe could make out.

They slipped under the tape and ignored the signs. Then used the key to the cottage Harry had given her.

Mrs Monroe hesitated. Josh had promised them it would be fine. Everything relevant to the murders had been removed and Cooper's solicitors had arranged for the place to be cleaned. Kezia had been disappointed. She was counting on finding some remnants infused with blood to activate a vision. But Mrs Monroe had felt nothing but relief.

She took a quick look at Kezia, her face barely visible in the dark. Life would be much easier if she'd never met her. Then she banished the thought.

'Ready?' Kezia said. 'Gloves.'

She found the gloves in her pocket and put them on. A snap of plastic as the dim figure beside her did the same.

Kezia pushed the door open and they walked inside.

It was chilly. And damp. Typical of old cottages as soon as they were left without heat for a while. She forced herself to accept that as an explanation and not to wonder if there was a lingering malevolent presence.

'Shut the door,' Kezia said.

'I have.'

She heard the rustling of cloth as Kezia fumbled inside the backpack she wore and produced the torch. Its light was faint, but enough to see that they were in a square, windowless porch. Layers of coats hung along two walls, with boots and shoes spilling out of racks beneath them. A faint smell of mud and straw still clung to them.

'Let's leave our shoes here.'

Mrs Monroe obediently removed her trainers. They were covered in mud and grass from the bridleway. Thank heavens she'd put thick socks on. She hoped very much Josh was right about how thorough a job the cleaners would have done. She didn't fancy treading in blood, whether dried or not.

Kezia opened the inner door. 'This leads to the kitchen,' she said. 'Elaine and Giles Cooper were found here. Giles at the table and Elaine on the floor.'

'But the bodies have gone, haven't they? Josh was sure about that.'

'Yes, of course.'

But Mrs Monroe couldn't shake away the fear they'd be still in place. Exactly as Josh had described them to Kezia. Lying in pools of congealed blood with early flies laying eggs in their wounds.

Kezia stepped inside. Mrs Monroe followed, her legs stiff and reluctant.

A harsh chemical smell. For a moment, she had to shut her eyes to stop them from watering.

'What is that?'

'Some chemical they used to clean, I guess.'

Kezia swung the torch over the floor by the stove. The slate tiles gleamed in the light running back and forth like a searchlight shining down on a prison camp, poking into corners and hunting for any fugitive traces. Nothing. She shone it onto the table. Again nothing but polished wood glistened in its beam. She crossed over to where Giles's chair had been, knelt down and examined the floor below. Then stood.

'Nothing. Absolutely nothing.'

She sounded bitterly disappointed, although Mrs Monroe felt the beginning of relief unlock her rigid body. Maybe they wouldn't find anything. The specialist cleaners knew what they were doing. Should she suggest they gave up and traipsed back to the car? She dearly, dearly, dearly didn't want to be discovered here. Josh had warned them the police patrolled from time to time. More since Boyes's murder so close by. There was no point though. Kezia wouldn't be satisfied until they'd explored every option.

'We might have more luck in the sitting room,' she said now. 'Where Charlie and Chloe were shot.'

While little Freddy lay sleeping upstairs. The child was lucky to have survived. Had the killer baulked at shooting him or just not known he was there?

Kezia disappeared through the door. Mrs Monroe heard her gasp of dismay.

'They've removed the carpet,' she said as Mrs Monroe joined her. 'And cleaned the wood underneath. Cleaned it really well.'

She shone the torch slowly over an expanse of pristine floor.

'Charlie was lying here by the window. It was full of plants when Josh found him.'

'Keep the torch away from the window.'

But Kezia had already moved on and was tracing the boundaries of the room with the light and searching for anything left behind by the all-too-efficient cleaners. She did one circuit, then returned for another, this time on hands and knees, poking the torch into every crack and fissure in the ancient stone walls. She was very supple, Mrs Monroe thought. And determined. The chill was penetrating her thick socks and she wondered how long before Kezia finally gave up. She felt weary. Weary to her bones. The nagging pain in her hip was worse than normal, too. Did she dare sit on the sofa? It was the only piece of furniture remaining. Everything else must be in storage. It was very low though and she wasn't sure Kezia was strong enough to haul her back up. She'd put weight on in the last week or so. Since she'd stopped smoking.

But that was only to be expected.

A sudden intake of breath from Kezia brought her back to the scene. She was kneeling by the stairs, her torch and head pushed into a corner.

'They missed a bit of carpet when they pulled it up. Just a few shreds caught on a splintery bit of wood.'

Mrs Monroe crossed over. Part of her hoped very much they would just be old scraps of carpet with nothing on them – or at least no blood. She'd be happier if there were no more visions. Or dreams. Or whatever they were. They took their toll on the visionary and the person who witnessed them.

'They're caught tight.' Kezia's voice was muffled but angry. 'I can't get a decent grip.'

She sat up abruptly and ripped off her gloves.

'No, Kezia!'

But it was too late. She dived back into the corner and a few seconds later she shot back up, clutching a few strands of wool. She held them out to Mrs Monroe.

'Take them quickly, please.'

CARPET

It's probably Chloe Cooper's favourite moment of the day, the quiet time after Freddy's bath when he's all clean and cuddly and smelling of baby soap. He doesn't really need a bath every day but he enjoys it so much it seems harsh to deny him. And now, after collecting up all the ducks and boats he's scattered around the bathroom, they're both in their tiny bedroom, Freddy muttering sweet nothings to his toys. It's her opportunity to sit still and let her thoughts go where they want to, because Freddy is quite happy playing by himself. She doesn't know why. The rest of the time he's demanding attention. But during this precious half-hour he chats to his toys in a language no one but he understands. The rest of the family think she's busy getting him to sleep, so no one is after her to help with supper or the wretched horses or feed the dogs.

She can't wait to move out. It'll be tough on her own but nothing could be worse than staying here. She'll manage. She loves Freddy but, for a time after he was born, the shock of having him and looking after him had overwhelmed her. Over the last few months though she's felt some of herself returning.

A dull thud comes from downstairs. She hopes her mother hasn't broken something. She could do without another evening of tears and anger. None of them care that her mother is prone to dropping things except her mother. It always makes her cry. But then anything and everything makes her sob at the moment. And it's this endless weeping that enrages her father.

It's all right for Giles. He'll slope off to his bedsit over the stables after supper. Spend the evening watching whatever he wants or gaming or drinking with a few of his friends. None of them know what he gets up to except perhaps the lad, Marty, who has a bedroom in the yard too. And he's unlikely to interfere.

Another thud.

She waits for the wail but it doesn't come. Maybe it's her father thwacking logs into the pile by the fire. He's incapable of doing anything quietly. His ever-present undercurrent of anger finds an outlet in slamming doors and throwing things around. There never were two people more unsuited to be married than her parents. She doesn't know why they've stayed together but then people of their generation often do. For no apparent reason. She's glad she split with Sean. There were a few times she wondered if she'd done the right thing.

Whether moving out from home and in with him would have been a better option. It would never have worked though. Especially with her father so against him. Still she's glad Sean slips in to see Freddy at the panto rehearsals. He claims he's come to take his mum home.

The tarot cards on her bedside table catch her eye. They were pushed through the door yesterday in an envelope addressed to her with a note inside saying to tell Giles. One of them is a king. That much she knows. The other has a picture of a baby on a horse. It made her think of Freddy, who loves it when Granddad sits him on a horse. Except someone has crossed out the infant's head with red biro. Very creepy! She picks the cards and note up.

Another thud from downstairs, this one louder, and then a groan from her father. God, she hopes he hasn't fallen. They'd be stuffed without him. The stables would fall apart. She runs quickly down the stairs.

She sees her father first. Lying by the window. He's clutching something red to his face although he's absolutely still. She opens her mouth to call for help and a sudden movement catches her eye. She swivels.

A figure stands there. Completely still as though they've been waiting for her. With a gun. A gun pointing at her. Something flutters behind the gun.

Her vision splinters into flying fragments.

THIRTY-SEVEN

KEZIA

SAME DAY

The pain is white hot. A white-hot hole in my chest. Burning down every vein and every artery. Juddering along every nerve.

Make it stop.

I curl my mind into a tight ball. Shrink from the crater where my heart was.

They shot me. I should be dead. Why am I not dead?

It's the pain. The pain is keeping me alive. I am nothing but pain.

Where am I?

At the bottom of stairs. I'm at the bottom of the stairs. I hold on to that. It's something real. Something concrete. I am at the bottom of the stairs.

Before the pain. Before the end. I was coming down the stairs.

No, that's not right. Something not right. Try again.

Where am I? I'm at the bottom of stairs. That's right.

I feel for the carpet. The carpet Mum loves so much. Where is the carpet? Where are my fingers? I can't feel my fingers.

Yes, I can.

Something cool and smooth. I feel something cool and smooth.

Not carpet. But wood. The pain recedes a small way. I have fingers.

The fingers are mine.

But the pain isn't mine.

The pain is Chloe's.

I am not Chloe.

Coolness quenches the burning. The pain ebbs. It's still there. Like a memory waiting to rise and overwhelm me.

But it's not my pain.

'Kezia.'

I hear a voice. I have ears.

'Kezia?'

Yes, the ears are Kezia's. The fingers are Kezia Heron's.

Kezia Heron's fingers feel the cool hard floor. Not carpet. Floor. Kezia Heron tries to move her fingers. They won't move. Not yet. But they will. Knowledge pours in. It's always like this. The confusion. The time when I am neither one person nor another. But I always come back. First feeling then movement.

I say the mantra to myself. The one my mother made me learn.

I am Kezia Heron. This is Kezia Heron's body.

My mother told me to watch the kittens. They would run away and hide when something shocked them. Then watch from a distance and wait. But they always came back.

It wasn't until I was older I realised sometimes they didn't.

I am Kezia Heron. This is Kezia Heron's body.

I came to lying at the bottom of the stairs. In the cottage where the Coopers were killed. A pair of legs wearing thick socks and black sweatpants faced my head. I followed them up. Mrs Monroe sat on a chair she'd found somewhere, her face's soft flesh sharpened by the light of the torch she clutched in her lap. She looked exhausted. How long it had taken for me to surface this time? Probably ages. I hadn't drunk my tea for days. The mixture of herbs and ashwagandha that kept all but the strongest attacks at bay also sped my recovery.

'Kezia?' she said.

'Yes,' I said.

'Are you back?'

'Yes.'

She let out a long, shuddery sigh.

'How long?' I managed to ask.

'Nearly two hours this time.'

Even when I was drinking the protective tea, it took a while to come back. The first time with Mrs Monroe present, when I'd picked up the cufflinks on the tray of objects her clients had brought with them, it had taken half an hour.

Mrs Monroe had been on the verge of calling an ambulance. I don't know which one of us was in the worse state. Both shocked. Me because I hadn't had an attack for so long, I'd thought they were a thing of the past. Her from witnessing it. It's not pretty. Doing the photoshoot afterwards had been hard.

'What did I say? Did you record it?'

I don't always remember what I've experienced, you see. Or at least not immediately. I thought it was to protect me from slipping back into whoever's mind I'd been in. My brain locked their memories and thoughts away and it was only later things came back to me.

'Not the beginning,' she said. 'I wasn't expecting you to... I thought we'd agreed to wait until we were home.'

That was true. But I'd taken my gloves off to get a firmer grip on the carpet fibres.

'Did I say anything useful?' And before she could recount everything: 'Don't tell me too much. Chloe is still very close to me.'

'It was Chloe, then?'

'Yes. It must have been her blood on the fibres. Where are they?'

'Here. In one of the plastic bags we brought.'

It lay on her lap next to the torch. I tried to reach out a hand to pick it up, but neither of them would work. Shit. Nothing would work for a while.

You couldn't see the blood on the bits of wool but one of them must have a minute amount. Enough to provoke an attack, especially in my state of heightened sensitivity.

'We're stuck here for a bit, I'm afraid.'

'Has the migraine come on?'

'Yes.'

A migraine was the easiest way to explain the aftermath of the attacks. What the doctors call a hemiplegic aura. Weakness to one half of the body. Mine was whole-body. I couldn't move for a while after the attack.

'Anything useful?' I repeated.

'You mentioned the tarot cards. The Sun and a king. And a note.'

The image of the Sun, disfigured with a red cross, broke through the barrier. Chloe Cooper had been going to show it to Giles.

A thousand needle-like stabs rippled down my arms and legs, making the muscles twitch and tremble. It was painful. Made all the worse by the paralysis that stopped me rubbing and soothing.

I waited it out.

My mother told me it was a reaction to experiencing an event from inside another person's consciousness. My nerves and thoughts struggled to reconnect to my body. The pain and trembling were the chemical and electrical signals jamming and releasing as they tried to travel along my neural pathways.

Mrs Monroe eyed my shaking arms as my heels tapped a drum roll on the floor.

'Was it bad to watch?' I asked.

She nodded. Her soft, white hair gleamed in the torchlight, giving her the aura of a Renaissance angel.

Sometimes the attacks are violent. I think of the visions as attacks. That's what they feel like when the urgency of the experience thrusts my own self away until I'm only aware of the other person, lost in experiencing what they lived through.

If that's what happens.

Was I part of someone else's life for a short time?

I could never be sure.

My mother thought so but she believed in every hocus-pocus, weird magic or power.

It could be a form of autosuggestion. Or a sort of self-hypnosis. Most of what Charlie Cooper supposedly experienced I could have pieced together myself from the things Josh had said the night he discovered the bodies and my knowledge of Charlie Cooper. All inspired by my desperation to find to help Marty.

'How long before you'll be able to walk?' Mrs Monroe asked.

'I'm afraid we'll have to wait and see.'

'Unless I can find a wheelbarrow.' She smiled. 'It's a pity I can't make us a cup of tea. I suppose you'll think it's too risky even if I washed up afterwards.'

I did like her.

At first I'd thought she was a complete charlatan like all the other tarot readers and psychic clairvoyants I'd met while I was growing up, but I'd come to realise she did have some traces of the gift, plus a kindness that stopped her abusing it.

'I wasn't planning for it to happen here,' I said.

'I know. You just got very angry with that bit of carpet.'

'In the car. I've got some herbal tea in the car. In a flask behind the passenger seat. If you could bear to go and get it, it would speed the recovery up.'

Exhaustion slowed my speech. The attack had drained me this time.

'Will you do that?' I saw that she was reluctant. 'You can take the torch. I'll be OK. But if I fall asleep while you're gone, you must wake me up when you get back.'

It was dark without the torch. And very quiet without her presence. And, after a while, cold. A good thing because it dulled and then stopped the occasional ripple of pain. Without them my head cleared. I let myself explore a little of what I'd experienced.

Had I seen the killer?

I didn't think so. Everything had shattered at the end. Maybe when I was less tired I'd be able to piece the shards together.

Why had the killer waited?

Did I think that or was that one of Chloe's thoughts?

The chill stroked my arms and soothed them.

Later, I thought. I'd think about it later when I wasn't so tired. So very tired...

I woke up lying curled against the bottom stair. Freezing. But no more pains. Plus I could move my arms. I stretched them above my head, glorying in the freedom, then wrapped them round myself.

My legs worked too, and I pushed myself up and took a few stumbling paces round the sitting room. The clouds had lifted while I'd been asleep so the moon's cold light gleamed on the empty floor.

'Mrs Monroe,' I called.

No answer.

Was she in the kitchen?

It was empty.

I guessed she'd come back and failed to wake me. Maybe with the morning coming, and desperate to get away, she'd gone looking for the wheelbarrow she'd mentioned.

I called her again. Nothing. She wasn't upstairs. I phoned her. No answer.

I went outside and had a quick look round but there was no sign of her. Back indoors, I put the chair Mrs Monroe had moved back into the kitchen, shoved the plastic bag of carpet fibres in my pocket and checked everything looked as it had when we'd arrived. Then, I locked the door and trudged back down the bridleway to the car, wondering if she'd gone back there for some reason.

No sign of her, and the flask of tea was where I'd left it behind the front passenger seat.

I began to worry. What had happened to her?

I called her name. Several times.

Then strained my ears to hear beyond the noises of the woods. The wind wasn't strong, but it was enough to fill the night with branches creaking and whispering.

Nothing.

As I turned to walk back to the cottage, a soft glint caught my eye.

My car keys.

Lying on the ground by the passenger door.

And now I looked harder, I saw scuff marks in the damp earth, as though someone's heels had skidded out from under them. Mrs Monroe? It must be. I knelt down and ran my hands over the dirt, hoping against hope that something would come to me. There was no sign of blood, but sometimes places retain an echo of what has happened for a short while.

Had she tripped and fallen? Wild thoughts of her wandering the countryside dazed and confused whirled around in my head. They were masking another explanation for her disappearance, though. The one I didn't want to think.

Most likely she'd fallen. Most likely she was lost or confused.

I'd walk back up the bridleway looking for her. And check the stables properly.

The sounds in the wood seemed louder now. And the moonlight was no longer welcome. I felt exposed and vulnerable each time I called her name. I searched the stables. Empty and quiet where once they'd been full of horses and people. It didn't take long.

Mrs Monroe was nowhere.

I rang Josh but there was no answer. He was probably asleep. Like most people.

I rang the hospital in Harrogate. Nothing. And then the ones in Leeds and York. They told me to call the police.

And then the thoughts I'd been damping down with all my force escaped.

I went into what used to be the tack room, where the owners made themselves coffee. It was empty now apart from the old mounting block. I sat on it.

Had Mrs Monroe been abducted? All that publicity she'd done. Claiming Marty wasn't guilty. There were people out there who didn't want Marty to be innocent. Dangerous people. People with tentacles that crept everywhere. Including into the police.

The Kingsleys.

Were they watching the cottage? Or still watching me?

No dead body, I told myself. You haven't found a body.

Of course not. The last place they'd leave her corpse was here. They'd dump it somewhere else. Somewhere it might never be found.

And why hadn't they taken me?

Was it a final warning? A last chance given to me because they knew David wouldn't want me killed?

The shaking came back, and a shadow of pain in my chest. Chloe's pain. I mustn't go back down. I dug my fingers into the rough wood of the mounting block, feeling its splinters. I was in the tack room. *I was Kezia Heron.*

Yes, Kezia Heron, who'd told a big lie and then persuaded Mrs Monroe to go along with it. If she'd been taken it was because of that lie. Because they thought she was dangerous.

I could barely remember why I'd lied in the first place. Embarrassment? A wish for Josh to carry on seeing me as a sensible and mature adult?

I'd go to her house. Maybe she'd had an accident. Fallen at the side of the road where the car was parked, or been knocked down by some late-night driver. If she hadn't been too badly hurt, someone might have taken her home. She could hardly have explained what she was doing there, after all.

I'd check her house first. And then call the police. Although I needed to think what to say to them.

A churned-up track off the bridleway caught my eye as I raced back to the car. Maybe Mrs Monroe, with only the faint light of my torch to show her the way, had taken the wrong path. It wound into the woods between the bridleway and the road. Dense bushes of brambles filled the space under the trees here and the moonlight barely penetrated. It was quiet too. Apart from the rustles of little animals and birds in the undergrowth. And big. There was so much more land than I'd realised.

I kept on calling Mrs Monroe's name, but even I could hear the lack of hope in my voice.

The track ended in a little hollow with a building. An old stone barn. I remembered Lauren telling me there was a barn here. Where Giles stored things.

Giles, I thought again. Always Giles. Sean saying Giles had dodgy friends. Giles and David.

I watched the building from under a tree for quite a while. No movement. There was no one there. I was sure of it. I slipped down to the nearest window and looked in. It was hard to make much out in the gloom inside. A couple of stainless steel tanks gleamed in the patchy moonlight that came through the window and reflected onto a stack of blue plastic containers in the corner on my left with a mess of orange tubing draped over them.

And a van in the middle.

A big one with peeled and faded paint. Not white, but the moonlight was too faint to tell what colour it was.

Farming detritus and a vehicle that was probably too old to be worth taxing and insuring. The sort of stuff that ended up in barns and garages everywhere. I wasn't sure what I'd been expecting. A cannabis farm – although it wasn't really big enough – or piles of boxes of illegal drugs.

There was no sign of Mrs Monroe. I walked back to the car, still calling, still holding on to rapidly fading hope.

THIRTY-EIGHT
KEZIA

SUNDAY

I drove straight to Mrs Monroe's house. The sky was lightening to a dark grey as I arrived. No answer when I rang the doorbell and hammered on the back door. It was too early to wake up the neighbour who I thought might have a key.

Back to the car for more waiting. My legs felt as though my shoes had lead soles and my eyes stung with tiredness. I couldn't sleep though. I stared without seeing at the lime trees lining this small suburban cul-de-sac. A few leaves still hung like damp rags from their branches.

Occasionally I tried Josh, but he never answered.

Around seven o'clock lights came on in the neighbour's house. With the help of the rear-view mirror, I made myself look less like a woman coming home from a wild party and knocked on her door. My legs were feeble and I staggered as I waited.

She opened the door on the chain and peered through the gap, a woman of about the same age as Mrs Monroe and still in her dressing gown with a glimpse of floral nightie underneath. Something whisked through my mind at the sight of the nightie, but it left no trace behind.

'It's Mrs Monroe,' I babbled. 'I'm worried about her. She came out with me last night and disappeared. She's not answering her door. Do you have a key? Could you check?'

And I sat down abruptly on her porch.

'Sorry,' I added. 'I've been so worried, I haven't slept.'

She eyed me for a few seconds. 'You picked her up yesterday?'

'Yes.'

She disappeared and returned a few seconds later clutching a key.

'Go and look,' I said. 'I don't think I can move.'

I knew she wouldn't find Mrs Monroe but I had to check. And sure enough, when she came back she shook her head.

'No sign. You said she disappeared. But how?'

I'd thought about this while I waited. Next stage would be reporting Mrs Monroe missing to the police, and I couldn't say we'd been at the stables. We'd broken several laws, I was sure, so there was every chance the police would arrest me.

I'd concocted a story about someone who'd seen her on television contacting her with important information about the killings and how we'd gone to meet them at Leeming Bar service station but no one had turned up. We'd driven back to Thorpe and stopped briefly where the bridleway met the lane - exactly where I'd parked in reality. I'd got out of the car to pee and when I'd returned Mrs Monroe wasn't there. It was a route we might have taken from Leeming Bar to Thorpe.

It satisfied Mrs Monroe's neighbour anyway.

'Will you go to the police,' I asked, 'and report her missing?'

'Surely you should do that. You were the last person to see her. I'll look after her dog though.'

It had been a vain hope. I nodded, but I gave her Hamish's number and asked her to call him and let him know where I'd gone.

Once I'd repeated my story to the officer at the reception counter, they put me in an interview room and made me wait. For hours. It was nearly lunchtime when the door finally opened and two offi-cers came in. Neither of them was DCI Carter. I couldn't decide if this was good or bad.

A sign on the wall announced the room was equipped with a remote monitoring system and a red light would be illuminated when in use. I couldn't see one, but my eyes were tired.

Anybody could be listening in. Everything I said might be going straight back to the Kingsleys. I needed to be very careful.

The younger officer introduced herself and her colleague: DC Gray and DI Burden. She made me repeat the story yet again and then went back over the details. DI Burden watched me closely throughout.

I didn't like him. He was sharp and thin, and I sensed his enjoyment of my discomfort. I thought he was waiting to pounce.

I was right.

He picked up the thread from DC Gray. 'You say you arrived at Leeming Bar Services at about eight p.m. and left some time around ten?'

'Yes.'

'And you were driving your car, registration CK53 XLD?'

Too late I saw my mistake. Too late.

'Yes,' I said.

'There's no record of that car in the services,' DC Gray said.

'Not at that time. Nor earlier. Not later,' DI Burden drove the point home. 'The car park is equipped with both CCTV and number plate recognition.'

To avoid people outstaying the free period. Of course it was. If I hadn't been so tired, I'd have remembered. I shrugged.

Burden's lips twitched.

'Clearly you think your friend's... her disappearance has some-thing to do with her vision about the killings at Cooper's Stables. Are you suggesting the person you were meeting at Leeming Bar followed you and abducted her?'

'Yes. Well, maybe. I don't know.'

'It seems a little unlikely. I understand no lines of enquiry came out of her interview with us.'

'No.'

'That must have been disappointing for you both. Your friend was determined to… to help with our enquiries into the killings. Is it possible this is a misguided attempt on her part to add credibility to her rather odd story?'

'Of course not.'

I hated him. With his thin lips curled into a half smile half sneer, he occupied the room as though it belonged to him and only to him.

'In any case,' DC Gray said. 'Mrs Monroe has been missing for a very short period of time. More than likely she'll turn up in the next twenty-four hours. People mostly do. Come back and see us if you haven't heard from her in a couple of days. Don't worry. There's every chance you'll get home and find a message.'

'I'd like to go now,' I said.

Before I started crying.

'Of course.'

I went back to the flat. I couldn't think what else to do. I was too tired to drive to the campsite where I'd spent the last two nights. Besides, the flat was more secure than the ancient mobile home I'd rented. If they were following me.

No sign of Josh. In fact, the flat was cold because he'd turned the heating down. he must have gone away.

I called him.

Still no reply.

Wherever he was, whatever he was doing, he wasn't answering his phone.

I had to do something. And quickly.

Because I was on the verge of passing out. The periphery of my vision was blurring and from time to time black spots whizzed over my eyes like speeding flies.

Hamish.

Maybe he could help. If Mrs Monroe had had an accident… Banged her head and suffered some form of amnesia. Or given a false name when she went to hospital because she hadn't wanted to be connected to the stables? Or simply got lost, in the woods at night. Some publicity might help find her.

In my heart of hearts I was convinced she'd been taken. But I had to try.

I thought I detected a certain reserve in Hamish's voice after I told him the same story about going to a service station. It sounded less credible with every repetition.

'I'll see what I can do,' he said. 'One thing though. The police have brought Sean Price in for questioning again.'

'When?'

'This morning.'

'How do you know?'

'I'm a journalist. Any idea why?'

I hadn't mentioned Sean during my interview. Although I wasn't convinced about his alibi. When I'd asked him about the light show at Fountains Abbey, he'd agreed with me that the rotating globe was good. Except there had been no globe, rotating or not, in the show when I'd seen it. I thought Annie, his mum, might have lied for him.

'No,' I said. 'I've no idea why the police are questioning Sean.'

'Well, let me know if you find anything out.'

'Sure.'

Then I passed out on my bed.

THIRTY-NINE

KEZIA

SAME DAY

I woke late evening to the sound of torrential rain. Still tired and still feeling as though someone had smashed me into little pieces and glued me back together carelessly so that the slightest knock threatened to fragment me.

But that was normal.

The attacks undid me. Their violence shook me. Being dragged into someone else's experience of great distress or terror or pain was not a gentle or mystical experience.

They've got worse over the years. When I was a child they were less disruptive, quieter, and afterwards I thought I might have been daydreaming. They got wilder when I reached adolescence. Until I had a bad bout at whatever school I was attending at the time. I went to so many it's hard to remember.

It was a brief foray into the mind of one of the younger boys after I picked up his bloodstained tissue. Blood is often the catalyst but not always. He'd been beaten up in the playground. I can still taste the blood in his mouth. And hear the crunch as a fist met his teeth.

The school called an ambulance for me. The hospital ran test after test. God knows I wanted them to find an explanation. There was no sign of anything amiss with my brain. No tumour, nor infection, nor injury. I hadn't had a stroke and it wasn't epilepsy. In the end they identified it as hemiplegic migraine because of the weakness in my limbs, and let me go, with instructions to my mother to bring me back in six weeks, or earlier if I had another attack.

We moved on again shortly afterwards, so I never went back. But my mother tried different herbs until she found a concoction that seemed to control the attacks.

At seventeen I announced I was leaving to live with Zina. My mother gave me two bags of the herbal tea and the recipe and told me to drink it every morning.

I didn't. I'd left home to get away from all that mumbo-jumbo.

The attacks came back. Until in desperation I tried the tea. It helped. Especially if I drank it a few times throughout the day, although the attacks never went away completely again. I did some research and worked out what I experienced could be psychometry – a form of extrasensory perception where you experience past events through the medium of someone else's personal object. In my case, it looked as though I reacted to a trace of themselves the person had left behind.

If you believe in that sort of thing, which I don't.

I absolutely don't.

I spent my childhood surrounded by mediums and clairvoyants, healers and medicine men, guides who would help you explore your previous lives or experiment with mind-altering substances to expand your consciousness. The list was endless. But they had one thing in common: they were all fakes and charlatans. Their motives were different. Some were out and out in it for money. Others got a kick from the awe of the gullible people they tricked, and a few, a very small few, genuinely wanted to help people.

I don't believe I have some telepathic gift. There must be a rational explanation for what happens. Some sort of fit perhaps, a little electrical problem in my brain, during which my imagination runs wild, creating a fantasy about someone I've met. I don't know. I keep on drinking the tea and try not to think about it too much.

And mainly that has worked.

I went into the kitchen and put the kettle on, took the bag of herbal tea out of the cupboard. It's a mixture of lemon balm, prickly ash, wood betony, chamomile and milky oats, along with a large dose of ashwagandha.

I grow most of them myself, but I'd run low on the ashwagandha I'd dried a few weeks ago and had bought some. I suspected it was a different root because I'd had the first attack at Mrs Monroe's a few days later, when I'd picked up the cufflinks to give to her and experienced the elderly man fainting in the clothes shop.

And then the attack sparked by the cloth in the ashes, when I'd thought I was Charlie Cooper.

I'd harvested some of my own ashwagandha afterwards, but I hadn't drunk any because of my delusion there might be some truth in what I'd seen. I'd wanted the freedom to explore it more. But now, I craved the peace the tea gave me.

I checked my phone as I waited for the kettle to boil. Three messages.

The first was from Hamish, saying he was sorry. He had no control over what the *Yorkshire Post* printed. There was nothing he could do unless Mrs Monroe was still missing when the next edition of the *Gazette* came out. But he'd let me know if he heard anything.

By anything, he meant a dead body. I knew he did.

The second message was from Lauren. She was at the Sunday panto meeting. My handbag was ready. Could she call by with it afterwards because there was something she needed to tell me. Something she'd just worked out because of what I'd said last time we'd met. And Becky was going to come by and give her something for me.

What did David's new wife have for me? Nothing good. That was for sure.

I checked the time. The panto meeting finished ages ago. I guessed Lauren had rung the doorbell but I'd been too deep asleep to hear. I called her back but she didn't answer.

The last was from Josh. Finally.

Kezia, he said. *I got your messages. And I'm sorry. So sorry. I'm coming back as soon as I can. Please just wait for me. Don't do anything stu— rash. We'll talk when I get home. Probably tomorrow. I'll try and call later. Please just sit tight.*

Sit tight. Wait. Don't do anything rash. How very sensible Josh was. And, of course, he was right.

I spooned the herbs into a mug, poured hot water in, but hesitated.

I wasn't sure I could swallow. My throat muscles had tightened. I should try, because the tea would alleviate the attacks.

I breathed the faint fumes from the tea. Everything calmed. Everything Josh had said made sense. I should do what he said. Wait for him. Let him sort it out.

Then I forced my hand to turn the mug over and pour every last drop of the tea down the sink.

Sod that.

I'd try the carpet fibres again. My memory of Chloe's experience was patchy. I'd relied on Mrs Monroe to tell me what I'd said.

I went to get the plastic bag of carpet threads.

CARPET

The attack started abruptly. As they always do. There was never a gradual transition, no soft landing. Instead Chloe Cooper's thoughts and feelings, the colours and shapes of her surroundings, the noise of Freddy's chatter burst into my brain and forced everything else out. I fought to keep some part of myself present. It was easier to remember afterwards and the period of recovery was less painful. Nevertheless it was hard not to lose myself in Chloe's enjoyment of this quiet moment at the end of her day.

Notice the things you didn't see before, I told myself. The things Chloe is barely aware of. The softness of the blanket she fingered as she watched Freddy. The photos of the two of them on the wall, mounted into a collection of frames. On the bedside table, a battered paperback. And alongside it the tarot cards. The Sun, and the other card. It was the King of Cups, sitting on a throne on a slab of granite floating in the ocean. And there was the note that came with it.

I'd forgotten about the note. I stuck it in my mind like a yellow Post-it and told myself to remember.

I heard the first shot, although it didn't register in Chloe's consciousness. She was too lost in thinking about going to London. She wanted to get away badly. I waited as Chloe considered all the things she'd need to sort out to go. Her thoughts slipped in and out easily like well-greased pistons and I suspected they'd been gone over time and time again. I felt the undercurrent of love for Freddy that flowed behind everything. If any part of Chloe still remained, I hoped she knew Freddy was being loved and looked after by Sean's family.

Chloe registered the second gunshot, but her mind interpreted it as a dish falling in the kitchen and lost itself in her parents and their unhappiness.

The tarot cards on her bedside table caught her eye. They had arrived with a note inside saying to tell Giles. A flash of the note whisked through Chloe's thoughts but it wasn't enough for me to see more than Giles's name. It wasn't long though. Just a couple of sentences. Typed not written, which was strange for a short note on a scrap of paper. I did my best to press the image into my memory. Chloe picked it up and decided to go and show Giles now.

Another thud from downstairs, this one louder, and then a groan from her father. Concern brought Chloe to her feet and she ran downstairs to see what was happening.

Her brain couldn't take in the details of her father lying by the window. She knew it was him. Because of the clothes and the red and swollen finger joints. He'd had arthritis for years although he refused to do anything about it. He clutched a lump of something red to his face. I fought hard not to get submerged in the horror of it all. I needed to see beyond the splintering of vision Chloe experienced. The moment arrived. A sudden movement caught Chloe's eye. She swivelled.

A figure stood by the fire. Waiting for Chloe. With a gun. A gun pointing at Chloe. And in the split second before the noise of the bullet fragmented Chloe's consciousness, I realised how hopeless it was. The room was dimly lit and the fire behind the figure with the gun cast an orange radiance onto the honey-coloured stone that lined the fireplace and created a black silhouette, its edge sharp against the soft light. Only the gun glinted in the reflected glow.

The gun fired. Chloe's vision began to splinter but in the split second before it fell apart I saw the figure recoil. A flutter of light-coloured fabric. And the sharp scent of newly crushed herbs.

FORTY
KEZIA

MONDAY

Rosemary and thyme, a hint of sage, some bay and chives, I thought, and maybe dill.

I woke.

Lying on my bed but not in bed. The clock said it was seven but not seven in the evening. It was morning. What was I doing here? And why was I listing herbs? A glimmer of memory stirred but it hurt. Instead I remembered Mrs Monroe.

And everything else flooded back in.

Mrs Monroe.

I'd slept for too long. I should have been out there doing something.

I listened for Josh. No sound of anyone in the flat. Not back yet then. I forced myself off the bed, found a pen and paper and wrote down everything I could remember from the attack. The tarot cards, the Sun and the King of Cups. Two more of the cards missing from Zina's deck. I picked it up from my bedside table now and let my hands shuffle as I thought.

The note. The note telling Chloe to tell Giles. Giles again. Why weren't the police investigating Giles?

I checked quickly. Nothing on the news sites about the discovery of a dead body. Nothing from Hamish. There was still a chance Mrs Monroe was alive.

I'd go back and get a better look at the barn on Giles's land. Maybe Mrs Monroe was there. Maybe she'd been unconscious when I called. And then I'd break into Giles's room above the stables. But before I went, I laid the deck out on my bed. One more try. I needed all the help I could get and for once I was desperate enough to believe they might have a message for me.

I ground myself in this moment, connecting to the Earth and drawing on its protective energy, I muttered with my eyes shut. *I come to seek answers in the tarot with a heart full of truth.*

It was something my mother made people recite.

Show me the way, no matter how hard it is.

And I chose a card.

The Empress.

Again.

Either the cards were mocking me, reminding me I'd turned my back on everything my mother stood for. Or it was a stupid coincidence.

Whichever it was, it was useless. The Empress with her lush fertility and maternal love meant nothing.

Unless it was a message from Chloe. Chloe, the mother whose love Freddy had lost.

Stop. Just stop. None of this is helping. Go and do something useful.

I grabbed my car keys and shot down the stairs, then ran all the way to the car park. No one was going to catch me. Last night's rain had left deep puddles in the unrepaired roads and pavements. I splashed through regardless. My speed dropped as I reached the car. My vision blurred again. Shit. I was going to faint. I leaned on the bonnet for a second. What was wrong with me?

Hunger. I hadn't eaten anything since... Since before going to the stables. More than twenty-four hours. More than twenty-four hours. The thought twitched an echo in my brain.

Sean Price's burger van was parked nearby. The hatch was closed but the door was open. Was his assistant, Megan, who Josh dropped into the conversation from time to time, there? Maybe I could cadge a sandwich and find out about Sean at the same time. I walked over.

But Sean stuck his head out when I tapped on the door.

'I'm not open yet.'

And then he recognised me from my visit to his parents' house and his gaze sharpened.

'Hello Sean,' I said. 'I know you're closed but if you had any sandwiches left from yesterday, they'd be fine. I don't want you to make me anything.'

I wanted to look inside. I had to look inside. Hamish had said the police had picked Sean up to interview him yesterday morning, so he was free when Mrs Monroe had been taken. I couldn't walk away without checking the van.

'Or just a bit of bread,' I babbled. 'Anything really. I'm worried I might pass out from hunger.'

'Let me see.'

He went inside and I looked round the door.

It was bigger inside than I'd thought, with enough room for two lengths of counter, one below the serving hatch and the other on the far side with a row of cupboards above, two gas hobs and a sink at the far end.

Mrs Monroe wasn't there. Not unless she was in the large fridge on my right. But as I watched, Sean opened it and pulled out some baguettes wrapped in cling film.

He saw me staring.

'All brand new and meeting all Food Standards Agency regulations. If you were checking up on me.'

'No, no. Why...'

'I've got cheese or ham baguettes left.'

'Cheese is fine. Two, if you've got them.'

That morning's copy of the *Yorkshire Post* lay on the counter. I caught a glimpse of a headline.

'Have you finished with this?'

'Take it,' he said.

The article was halfway down the front page.

SO-CALLED PSYCHIC 'DISAPPEARS'

Mrs Monroe, the medium who lambasted the police for careless work in the Cooper's Stables massacre, has been reported as missing, police confirmed today. Her neighbour claims she disappeared while on a mysterious late-night hunt for more information about the case.

The police have issued a statement: 'Only 3% of people reported missing fail to return within a week. We do not believe Mrs Monroe's disappearance is linked to any ongoing investigation nor do we believe her to be at risk. No new lines of enquiry resulted from her interview. While we encourage the public to come forward if they have information that may assist us, a small number of habitual callers and publicity seekers waste a large amount of police resources.'

I stormed out of the van with my sandwiches, forced two large mouthfuls down and called Hamish.

'I didn't write it,' he said. 'And I didn't think it would be as nasty as it is.'

'They're implying it's all a publicity stunt.'

He was silent for a few seconds.

'Are you sure it isn't?' he said at last.

I cut the call, got into the car and threw the baguettes on the passenger seat. He called back. I thought about ignoring it, except I might need him.

'Yes,' I said. 'I'm sure. Very sure, Hamish. What the police aren't telling you is that I was there when she disappeared.'

'You reported her missing.'

'Yes.'

'So the police told us, off the record, that the person who'd reported her missing told a lot of lies. CCTV images proved it.'

Shit. Never lie. Every lie I've ever told has come back to bite me. Several times.

I told Hamish the truth about Mrs Monroe's disappearance. Every last bit of it.

'So you think she was taken by someone who doesn't want the police to keep investigating the Coopers' deaths?' he said when I'd finished.

'Yes.'

'How did they know you were at Cooper's yard? Are you being followed?'

'Maybe. But I couldn't have been that night. I checked there was no one else around.'

'There are other ways of tracking you than following you in person. Check your car.'

'My car?'

'For a tracker.'

'OK. Listen, Sean Price is free.'

'Are you sure?'

'I've just seen him.'

'Did you ask him why they interviewed him?'

'How was I supposed to do that?'

'I'll call him.'

He rang off and I got out and walked around my car. It looked normal. The plus side of it being bright orange was that it was easy to see if I'd picked up anything that shouldn't be there. I ran my hands under the wheel arches. Nothing.

I grabbed a plastic sheet from the boot and laid it down on the far side of the car from the burger van although Sean had shut the door firmly behind me when I'd left, then looked underneath. And found it. A small black box on a flat area of the chassis towards the back, held in place by a strong magnet. I flipped it off and crawled out.

A tracker, for sure. Not difficult to do. My car was always here in the car park. It was quiet at night and placing the tracker would only take a minute or two.

My phone rang. Hamish again.

His voice was sombre.

'Kezia. I'm really sorry but we're getting reports of a body found in Thorpe. A woman.'

No. Please, no.

'Where?'

'In the river. Under the footbridge by the Water Rat. Between it and the old church.'

I knew it well. It was a short walk from my studio and not far from the centre. I could walk but it would be quicker in the car. I just needed to get rid of the tracker.

I went back to the burger van and stuck it under the rear valance.

FORTY-ONE
KEZIA

SAME DAY

I drove to the Water Rat car park and ran to the footbridge. A narrow wooden walkway over the river. Word travels fast in Thorpe. Already twenty or so people had gathered and were watching an ambulance reverse slowly back up the road. No flashing lights. No siren. Whoever it was carrying was beyond the need for urgent care.

The onlookers moved back to let it through. Everyone was silent, even after the ambulance had turned into the main road and left, a mark of respect no one liked to break. Gradually the occasional whispers grew into muttered conversations and became chatter.

'Who was it? Do they know?' I asked a young woman.

'A woman. Don't know her name.'

'In her sixties?'

'No. Quite young, I think. Dark hair from what I could see. Dead, though. She was half in and half out of the water and under the bridge, so no one saw her first of all. It was slippery with all the rain last night.'

'What was she wearing?'

'Jeans and a grey top.'

Relief relaxed my muscles and I staggered a little. Mrs Monroe hadn't been wearing jeans. Mrs Monroe never wore jeans.

'You all right?'

I nodded. I was more than all right. It wasn't Mrs Monroe. I turned to go back to my car but then a man with a shopping bag spoke to us.

'I heard it was the woman who the runs the leather shop off the market square. They found her bag in the shallows.'

I turned back.

'You mean Lauren...' I couldn't remember her surname. 'She makes handbags.'

'That's the one. Someone said she'd just split up with her partner, so maybe it wasn't an accident. You sure you're all right, you look very pale.'

I pushed past them and towards the bridge. Most were leaving now, picking up their bags and their lives and getting on with their daily routine. This death was nothing but a short interlude. Something to tell family and friends later and maybe a reminder of how quickly a life can be over. Sometimes before it's barely begun.

Lauren? Was it Lauren?

I rang Josh. He answered. He was in his car.

'I'm on my way back,' he said.

I told him what had happened. 'Is it Lauren?'

'I've been away from work. Let me check.'

I wheeled round and walked a few yards down the path along the river, then turned to watch. A white-suited officer examined the bridge's handrail, while down below two others trudged back and forth over the curve of gravel the river washed round at this point.

Think, Kezia.

But my brain wouldn't work. Its mechanism had jammed and it repeated the same phrases again and again. *Please no. Not another death. Please no. Not Lauren. Not lively, talented, determined Lauren. Please, no.*

I sat down on a bench and gripped its smooth wood to anchor myself. Took a few breaths. Focussed on the distant sound of cars on the road the other side of the houses.

Was it an accident? If it was Lauren, she wouldn't be the first to fall off this bridge. The rails weren't high. She'd have been at the panto meeting at the old church on the other side of the footbridge.

My phone rang. Josh.

'It is Lauren,' he said straight away.

'How?'

'Too early to say but head injuries consistent with a fall from height. Discovered by a dog walker a couple of hours ago.'

'When did it happen?'

'We don't know exactly but she slipped out of the panto rehearsal to meet someone yesterday and no one's sure if she came back. Raymond is being interviewed now.'

'She rang me, Josh. Yesterday morning. She left me a message, saying she had something to tell me. And Sean was brought in for an interview by your colleagues then. What was all that about?'

'Look, I'll see what I can find out and call you back.'

I wandered a few steps back upriver as I waited. The water rattled against the gravel. I don't like water. Always shifting. Formless and secretive. If it contained the answers it would never tell me. My eyes followed its flow downstream.

Something was caught in the bushes where the gravel ended and the water reached the bank. I wouldn't have noticed it if it hadn't been so familiar.

My handbag. The one Lauren had mended. Had she dropped it as she fell?

I walked downstream, waited until none of the officers were looking in my direction and grabbed it, then walked smartly away. If they'd turned round they'd have seen nothing remarkable. Just a woman, neither old nor young, going up the path with her handbag slung over one shoulder.

A very wet and shiny handbag.

Josh called as I reached the car.

'Sean Price wasn't released until this morning. He was brought in because of a problem with his alibi for the Coopers' murders. Turns out he gave the police a false one. He was only with his mother at the restaurant early on. He asked her to cover for him afterwards because he was at a poker game. He didn't want Lauren to know. But it checks out. And he's in the clear for Lauren's death. If it is suspicious. He was locked up in the cells last night.'

Part of me was surprised the police had checked Sean's alibi at all. 'I thought you'd closed the case with Marty's arrest.'

'Nothing is closed until we get a conviction. The police aren't as...' His voice trailed away.

'The police aren't as what? As bad as I think they are? As corrupt?'

But Josh was silent. I let the seconds roll by and thought rapidly.

'Did Lauren tell the police about Sean?'

'No. Someone saw him leaving the game early Monday morning and rang to report it. People are still suspicious of him and his involvement with the Coopers. But the other poker players have confirmed he didn't leave until after midnight. The Coopers were long dead by then. Not that we've ever released the time of death.'

So definitely not Sean, then.

Lauren said she had something to tell me. What could it have been?

'Look, I'll be back later.' Josh interrupted my thoughts. 'Things are happening. I can't talk about them but everything should be clearer soon.'

I had a good look at the handbag.

Lauren had done a lovely job. The new piece of leather looked as though it had always been there and I loved the printed fabric of the lining. So pretty with its clusters of green herbs. Herbs again. Lauren had added a deep pocket at one side. I slipped my fingers in it and found a damp envelope with my name on it.

It contained a tarot card. The Tower.

From the Rider–Waite deck, of course. The card the woman had given me for David. The one I'd left at the house. This must be what Becky had given Lauren for me. I turned it over. Sure enough, Zina had marked it. A subtle mark no one but I would have noticed. It was confirmation. The deck the cards had come from was the one David had.

I scribbled a list of the cards missing from Zina's pack and what I knew about them on the back of the envelope.

The Tower – David had sent it as a threat to the strange woman.

The defaced Sun and King of Cups – sent to Chloe with a note to tell Giles. Threat?

Death and the King of Pentacles – found at Boyes Farm.

Ten of Swords – don't know but think Josh might.

King of Swords – don't know.

King of Wands – don't know.

Forget the meanings of the cards. Think of their appearance. Death, the Tower and the Ten of Swords – three of the scariest looking cards in the deck. And the Sun – a lovely card with the infant riding a horse. Unless you put a big red cross through the child's face and sent it to a riding stables.

All meant to frighten.

And the Kings. All the Kings.

Kings for the Kingsleys. Of course, they were.

Had Becky found the Tower in the house? I thought so. But why send it to me? She hadn't been happy when I left after seeing her and David. Had she too suspected he was more involved with his family that he claimed? Was it a warning to me?

A strange fury took hold of me. Sort of icy but raving. It was all too much. Too, too much. I was going to see David. Sod the Kingsleys. It was time he made all this stop. He had to stop it.

There was no answer when I rang the doorbell. The windows were dark and no cars were parked outside. They were out. Nevertheless I hammered on the door a few times, until my rage seeped away.

This was stupid.

As I turned to leave, a voice called my name. It was Mrs Ramsay, my old neighbour, standing in her open front door and leaning on her frame.

'Kezia,' she called again. 'I thought it was you but I wasn't sure I'd make it to the door in time.' She beckoned me.

The Ramsays were a lovely couple. They'd run the local post office until retirement and now enjoyed themselves, letting the house slowly moulder around them, preferring to expend their energy on seeing their numerous friends.

'I can't stop, Mrs Ramsay.'

'But we never see you any more. Why don't you visit us? You're always welcome, you know that. I suppose it's because of her.' She jerked her head at my old house.

'Actually I need to speak to her. Do you know when she'll be back?'

'She's gone away, I think. Put a lot of suitcases and boxes in her car and drove off a couple of hours ago.'

Becky had gone away? A holiday? Or for good? Not that it mattered; it was David I needed to speak to.

I detached myself with promises to come back soon. Time to go and look in Giles's barn in daylight.

FORTY-TWO
KEZIA

SAME DAY

I left the car a few hundred yards away from the bridleway and walked. The tracker was still stuck to Sean's van but I wasn't taking any chances. It was easy to check if someone was following me on foot. I stopped for a few minutes to say hello to Bathsheba and took the opportunity to survey the road in both directions. All clear. Bathy came over straight away and nuzzled my face. She hadn't been clipped for a while, nor had Harding, but no one would be riding them over winter. Not now Marty was locked up.

Marty. That was all that mattered. Marty and Mrs Monroe.

'Did you see what happened to Mrs Monroe, Bathsheba?'

Probably not. Although she'd remember if she had.

I crossed over to where I'd parked on Saturday night and searched the ground. Last night's rain had turned it to thick mud that clung to my boots and made each step heavier and heavier. There was nothing but wet earth and puddles. The ditches at the side were full of brown water with patches of green scum floating here and there. The footprints we'd left on Saturday night had disappeared, smoothed away by the rain.

I combed the ground the other side of the gate. It was less

muddy here, although the stones and grit that littered the surface were slippery. The fear that I'd been battling to keep down rose back up again and tightened my throat.

It was all my fault. If I hadn't used Mrs Monroe as a front, they'd never have taken her.

I shook my head. No time for this. And then I saw it. Over the fence, something glinted in a clump of grass. I climbed over. It was Mrs Monroe's phone, half covered in mud but otherwise intact.

Nothing left in the battery. Anyway I didn't know her passcode.

'You're on private land.'

I turned.

A woman in a Barbour, tweed cap and boots stood on the track I'd left. A long bag was slung over her shoulder. I registered the shotgun, held loosely but comfortably in one hand.

I knew her but the memory took a minute to surface. Dirty blond hair tied back tightly under the cap, and skin whose sallowness made it look faintly grubby. She was the woman who'd brought the Tower to my house all those months ago. The card I thought Becky had sent me.

'Who are you?' I asked.

A glimmer of surprise disturbed her hard features and her grip tightened on the gun, then relaxed. She pushed her cap further back, revealing the scarred eyebrow.

'Wanda Stainthorpe.' Her voice was matter of fact. 'You're on my land.'

Wanda Stainthorpe. The elusive owner of the pheasant shoot whose land adjoined the Coopers. The one who'd gone away. Except now she was back.

I didn't think she remembered me, but then she'd barely looked as she thrust the Tower into my hand and delivered her message for my husband.

She jerked her head in the direction of the fence and I meekly climbed back over.

I should ask her about the Tower and what she'd meant. Except

I didn't know where to start and, as I tried to think, she climbed over the fence herself and walked back into her woods on her side of the bridleway. She chose a rock and sat on it, removed a pouch from another pocket and began rolling a cigarette, the gun balanced over her knees.

Clearly she was waiting. For me to leave? Or for something else? I had a feeling she wouldn't hesitate to shoot me if she deemed it necessary.

Wanda finished rolling her cigarette, shot a glance in my direction, then rose smoothly to her feet and walked away.

I breathed a sigh of relief. Still, I wouldn't go back onto her land. Not now. I'd wait until I'd checked the barn and stables and then come back.

I trudged up the bridleway until I came to the turning towards the barn on Cooper's land. It was nothing more than a space between the trees really. Easily missed if it hadn't been churned up by a vehicle.

The barn was not as tumbledown as it had looked on Saturday night. The windows, although filthy, were recent and heavy-duty doors had been installed at one end, locked with a chain and padlock. The same scene as last night met my eyes when I stared through the grimy windows: steel tanks, plastic containers and tubing and the big van in the centre with its peeling paint. Light came in from above, now, and lit the faded logo on its side.

I almost laughed. The name was unreadable but the picture showed a burger with crisp onion rings piled on a meat patty and a frill of lettuce under the bun. An old burger van. Doubtless Giles's old burger van. Left over from his failed catering service.

I'd left Sean's burger van in the square to find a much older version here. I remembered the Deliveroo bike I'd seen coming out of here all those months ago and wondered if Giles had been running a takeaway food business on the quiet, far away from the reach of the Food Standards Agency Sean had complained about.

The light came through a tarp-covered hole in the roof and, when I walked round the back, I saw the reason why. A tree had crashed down and smashed the tiles, probably in Storm Beatrice a couple of weeks ago. It had left a gaping hole, loosely covered with tarpaulin that flapped and smacked in the breeze. The tree had taken the power out too. The pole lay on the ground with a loose cable a few yards away. If Giles had been running an illicit take-away business that would have put paid to it.

I'd take a quick look. It wouldn't be too difficult. The tree still leaned against the roof and I could scramble up it even in my boots. But when I reached the top and pulled the tarp aside, the van roof a few feet beneath me was all that was visible. I loosened one of the cords holding the tarp in place, squirmed through the hole breaking a few more tiles, and lowered myself down, then dropped the last foot, grabbing the burger van chimney to stop myself toppling over and falling to the ground.

The far side of the barn, now visible, although steeped in gloom contained nothing but neat stacks of plastic containers, metal drums and canisters of gas. A faint smell of something acrid and sharp filled the air. Cat pee? Or some other animal that had sneaked in. A fox maybe.

I squatted down on the roof and held on, despite the layer of greasy dirt, so I could stick my head over to look more closely. I didn't fancy going down there. It might be difficult to get back onto the van roof when I wanted to get out.

I called Mrs Monroe's name a few times, although there wasn't a whisper of movement.

I crawled over to the filthy roof light and swiped a layer of muck away with my coat, then peered into the van. Too dark to make out much. I shone the torch in and a weirdly familiar sight flickered back at me. The interior was similar to Sean's van, without the cleanliness and organisation. There was a sink and a large gas hob, but, under the litter of glass jars and tubes, plastic bags and funnels, stained filters and utensils, the counters were melamine instead of stainless steel. A Bunsen burner and a set of scales lay amid the detritus and two yellow suits with what looked like gas masks were slung over a chair. At the far end, any resemblance to Sean's van vanished. Someone had ripped out the counter and replaced it with a large white tank. A long tube came out of its top and ran down to the counter. Smaller tubes came off it and fed into white plastic containers.

Whatever Giles had been doing, it wasn't cooking burgers.

I wouldn't have had a clue if David and I hadn't spent lockdown watching all the TV programmes we'd missed on box sets and catch-up. David had adored *Breaking Bad*. We'd watched it together and then he'd watched it again. The inside of Giles's burger van was very like the inside of the RV Walter and Jesse had used to manufacture methamphetamine.

I was sure that was what the barn was being used for. Maybe not meth, but illegal drugs of some sort. A shiver ran through me as I wondered if *Breaking Bad* was where the idea had come from. If it was David's idea. If he'd been dragged further into his family's business than he'd claimed.

I wasn't staying to find out. Mrs Monroe wasn't here and the police needed to deal with what was in the barn. Thank God for Josh. I took a couple of photos, although they weren't very clear.

Getting out was harder than getting in. The hole in the roof was a foot away from my outstretched arms and I thought jumping and grabbing would only bring more of the tiles down. In the end I balanced myself on the van chimney and seized the end of a wooden beam before pulling myself up and out.

FORTY-THREE

KEZIA

SAME DAY

I was halfway down the roof when the sound of cars coming down the track startled a flock of starlings out of the trees and into a giddying swirl through the grey sky. I froze, clutching the tiles.

Someone was coming. What should I do? I didn't dare risk jumping down. For the moment I was unseen, flattened alongside the tree on the far side of the roof. Even if they came round I didn't think they'd see me from below. I waited.

The cars arrived.

Doors slammed.

The garage doors scraped open and the sound of voices came from below.

I had to know who was there.

I squirmed back to the hole, lifted the tarp cautiously and peered in. Below was flooded with light from the open door that filled one gable end. Two big Land Cruisers were backed up to the entrance. Two men hurled containers and canisters from the pile on the floor into them.

The burger van engine started up and a third man leaned out of its window and gave a thumbs-up sign.

'Let's see how far down the track it'll go before we have to tow.'

It was David.

David.

Now arguing with one of the two other men, who wanted to rig the tow bar in the barn.

'In the dry,' he said. 'Much better than when it gets stuck. Which it will.'

'Be quick then. We can only hold them off for so long.'

Hold who off? Did he mean the police?

'I told you last time it was knackered. It needs to be parked up and left. Where are you taking it now?'

'I'm waiting for a call. No time to sort anything out. Beresford said to get here and shift it fast.'

The man knelt down at the front of the van out of my sight. I'd seen enough though. Enough to work out they were clearing the barn out, and fast. In a short while there'd be nothing left except the faint smell, which must be chemical rather than animal. Did I dare call Josh from up here?

No.

But I'd text him and send him photos. I slipped down the roof, turned onto my back and wedged my feet against the tree as I texted him.

It didn't go. Neither did the photos. No service.

The men were all in the barn and with the van engine going they wouldn't hear much.

I didn't let myself think. I slithered down the tree, hit the ground and ran in the opposite direction from the open garage doors, only turning round once I was deep in the woods.

Thank God for the brambles because the trees here were young and spindly. Scrub oak bent into twisty shapes by the winds that whistled through in winter. I doubted anything flourished. Except brambles. And even they were thin. No need to lift my head over the top to see what was happening. I could see through. The men had emptied the barn and got the van out onto the muddy track. One of the men hosed down the interior. The electricity might be out but there was a plentiful and strong supply of water.

I whisked round to head away, but a shout made me turn back.

No! One of the men was staring in my direction and pointing. The jerk of my movement must have caught his eye. I froze.

The starlings saved me. The man's sudden cry startled them back into the air and as his eyes rose to watch them, I flattened myself and crawled out of his sight, then broke into a crouching run until I was out of sight. Then I stood and fled.

I reached the bridleway and bent double, hands holding my aching sides as I grabbed breaths.

Still no phone signal. I'd walk up to the stables. There was definitely signal there. Everybody used their phones on the yard. But as I moved a sharp click turned my blood to acid and stopped me dead. I looked round slowly.

Wanda Stainthorpe stood there. Every muscle from her tight legs through her still centre and down her arms was focussed on the gun she held and pointed at me. It was part of her and her shooting stance as natural as a cat's crouch to stalk its prey.

'A lookout,' she said. 'I wondered why you were first here and why you waited for me to leave. Did you call to tell them the coast was clear? They're cleverer than I thought and more stupid. A lookout is easy pickings and generally can be made to talk.'

'What do you mean?'

'Ploy number one. Play the innocent. Buy your husband time to get everything away before the police arrive.'

So she had recognised me.

'He's not my husband.'

The words came out before I could think. But it didn't matter. I thought she was on the side of the angels. It was a pity she thought I wasn't.

'Mistake number one,' she said. 'How do you know who I meant?'

'Because you mean David Kingsley, who's back in the woods, supervising the removal of an old burger van the police will be very interested in. And he's my ex-husband. I left him after you came round with the tarot card. The Tower. I have nothing to do with what they're up to. I'm looking for Mrs Monroe.'

'The psychic woman.'

'Yes. She disappeared here on Saturday night.'

'She'll be dead.'

I knew this really.

'I'm trying to call the police.' I held my phone out. 'Look, you can read the text I was trying to send. I took a couple of photos too.'

She gestured for me to put the phone on the ground and move back, then she picked it up and read it.

'Who's Josh?'

'My nephew and a police officer. He's been helping me.'

'Local police force?'

'Yes.'

'Not much help then. They're rotten to the core. The Kingsley family knows what's going on before the local force has put the phone down on you.'

Despite the harshness of her words, she'd relaxed a little. She clicked the safety back on the gun and held it upright.

'Not Josh,' I said.

'We'll find out. Your text has gone. Let's see if you're luckier than I have been.'

'Can I have my phone?'

'No. I'll keep it for a while.'

'But I need to call Josh. I don't want them getting away. They've killed the Coopers and another friend and Boyes—'

'Quiet.'

She was right. Anger had turned my volume knob up to full.

'I want them to pay,' I muttered.

'So do I. That's why I came back. I didn't like Charlie Cooper, and Giles was a stupid and unethical man – a dangerous combination – but no one deserves to have that happen to them.'

She shut her mouth.

The sound of cars wiped the questions from my brain. Wanda

was over the fence into her land in a couple of seconds and I stumbled after her.

'They're leaving,' she said. 'Shit.'

She crouched down and ran through the trees in the direction of the noise. Car doors slammed followed by the howl of an engine revving. She circled round, creeping along until we were on a small rise looking down to where the track to the barn met the bridleway. There were no trees here, but the blackthorn flourished. Its close-meshed twigs with their covering of bitter purple berries and fast-fading leaves provided cover. We edged as close as we dared.

They were there. The two Land Cruisers and the van. But they weren't going anywhere. The van, driven by David, was deep in the mud. One man watched as the other tried to haul it out with a Land Cruiser. Its spinning wheels spattered gobbets of mud. More shouting, and the three of them grouped round the back of the van. Voices rose and fell.

'Where are the bloody police?' Wanda hissed, half to herself.

'It'll take Josh a while to get things organised.'

'Not your Josh. I have contacts in the police elsewhere. High up. I called them yesterday. As soon as I realised your husband had brought the van back here.'

'He's my ex-husband,' I hissed back. 'And it doesn't look as though your contacts have come through either.'

'I don't know what's going on. They said they'd deal with it. And then this morning they asked me to ring Thorpe station and report it. I told them the locals were leaky but they said it would be fine. I guess something went wrong. Because you turned up within half an hour of me making the call.'

'I told you, I'm nothing to do with it.'

A half-smile curved her pale lips.

'I almost believe you.'

'I've never been a part of it.'

She gave a half-laugh, more like a bark than the sound of genuine amusement.

'Shh,' I said.

'They can't hear us over the engine noise,' she said. 'So when I brought you the card that your husband sent me after warning me to keep my mouth shut about what was going on in Giles's barn, are you telling me you didn't know why I'd come?'

'No.'

'You knew the card, though. I saw that in your face.'

'It's a tarot card. I know tarot.'

'Maybe you chose the next one?'

'What next one?'

'The one your husband left pinned to the broken fence posts when they'd destroyed my pheasant pens and set their dogs loose on the young birds. After I'd rung the police to make an appointment.'

'What card?'

'A King. The King of Wands. I got the message. David Kingsley. He'd told me to remember the name.'

Bingo. The Kings. The Kingsleys. I was right. They were calling cards.

And this was confirmation David had provided more than legal services for his family. And for a long time. Threatening people and damaging their livestock. It was horrible. I'd asked him at that awful meeting at his house, when Becky took the cups to the kitchen, if he knew anything about the Coopers' massacre. He'd promised me he didn't. And I'd believed him.

Had I been wrong about that too?

David turned the van engine off.

'Shhh,' I whispered.

A sudden silence filled the air. No breath of wind rustled through the trees. No noise of distant traffic. Nothing but the men arguing what to do.

David had lied and lied and lied to me.

I tried to shut the thought out. Tried to focus on the feel of dampness under my hands and the mushroomy scent of decaying leaves. And another smell. Lighter and fragrant. I looked down. Yarrow. Wild yarrow. I'd knelt on its ferny foliage and the crushed leaves gave off an aromatic scent. Yarrow is for protection. For warding off negative energy. Evil spirits if you like. Witches use it to make their protective circles. A stupid idea that it might help us came to me. I picked a couple of sprigs and put them in my pocket.

A shout dragged my attention back to the scene below. A man in a dark coat ran up the bridleway. Ran right up to David and started arguing with him. Stray phrases carried through the stillness. Enough for us to realise he was telling them to leave the van and get out of there fast but David was refusing.

'What's going on?' I was whispering to myself really but Wanda answered.

'He could be the lookout. Someone they left down the bottom of the bridleway?'

'Maybe the police are here.'

The noise of the van engine starting reached us.

'Let's hope so, because the recent arrival knows what he's doing. They're going to use both cars to pull.'

Her whisper was prickly in my ears.

Under instruction, the Land Cruiser from behind the van drove in between the trees and round the two stationary vehicles, then reversed back to stop in front of the other Land Cruiser. They started fixing a towing iron between the two cars and piling branches on the mud before the front and back wheels of the burger van.

'It might work.' Wanda's words were no louder than the rustle of leaves, whispered into life by a breath of wind.

Part of me wanted nothing more than for the men to leave but I hoped she was wrong. If they got away, we'd have nothing except our account of what had happened and a few indistinct photos on my phone.

'Listen.' She pulled me down behind the brambles. 'I can stop them leaving, but I'll need your help.' She unzipped the bag from her shoulder and took out a plastic box of bullets and another gun.

'It's loaded,' she said. 'As soon as I've fired two shots, pass it to me and reload mine. Do you know how?'

I nodded. She looked doubtful.

'It's not difficult,' I said.

'Just don't point it at me while you're reloading.'

'Are you going to shoot them?'

'Not unless I have to. I'll shoot out the Land Cruisers' tyres, but if they've got guns they'll come after us. Can you shoot?'

'I've done clay pigeon shooting.'

'Same principle.'

I wondered how much damage she could do. We weren't that near.

'Shouldn't we try to get closer?' I muttered. 'Be sure of hitting the tyres.'

'I won't miss. I never miss.'

When we peered back over the blackthorn, the combined strength of the two Land Cruisers was slowly dragging the van out of the deep mud and onto the bed of branches. A few more yards and it would reach the better surface of the bridleway, and from there it would be an easy run to the road.

Wanda took a long slow breath then, rose to her feet, pressed the gun into her shoulder and fired twice in rapid succession. Then she dropped back down, seized the other gun from me and passed me the first.

It had all been too quick. I hadn't expected it to be so quick. I fumbled for the bullets and knocked the box over. She fired again twice. I scrabbled for two bullets, broke the gun, rammed them in, then shut it and held it up to her.

She took it and passed the other gun back. I reloaded it but more smoothly this time. She hadn't fired again. She still had the gun pointed towards them but she was motionless.

I risked a look.

I thought she'd missed. The tyres on our side of both Land Cruisers looked intact. I'd expected them to be shot to pieces. Like in a film. But as I watched, I realised they were flattening, and fast.

'Good shot,' I breathed.

'They've got guns. Get down.'

A dull crack split the air.

Wanda spun round and shot straight back, twice, and I heard a loud scream.

'One down.'

'Is he dead?'

'No but he won't be running around. I've bought us some time. That's all.'

She reloaded the gun as she spoke and pulled a handful of bullets from the ground into her pocket. I hoped the mud wouldn't stop them firing.

'Won't someone hear the shots and...?'

'Call the police? That's not helped us much so far. Besides, the sound of shooting here won't surprise anyone. You stay here. Keep the other gun. Fire at them from time to time. But through the bush. Don't stand up.'

'What are you doing?'

'I'm going round. I won't let them reach you. How many of them are there?'

'Four with the one who just arrived. No, three. If you're sure you got one.'

'I'm sure.'

And with that, she turned and slipped away up the slope. I watched her until she disappeared, her dirty green coat and trousers blending into the background fast.

A sudden movement down at the van. A glimpse of sleeve and what I thought was a head appeared. I raised the gun and pressed the trigger. Nothing happened. The safety! I'd left the safety on. I slid my thumb forward and pushed it off. The gun jerked and fired, then slammed back into my shoulder. It hurt. Shit. The trigger was hair-light.

But it had done its job. Nothing moved below except the Land Cruisers slowly sinking. Hopefully the men thought I was the shooter who'd taken out the tyres with such proficiency. How long before Wanda got into position?

A crack whipped through the cold air, followed by an echo

somewhere behind me. A bullet. I was sure. It had hit something behind me. I kept my head down, pointed the gun and fired back.

Reload! Reload! My brain screamed. I did. With less fumbling this time.

Nothing moved down at the cars. Were they circling round to trap me? Could Wanda really stop them coming up from behind? I cast a swift eye up and down the bridleway. They'd have to break cover to cross it.

Still no movement down by the van. No movement on the bridleway. Nothing down by the cars. No—

Then I saw her.

She stumbled into view, coming round the bend from the stables.

Still wearing sweatpants and trainers. Her light-grey hair lank and flattened on one side.

All alone and staggering towards the men. The men and their guns.

I stood up.

'Mrs Monroe,' I screamed. 'Get out of here.' And waved my arms and yelled her name again.

A man appeared a short way in front of her. Then another. I screamed again.

A loud crack. The first man fell to the ground as I dropped down behind the blackthorn and swarmed sideways until I could see the bridleway through a gap.

The man on the ground wasn't moving. But the other was still standing. Why hadn't Wanda shot him too? She had two shots before she needed to reload.

And then I saw he wasn't alone. He held Mrs Monroe tight to him. My ex-husband, David, held Mrs Monroe tight to him as he turned round and round with her head buried in his shoulder. As if in a lovers' embrace, without a hair-breadth of air between them. Except his hand wasn't caressing her hair. It was holding a gun pressed against it.

The world stopped.

FORTY-FOUR

KEZIA

SAME DAY

'Come out,' he yelled.

Come out? Did he think I was stupid?

'I'll shoot her if you don't.'

Surely he wouldn't. He must know he was a dead man without Mrs Monroe as a shield.

'I won't kill her. But there won't be much left when I've finished.'

The sense of what he'd said hit my brain at the same time as a shot resounded through the trees. A tight scream followed. Not Mrs Monroe's voice. A man's.

I hoped against hope the scream came from the fourth man still behind the cars and that Wanda was somewhere now taking cold and efficient aim at David.

If it was safe to shoot. Even if she got him in the head, might some dying reflex press his finger on the trigger?

'Come out,' he said again. 'Or do I need to shoot her knee off to get your attention?'

He had my attention. Every scrap of it. I needed to get his. I needed to get his gun pointing away from Mrs Monroe.

I'd lost the power to stop myself anyway. I couldn't stay here and listen to him shoot bullets into Mrs Monroe's body.

My legs pushed me to my feet and I started walking down to meet him, my gun pointing towards him. It felt more like a shield than a weapon.

I stopped once I reached the path, and stood a few yards away from him.

'Kezia,' he said. Then, 'Kezi. Oh no.'

He hadn't known it was me. Of course he hadn't.

I knew what he was thinking. Nothing supernatural about that. I'd lived with him for over twenty years. His mind was leaping ahead. He always overthought things. It was one of the reasons he was such a good solicitor, always combing the details of his clients' cases, looking for dangers that might catch the unwary out.

I looked into his eyes.

The laughing David I'd married was no longer there. The one who'd sworn with me that we'd walk our own path and leave our families behind.

This was the David I'd caught glimpses of during the final months of our marriage unravelling. A David I'd tried to pretend didn't exist. A David desperate to escape the mess he'd got himself into.

And that frightened me more than anything, because Mrs Monroe and I were the only things standing in his way.

Any moment now he'd realise I hadn't shot the tyres out. That it couldn't be me who'd picked his colleagues off one by one. That there was someone else out there. He'd realise he needed to cut his losses and get himself away. I had to distract him. But how?

'What are you doing, David?'

His face blanked. Wrong question.

'It was my fault,' I said. 'Wasn't it? I should have realised there wasn't much money. I should have got a job. I shouldn't have spent so much. Keeping Bathy was so expensive. I'm sorry, David. I'm so sorry.'

Nothing. Not a hint he'd heard me. Except he hadn't shot me. Not yet. I tried a bit more.

'You had to borrow money from your uncle, didn't you? To get us out of the hole we were in?'

His face shifted. He was listening.

'It was only to buy into the burger van,' he said. 'Giles was full of ideas. And Sean, too. I thought it would make money. And then I was going to buy more vans. Or invest in different small businesses. Give other people starting up a chance.'

He sounded briefly like the old David. The one who was consumed by each passing passion. Had I missed this one? Somewhere in between the sportsman and the athlete, he'd seen himself as an investor. A benefactor making people's dreams come true.

It crossed my mind that the first David I'd met, the man determined to turn his back on his family and make it on his own, might have been as ephemeral as all the other Davids.

'But Covid happened,' David said. 'And Sean walked out. I realised he was the worker and the one with the flair...'

I could see how it had played out. Pressure from his uncle to repay the loan. The idea of converting the van to manufacture something more profitable. David's idea? His uncle's? It didn't matter.

I had to get Mrs Monroe away from him.

'I didn't kill them, Kezia.' David's voice broke through my thoughts. 'I told you when you came, I had nothing to do with the Cooper deaths.'

And God help me, I still believed him. He must have seen it in my face.

'I did send Chloe the tarot cards. You were right about that. Storm Beatrice took the power out in the barn here and we had a batch in progress. It only needed purifying and finishing. I'd sold it already and I had to find a way of getting it done. So I told Giles to make his father let us use the stables. Just on the Monday. That was all. The stables were closed anyway. I needed to put pressure on him. But I had no need to kill them because Giles caved in and persuaded his father. So I drove the van over on Sunday night. After the stables had closed. I found them all then. I had nothing to do with their deaths.'

Still he clutched Mrs Monroe to him. Although I thought it was a reflex. I bent down slowly and put the gun on the ground. It was useless anyway. David knew I'd never shoot him.

'Let's go,' I said. 'Leave her. We'll take a Land Cruiser and get out of here.'

'They're attached to each other.'

So he'd already considered it.

'I'll undo it.'

For a moment I thought he might agree. He was stressed. And desperate. Maybe the years of being together would overrule the months apart and the easy trust we'd had in each other would snap back into place.

'Come on,' I said.

But he hesitated. The moment passed. A weird smile broke his face.

'I'm sorry,' he said.

He was going to shoot me. I saw it in the hardening of his stance and the tensing of the tendons in his hands. He took the gun away from Mrs Monroe's head and turned it towards me.

Now, I thought. Now, Wanda. This is the moment. While he's still coming to terms with the reality of shooting me. It won't last long. What are you waiting for?

'David,' I said. 'I love you.'

His mouth opened on a quick inhale. Horror flooded his body. He jerked the gun away from me. And then there was a crack. He fell.

Mrs Monroe screamed.

Something barrelled into my side and knocked me down.

Then nothing. Except breathing. Raspy breathing. Mine? I held my breath. Not mine.

I raised my head.

'Stay down.' The voice was close to my ear. I turned.

A man lay on the ground next to me. Unshaven and crumpled. Breathing heavily. Carter. DCI Carter.

He seized my gun lying on the ground between us, broke it and took the bullets out. Then picked up a walkie-talkie, fumbled around in the dirt and found the earpiece, which he rammed into his ear.

'Carter,' he said. 'Update.'

He listened for a few seconds.

'A firearm here. But made safe.'

He got to his feet and held an arm out to me. I ignored it and stood up on my own. A police officer, bulky with vest and helmet, knelt by David's body. Beyond him, another leaned over Mrs Monroe, now sitting on the grass.

'You OK?' Carter asked. 'You nearly got yourself shot.'

'I don't think he would have. That one is David Kingsley.' I pointed to David's body.

But Carter had gone over to the other body. The first man shot by Wanda as David grabbed Mrs Monroe. Carter rolled it over. It was the man who'd arrived later. His dark overcoat flapped open, revealing a police uniform underneath.

'Beresford,' he said, and then something I couldn't make out.

Behind him, more officers emerged from the trees. All wearing vests and helmets. All carrying guns. One came over and examined mine.

'Bag it,' Carter said.

'The van,' I said. 'It's a drug factory. That's what this is all about. David's family. The Kingsleys. They're behind all this. Nothing to do with Marty. Nothing at all.'

He ignored me.

'Stay here,' he said and gestured to one of the officers to keep me.

I ignored him in turn and went over to Mrs Monroe.

'Are you all right?'

It was the stupidest of questions. She shook and shivered so the silver blanket the officer had wrapped her in glittered in the dull light. She looked tiny somehow.

'She's been drugged, I think,' the officer said. 'She's not making much sense. Look at her eyes.'

Her pupils were huge and black in her crumpled white face and her lips red and raw. Strands of yellowy-white clung to the skin round her mouth. Adhesive, I thought. They'd stuck tape over her mouth.

'She's been missing since Saturday night,' I said. 'She takes pills for her blood pressure.'

'Don't worry. She's going straight to hospital. They'll check everything there. What's her name?'

'Mrs Monroe.'

'First name?'

'I don't know.'

A raspy croak came out of Mrs Monroe's lips. We bent to listen.

'Antonia,' she repeated.

'What happened?' I asked her.

It was another stupid question but I couldn't seem to come up with any sensible ones.

'Thirsty,' she managed to get out.

'We'll get you something as soon as you've been checked over. The ambulance will be here soon.'

Two paramedics arrived and pushed past me to squat beside Mrs Monroe, but she waved her hand at me.

'Knocked me on the head,' she said when I knelt down. Her voice was stronger now. 'Just came to. Looking for you.'

'Mrs Monroe. You've been missing for nearly two days.'

'Two...?'

'Don't you remember'?

'Maybe. Bits. Sleeping.'

'Where? Can you remember?'

She shook her head and winced.

'No.'

'Or who. Did you see who did this to you?'

She didn't shake her head this time but gazed past me.

'Yellow.' She managed to get out.

I waited.

'Yellow flowers.'

'In a vase? A garden? On a shirt?'

'No. Pillow. Yellow flowers on the pillow.'

A pillow with yellow flowers? She was confused. They must have taken her somewhere though, then brought her back here. Why, though? Why hadn't they killed her?

'My wrist,' she said. 'It hurts.'

The paramedics pushed me out of the way.

Wanda strolled down from the far side of the bridleway. She was on her phone, carrying her gun safely in the other hand. Officers shouted at her to stop and put her weapon on the ground. She obeyed the second part but carried on walking to me as she finished the call.

'Did you shoot him?' I asked. 'David, I mean?'

'No comment,' she said, and for a brief second a tight smile broke her blank expression. Officers surrounded her.

'And you are?' Carter had come up behind me.

'Wanda Stainthorpe,' she said. 'I'd like my guns back when you've finished examining them.'

'Wanda Stainthorpe. I am arresting you on suspicion of murder. You do not have to say anything but it may harm your defence if you do not mention, when questioned, something which you later rely on in court.'

I listened in disbelief as he said the familiar words.

'You can't arrest her.'

'Of course he can and he has to. But don't worry, it won't be for long.' Wanda held out her arms and Carter snapped handcuffs round her wrists.

Carter turned to me. 'Kezia Heron, I am arresting you—'

'She didn't shoot anyone,' Wanda said.

'I worked that out. I am arresting you on suspicion of murder.'

And once again he repeated the police mantra. He shifted his gaze to an officer standing by me. 'Hand-swab them both then take them to the station. Separate cars and separate rooms.'

'You can't do that,' I said.

He ignored me.

'What about Marty? You'll release him now, won't you?'

He turned his back on me, but I shook the officer holding me off and grabbed his arm.

'You'll release Marty now, won't you?'

'No.'

'But... The Kingsleys. Miles Kingsley. He's behind all this. Not Marty. You can't still think it's Marty.'

Something on him buzzed and he reached into his coat pocket and pulled out a phone. His eyes narrowed when he saw the number.

'Sir,' he said. The creases above his brows deepened as he listened. He looked briefly over at Wanda, then walked out of earshot. I thought he was arguing.

An officer rolled a damp swab over my fingers, then snapped plastic bags round my hands. I realised I was actually being arrested.

'Let's go,' the officer said to me. But Carter lifted his head from his phone and held up a hand.

'Take them to the cars. I want them out of the scene. But wait for me there.'

We traipsed back to the gate.

I thought of resisting but the officer holding my arm had handcuffs at her belt. Besides, I needed to get this over and done with as soon as possible so I could make a fuss about Marty.

We reached the gate. A chilly-looking officer wrote our names on a clipboard as we ducked under the black and yellow tape. The last of the adrenalin leached from my blood and I felt cold. I shoved my hands in their plastic bags into my pockets, glad they hadn't cuffed me. I felt the yarrow I'd picked earlier. I'd have liked to think it had helped but really it was all down to Wanda.

Josh was waiting in the lane.

'Can I have a quick word with her?' he said to the officer escorting me.

'Make it quick.'

'Josh, they— Carter still thinks it was Marty.'

'I know. I know.'

'Can't you do something?'

'Kezia. It wasn't the Kingsleys. They had no reason and there's nothing linking them to the scene. We heard everything David said to you.'

David's words flooded back. Josh was right. The Coopers' deaths had wrecked his plans. Wrecked the Kingsleys' plans.

'Were you there?'

'In the background. Waiting. Only Carter and the firearms unit were allowed to get close.'

'Waiting for what?'

'For someone to turn up.'

'Who?'

He cast a quick look around at the waiting officers standing tactfully a few metres away and dropped his voice.

'Beresford. The sergeant at Thorpe. I'll explain later.'

The officer escorting me signalled to Josh that time was up and he moved away.

The narrow lane was blocked with vans and cars. Most were police but one was unmarked and windowless. Probably for the bodies.

So many bodies. The Coopers and Boyes. And now, David.

And, with a jolt, like an electric shock, I remembered Lauren. How had she got involved in this? How had she got herself killed? Because Becky had given her a tarot card for me?

I thought back to the message Lauren had left. She'd worked something out because of what I'd said last time we met. Was that it? Nothing to do with the envelope Becky had given her for me?

Last time we'd talked had been in her shop. What had I said? She'd told me she and Sean had split up. because of his gambling.

We'd discussed the Coopers and Freddy while choosing material for my handbag – the lovely scrap of burgundy leather and the cloth with its pretty pattern of herbs. I felt the yarrow in my pocket again. Herbs. Herbs everywhere. In my tea. At my allotment and in the pots at the studio where I'd tipped the ashes with the charred cloth that I thought belonged to the murderer.

Chloe Cooper smelling herbs. And that strange fluttering at the edge of her vision when she'd been shot. Charlie Cooper had seen it too.

And then I remembered the roses. The smell of roses in the first attack at Mrs Monroe's house as Bill had fallen to the ground, still clutching the rose-patterned blouse he'd wanted to buy his wife.

Maybe the herbs weren't a scent?

And why had the shooter waited? Why had they waited downstairs? Why hadn't they gone straight upstairs and killed Chloe? They'd killed the other three Coopers in quick succession, why had they waited for Chloe?

Because they *had* gone upstairs eventually. Josh had said there was mud on the stairs when he'd told me about his terrible fear he'd find Freddy's corpse in one of the bedrooms.

Freddy...

And everything shifted in my head.

Until it formed an entirely different picture.

I considered my picture as officers escorted us to two cars parked alongside Bathsheba and Harding's field on the opposite side of the lane and boxed in by the vans. What did it mean?

Wanda looked over the top of the cars at me.

'Tell them everything,' she said. 'Every little detail. It will be all right.'

She smiled, quite a pleasant smile for her, as one of the officers placed a hand on her head and ushered her into the first car.

She was wrong though. Everything wasn't going to be all right. Carter was determined to pin the murders on Marty. The real murderer was going to get away.

'I can manage,' I said as another officer put her hand on my head, but she insisted.

What was I going to do?

I stared out of the window. Bathsheba had retreated to the far corner of the field, by the old barn. Harding stood near her but looked in our direction from time to time.

Carter suddenly arrived and spoke to the officer standing by Wanda's car. He opened the door and Wanda got out. They talked. I could only see the back of Wanda's head, her ponytail still neat and tight under her cap. Carter, facing me, was unmistakeably furious though, spitting words out through white and tight lips. After a while, Wanda shoved her hands forward and he undid her handcuffs, then flung them into the back of the car.

Wanda strode up the road without a backward glance. What had just happened? Why had they let her go?

'What was all that about?' I asked the officer in the front of the car. He exchanged a look with his colleague, who was clearly as desperate to know the answer as I was.

'No idea,' he said. 'All over now. They're moving the vans and then we'll go.'

All over.

Except it wasn't.

I thought about trying to tell the police what I now believed had happened. No point. They wouldn't believe me. I had another idea. Probably not a good one but I was tired of trying to do things the right way. It hadn't worked so far and I couldn't see any reason why it would work in the future.

The vans alongside us started to move away, leaving us free to set off. It was now or never.

FORTY-FIVE
KEZIA

SAME DAY

'I'm feeling sick,' I said. And then, 'I need to get out.' I let my breath come in panicky gasps like someone about to vomit and made a retching noise, undid the seatbelt and fumbled with the handle. The door was locked. Of course. 'Please. Please let me out.'

They gave each other a quick glance and then one of them got out and opened the door for me. I stumbled out and round the side of the car, knelt over the ditch and retched until I produced some yellowish liquid that burned my throat.

The officer stood over me the whole time.

This was no good.

I stayed there while I thought.

'If I could just sit for a few minutes,' I said.

I staggered to my feet and sat back in the car. Leaving my legs sticking out though.

'Could you leave the door open, please. In case I need to be sick again.'

She shrugged but did as I asked.

A van drew up alongside us. My officers stepped away and started chatting to its occupants.

I had a chance. While they were distracted. I only needed a short start, but it still took every ounce of grit to force myself to move.

I counted to three, shot out of the car and was over the fence before I heard shouts behind me. I raced across the field, tearing the plastic bags from my hands.

They must have hesitated a few seconds, not realising what I planned to do and thinking I'd be easy to catch. I was a middle-aged woman, shaky and tired from a vile ordeal, and they were young and fit. Bathy's head collar hung from a nail at the entrance to the barn. Still attached to its leading rope. I snatched it and tied the other end of the rope to create a makeshift bridle, then looked back. They were only starting to climb the fence.

'Bathy,' I said.

But she'd already come to me, seeing the head collar in my hands. She bent her head obligingly as I pulled it on and clipped it shut.

Over by the cars, officers yelled. They'd worked it out.

I ran and jumped, then scrabbled my way onto her back. It wasn't pretty but she helped by standing stock-still.

My beautiful, wonderful horse.

I felt the muscles ripple across her back. She was excited and ready for anything after weeks stuck in the field.

If only we had more time.

More shouting and Harding came into view. Unsettled by people running towards us. Excited by it. He shook his head and moved away from them, walking and then breaking into a canter before swerving round at the fence and coming back at a full gallop, his hooves thudding into the ground.

The police were nearly upon us. Bathy danced, still happy but a little unsettled too by the noise and people. We were too close to the fence here. She needed some space. A quick glance back told me it was too late. The police were nearly upon us.

Then Harding galloped towards them.

Just letting off steam. But impressive nevertheless.

Enough to make the police stop.

I had a chance.

I forced myself to stay calm, and made Bathy take as wide a circle round as I dared, then pointed her at the fence. As she started cantering, I knew she'd understood. She didn't hesitate. Went straight up to the fence, paused to gather the energy to power her hind legs for the jump, then lifted and soared over the wooden rails.

I patted her again when we landed, told her what a clever girl she was and urged her onwards and onto the moors. She needed no further encouragement and broke into a gallop.

The sound of hooves smacking the ground came from behind us.

Shit.

One of the police officers could ride.

But as I darted a quick look over my shoulder, I saw lovely, lovely Harding, riderless and galloping along behind us. Of course. He loved an outing. He'd been stuck in the field for weeks. And Bathsheba was his fieldmate and his stablemate. He wasn't going to stay behind.

We pelted across the moors until I was sure the police would never find us let alone catch us, then I slowed Bathy to an easy canter, then a walk. Harding matched us.

I shut them in a field near a cottage with children's toys scattered over the back garden, undid Bathy's collar and tied it to a fence with the rope. I'd text their whereabouts to Josh later.

After I'd made a couple of phone calls, I walked up the long straight road that was the village centre. It was mostly old stone cottages, the sort that are now too expensive for local people and are either Airbnbs or second homes. This village had clung on to its pub though, plus a post office cum general store and an award-winning butcher with a clientele from miles around.

I still had ten minutes to wait. I spent it eyeing up the hot sausage rolls. I was hungry. And thirsty. I had no money though. I was wondering whether I dared steal a bottle of water when my taxi arrived.

'Thank you, Sam,' I said as I got in. 'I couldn't think who else to call.'

A voice from behind me said hello.

'And hello to you,' I said, turning to smile at the child in the car seat in the back. For a moment I couldn't remember if Sam had a little girl or boy and, wrapped up in a puffy all-in-one suit with a hood, with only plump face and hands visible, it was hard to tell.

'I had to bring her,' Sam said. 'Couldn't find anyone to look after her at such—'

'Short notice.' I finished the sentence for her. 'But thank you. You came all the same.'

'I'm four,' the little girl said.

Her name came back to me.

'Hello, Ellie who's four years old,' I said. 'I'm forty-seven.' I didn't tell her my name. Who knew what the fallout of my running from the police would be? Better for Sam if nothing connected her to me.

'Where are we going?'

I told her.

'There's tea in the flask,' she said as she reset the maps app on her phone.

'Sam, you're a life-saver.' I glugged a few mouthfuls, then sipped at the rest as she drove away.

'Want to tell me anything?'

'Do you mind if I don't?'

She shook her head. 'Do *you* mind if I put her tape on?'

'Of course not.'

The Wheels on the Bus filled the car. Sam and Ellie sang along while my mind leapt into the near future. I wasn't sure what I was doing. But I had to try.

I couldn't let the murderer get away with it. Four people killed. Five, if you included Lauren. Marty's life nearly destroyed. For a few seconds tears smeared my vision. Tears of rage. I hissed a breath in through clenched teeth.

'OK?' Sam said.

'Yes. Very much OK.'

I needed a plan. That was what Zina always said. To get anywhere in life you needed a plan. Maybe that was where I'd been going wrong. I came up with one; a simple one. Go there. Break in. Find evidence. There must be some evidence of Mrs Monroe's presence. Call police.

'Drop me just before the bridge,' I said as we neared my destination. 'I'll walk the rest of the way.'

She did as I asked.

'How much do I owe you?'

'Nothing. This one's on the house.'

I didn't have it in me to argue.

'If you were anyone else, I'd make you go home,' she added. 'What are you doing?'

'I wish I knew.'

'Kezia.'

'I have to see this through. If I don't get in touch in the next few hours, will you call... Call the police and tell them you dropped me here.'

'Kezia.'

'Only if I don't call though. I don't want you involved.'

I waited until she'd driven away and walked slowly over the bridge, stopping to gaze down at the river's brown, turbulent waters. The banks rose steeply here and the river tore through a narrow channel. If you fell in you'd be swept away in no time. It was the ideal place to get rid of a body. It might well not surface until it came to the flat waters of the Humber estuary. Yet they hadn't used it to get rid of Mrs Monroe.

And that gave me hope I was right.

FORTY-SIX
KEZIA

SAME DAY

It was at the end of a long and winding track through fields of sheep. A small cottage hidden in a cluster of graceful lime trees. And very close to the river. Exactly as Alan had said when I'd rung him after leaving Bathsheba and Harding in the field. I could hear the water now, although I couldn't see it. Stone built, two up and two down, the sort of place that used to house agricultural workers and their families but now sold for hundreds of thousands of pounds to people with money.

People like Dennis Price.

Mrs Monroe had been kept here. I was sure of that. In one of the upstairs bedrooms. No houses nearby. Nothing but sheep. No risk of her being heard, if she woke up enough to scream. If I could get a look upstairs, I'd see soft cotton pillowcases with a pattern of flowers on them. Yellow flowers. Exactly as Mrs Monroe had described. Probably sewn by Annie.

Did she know what her husband had done?

I wasn't certain.

But she'd have probably approved. She was a great one for

putting family first, and that was what this was all about. She'd do anything for Sean. And for Freddy.

And then I heard the faint sound of an excited child. Freddy must be here. Round the back.

Who was with him? The killer? I peered round.

Freddy and his granddad played football on a stretch of grass at the top of a short, steep bank leading down to the river, although a makeshift barrier of plastic fencing stopped the ball – or Freddy – from rolling into the rushing water below.

They weren't really playing football. Dennis kicked the ball towards the toddler, who ran after it and threw himself down and over it to stop it rolling away, then screamed with joy.

They were both utterly absorbed.

Dennis hadn't heard me arrive, but he caught sight of me and came to an abrupt halt mid-kick. The ball trickled slowly towards Freddy, who, tiring of the game, sat down with a thump and started examining the grass between his wide-flung legs.

The pleasure on Dennis's face faded.

He knew why I'd come.

Something I'd said or done when I'd asked him all the questions during my visit with Alan had made him suspicious. Maybe he'd recognised me as the woman who'd gone with Mrs Monroe to the police station. Our faces had been in all the local papers and he'd have scoured them, worried about anything casting doubt on Marty's guilt. Easy for him to put the tracker on my car. He knew where I parked it. He knew what colour it was. Alan had said he worked in electronics, so he knew about these things. He'd tracked us to Cooper's cottage and panicked.

He'd abducted Mrs Monroe. Not the Kingsleys. She'd be dead if it had been the Kingsleys.

'I worked it out,' I said. There didn't seem much point pretending. Really I should have left as soon as I'd heard Freddy playing and realised they were here. I should leave now. But I wanted an end to this.

'I worked it out,' I said again.

Dennis had burned the bloodstained cloth in Alan's incinerator. To destroy the evidence linking the killer to the Coopers. Probably when he picked Alan up early Monday morning to go down to the cottage. Alan kept his fishing tackle in the allotment shed, so Dennis often met him there.

Alan would normally be here. It was a Monday. The day the two fished together, but Alan had told me Dennis had cancelled last night. Said he and Annie were taking Freddy to Lightwater Valley Adventure Park. I'd thought I'd be able to search the cottage, but for some reason Dennis had lied.

The killer came out of the cottage now, holding a laundry basket piled high with sheets and pillowcases. She took a moment to watch Freddy lever himself up and trot after the ball. Delight melted her features. From the curls of her dark brown hair with its strange streak of blond to the loose folds of her flowery dress, she oozed nurturing.

She saw me.

I remembered the tarot card I'd chosen twice now. The Empress. She was the Empress. Not my mother. Annie Price put down her basket and held out her arms to Freddy. The boy ran to her and she picked him up and cradled him, pressing her face against his.

A breeze came up and fluttered the folds of her dress, patterned with sprigs of honeysuckle. For a moment I could smell their scent as though the wind had blown its traces towards me.

Sense confusion.

That's what had happened in the visions.

A fluttering of a skirt or dress as the force of the shotgun blast made the shooter recoil. The pattern of herbs barely seen by Charlie Cooper and his daughter, Chloe, but nevertheless registered somewhere in their brains and emerging as a half-remembered scent.

A skirt or dress made by the clever fingers of an adept seamstress like Annie. And, maybe, just maybe, she'd given the scraps to her son's girlfriend, Lauren, who in turn had used them to line my handbag.

But it was all too nebulous to tell the police. And too nebulous for me to accuse her to her face.

Besides, I wasn't sure.

So in the end, I stuck to the everyday stuff.

'Sean's alibi.'

I spoke to Dennis. Somehow I couldn't bring myself to talk to Annie. Not with Freddy in her arms. Anyway, he was my only hope. I didn't think he was a murderer. He'd abducted Mrs Monroe rather than killing her. And he'd let her go when the police's dismissal of her disappearance had made him realise she wasn't dangerous.

'The police discovered Sean wasn't with your wife all Sunday night when the Coopers were massacred,' I said. 'He had a meal with her and then they went their separate ways. They brought him in for questioning but his new alibi checked out, so they released him. But it's left your wife without an alibi for the vital hours.'

'My wife?'

'Your wife. She went to the Coopers' that Sunday night. Took Cooper's gun and shot the family. She knew where Charlie Cooper kept his gun because he'd fetched it to threaten them the last time she went there with Sean.'

He said nothing. The blood had drained from his face while I spoke, leaving it grey and making the strange lumps stand out all the more.

'She waited. She shot Elaine and Giles and Charlie straight away. Then she waited in the sitting room. I could never work out why. I thought maybe the killer hadn't meant to shoot Chloe. But then why hadn't they left? And then I remembered Freddy. Your wife couldn't bear to shoot Chloe in front of him. But she had to kill her. There was no point to the others' deaths if Chloe was still alive.'

I waited to see if he'd protest. He didn't.

'And then,' I said. 'I think Annie went upstairs to check Freddy was safe in his cot and wouldn't come to any harm if he was alone for a while. It was all because of Freddy. Because she'd learned that afternoon at the panto meeting that she was never going to see him again if she didn't do something. Chloe Cooper was going to London. It was supposed to be secret but everybody knew. I guess they overheard her talking to Raymond. Or she told too many people.'

Dennis said nothing.

'And Chloe leaving was going to put an end to Annie's Sunday afternoons with Freddy. I imagine he spent most of his time with the sewing group. While Chloe rehearsed. It must have been a terrible blow for Annie when she learned she was going to lose even that small pleasure. Wasn't it, Dennis?'

Still he said nothing.

'I understand how she felt,' I added.

He looked over to where Annie had been standing with Freddy in her arms.

She was no longer there. Nor was Freddy.

'I don't think so.' His voice was so low that for a moment I barely made out his words. 'I don't think you do understand. You don't have children. I suppose you never wanted them. But Annie, she was meant to be a mother. It was all she wanted. And there was no reason why she wouldn't have been. If it hadn't been for me.'

Part of me desperately wanted to hear him out. I wanted to be sure I was right, and I'd expected an outright denial rather than this acceptance of my accusation. But Annie's disappearance worried me.

'It nearly killed her when I said we couldn't have any more children after we learned Sean had inherited my illness.'

'I'm sure she had her reasons,' I said, trying to see where Annie had gone. 'But nothing can justify—'

His hands grabbed my shoulders and shook them until I looked at him.

'You're not trying to understand,' he said. 'Put yourself in her shoes. She was a young woman. She wanted a family. She'd married me in the face of a lot of opposition from her family and her friends. I know that. I would have set her free. She could have married again. Had the huge family she wanted. But she didn't. We stayed together and she made the best of it. She had Sean, after all. And for a long time everything seemed fine.'

He took a deep breath and his grasp on my shoulders loosened. I wondered if I could wrench myself away. But when I twitched, his hold strengthened.

'Then we reached the age when all our friends had grandchildren,' he went on. 'Once again there were children everywhere. I knew Annie found it hard but she soldiered on. Until, out of the blue, Chloe Cooper became pregnant and Sean was the father. Annie lived the seven months between us finding out and Freddy's birth as though they were the last months of her life. Never sure if Chloe was going to have an abortion. Never sure how the baby would be. And then Freddy arrived. And he was perfect. It was as though all her Christmases had come at once—'

I cut him off.

'Except Charlie Cooper wasn't keen on letting Sean and therefore your wife see Freddy,' I said. 'And then he stopped the contact completely. So all she had left were her Sundays when Chloe brought Freddy to rehearsals.'

Something hit me in the back and I stumbled. My legs failed to rebalance me. They crumpled and I collapsed forward onto the grass.

Dennis looked beyond me to where I had been standing. I turned my head.

Annie stood there. An overall over her dress, wearing rubber gloves.

'Annie,' Dennis said. His voice was full of pain.

'We'll put her in the river,' his wife replied. 'Don't worry. She'll be gone in no time. It runs much faster here than in the centre of Thorpe.'

I should get up but I wasn't sure I could. The fall had knocked the breath out of me and I felt strangely shivery although my face was sweating.

'You'll need to get the hose out and rinse the grass.'

'Annie, it's no good.'

Time to tell her it wouldn't work. That Alan knew I was here. That I'd told Sam to call the police and tell them where I'd gone if I didn't get in touch. But my voice had disappeared. Some connection between the words in my brain and my mouth had been broken. I forced myself to take a deep breath. And a sharp and agonising pain tore through my back.

What was that?

Above me the Prices were exchanging terse and bitter words, but I didn't have the strength to look up at them, let alone speak. Instead I gazed at the grass, damp in the early evening air. A dark red patch stained it. And was spreading. Dark red and still gleaming with damp.

Blood. My blood.

I'd been stabbed.

I reached an arm round. A further stab of pain. The knife was still there. Should I pull it out? I wanted to pull it out. I hated having it stuck in my back. But would it make it worse?

Hands grabbed my legs. I forced myself to look. Annie had seized them and was gesturing to her husband to take my arms. She tried to roll me onto my back. Onto my back with the knife sticking out. I kicked at her.

'People know I'm here.' I found my voice.

The effort of speaking unlocked my body and I forced an arm round my back and tugged at the knife. It came out. Pain screamed through my body. Blood felt damp against my skin. I passed out.

The feel of hands round my ankles brought me back. Dennis knelt at my feet. He tugged my boots off and slipped a noose of rope round my ankles, pulled it tight. He'd already tied my hands in front of me.

'Alan knows I'm here,' I said.

He heard me.

'Alan thinks we aren't,' he said. 'He thinks Annie's dragged me to Lightwater Valley Adventure Park. We'll go there now. Just to be sure.'

'Sam knows I'm here,' I said. 'She dropped me.'

He picked up my bag, found my mobile phone. His wife came out of the house.

'Freddy's fast asleep,' she said.

'Good. Get a cloth.'

She went back in.

'Why are you doing this?'

He ignored me. I tried to sit up but trussed as I was it was impossible. I screamed. He slapped a hand over my mouth, then wound parcel tape round and round, so tightly he ground my lips into my teeth.

He took the cloth Annie brought and wiped the blood off my right hand, then held my finger against my phone.

'I'll put it in the wash,' Annie said.

'No. I'll burn it. Everything must be burned. Anything she's been near. Plus the clothes we've got on. I'll burn them, but here this time.' He went back to my mobile phone and scrolled through it. 'Sam. Sam taxi. I guess that's who she means.' He typed a few words. 'I'll get the bus into Thorpe afterwards. Take her phone with me. Leave it in the car park. If they trace it to here it'll look as though she left and dropped it.'

I wondered what he'd messaged Sam. Something short and sweet, saying everything was fine and I was going home. It wouldn't succeed in the long term. Josh would work it out – but I'd be dead by then.

'Take her legs,' he said.

I bucked and twisted and fought them every inch of the way but little by little they half-carried, half-dragged me down to the riverbank, where they dropped me on the grass. A couple of feet away the water ran smooth-surfaced and still. Almost inviting.

'I'll have to knock her out.' Dennis looked around.

'Can't we just put her in?'

'Need to remove the ropes and the tape. In case the body's ever found. It must look like an accident.'

'Pity I stabbed her. Can you do anything about that?'

Annie waited while he thought.

'Her body will be battered and torn enough to hide it. Fetch me the mallet, will you. It's under the stairs.' He sighed. 'I'll have to get rid of it too. Try not to touch anything else until we've had a shower.'

She nodded. Walked slowly back up the garden, her feet dragging a little and sighing. A little less Empress-like now, she was simply a tired woman with one too many jobs to do. Mr Price looked tired too. If only I had the use of my hands and feet. I could overpower him easily. Even against both of them, I could put up a good fight.

He looked down at me and sighed again.

'I'm sorry,' he muttered. 'Annie's never been good at seeing things through. I've always had to sort out her messes. I knew she'd done something when she came home on Sunday night. There was blood on her dress. She said it was pasta sauce from the restaurant but I knew it wasn't. She was strange. And smiling. And chatty. But she asked me something odd. How long did I think a toddler would survive without water? So when I learned about the Cooper killing, I worked it out.'

Annie appeared at the top of the bank. 'I can't find it.'

'Shelf above the door,' he said patiently, and then to me: 'She... She won't do it again. It was a one-off.'

I didn't think he knew about Lauren. I didn't think he knew Annie had slipped out of the panto meeting to accost Lauren on the footbridge. Smashed her over the head with something and pushed her in.

When I'd seen Lauren in her shop, she'd told me Sean had been gambling. I thought she knew it was the evening of the Cooper murders and she'd worked out that meant Annie didn't have an alibi. And she'd told me in the church that Freddy's trauma, his inability to sleep through the night, came from being left alone for twenty-four hours after the killings. According to Annie, that was. But how had Annie known how long it was? The police had never released the time of death, instead asking everyone to account for their movements from Sunday evening until the bodies were discovered on Monday evening.

None of it was outright proof Annie had killed the Coopers, but it might have been enough to make Lauren wonder. And enough to make her ask Annie a couple of questions. I didn't think I'd ever know. But whatever it was, it had been enough for Annie to get rid of her.

Dennis looked up. 'You found it then.'

Annie came down the slope carrying a large wooden mallet. Its weight dragged down her arms and she walked jerkily. Fear swamped my body. I could see the immediate future. The mallet raised and smashing into my head. The blood and chips of white bone flying out. I'd never survive it.

Dennis hurried up the slope to take it from her.

I didn't want to die. I wanted to survive. There were things I wanted to do. Little things like ride again. Like see Marty and check he was OK. Talk to Mrs Monroe. And bigger things too. Like work out the shape of the next part of my life. I'd been treading water for so long.

Terror burst into an open flower. Yet through its centre ran a calm fierceness. There was only one way out of this. I couldn't fight. I couldn't scream. I couldn't run. I couldn't even stand. So I took a deep breath and rolled over and over until I dropped off the bank and into the river.

FORTY-SEVEN
KEZIA

SAME DAY

A splash and the water closed over my head. It was cold. I rose back to the surface and tried to take a great gulp of air. Shit. I'd forgotten the tape over my mouth. I threshed around as much as my tied legs and arms would let me, then promptly sank again as the water infiltrated my clothes, turning them into heavy weights. My knees hit the bottom and the current seized me and whisked me away, scraping my legs through grit and mud.

I was a stone, dragged along the riverbed. Stones sink. Stones can't swim. I can't swim.

I hate water. Nebulous. Shape-shifting. Insidious stuff. Water gives way. It doesn't hold. It doesn't hold.

And yet it pulled and tumbled me. Strong and forceful. I fought back. I kicked back. My lashed feet smacked the bottom and propelled me up until my head broke out. I forced air in through my nostrils and sank again, hit the bed, then kicked myself up once more.

This time when my head broke the surface I kept on kicking, bending my knees and thrusting down. I stretched my arms out in front of me and somehow I stayed up.

I'd travelled. The bank I'd rolled off was already metres away. Mr Price stood staring after me and behind him figures ran down the bank. In uniform. The police? If only I'd waited.

The river whirled round a curve and they were out of sight.

This was OK, though. I was managing to keep my head above water. Managing to breathe. Despite the tape. The river must widen at some point. Become shallow and slower. I thought of the gravel beaches that lined it at Thorpe. The children paddling in summer.

But Thorpe was miles from here. And the water was cold. Mustn't think about that. Mustn't think about the iciness chilling my flesh, slowing the blood and freezing the muscles. Think of something else.

What if the river never widens? What if it flows straight into the sea?

Think of something else. Keep on kicking. Keep on breathing and think of something else.

The Empress. Annie Price. No, the tarot was wrong. Annie Price wasn't the Empress. Annie Price brought death, not life.

And I was back with my mother. The old Empress. Fertile. Passionate. Following each new desire wherever it took her and dragging us children along. Giving us no choice. No stability. No grounding. No future.

Anger flickered.

Look what you've done, I told her. *Look where the childhood you gave us has brought me. Did you never question your life? Think about the effect it had on us? Look at me. I've spent my whole life getting away from you. Trying to become everything you weren't. And I've failed. Failed. It's time someone told you how wrong our childhood was. How awful you were. How awful you are. A dreadful woman. Immoral. Selfish. Stupid. Blind to everything but what you wanted.*

Rage sent fire to my muscles and I kicked harder. Felt warmer. Could I thrust my way through the current and to the bank? I tried. My legs jerked and pumped and flailed against the current. My arms pushed and pulled. I snatched at the air. But when I cast a desperate look at the bank, it was no closer. The current was too powerful.

My thoughts erupted in a despairing scream. Smothered by the tape.

My head slammed into something. A brief moment of shock. Of stasis. The water whirled, seized me again and would have dashed me away but I forced myself round, lifted my arms over the obstacle and clamped it to my body in a desperate embrace.

It was a small tree. It had fallen into the water, tearing a great chunk of bank away, but still had its roots buried into the earth. Storm damage.

I clung to it and found I was weeping. Warm dribbles of water on chilled flesh. And with the tears came strength. I edged my way to the bank. Inch by inch. Too terrified of losing my precious grip to go any faster. And by the time the rescuers arrived, I'd nearly made it.

THORPE GAZETTE

Shortage of space has forced us to suspend our series of articles on *Little Known Historical Facts about Thorpe and its Surroundings*. Fans of this series will be pleased to hear it will return next week with a section on spur making in Thorpe in the 6th and 7th centuries.

COOPER'S STABLES SHOOTINGS

A couple, both aged 65, have been charged in connection with the recent murders at Cooper's Stables where Charles, Elaine, Giles and Chloe Cooper all lost their lives. Although enquiries are ongoing, police are not looking for anyone else in connection with this case. The 17-year-old who was previously detained has been released without charge. The case has been of great local concern and residents will be pleased at the relatively speedy resolution to these tragic events.

ARRESTS MADE IN PETER WALKER MURDER CASE

The *Thorpe Gazette* has ceaselessly campaigned for the police to devote more resources to solving the abduction and killing of young Peter Walker over a year ago. The effects of the tragedy still echo through the local community.
We understand from sources within the police that arrests have been made and that officers are confident charges will be brought. While we welcome this news, we feel there are lessons to be learned from the handling of this case.

WOMAN RESCUED FROM RIVER BURN

The expertise of North Yorkshire Water Rescue Services was once again called into service to extract a local woman, Kezia Heron, from the swollen waters of the River Burn last Monday. The unit arrived promptly at the scene following calls from local residents and executed a textbook rescue. Ms Heron was taken to hospital, where she is expected to make a full and speedy recovery. Ms Heron told our correspondent that she was deeply grateful to the rescue services for their intervention. North Yorkshire Water Rescue Services have issued the following statement:

Last year more than 250 people accidentally drowned in the UK, with most of them never intending to enter the water. We cannot stress enough how important it is to take care while walking or running next to water, particularly after heavy rain when river levels are high and currents strong. If you are walking a dog and they end up in the water, do not go in after them.

It would do us well to heed their warnings. Let's not forget the recent and tragic accidental death of Lauren Wargrove, who fell from the footbridge in the centre of Thorpe last Sunday. A petition has been launched by concerned locals to reinforce the footbridge barriers and can be signed using the link below.

MISSING PSYCHIC FOUND

Mrs Monroe, the local psychic reported as missing last weekend, has been found. She was discovered wandering in the woods on the Stainthorpe Shoot by the owner Ms Wanda Stainthorpe. 'The poor woman had clearly suffered a terrible fall,' Ms Stainthorpe told us. 'She was confused and in great pain. Luckily I was walking the dogs and came across her. Otherwise she could have wandered for days. We rarely have occasion to visit that part of the estate since vandalism forced us to move the pheasant pens elsewhere.'

The police, who, in the *Gazette*'s opinion, issued an unnecessarily hostile statement when Mrs Monroe was reported missing, said they were pleased to hear she had been found. 'People generally turn up within a week of being reported missing,' a spokesperson told us. 'We would however like to take this opportunity to publicly thank Mrs Monroe for her attempts to assist us with recent enquiries.'

If you're interested in a psychic consultation or tarot reading with Mrs Monroe, please see her advertisement in this edition of the *Gazette*.

TRAGEDY ON BRIDLEWAY

Two men were killed when trees, weakened by Storm Beatrice, fell onto the bridleway between the B275 and the B56. The dead have been named as local solicitor, David Kingsley, and Police Sergeant Beresford. Residents of Thorpe will be sorry to hear of Sergeant Beresford's passing. He was a fixture at Thorpe police station for decades and his contribution to community policing much appreciated. The funeral will take place next week and, in lieu of flowers, a JustGiving page has been set up to fund a bench outside Thorpe police station in his memory. Link at end of article.

The bridleway will be closed on public safety grounds for the next two weeks while a survey of remaining trees takes place and any urgent remedial work is carried out. Thorpe Town Council asks residents to respect this closure and reminds them fines will be imposed for any infraction. A council member also took the opportunity to squash rumours that there had been a shootout in the woods along the bridleway. 'The presence of paramedics and police in the vicinity was purely in response to the tragic accident. Yorkshire can be a wild place but we're not the Wild West. Or, at least, not yet.'

THORPE PANTO CALLS FOR HELP

Can you sew or paint scenery? Thorpe Panto is urgently looking for volunteers to help with the production of this year's panto, *Puss in Boots*. Raymond Mason, the panto's director, told us, 'Getting the panto ready is a lot of fun. We have an active and willing team but we are always on the lookout for new help, particularly people with sewing and painting skills.'

FORTY-EIGHT

JOSH

MONDAY

Lovell was packing up the investigation room at Thorpe station when Josh went in, piling papers and office supplies into one of several boxes. It had been a whirlwind of a week since the shooting in Cooper's woods and the aftermath. He'd spent it at headquarters in Northallerton being interviewed by a series of tough and unsmiling officers about what Mrs Walker had told him and why he'd taken the story straight to the Independent Office for Police Conduct via his friend from police college who'd gone to work for them at Canary Wharf.

Now, he had to face Carter. One final interview before he could return to Local Policing. He wasn't looking forward to it. No matter how circumspect he'd been when interviewed, it was impossible to hide his initial suspicion of the man.

'DCI Carter,' he said to Lovell. 'Here to see him.'

'He's not back yet. He's at a press conference in York.'

Josh thought of waiting in reception, but the new sergeant running the station didn't like officers hanging around.

'You're packing up then?' he said.

'Yes. The rest of the investigation will be run from York.'

'I was surprised you were still here actually.'

'Ah yes. You've been on leave, haven't you?'

Josh couldn't tell whether Lovell knew where he'd actually been. He gave little away. As Josh planned to do in the future. Along with his new fitness regime. The one good thing about last week was that he'd lost weight. He'd had neither the appetite nor the opportunity for large meals and snacks. This time he was going to keep the weight off.

'Carter wanted every detail of what David Kingsley said confirmed independently,' Lovell said. 'So I've spent most of the week tracking the movements of Giles Cooper's burger van.'

He pointed to a whiteboard displaying a grid in green marker pen.

DATE	VAN	CONFIRMATION
End 2023	Van in barn in Cooper's woods	Statement WS
Fri 11/10	Storm Beatrice takes out power to barn	
Sun 13/10 night	COOPER FAMILY KILLINGS	
Sun 13/10 night	Van driven to stables. No access. Left	Statement GY
	Van driven to car park behind Sainsbury's, Thorpe	CCTV Refs 393, 399, 412

Tuesday 15/10	Van leaves car park	CCTV Refs 563, 587, 592
	Van taken to Boyes (?)	Statement GY but vague as to when Note: camera at Boyes turned off Tuesday night
Wednesday 23/10	BOYES KILLED Van moves to barn (straight away?)	WS statement van in barn on Friday 25/10

'GY?' Josh asked.

'The neighbour opposite the entrance to the stables.'

'So he did see a burger van?'

Lovell nodded. 'Storm Beatrice brought a tree down onto the roof of Giles's barn and it also took the power out. They were planning on doing a manufacturing session on Saturday but without power they couldn't. We know Giles was racing around on Saturday and Sunday trying to get an electrician to sort the problem out. The stables were nearby and closed to owners on Monday. We think using the stables was what Charlie and Giles rowed about on Sunday. But Charlie did agree. It may be he sacked Marty to keep him out of the way. The Coopers' deaths stymied David Kingsley's plans.'

'Do you think Kingsley went in and found the bodies?'

'It's what he said. He didn't take the van back to the barn anyway, which suggests he knew the woods might well be searched. He parked it in the middle of Thorpe until they strong-armed Boyes into letting them go there.'

'Boyes?'

'He knew some of what was going on. Wanda Stainthorpe told us there were signs last year. Things you'd notice if you lived nearby. Chemical odours and, in the early days, they dumped the waste in the woods. The entrance to Boyes's Farm is down the road from the bridleway, so maybe he noticed the youngsters on mopeds they used to deliver the product. We know Boyes rang us around then and made some accusations, but he was fairly drunk and when it was followed up he said he'd been mistaken. In between the call and follow-up, his dog was badly injured and lost its leg.'

'A warning?'

'Probably. But the dog died last week, so we think Boyes decided he had nothing left to lose. He rang again and spoke to Beresford.'

He broke off from his packing and gave Josh a look.

'But you know about that.'

'Yes.'

Josh didn't know how Carter had discovered it was Beresford passing information to the Kingsleys, and one look at Lovell's tight face told him it wouldn't be worth asking. The silence surrounding Beresford's activities was complete.

Lovell resumed his packing, but there was one more thing Josh was curious about.

'Wanda Stainthorpe. Why did Carter release her?'

'I'm not a hundred per cent sure. She was in the army, you know. A sniper unit. She's a crack shot. She's supposed to have retired but I wonder if she has completely. Anyway, she has friends in high places and one of then called the chief constable. Carter had no choice.'

Carter pushed the door open. He wore a suit and his hair was neatly brushed.

'Bit of news.' He handed Lovell a piece of paper. 'You going to apply to join us, Lovell? You'd be very welcome.' He gave Josh a copy too.

It was a press release.

SPECIAL UNIT TO TACKLE ORGANISED CRIME

A special unit to tackle organised crime throughout Yorkshire has been set up as a joint initiative between the Humberside, North

Yorkshire, South Yorkshire and West Yorkshire Police Forces. The unit will be based in York.

Chief Constable Larber said, 'Such an initiative is long overdue. Organised Crime Groups do not respect police force or county boundaries and significant time and energy has been wasted in previous operations due to the necessity of complicated liaison work with neighbouring forces. This is a very positive outcome. The new unit will be headed up by Detective Chief Constable Carter.'

So Carter was off the hook. Big time.

Josh followed Carter to his office. Carter signalled to him to sit. A good sign? Then sprawled himself over the chair behind the desk. Josh remembered his genial manner when he'd interviewed Mrs Monroe and Kezia and told himself to be careful.

'Anything you'd like to ask?' Carter said.

What did he mean? Was it a loaded question?

'Beresford,' he said anyway. 'How did you know?'

It was a fair question.

'I've suspected information was getting to the Kingsleys via someone in Local Policing since Peter Walker's death. You know his time of death indicates he was killed shortly before his body was found, which was within hours of the Walkers asking me to come over to talk to them?'

'Yes.'

'Kenneth Walker told his family liaison officer he wanted to talk to me privately. She left me a message here. I told very few people about it. And I trusted them all. Not that it stopped me asking ACU to look into them. But it wasn't until Boyes was killed that I considered Beresford. He ran the station. It was more than likely he knew about the Walkers' message. Very little happened in Thorpe station without Beresford knowing.'

It was true that Sergeant Beresford had kept a close eye on everything no matter how mundane.

'You said you only considered Beresford when Boyes was killed. Why was that?'

'Boyes called Beresford to report what David Kingsley was up to. After his dog died. You knew that?'

'I knew they'd spoken.'

'Beresford passed the information straight on to the Kingsleys and buried the call in a routine report that focussed on Boyes's drinking. The Kingsleys killed Boyes early Wednesday morning and did a swift clear-out, moved the van but were planning to come back and check properly. However, Harry Appleton turned up, discovered the body and called it in to Thorpe police station.'

'He spoke to Beresford too?'

'Of course. So Beresford reported it to us – he couldn't very well delay – then raced down to the farm to check everything. According to Appleton he shot round the outbuildings and the house as soon as he arrived. Told him he was making sure no one was there.'

Carter loosened his tie, then thought better of it and removed it completely.

'He'd known Boyes reasonably well, so his speedy arrival wasn't suspicious on the face of it. But Appleton was insistent he'd seen tarot cards in the kitchen, although we never found them. Beresford was the only person who could have taken them. It was enough to look into him and realise he had more money than you'd expect.'

Beresford always knew everything going on in Thorpe, Josh thought. And he was always chatting to his cronies in other departments.

'It wasn't enough to be sure of a conviction,' Carter continued. 'And then I received a call. A call from someone with information that the van was now back in the barn on Cooper's land, provided by Ms Stainthorpe. Information that no one but me knew. So I decided to trap Beresford. Ms Stainthorpe was asked to call Thorpe station and report the van on Monday. At the same time I told Lovell to get Beresford to provide local officers to do another sweep through the woods. Immediately. I knew they'd have to move the van again and we were waiting and watching. As you know.'

'Yes. I didn't know who you were waiting for though. Apart from Kingsley.'

'For a time, you know, I thought the informant was you.'

'Me, sir?'

'Yes, Mason. With your connection to Kingsley and your attempts to divert us with stories of visions. Still, I gather my suspicions were reciprocated.'

He waited, then smiled wryly when Josh didn't respond.

'And then, of course, Ms Stainthorpe took matters into her own hands, egged on by your aunt.'

Wanda and Kezia had done well. Very well. It wasn't their fault they were caught up in so many layers of deceit. Part of him wanted to stand up for them. And for all the others who'd been trapped in the web. Marty and Harry, Mrs Monroe, Mrs Walker even. All of them trying to do their best.

'So might you think of applying for a job in the new unit, Mason?'

Was he being invited? He couldn't tell. Carter gave so little away.

He was sick of trying to second-guess everyone anyway, of always being the last person to know anything. And he was finished with trying to impress Carter.

'Probably not, sir.'

'Ah. Happy in Local Policing, then?'

'For the moment, yes. I like being able to help.' He couldn't stop himself from biting out the word help.

'Yes. Crime can be a bit dispiriting, I suppose. So many criminals. You forget the general public can actually be perfectly pleasant and honest.'

'Yes.'

'Well, if you change your mind let me know. You did the right thing by going to Canary Wharf, by the way.'

Josh stood. But Carter had another question.

'How much of this are you going to tell Ms Heron?'

Everything, he realised. She deserved it.

'How much can I?'

'There's not much she can't work out anyway, but try to ensure she keeps it to herself. Particularly that Beresford was in the pay of the Kingsleys. It would be better for community policing if that didn't get out. The essential trust between the police and the public is a fragile beast. But your aunt strikes me as the sort of person who can keep her mouth shut. Has she ever thought of joining the police?'

For a second Josh thought Carter was making fun of him. Except his face was perfectly serious.

'No. I think I can safely say the thought has never crossed her mind.'

'Pity. Someone with her skills might be very useful in crime scene investigation. That'll be all, Mason.'

FORTY-NINE
MRS MONROE

SAME DAY

'Your skills,' Mrs Monroe said when Josh had finished explaining. 'What did he mean?'

'Photography, I imagine,' Kezia said quickly.

Mrs Monroe smoothed the hospital sheet and remembered Josh didn't know the truth about the visions. She wondered if DCI Carter suspected. He'd struck her as more perceptive than Josh and Kezia gave him credit for. Maybe that was why his accusations of lying had stung so much. Had he guessed? She'd never know. Mind you she'd thought she'd never know a lot of things. She'd been a little startled when Josh and Kezia had arrived in the hospital so that Josh could explain everything. Kezia had insisted she be told too.

'How did the police get to the Prices so quickly?' Kezia asked.

It was one of the few things Josh hadn't mentioned. Really, he'd been very forthcoming.

'Alan,' Josh said. 'He got my number from my mother. He was worried about you and feeling guilty.'

'I suppose he told you about Dennis Price picking him up from the allotment on Monday morning when they were going fishing. And noticing afterwards that the incinerator had flared up again.'

'Why didn't he tell you when you asked before?' Mrs Monroe said

'I think Alan desperately wanted it to be Marty. Plus he couldn't believe Dennis was involved.'

She pushed back the chair with a grating noise and went over to the window. There was only a view of a yard and the bins from here, but Mrs Monroe didn't mind. She was lucky to have a private room, although it might be a bit livelier in one of the wards. Still, she mustn't complain. It was all working out well, especially since the orthopaedic surgeon who'd fixed her broken wrist had said he'd bump her up the list for her hip to be replaced. Good thing she'd managed to keep off the ciggies. Although being drugged and helpless and then stuck in hospital had been useful.

'Annie Price,' Mrs Monroe said. 'Who'd have thought it.'

'Well, you're in a minority. Quite a few Thorpe inhabitants have stories about how awful she was and how they're not surprised.'

'That's fairly normal.'

'Some of the stories are pretty bad,' Kezia said. 'She was missing a conscience, I think. Did Carter admit how wrong he was about Marty?'

'No. But I wouldn't expect him to,' Josh said.

'Typical.'

'Do you want a lift, Kezia? I need to go.'

'No thanks. I'll make my own way.'

Once he'd left she came back to the bed and sat down again.

'He's grown up a bit,' Mrs Monroe said.

Kezia laughed. 'You mean there were things he didn't tell us. Like exactly what Mrs Walker told him.'

'He was a little vague about the details.'

'Whatever it was, it sent him charging off to London. I wonder if it was something awful about David. He knows how unhappy I am about him.'

If Josh had become more reticent, Kezia was more open. Mrs Monroe waited.

'It's grief really. I mean, I never really grieved our divorce. Too bitter, I guess. And now it's caught up with me. At the moment I can't bear it, can't bear thinking about who David became at the end. And wondering if that was who he always was. If I've been a blind fool all these years.'

She breathed a couple of shuddering sighs, then put her hand onto the cool steel of the bed rail. Anchoring herself, Mrs Monroe thought.

'But it's a process I need to go through. I know that.'

Mrs Monroe laid her hand briefly over Kezia's.

'You can talk about it to me. If you want,' she said. 'I know you think I'm an old fraud but I—'

'I don't. Of course I don't.'

This was so patently untrue Mrs Monroe couldn't help laughing. Kezia stared at her for a second, then joined in. Neither of them could stop. They were still helpless with it when a passing nurse stuck her head round the door to check everything was all right.

'Thank you,' Kezia said. 'Thank you for not giving me away. And don't ask me why I lied about the... the attacks, because I'm not sure. Not yet anyway. Did Marty come and see you? I told him to. I told him how much you'd helped.'

'Yes.'

He was a nice boy. Awkward and not sure what to say to her until she'd asked him about the horses Kezia had escaped on. Then he'd talked. And talked. Until Harry had rescued her and taken him away. A job interview apparently. Organised by his tutors at college so he could continue his course.

'Did he get the job?'

'Yes.'

'So all's well that ends well.'

It wasn't true, she realised. And this time, not funny. It hadn't ended well for the Coopers. And it hadn't ended well for Lauren.

'What's next for you?' Mrs Monroe asked. 'Your back, where Annie Price stabbed you, has it healed?'

'Nearly.'

'They didn't keep you in for long.'

'I discharged myself. My mother always said you should keep out of hospitals.'

'Probably right. The food isn't going to help anyone get better.'

'I brought you some fruit and, if you fancied it, a herbal drink I make myself. It's good for healing.'

She put the fruit on the table and opened the cupboard beneath. 'I'll put the bottle in here in case the nurses— You've got a tarot deck!'

'Ah yes. The surgeon – the one who did my wrist – he's very interested in tarot and he'd seen me on the television, so he brought some cards in and I've given him a few readings.'

Kezia riffled through the cards, then looked at their backs.

'I don't mark them,' Mrs Monroe said.

'I can see that.'

'I suppose you know how.'

'Of course I do.'

They grinned at each other.

'Let me do your cards,' Mrs Monroe said. She wasn't sure why.

'What would be the point? I don't believe in it at all.'

'Well, neither do I.'

As soon as she'd said the words, Mrs Monroe felt a degree of surprise. Was that true? Did she really not believe in them at all?

'There might be something in it,' she hedged, waiting to see if Kezia would soften her stance too.

She didn't.

'Sometimes they help clarify things,' Mrs Monroe added.

'I don't need anything clarified. I've already made a lot of decisions. Ones I should have made ages ago.'

Mrs Monroe waited.

'I'm going away for a few days. To see my mother.'

'That'll be nice.'

'Probably not actually, but it's something I should have done years ago.'

How long was it since Kezia had seen her mother, then? She decided not to ask.

'Then I'm moving out of Josh's flat. I've been there far too long. And I'm going to find a proper job. One that actually pays money. I can't live on photography.'

'What job?'

'Um, not sure yet.'

'Maybe you should do what DCI Carter suggested and train as a crime scene investigator, because—'

But Kezia cut her off. 'The visions are as fake as tarot card reading. They're... they're autosuggestion. I was desperate to find something to exonerate Marty and... well, I made myself see all those things.'

Mrs Monroe kept her thoughts to herself. There was no point arguing with someone who was so adamant.

'Just three cards,' she said. 'Go on. Just for fun. One for the past, one for the present and one for the future. The classic reading. Go on Kezia, just to make me happy.'

Kezia gave her a wry look, then chose three cards and laid them one by one on the table stretched over Mrs Monroe's bed.

Mrs Monroe turned the first over.

The Six of Cups.

'It means—'

'I know what it means,' Kezia snapped. 'Something unresolved in the past. Sorry, I shouldn't have spoken like that. It's just... When this all started, back at Zina's salon we were fooling about with the tarot deck and Lauren picked this— No, I'm wrong. She didn't. I chose it.'

She bit her lip and thrust her hands into the loose sleeves of her jumper, hugging herself, despite the hospital's warmth.

'Maybe I should have paid more attention,' she said, then turned the second card over. 'My present.'

They both looked in silence.

The card showed a blindfolded woman, seated and holding two swords in a diagonal cross in front of her. Behind her lay water filled with islands of rock.

The Two of Swords.

A card notorious for meaning indecision, which was accurate enough. But it was the blindness of the woman that struck Mrs Monroe most and the way she crossed the swords in front of her as though trying to protect herself from an unseen foe. The rocky islands in the water symbolised obstacles, but Mrs Monroe realised how beautiful the scene with the thin crescent moon above was. Really the woman should throw the swords away, stand and take her blindfold off, then turn and drink in the view.

She wasn't going to say that though. She wished now they'd never started.

Kezia reached out to turn the third card over. The one that represented her future. She didn't, though. Instead she gathered all three cards up and shoved them back into the deck.

'If you don't mind,' she said. 'I'd rather decide what I'm going to do with my life without any help from the tarot.'

A LETTER FROM THE AUTHOR

Dear reader,

Huge thanks for reading *The Dying Hour*. I hope you've enjoyed Kezia's, Josh's and Mrs Monroe's stories; I had great fun writing about them and the other inhabitants of Thorpe and it's a pleasure to share my writing with you. If you want to join other readers in hearing all about my new releases with Storm and bonus content, you can sign up here:

www.stormpublishing.co/jane-jesmond

And if you want to know more about my books and me, you can sign up for my newsletter:

jane-jesmond.com/contact

If you enjoyed this book and could spare a few moments to leave a review that would be hugely appreciated. Even a short review can make all the difference in encouraging a reader to discover my books for the first time. Thank you so much!

The spark that ignited *The Dying Hour* was my fascination with the supernatural. Particularly the ability of objects and places to retain an atmosphere of their history. I'm thinking of Stonehenge, of Culloden, of the Colosseum in Rome and the prehistoric copper mines in Llandudno but also of small objects such as a flint arrowhead, or a fossil found on the beach. They all have stories to tell and I wanted to explore how this might play out within the framework of a murder mystery.

Like Kezia, I am, however, deeply sceptical about many of the people who claim to have psychic insight or superhuman skills. I suspect I'm not alone in this. But it doesn't stop me loving writing about strange happenings all the same.

Thanks again for reading *The Dying Hour* and I hope you'll stay in touch.

Jane Jesmond

jane-jesmond.com

 instagram.com/authorjanejesmond

 facebook.com/JaneJesmondAuthor

 x.com/AuthorJJesmond

ACKNOWLEDGEMENTS

I am so grateful to the people who go out of their way to help me write my books by sharing their knowledge. Thank you, this time, to Kate Bendelow for her advice on crime scene investigation, to Madeleine and Ruth for advising me on everything to do with horses and stables, to Mike for answering my queries about cars and technology and lots of other things, and, of course, to Michelle Kiedron for doing her best to keep me on the straight and narrow where policing is concerned. If there are errors in this book, despite all their help, I can only stress that these are all down to me.

Thank you to everyone at my publisher Storm, particularly to my editor Kathryn Taussig for her insightful comments and to editorial operations director Alexandra Begley for all her help. Many thanks to my agent Amanda Preston, always brilliant, but especially for holding my hand during the rather wobbly start to this book.

My writing process involves burying myself in each book for six to seven months, then emerging with a vaguely readable draft that I need feedback on. So a huge thank you to Nikki Hughes and Fiona Erskine for tackling the manuscript at this stage and thank you to Madeleine Hill and Jonathan Crowe for reading later versions.

Andrew Wille, creative writing mentor, teacher and editor, read a draft when I was feeling fairly despondent about the book, and helped me find the magic again. His classes on writing craft are a constant inspiration.

A final major thank you to my husband Alex, without whom

I'd starve while writing each book. Thank you for not minding when I don't hear you because I've suddenly had an idea and am seeing if it could work, and for listening when I ramble on about a gnarly plot point that only a saint could find interesting.

www.ingramcontent.com/pod-product-compliance
Lightning Source LLC
Chambersburg PA
CBHW010606310726
48969CB00010B/2592